A Note from the Author

Hello.

Every time someone enjoys one of my books, I have a little 'yay' moment, so thank you for that.

Bug Magic is the second book in the Paranormals of Ahl series. If you haven't read The Dragon Problem, Book 1 in the series, I suggest you start there, or some things might not make sense.

Trigger warnings and heads-up:

1. A heavy reference to past child abuse.

2. References to torture.

3. Violence throughout the book.

4. Profanity.

5. A romantic theme between a dragon shifter and a mage.

6. I'm not a spicy writer. The love scene(s) are fade-to-black.

7. The romance has an age gap (I know some people don't like that).

BUG MAGIC

The Paranormals of Ahl Book 2

ML CONKLIN

CHAPTER ONE

DRAKE

Drake wrinkled his nose against the putrid stench of decaying food as he slipped through the back door. Dirty dishes, discarded receipts, and other garbage littered the kitchen. Unopened mail piled on the counter amid the other garbage told him he missed her.

The weathered two-story house on the outskirts of what the humans called Philadelphia was the third one he found in his year-long hunt for the second queen. She remained elusive and a step ahead of him. As if she knew he hunted her. The narrow staircase groaned as he climbed them. He stopped at the top and stretched his foot.

'Creeeak.' The sound echoed off the walls of the otherwise silent house.

He peered back down the stairs and waited. When the house remained quiet, he moved into the room. Half-empty glasses and some sort of human bottles sat abandoned on the nightstand. The blankets on the bed were a tangled mess, and clothing littered the floor. The distinct scent of decaying flowers and stale alcohol indicated it hadn't been long since the second queen had lived in the house. His stomach soured.

Moving to the bathroom, he peered in. It held nothing but a bar of soap. He eased out of the room.

Halfway down the stairs, he froze. Was that a swish of clothing? Drake amplified his senses.

"This is not your task, First." A dry voice floated up the stairs.

"What are you doing here, vampire?"

Tarquin appeared on the landing. "This is my case."

They'd run into each other a few times during his hunt for the second queen. "She's no longer here."

"Of course not." Tarquin pushed past him and disappeared into the bedroom.

"It is as if she knows when we're coming."

"Yes." Tarquin's blank brown eyes revealed no emotion as he emerged. "Odd since I do not report my whereabouts."

"Nor do I." Jenella opened the bond as they entered the kitchen, and his heart fluttered. "Jenella's in Ferine."

"She is finishing up a relocation case." Tarquin shuffled through a stack of papers. "I do not know why she bothers with the mundane. It is a waste of her talents."

"She is appeasing her brother. Same as you." Drake picked up the stack of mail. He thought it clever that humans had an organized, affordable service for sending messages. Although, with all their electronic gadgets, he didn't understand why they still used it. The mail was addressed to Amanda Smith. "She's up to something." He handed an envelope to Tarquin.

"She is hunting for the other Firsts and hides her intentions well." A note of pride rang through Tarquin's voice.

The familiar pang of longing made him pause. He'd requested she wake the other Firsts to save them from the hellish half-sleep not long after her incredible magic woke him. It didn't surprise him that Jenella kept her word. Unlike her mother, she was honorable. "Has she found any of them?"

"I am not the foremost authority on all things Jenella."

"Noted."

"What do you plan to do when you find the former queen?" Tarquin asked as they slipped out the back door.

Drake breathed the fresh air to erase the disgusting odor of the house. It didn't help. It coated his sensitive nose and would for a good while. "Eliminate her."

Tarquin narrowed his eyes. "That is not wise."

"What do you propose I do?"

"Tell Jen the truth."

"You say that as if you've been honest with her."

"I am working for the Regent. You are not."

"The Regent forgets he works for the Queen." Drake leaned forward. "That means you also work for her."

"Your point?"

"That you have the balls to criticize me when you lie to her face."

The vampire turned toward the back gate. "Oh, yes. It is my fault that she doesn't know her mother is alive."

Drake shook his head. "The information won't sit well with her."

"Correct. Which is why I will not utter a word." Tarquin disappeared.

The world went dark, and sharp pain radiated through every inch of his body as Drake morphed into his dragon form. He shook his head as his vision and perspective adjusted and launched into the air. Dishonesty would kill any chance he had with Jenella. Yet, revealing the secret would also alienate her. She would hate him no matter what he did. He'd gotten the information by listening to a conversation that wasn't his business. It wasn't the first time he wished he could go back and make different choices. He dismissed the thought, launched into the sky, and flew toward Ferine.

CHAPTER TWO

JEN

Tall trees cast long shadows along the edge of a bubbling brook that flowed over rocks, making a joyful sound. A combination of trees, damp earth, and wildflowers perfumed the air. The place was perfect for a family of trolls to live. Perfect, if I overlooked the elves lurking in the trees, armed with various weapons, the three troll kids bickering on the center bridge, and the two dragons circling overhead. I doubted anyone else noticed the dragons because of their cloaking magic.

My troll clients were silent as they examined the three bridges and ignored the ear-splitting shrieks their kids made every few seconds. I scanned the trees where I sensed the elves. A tickle of excitement danced in my stomach. I'd never been in the pocket of Ferine before, nor had I met so many elves at one time. A branch near the kids wiggled. We needed to move this along before the elves got twitchy and killed my clients. "Will this work for your family?"

The patriarch of the troll family shifted from one foot to another. "Are you sure no kelpies reside in this water?"

It was a fair question. Kelpies and trolls were always fighting each other. The Troll King liked to charge the kelpies when they passed under bridges. The Kelpie Queen retaliated by driving the trolls out and taking over the water underneath them. They'd brought their dispute to the crown who ruled over all paranormals, or me and my brother, multiple times. Not that they knew I was the Queen of Ahl. I wore undetectable glamour made by one of the most powerful dragons in the world when I did my detective work.

The feud between trolls and kelpies continued, no matter how many solutions we offered. The ongoing tension between the leaders unsettled their people. That they couldn't come to an agreement bothered me, so I jumped at the chance to help the troll family move to better bridges. "This stream is too small for kelpies. The bridges are on Greenwood Elf land, and they agreed to allow you to live here if you meet their conditions." I'd spent hours negotiating with their stern-faced chief through a projection spell. He had a reputation for his temper and handled uninvited guests with violence. I liked the guy.

The matriarch's eyes narrowed. "And what are those conditions?"

I pulled out my phone and brought up the list of demands. "You must respect the environment. They won't charge you rent if you allow the elves to pass over the bridges for free. The Chief would like to discuss a noise ordinance and a few other things with you in person. He also wants you to help defend the land from trespassers."

"Those are acceptable terms."

"Yes. We can live with that," the patriarch added. "Did the elves agree to allow us to use all three bridges?"

"Yes." My eyes slid toward the trees.

"Very well. If you'll excuse us, we wish to have a private discussion."

"Sure. I'll wait at the rocks." I headed toward my guard, Tracy, who sat on a boulder working on her phone. Not that she had anything to guard me against. Since we'd taken out a demon and rescued the Dragon Queen, I'd stuck to helping regular paranormals with small things. I helped an ogre find an antique lamp stolen from his home and caught a gremlin who kept raiding a hive of pixies to steal their magic dust. My favorite case was in a pocket named Pyron, where I tracked down some stolen jewels for a mid-level tech mage.

I'd spent a lot of time helping the Rübezahl. The mountain guardians insisted I go to the pocket of Mage Mountain about once a month to solve some minor problem. One time, they hired me to find the person responsible for leaving footprints on the corner of their land. The tracks in the snow led to the mountain and then disappeared. It turned out to be a young goat shifter who got lost and veered the wrong way. He didn't realize that he'd encroached on their territory until I explained it to his parents.

Another time, they hired me to warn a sasquatch family to stop running past their village screaming at night. It took me three days to track them down and warn them. The sasquatches claimed they'd come through the entrance on that side once. They'd messed with some human bigfoot hunters and were a little too wound up. In the end, they promised to be quiet in the future when they raced through the gate near the village.

The simple cases allowed me to meet a lot of regular paranormals and become a pretty good detective.

More than that, they allowed me to travel to other pockets, or small individual realms scattered around the world, where paranormals lived. Every time I went to a new one, I scanned for anomalies. I wanted to find the resting places of the Firsts, the paranormals who created the magical races. My mother had put them to sleep against their will before she died and I planned to right that wrong. Plus, I'd promised Drake, another First, to look for them.

The trick was not to tell anyone what I was doing. Especially my brother. He'd have a fit if he knew why I took cases in the various pockets. So far, I knew the general vicinity where two Firsts rested. I needed to catch a case that would take me back to those pockets and then try to repeat the magic I used to wake Drake.

My stomach fluttered at the thought of him, and I shifted on the rock. The minor cases gave me cover to search and made my brother back off with his safety measures. They also beat being kidnapped by the Bellicose, a group who wanted to eliminate me and take over the throne. And they were so much easier than fighting mind-controlled dragons and demons. Or so I told myself. If I bothered digging a little deeper, I'd have to face the fact that I was bored and restless.

Tracy dragged her eyes away from her phone. "Hey. You about wrapped up here?"

"I hope so. They seem to like this area."

"Good. I've booked a hotel for tonight. I mean, we can see if there's a transport heading back to Allure if you want, but I have a couple of potion clients in Ferine that I need to see."

"That's fine." I pulled out my phone to check my messages. Verity, my assistant, sent one outlining the queen's schedule for the next week. As queen, I had to remove my glamour and make appearances at the castle now and then. I tried to avoid it because I loved my freedom and wasn't ready to take the throne. Besides, the one time I'd stepped up and tried to lead, my brother slapped me down, so I left him to carry out the duties as regent.

The second message was from an old acquaintance, Colonel Ballard. A level-headed and competent bear shifter who led the enforcers in the pocket of Hospa. I'd met him when mind-controlled dragons kidnapped us a while back and he'd later saved my life. His message asked me to call him when I had a moment. I slipped my phone into my pocket and stood as the troll couple approached. "Do you like it?"

"This place is acceptable," the matriarch said.

"Great. Would you like to meet with the Elven Chief?"

"Yes."

I whistled, and elves melted out of the woods from every direction. The Chief signaled the other elves to hang back as he glided toward us. He didn't look any different from the other elves, with his long brown hair and bright blue eyes. He wore a green long sleeve T-shirt and khaki cargo pants. I introduced the two parties and waited while they worked out the rental agreement. When the magic contract settled over them, I collected my payment, and Tracy and I headed down the trail toward our car.

The pocket of Ferine was nestled in the rolling hills of a state humans named Pennsylvania, on the outskirts of a town called York. It held a picturesque, medium-sized city with charming architecture and several types of paranormals. While Ferine didn't come close to rivaling the bustle of the capital where we lived, Allure, it held a certain charm that I adored. The downtown area had a range of accommodations for visitors, everything from luxury to basic, with a smattering of boutiques and a few restaurants.

The sweltering heat of late summer mirrored the human world, but the pocket had clean air thanks to the wards that kept it contained and included air filtration. Unlike Allure, Ferine allowed human vehicles inside. Against Tracy's wishes, I'd rented a car with air conditioning in the human world.

I slid into the driver's seat, started the car to cool it down, and called Colonel Ballard. He answered on the first ring. "Colonel Ballard."

"Hey, Colonel. This is Jen Hendrix. You sent me a text?"

"Oh, hey, Jen. Yes. A friend of mine needs some help and doesn't want to involve the local enforcers."

I perked up. "What kind of help?"

"I'm not sure, exactly. He oversees a pride of leopards in Ferine and asked if I'd recommend a competent and discreet detective. Since you single-handedly rescued the Dragon Queen from my pocket without alerting the multiple spies, I recommended you."

He referred to my first case where I'd gotten myself kidnapped by chimeras. I wasn't conscious when they dragged me into his pocket and locked me in a cage. But he ignored that fact. "Right. Sounds dangerous to me. I try to avoid dangerous cases these days." I'd almost died trying to save the Dragon Queen, Deva.

"He didn't give me the impression that this one is dangerous. The pack needs someone with magic to solve a puzzle."

I tapped my knee as I considered it. I didn't have another case lined up, and I trusted Colonel Ballard's judgment. "Okay. I'll talk to him, but I make no promises. It just so happens I'm in the pocket of Ferine."

"Great. When can I tell him to expect you?"

"We'll head over now." After I got directions to the compound, I ended the call.

As I pulled away from Elven territory, the car's tires kicked up gravel. We skidded around a corner, and I stepped on the gas, rocketing toward the other side of town. Another car pulled out ahead, and I slammed on the brakes, swerved around it, and took the corner leading to the shifter compound too fast. The car fishtailed onto the dirt road, and I fought to recover. Excitement bubbled in my stomach as I swung into the gravel parking lot and skidded to a stop somewhat inside a parking spot. "You can work on your potions while I solve this if you want," I said, as we climbed out of the car.

Tracy shook her head. "No. I'll work around your case."

We stopped in our tracks just inside the gates to the compound. Thick, inky black tendrils of magic oozed down the main path. Small offshoots stretched out in every direction and thinned into points. One led up the front steps of a cottage, while another wrapped around a tree. That one wiggled. I shuddered. "Ick. Are you seeing this?"

Tracy leaned forward. "Yeah. I'd think it was a black ant colony if it wasn't magic. Stay here. I need my potions."

I tiptoed toward it. A tendril split off and crawled toward me. I shuffled back a few steps and it followed. The magic slithered, or maybe oozed, in what looked like slow-motion. A shiver ran down my spine with the sense of dread radiating from it. When I moved left two steps, the tendril followed. I moved to the right and watched it change directions. I backpedaled until it stopped following me. A hand clamped on my shoulder. *"Gah!"*

"Geez, Jen. Jumpy much?" Tracy adjusted her bag. "Did that stuff follow you?"

"Yes."

She pulled out a vial and crept toward it, taking slow, deliberate steps, then extended it toward a tiny tendril. Another one oozed from the left like it was trying to box her in.

I latched onto her arm and pulled her away. "Touching that stuff is not a good idea. Can you feel the vibe coming off it?"

Tracy shook my hand off. "No, I mean, yes. I can feel it, but how are we gonna figure out what it is if we don't sample it?"

I examined the nondescript cinderblock building that served as the main office of the leopard pride. "This is a bigger problem than Colonel Ballard let on."

"At least it's not boring like your usual cases."

"Yeah. Let's find out what they want us to do."

The heavy door swung open with little effort as we stepped inside. It was just as bland as the outside, with its cement floors and medium gray walls. Small windows dotted the left and right sides high on the wall. A small, ancient desk sat in the middle, a young shifter sitting behind it. The man checked us in and pointed to five ancient wooden chairs in a corner that somewhat resembled a waiting area.

Chairs so uncomfortable it didn't take long for my back to ache. After a few minutes of suffering, I stood, stretched, and moved to the far wall, where pictures of past and current royalty hung.

The first picture showed the unassuming, if not bland, face of Jonas, the First who created the shifters. The only First my mother didn't put to sleep. Around the time of my mother's birth, he turned the shifters over to his son, Morten, whose stern face graced the next picture. After he started a war by separating the different types of shifters into classes, he was forced to turn leadership over to someone not born of Jonas's line. With his amber eyes, dark hair, and menacing expression, Gabriel, the current Shifter King looked competent and lethal in the last picture.

Three additional paintings hung under them. On the left was a portrait of the first queen of Ahl, who created the coalition by merging the warring supernatural factions into a combined society. The next one showed the second queen, who created the pockets that we lived in. The last was of the current queen. I scowled at it and returned to the rickety chair. "It must have been hard to organize the supernaturals into a coalition, especially during such brutal times."

Tracy shifted toward the pictures. "Yeah."

A man with messy hair and a five o'clock shadow emerged from the back office. He escorted another man with sad eyes toward the front door and leaned in close to say something to him. Shifter packs formed from multigenerational families. When an Alpha became ineffective or retired, they used a highly civilized process to choose the next one. The most respected senior members took physical and written leadership tests, and the one with the highest scores became Alpha. The test scores were also used to rank the upper pack structure. It helped focus their competitive streak on productive things like physical fitness and academics.

The process was much better than their previous system, which allowed anyone to challenge and fight to move up in the pack. That system caused a lot of problems during the shifter wars because many alphas were physically strong but had no leadership skills. It caused entire packs to get wiped out. Gabe and Linda, the current Alphas restructured the process after the war.

Based on their body language, the guy with messy hair was the alpha. Once the other guy left, he took a deep breath and approached us. "Detective Hendrix?"

I offered a polite smile as I stood. "That's me. This is my assistant, Tracy." Like me, Tracy wore glamour to hide her identity. I introduced her as my assistant rather than my guard because low-level mages, like I was pretending to be, didn't have guards.

"I'm Alpha Roberts, the head of this family of leopards." He bared his teeth in what I assumed was a smile. "Thank you for making the time to meet with me." He turned and strode toward his office, expecting us to follow. We shared a look, then scrambled to catch up.

Alpha Roberts closed the door and offered us seats in more rickety chairs. He slunk behind his desk, pulled a file out of his drawer, and nodded as if he agreed with himself on something. "Colonel Ballard said you were one of the best detectives he'd ever worked with."

I wasn't even in the top one hundred. The Director of the Private Investigative Supernatural Division, or PISD, would never allow me to become the best. Not because I wasn't good at solving cases, but because he was my former best friend. The 'former' part placed me at the bottom of most of his lists because I'd ended our friendship and lowered his social status, which was all he cared about. "What steps have you taken to eliminate the magic outside?"

"None. It's diseased."

"Colonel Ballard is a good man, but I don't normally take these types of cases. I'd be glad to refer you to my mentor."

His forehead creased. "No offense toward Consort Tarquin, but I would prefer you take the case. Ballard said you were good at solving magical problems and reversing spells. He said you don't give up no matter what you face."

That part was true. Especially if people were in trouble. "Right. I'm not sure I'm your best choice for this job. That magic running through your compound isn't anything I've ever seen before."

He nodded. "Let me give you the background and then you can decide."

This alpha wouldn't take 'no' for an answer. My involvement would draw attention to me, which was the last thing I wanted. My brother would have a fit if I chased after magic that was most likely created by the Bellicose, but it *was* my responsibility to protect the people. I'd have to solve it or hand it off to someone else before I continued my search for the Firsts.

I rubbed my eyes. "I'll hear you out, but can't guarantee I'll take the case."

"My sister's mate was the man you saw me walk to the door. Two of their children got infected." He tapped his fingers on the desk.

"We'll take it," Tracy said.

My head whipped toward her. Tracy never spoke up in meetings with potential clients. The magic had her worried. I cleared my throat. "Um."

She rested a hand on my arm. "If we take this case, Jen will need all the information you have. If it gets too dangerous, she'll need to hand it off to someone more qualified."

He hesitated for a second, then slid the file to me. "That's acceptable. This is the information my trackers gathered. We can't see magic, but we can smell it. I sent three of my best trackers to follow it and they all fell ill within an hour. I've been around for a long time, and I've not seen anything like this. It... the magic, I guess, is like a disease that infects upon contact and makes us useless for a time, followed by extreme violence." He leaned back in his chair. "It makes our pride vulnerable. I want you to figure out how to eliminate it from my compound. After that, I don't care what you do with the information."

Tracy was right. I needed to know what was going on, even though I didn't like it. I saw first-hand what mind control magic did to the dragon community and didn't want that for the shifters. They didn't have as many magical defenses as the dragons, and were more susceptible. If left unchecked, the diseased magic would take over entire packs of shifters. "Have your trackers recovered from their exposure? Or has it gotten worse?"

"It's worse. It transfers like a disease and I fear they won't recover on their own."

"Right. Based on how it followed us outside, it gravitates toward magic. I suggest you keep anyone not infected away from the pack members affected by it."

He nodded. "We've already quarantined the infected. I've ordered my pack to maintain distance. Ballard said you'd figure out a reversal spell."

"We can try, but I can't make any promises."

"Then I would like to hire you to research it and find a cure."

It didn't seem so dangerous to me unless I factored in the possible Bellicose involvement. Even then, I didn't want a detective less powerful than me looking into it. Especially if it was contagious. Colonel Ballard saw me reverse a spell once, so that's probably why he recommended me. This magic was different, though. I didn't really want to take the case, but I itched to figure out why it felt so awful. "Okay. We'll take your case. I can't promise you I won't involve the enforcers because magic that makes shifters sick and violent is a big problem."

He ran a hand through his hair. "I understand. While I don't have a problem with their involvement, I would appreciate it if you didn't let them push you out. I need this solved as fast as possible and don't like dealing with red tape."

"Oh, they won't keep me out of this." I realized the words came out clipped, so I cleared my throat. "Is there a number I can call if I have questions?"

He scribbled a number down on a piece of paper and handed it to me. "Call this number and talk to my second. There is a thirty-thousand-dollar bonus on top of your regular fee if you heal my infected members within one week."

I tried to keep my expression neutral at the mention of the money. Not because it was a lot of money. It was. But I wondered why they didn't use some of it to buy decent chairs. Preferably ones made in this century.

We made a magical contract, and the Alpha dismissed us.

Free of the torture chairs, we stepped out of the building, and I inhaled the fresh air. Unlike the forests near Allure, which smelled of pine and fresh water, the woods of Ferine smelled heavier—like vegetation, damp earth, and blooming flowers. The trees were different, too. They were a mixture of oaks rather than the pine, fir, and spruce found in Allure. I loved the diversity and wondered if I could learn to create such magnificent pockets.

I screeched to a stop in the paved hotel parking lot. The car wasn't between the lines, so I threw it in reverse, stomped on the gas, then put it in drive. It sped forward too fast, so I slammed on the brakes. We stopped an inch away from the side of the building. An ear-to-ear smile spread across my face. "Driving like a human is so fun."

"Is that what you were doing? Because it seemed like you were trying to kill us." Tracy held out her hands for the device that started the vehicle.

The smile melted off my face. "What do you mean? I got us here in one piece."

She shook her head and opened the door. "I'll drive from now on."

I didn't think I did *that* bad.

Tracy and I made our way into the hotel and I settled in my room and ordered food from the small magichef found in all the hotel rooms throughout the pockets.

I opened the file the alpha gave us. The mother was shopping in the human world when she stopped to admire a purse. Her son got bored, so he told her he would meet her in the food court. When she got there ten minutes later, she found him slumped over a table. She mentioned she got an eerie feeling from the place, but in her panic, she didn't care. The pack sent their best trackers out. They went catatonic before they made it to the edge of the mall's property. As soon as they woke up, they attacked everyone around them. The Alpha restrained the infected and locked down their compound.

With so little information about the magic, I was going to have to start from scratch. Not that I expected shifters to have much information. We'd have to start at the mall.

By the time I closed the files and finished my notes, it was well after dark. I texted Tracy, who had her own room, then logged on to the PISD's website and registered myself as hired for the case. The PISD licensed and governed private detectives. We worked independently, so I only had to add the nature of the case, the location, and who hired me. Registering our cases was a new policy. There had been a slight problem in the past where I might or might not have poached a case from a powerful vampire, who also happened to be my mentor. Quin didn't lodge a formal complaint, but he *did* mention it to a staff member who freaked out and took it to her boss. The new director added a rule requiring us to log our cases to avoid Quin's ire.

After getting a confirmation, I closed my laptop and set my wards. Witches created their own, but mages didn't have that skill, so I relied on Tracy for mine. Lucky for me, she was the most powerful witch I'd ever met. I double-checked them, took a shower, and flopped onto the bed.

I looked down at what used to be my favorite white nightgown, now tattered and dirty. Blood trickled from my face and dripped onto it. A tear joined the blood. I used my shredded gown to wipe my eyes. It didn't do any good to cry. I had cried, begging my father not to leave me and trying to tell him about the cage. I cried as I pleaded for my mother to stay. They said they were busy. They didn't have time. My parents always left, and the man took their place. And I ended up in the cage. I huddled in the corner. The smell of filth, suffering, blood and urine made my stomach churn. I wished I was big enough or had enough to hurt the man and run away. I wanted to get out of the cage. Pain exploded through my body as my bones reset themselves.

Heart pounding, I flew from the bed. A bead of sweat trickled down my back. Rain pattered against the window as my eyes drifted toward my wrists. I reminded myself that Jaques was long gone, and I was in a hotel room, not a cage. I snatched a bottle of water from the nightstand and gulped it down as I paced around the room, listening to the rain as I tried to stop shaking. Those dreams sucked, and I worked hard to deal with my trauma. As a result, I hadn't had one in months. The dream proved that I'd probably never be whole. I stumbled to the bathroom, splashed water on my face, and took some deep breaths. I sank onto the bed and opened one of my mother's diaries.

My grandmother's diaries were interesting. They contained a lot of history about the Coalition that wasn't written in the history books. My mother's diaries? Not so much. She bragged about how great she was and didn't give many details. By the time I got halfway through with them, I figured out why people hated her. Her writing was a great sleep aid, though, so I started reading. It didn't take me long for my eyes to droop, so I set it aside and fell into a deep, dreamless sleep.

Chapter Three

JEN

The mall where the shifters first spotted the magic seemed almost deserted. Tracy and I headed toward the shop where the woman split with her son. According to Tracy, it looked like a normal human store. I'd seen a few of them since becoming a detective and found them strange with all their bright colors and rows and rows of items. It was a sharp contrast to the simplicity of the small shops in the pockets where you chose an item from a magically enhanced tablet and it appeared. I'd never been to a human mall with so many shops. I fought the urge to abandon the case and explore as we made our way through the wide corridors.

The shop wasn't open, so we followed the scent of fried food to the area where the kid got infected. As we walked, I scratched my arms to stop my skin from crawling. The feeling was more ominous than the mind control magic used on the dragons during my first case.

I craned my neck to see where the trail led. A table at the far edge of the abandoned food court had a thick coat. Like the shifter compound, inky black tendrils flowed out from the table in every direction and thinned to sharp points. They scattered across the floor, up the support beams, into the restaurants on the ceiling. I hopped back as a tendril above me oozed down.

My lip curled as I shook out my hands to erase the heebie-jeebies. The tendril followed me. I eased way back and watched several others slither toward us. "Are you seeing this?"

"Yeah. I want a sample." Tracy removed her hand from my arm. "But no way I'm touching that stuff." She backed away. "What if it gets another kid?"

My stomach fell. I hoped the kid who got exposed didn't become a violent, mindless puppet like the dragons did. Dragons were powerful and dangerous, but shifters outnumbered them by at least a thousand to one. I eyed the surrounding businesses. "What do they call the individual magichef places? Restaurants or eateries?"

Tracy chuckled. "Fast-food restaurants. And they don't have magichefs. They cook food like Ara does."

Ara, the Vampire Queen, liked to cook like a human and made some of the best food I'd ever eaten. "Right." I wasn't as ignorant as I once was, but I still struggled with some things, especially in human society. I shook it off and focused on the problem. The Bellicose operating in the human world was not good. An image formed in my head of swarming ants carrying a teenage boy out of the mall. "You're right. We need to sample this stuff. Let me try a touch of dissipating magic."

Unlike most mages, I had three pools of magic. Healing magic made up the smallest one. The magic I was born with was a medium pool. I called it my inherent magic. Then, there was the massive well of ruling magic. It usually protected me, but it had a mind of its own and I couldn't always control it. I tuned my inherent magic to a dissipating spell, tiptoed toward the thinnest tendril of diseased magic, and zapped it. Given the situation, the ruling magic was unusually quiet, and I was grateful. I didn't need it beating down the humans who surrounded us. The stream cut through the tendril and splattered against the wall. It engulfed my magic.

We shuffled forward.

The glob exploded.

Tracy screeched.

We fast-walked down the corridor.

She came to an abrupt stop and spun toward me. "What the heck was that? Did that thing eat your magic? Did you just use black magic?"

"No. What the hell?" I waved my hand toward the mess. "That stuff just ate a complicated dissipating spell. What the hell is it?" The ant-looking stuff wiggled in celebration. My stomach twisted.

"Which of your three magics did you use?"

"Inherent. Healing wouldn't do anything, and the ruling magic stayed silent."

Tracy edged closer to the mess. "You really need to fix that. So, your magic excites it. Let's see if I can do something with a potion I've been working on." She pulled out a small vial of purple liquid, screwed the cap off, and flicked a drop toward it. When the potion hit the splatter, the black stuff swarmed. The pile of ants exploded again.

Our wide eyes met.

I turned and walked away. "We need to contact the leaders in Ferine and warn them about this, so paranormals don't come here. We should also alert the local enforcers."

Tracy ran to catch up. "We can't leave it. What if it feeds on humans? We have to do something, Jen."

"We will. But we need to figure out *what* to do. We can't just keep throwing magic at it. Imagine the explosion if it got one of us." I twisted around to make sure the glob wasn't following us. "For now, let's alert Ferine. We can work on a way to dissipate it and come back." I pointed to the humans working in the food court. "Look, it doesn't touch the humans, so they'll be fine."

She leaned over, put her hands on her knees, inhaled twice, then twisted her head toward the humans. "Okay, I see what you're saying, but you need to promise we'll fix this."

"You have my word." It was easy to make a promise about something I already planned to do. My head tingled as the magical contract settled into place.

She flinched. "You didn't have to contract it."

"What are you doing here?"

"*Gah!* Damnit Quin." My detective's mentor and the Vampire Consort loved to show up at the worst times. It was part of his charm.

"Oh, yes. Let's cause a scene rather than using our senses."

I rubbed my arms against the chill of his presence. "We're in the human world. I shouldn't need them." I raised a hand before he made another sarcastic remark. "Aren't you supposed to be trying to find that supposed king?"

"Yes." He rubbed his nose. "Something smells rotten. Perhaps the food?"

Tracy latched onto his arm and pulled him back. "It's magic that acts like a disease. I'm pretty sure the Bellicose created it."

"Ahh. So, you are poaching another case," he mumbled. "May I have a magic sight potion?"

Tracy dug into her bag and handed him an orange potion.

Quin drank it, blinked, and shook his head. His image flickered as the magic surged through him.

"You made a potion that works on vampires?"

"Yeah. Several, actually. Quin wanted magic sight, so it was one of my first inventions. I also have potions that repel vampires. I'm working on one that will allow Quin invisibility, though that one's tricky." Tracy dug through her bag. "I don't have many with me." She loved talking about her potions. Her ingenuity amazed me.

Quin leaned toward the oozing magic. "The sight is adequate." He pointed toward the food court. "This differs from the previous magics."

I folded my arms. "What previous magics?"

"The ones I destroyed, of course." Quin took two steps forward. "It seems they cannot keep their labs secret or intact when I am near."

"I hadn't heard that you've taken down labs." My brother, who raised me and served as the regent to my throne, had a habit of withholding information, so it didn't surprise me he didn't mention the labs. It still stung, but I let it go. "Yet you can't find their so-called king?"

"Oh yes. Let's pretend I am incompetent." His furrowed brow contradicted his casual tone. This magic had Quin worried. Which worried me.

"Let's not," Tracy said. "Let's not argue, either. We need to focus on fixing this."

She was right. We had a job to do. "We were going to report it to the leadership in Ferine and try to make a dissipating spell."

Quin shook his head. "I would not recommend that until you have more answers to their insufferable questions. Magic does not affect me, so I will gather a sample." He held out a hand.

"No," Tracy protested. "It makes shifters lethargic and then violent. We can't risk you going berserk in a human mall."

He dropped his hand and waltzed right into the magic.

Tracy flung her arms out. "You'd think he'd listen to me about this, considering I know more than him about it."

I didn't reply. I had faith that Quin knew what he was doing. He was right that vampires, especially ancient ones, were immune to most magic. Tracy's potions and spells were the exception.

He strolled past the splotch our magic made, and I sighed in relief when it didn't reach for him. He opened his mouth to say something, then paused. His eyebrows drew together, and he shifted his attention to his shoes. A steady stream of ant-looking things crawled across his shiny dress shoes, wrapped around his legs, and slithered under the cuffs of his pants.

"Oh, no. Don't..." Tracy ran straight into the stuff to help him. "Go in that."

Where the tendrils were hesitant to attack Quin, they latched onto Tracy fast.

Quin attempted to brush the stuff off his expensive suit. "Perhaps it affects vampires."

"We gotta do something about this. Quin, stop it. Geez. We need to figure this out. Jen, stay back. I'm going to find a table and work on a neutralizing spell." Tracy grabbed his arm, and he allowed her to drag him toward a table.

I eased back as I watched them. Why would someone use this in the human world when they'd already spread it to the shifter compound? Why not add it to the wards that contained the pockets? If I were an evil mastermind, I'd do that first, so that everyone became a violent mess. Then I'd swoop in and save the day with a dissipating spell. If that's what it even did to them. The only information we had came from the Alpha. Too many questions.

Two humans gave me inquisitive glances as they passed. Right. Not a good idea to loiter in the middle of the corridor. I went back down a device with moving stairs that Tracy called an escalator and circled back to the other side of the food court. I found a table that wasn't infected near them and pulled out a chair. "Let's figure this stuff out together."

We were still stumped an hour later. About fifteen minutes in, Quin stopped making sarcastic comments, grabbed his head, and collapsed on the table. He hadn't moved.

Tracy came up with several potions and spells that worked on demon magic since the dragon incident. She called them anti-demon potions, though I voted to call them anti-Jaques spells. Jaques was the brother responsible for my childhood trauma. I discovered that he also somehow had demon magic. As a kid, he'd use it on me and I developed magic to counteract him. My memories from that time were a little sketchy, So I didn't remember most of the details.

Tracy was particular about her spells. If anyone could figure out how to dissipate the stuff, I'd put my money on her. She cast a spell and sent it toward Quin. The black magic retracted, but it didn't dissipate, and he didn't wake up. Her skin was ashen after an hour of trying different spells, and dark circles formed under her eyes from the magic infection. Or maybe infestation. I wasn't sure what to call it. A tendril of magic crept toward me, and I moved a couple tables down. "You okay, Tracy?"

"Uh huh."

Quin's head popped up.

My spine snapped straight. "Um, Tracy?"

She didn't have time to move before his hand clutched her neck.

I jumped out of my chair. "Shit, shit, shit. Hang on, I'm coming."

Tracy threw a spell.

He released her and stumbled out of his chair. A red sheen flooded his eyes and long claws extended from his hands and feet, ripping through his designer shoes. A few humans screamed and ran out of the food court. He launched himself at me. I flashed away.

He spun and lunged at me again.

Trembling, I swung my head around to find a place without humans. I spotted a sign that said 'restrooms' and flashed into that hallway. Stabbing pain pierced my shoulder as Quin's claws dug into it. His fangs sunk into the back of my neck. The ruling magic vibrated, begging to beat him down. I let it go.

I barely registered the humans gathered at the hallway's entrance, their phones out and held up. The ruling magic smashed into Quin, and he flew toward the men's restroom. He didn't fall like I expected. Instead, he used his unnatural agility to keep his footing and went fluid. I lost him for a second. A jolt of agony surged through my stomach. I glanced down, my eyes widening at the holes his claws left. I sent healing magic through myself, tuned my inherent magic to a sleeping spell, and shot it toward Quin. He was already gone.

I swung my head toward the humans. A spell blanketed them, and they shuffled back toward the food court as Tracy joined me in the hall.

I sensed Quin but didn't see him. I tilted my head back and looked up at the ceiling. Tracy turned in a slow circle. He disappeared from my senses.

Screams and shouts erupted from another area of the mall. Adrenaline shot through me and I sprinted toward the sounds. The second most powerful vampire in the world going crazy and being set loose on humans was not something anyone wanted. I rounded a corner, Tracy on my heels, and we screeched to a stop.

Quin slashed his claws across the chest of some type of uniformed man. Humans had so many types of authorities that I could never keep them straight, so I wasn't sure which kind he was. His shirt was lighter blue than his pants and he wore a badge.

I threw a knockout spell.

The man in uniform sunk to the floor.

Quin charged me.

A shield formed in front of my face. Tracy shoved me behind her and braced both hands on the shield. I locked mine on her back. Quin bounced off it, sending a jolt through my arms. He shook his head, then charged again. He bounced off and started beating his fists against it.

Tracy shook her head as if to clear it. "This magic's got a hold of me. I'm going down in a minute. This is a protection spell meant to guard against mosquitoes mixed with your anti-demon magic. Learn it." She shoved the shield into my hands and conjured another.

A fist barreled toward me. I raised the shield just in time to block. Quin hammered against it, his massive strength making me feel like a fish trying to hold off a bear. With each blow, my arms got a little weaker. I used my inherent magic to bolster them, braced one heel against the wall, and shoved. He didn't budge.

The magic made him dumb, I realized. Anyone with an ounce of intelligence would have abandoned the shield and gone for my legs. And he was a seasoned fighter who would have already killed me if the magic didn't make him so stupid. It gave me a small piece of information about how it worked, but it didn't fix the infection.

Tracy's spell wasn't complicated, but I barely absorbed it before Quin crashed through the shield, his normally blank face twisted in rage.

We smashed into the wall as I tuned my inherent magic to the shield spell. At the same time, Tracy collided with us from the side. All three of us skidded across the floor. Pain exploded through my head as we slid to a stop. Quin kicked me in the side, his claws digging into my ribs. The ruling magic lashed out. It tuned itself to Tracy's new spell and wrapped itself around them. Then it smashed them against the ground three times and solidified so they couldn't move.

With a grunt, I slithered toward them. Spots danced in my vision. My entire body screamed in pain with every movement. I had to stop and wheeze a couple of times so it took what felt like forever to reach them, though it was only a few seconds.

If my magic ever merged, I'd be able to use the wild magic in the air to cast spells like a witch. It was a big 'if' because I'd been trying to fix my magic for most of my life with no results. Until then, I had to use the pools of magic inside me and hoped I tuned it to the right spell. All it took was missing or misinterpreting one element, and the whole spell would implode.

I stretched my shaky hands out, touched my friends, coated them in the dissipating magic, and ran healing magic through them for good measure. I gasped for air, gritted my teeth against the searing pain, and ran both through myself just before everything faded to black.

"I mean, I figured since this magic looks so much like bugs..." Tracy's voice brought me out of my trance. "There you are. Are you okay?"

"Did it work?" I croaked.

"Thank the fates you're alive. And yeah, it worked. I guess it took Quin attacking us for my brain to engage."

I cracked an eye open. We were still in the human mall based on all the marble and perfumed air. I tried to act like my head wasn't spinning as I sat up. The swaying was my first clue that my acting skills were off, followed by a steadying hand on my arm. "What about the humans?"

"Are you okay, Jenella?" The sound of the deep voice made my chest flutter.

The scent of wood smoke and Drake washed over me, and my brain decided everything would be alright. Grass-green eyes full of concern entered my vision. I shook my spinning head and threw out a hand to brace myself. Those thoughts were a big nope for me. "Hey, Drake. Stalking me again?"

His chuckle sent heat through my body. The traitor. "I was in the area and felt your distress."

I cradled my head and swallowed. "Uh huh. That's believable. Did you not realize I can sense cloaked dragons?"

"That's great. But right now, we need to clean up this mess." Tracy's voice broke the awkward silence that followed.

I'd never told anyone that I sensed cloaked dragons. In my defense, I never would have admitted it if my head wasn't reeling. I stumbled to my feet and would have fallen if Drake hadn't caught me. Bastien, Tracy's match and the Prince of Dragons came into focus beside Tracy, the usual deep scowl on his face. "Hey, Bas." My eyes drifted toward Quin, who leaned against the wall next to the unconscious man in uniform. No other humans were in sight. "Where did all the humans go?"

"We intercepted some and changed their memories. The others are in a trance. What in the hell were you three doing?" Bastien growled.

"That's quite a talent you have, Bas." I released my death grip on Drake and leaned against the wall. "Why does my head hurt so bad?"

"I slammed it on the floor or the wall. I mean, I wasn't in my right mind, so I'm not sure which," Tracy answered.

"Okay." I ran more healing magic through my head and my vision cleared enough to focus. "Better. We were working a case." I pointed down the hall.

Tracy put a hand on my arm and launched into the story, starting when we found the magic in the food court and ending with me healing my friends. "So, yeah. That's what happened."

Drake's magic brushed my skin, and my clothes returned to a serviceable state. He ran his eyes over me, then tilted his head toward the food court. "Bastien and I will take care of the humans. How fast can you clean up the magic?"

I tuned my inherent magic into the neutralizing spell and tested it in a small area. It worked, but my head still pounded, and I swayed with the effort. "A while."

Tracy grabbed my arm. "I already sent a spell out to disable cameras and phones. I'll clean the seating area. Jen can help when her brain reengages."

"Do it fast and leave the human world," Bastien ordered.

It took another hour. As my head cleared, I helped more. By the time I became coherent, the number of humans had increased tenfold. We had to be creative. I pretended to play on my phone and aimed my magic at the walls and ceilings. Tracy sat at a table, weaved spells, and sent them out in sheets. Quin hid himself in the corner and watched over us, though it was a mystery as to why.

Eventually, we dissipated the last of it and headed to our car.

Tracy yawned. "I need food and sleep before we do anything else."

Quin appeared beside her. "I apologize."

He moved slow enough for me to sense, so I didn't jump. "Don't apologize. It wasn't your fault." I paused. "What did it feel like?"

"Like I gave into bloodlust."

Tracy hit the button on the human gadget, and the car doors clicked as they unlocked. "For me, it felt like all the anger I'd ever repressed came to the surface. I had no choice but to take it out on you."

I opened the passenger door. "You two were lethargic. Quin flew into the rage a few minutes before you did. So, is it because he is older and has more rage? Or because he's a vampire who is susceptible to bloodlust? And when it hit you, you didn't recognize me as a friend. You also didn't attack each other."

Tracy nodded. "Yeah. We recognized each other, though. I believed he was an ally, but I had the overwhelming urge to kill you."

"Quin?"

"I did not catalog my thoughts. However, I failed to draw my sword or filter the magic out of your blood as I ingested it. Both automatic responses."

I pointed at him. "You weren't as graceful or fast as you usually are, either. And Tracy didn't use her potions."

Tracy ran her hands over her face. "So, you're saying someone else was in charge?"

"Either that or someone programmed the infection to dumb you down. There wasn't any nuance to your actions. They were clunky at best." I tapped my chin. "It's something to consider."

Tracy nodded. "Right. But I'm too exhausted."

"Me, too. Let's head back to the hotel and take a power nap."

Quin pointed to the far end of the parking lot. "A trail of that magic leads from the mall. I will follow it. How long must you rest?"

"A couple of hours." I snatched the human car gadget out of Tracy's hand.

"I mean, I probably won't be a hundred percent with a quick nap, but I'll have a lot more energy than I do now." Tracy held out her hand. "You aren't driving."

While taking my safe cases, I'd learned to function somewhat like a normal person. I no longer blew up magichefs and cleaned up after myself. I even talked to other paranormals without second guessing myself most of the time. There were still things I struggled with, though. Where Tracy drove slow and followed the rules, I saw things like speed limits and stop signs as suggestions that ruined all the fun.

I made a big show of being annoyed as I handed it back to her. "I'm calling Mat. We also need to alert the local enforcers."

"Of course. Let's complicate the situation," Quin scoffed.

"The last thing I want is to complicate things. But I'm positive this is the Bellicose. Mat needs to know about it." My brother wouldn't be happy I took the case, but he still needed the information.

"Very well. Tell Mathias. But do not involve the enforcers yet." Quin disappeared.

We bought burritos from a street mage outside the hotel and headed toward our rooms. Chills ran down my spine as I wondered what would happen if that magic went unchecked. Whoever made that stuff needed to be stopped.

"Is your call to Mat going to be an informational call or an argument?" Tracy asked.

Mat and I didn't argue as much as when I first became independent, but we still butted heads occasionally. "Informational only. I hope."

"Good luck with that. Let me know if you need a friend to lean on."

I liked the idea, but I always tried to remember that Tracy was my guard, not my friend. If she wanted, she could walk away from me and never look back. I doubted she would, but it always rattled around in my head. I'd led a very sheltered life where I never got too close to anyone. Growing up, I had one friend. And he only befriended me to raise his status, so I'd severed that relationship. "Okay."

She smirked. "Good. Because I've never really been your guard. I mean, you don't really need one. So consider me a friend who has your back." She stabbed the elevator button. "Since that's settled, we need to report this to the enforcers, no matter what Quin says. The damage that magic might have done if we hadn't found it bothers me. What if it's all over town and takes over a pocket?"

Hope bloomed in my chest at her declaration of our friendship. I squashed it and focused on the case. "Quin's right about investigating more before we act. I'll ask Mat to hold off on sending in the enforcers. That might keep them from resenting me like the ones in Hospa did." When I got kidnapped by dragons with my now assistant, Verity, I made the mistake of calling Mat's match, Emine, the head of the enforcers. The detectives in the small office in the pocket of Hospa didn't like that. As a result, I tried to be careful about involving my family in my detective work.

We stepped off the elevator on our floor. "For now, let's rest so we can go back out there before Quin gets himself in more trouble."

Chapter Four

JEN

My phone buzzed an hour later. I pried my eyes open and saw my brother's name. "Mat. What a coincidence. I was just going to call you."

"Were you? Wise, since I haven't heard from you in over a week." Mat, ever overprotective, hated not knowing where I was or what I was doing. He fought his nature to allow me to grow into myself and took care of most of my duties at home. I checked in with Verity daily but only called Mat once a week. My assistant, a mage with juror magic, was the most efficient person on the planet, so I didn't need to make too many personal appearances.

"Yeah. Sorry about that. I got caught up in finding a home for a family of trolls, and when it wrapped up, I caught another case. Which is what I need to talk to you about."

"There are far more important things than the next case."

"You don't need to lecture me about my duties." We had those conversations all the time. It was like how other people said, 'Hi, how are you?'

"Agreed. Let's discuss your fight with Tarquin in a human mall."

"How did you find out about that so fast?" At least my brother didn't show up in person. I called that progress.

"The humans put the video on the internet. What have you gotten yourself into?"

I rubbed my eyes and sat up. "We thought we got all the cameras."

"One can never catch all the cameras in the human world. They have them everywhere."

Mat raised me and was older than me by a couple of centuries. Mages of Ahl, like most paranormals, could live forever if we were lucky. Being over two hundred years old, he was in his prime. Even though I was almost thirty-seven, older paranormals still saw me as a baby. "I'm working with Quin and Tracy, so I'm safe."

"Except Tarquin attacked you." My brother's rough voice turned into a growl.

"Well, yeah, except then. But I handled it." I didn't mention Drake and Bastien hovering around because it felt too personal. "We came across a strange new magic. It's different from the mind control that took over the dragons. It makes people lethargic and then violent. Quin got infected and lost his... Quinness... He forgot about his sword, that he could disappear, and he wasn't as graceful or a good fighter. Tracy forgot about her potions and spells when it hit her. The stuff grew when magic touched it. It stretched out feelers and exploded."

"What?"

"I'm not explaining this well. It fed off our magic and grew when we tried to stop it. Quin's immunity didn't work against it." I paused and gathered my thoughts. "It looked like a colony of black ants. Have you heard of that before?"

Silence.

"Mat?"

"Tell me the story from the beginning."

I told him again, adding as much detail as I remembered. When I finished, I felt his anger and worry bleed through the phone.

"You need to come home. This is dangerous, and you don't need to involve yourself. If the magic is as bad as you say, you should be nowhere near it."

"I'll come home when we solve the case. Besides, Tracy figured out a way to neutralize it, so I'm fine. Have you heard about it before?"

"No. But I'm sure the Bellicose is behind it, so it could be a trap."

"It is a trap. But I'm not the target. It seems to be aimed at shifters, although I can't say for certain. I need to investigate that more."

He sighed in exasperation. "Since you won't listen to logic and leave, I'll notify the enforcers and send you some help. That is non-negotiable."

"You can send help, but tell them to stay back. Quin doesn't want enforcers stepping all over this magic until we learn more. Like I said, Tracy's discovered a way to neutralize it, so we're fine." Mat would send someone, anyway. An entire army, if he could. I planned to solve the case before help arrived. "I'll ask Verity to notify the Leadership Council so they can take care of their people. Deva needs to know right away. And maybe Gabe and Linda, since this magic is targeting shifters." Deva was the queen of dragons and extremely powerful. I saw her every couple of weeks when I went to the Dragon Headquarters to renew my glamour. Gabe and Linda led the shifters.

"I'll notify Deva and Gabe, but not the Council. No reason to get everyone stirred up until we have answers."

"Okay. And I'll be fine. I'll check in with you when I'm not in the field. I promise I'll stay safe."

"You better." He paused. "You think my worry for you is a burden, but your safety is vital to our future."

Not interested in having that argument again, I placated him. "Like I said, I'll be careful."

"I don't believe you." He hung up.

The sour mood from our conversation lingered as I texted Tracy and headed out to meet her. She waited in the hotel lobby, face in her phone. Even when wearing the glamour earrings that dulled her looks, she was stunning. The way people stared at her made me glad I was more cute than beautiful. Wearing my glamour earrings, I wasn't even cute.

Tracy spotted me and slipped her phone in her pocket. "Quin found something. Are you ready to go?"

"I can drive." I held out a hand.

She shook her head. "Not a chance. You're a terrible driver, and I doubt you'll ever improve. You don't think the rules apply to you and go way too fast. I mean, I have things to do and want to live to do them."

She was right that I hated following the rules. I was trying to change that mindset because I wanted to be a decent person. I didn't want Tracy to fear for her life, so I'd let her drive. "Okay. You can drive."

"Stop doing that. It's annoying." She strode toward the door. A male witch hopped in front of her to open it.

The witch let the door go before I got through, and I had to jump forward to keep from getting hit. "How can you stand that?"

"What?"

I pointed back toward the door as we got into the car. "The guy tripping over himself to impress you. How does that not drive you crazy?"

She started the car. "I'm mated to the Dragon Heir. I don't have to deal with it because he usually does. When he's not around, I use it to my advantage at every opportunity. Besides, you don't have any room to talk."

"I have never had that problem in my life."

"Suuuure, you haven't." She rolled her eyes. "I've seen first-hand how people trip over themselves to be noticed by you. Every eligible mage in Allure has visited the castle to see if you're their match. You're just good at ignoring the obvious." As we pulled onto the street, she shrugged. "To answer your question, I've been me my whole life, so those things seem normal."

"Sure. But it seems like it would get as old as all the bowing."

"I mean, the glamour helps, so it's not as bad when I'm wearing it. It's one reason my grandmother hates me. That, and she resents my power. I draw attention away from her, and she can't handle it. She's so jealous that she turned the witches against me and had me shunned. I mean, I don't care after what she did to my mother. One day, I'll be her end." Her knuckles on the steering wheel turned white as she spoke. "I'm not ready yet, but one day."

Tracy's grandmother killed her mom and tried to kill her when she was a kid. "Let me know when you're ready and I'll do what I can."

She chuckled. "It's a tricky situation because she's the President of Covens. She's on borrowed time, though. The witches are losing faith in her. As soon as she's voted out, I'm going to bring her down." Her voice was as casual as if she were discussing the weather, though her shoulders were still tense.

"I saw my parents killed in front of me. Mat got justice, but I never did, so I get it."

Tracy's face softened. "Yeah. I suppose you do."

"Mat and I fight a lot, but I owe him everything. He gave me a great childhood and I need to remember that." Heartbroken himself, instead of giving in to his grief, he pulled it together and took in a sad, abused child he barely knew and made a life. He did it without making it seem like work. Granted, he withheld information, lied, and was way too overprotective, but he still did his best.

"Yeah. My dad did the same. He didn't want to be involved in politics but ran for Vice President to protect me. He hates working with my grandmother. To him, the position is a way to monitor her."

"Maybe you and Bas should go public. I bet most witches would stop harassing you out of fear. My bullies took off the minute he became my guard when I was a kid."

"I don't want to use Bas. I love him too much for that."

"He wouldn't see it as using him. He'd see it as an opportunity to play a new game."

She let out a strangled laugh. "He so would. Another reason not to do it. His temper makes him dangerous, and I couldn't stand it if he got in trouble because of me."

"We are both so screwed up."

"No. No, we're not. We're two formerly broken girls who grew up to be kick-ass women."

I didn't believe I was a kick-ass woman, but I didn't want to ruin the moment. "Yeah."

We parked on the street in an industrial area, and she twisted in her seat. "We leave this discussion here, but you can always talk to me. I won't betray or use you like people have your whole life. It isn't healthy for either of us to keep this stuff bottled up. I will keep this to myself, too. We're friends now, which means we trust each other. I'm not going anywhere, and I'll always make time for you." She crossed her heart.

Tears sprung to my eyes. No one had ever said anything like that to me before. A small part of the hollow loneliness that always hung in my heart eased. "You're the best friend I've ever had." I sucked in some air. "Your secrets are safe with me. I'm not going anywhere except the stupid palace, so you can always find me."

She chuckled. "You will not get trapped. I won't allow it. If I can't spring you from your office, Drake or Quin will. You have people now. Besides, I don't think Mat's goal is to lock you in. He just loves you and wants you to be safe."

I couldn't help the sappy smile that spread across my face as we stepped out of the car. She was right, and I planned on figuring out a way to keep my freedom when I took the throne. I wasn't going back to my bubble.

The late afternoon sun and humidity made the air feel like soup. Sweat trickled down my back as we walked toward a massive warehouse. Two stories high, it took up an entire city block. The building was unremarkable, with its white concrete walls, a semi-flat metal roof, and lack of windows. Quin stood next to the man-door on the loading dock in the shade, wearing dark sunglasses. His head tilted toward a building down the street, where I sensed Bastien and Drake land.

His focus shifted to us as we approached. "What took you so long?"

Tracy waved a dismissive hand. "We got here as soon as we could. Human transportation is slow."

He flashed a bone-chilling smile. "That is precisely why I steer clear of it." He opened the door and waved a hand for us to go through.

The warehouse was big from the outside, but inside, it was cavernous. Squares of wood held boxes piled high in rows upon rows of metal shelving. I leaned toward one by the door and read a label on a box. "Cereal. What does a cereal warehouse have to do with anything? And where are all the workers?"

Quin motioned us to follow him and pointed toward two tiny offices and a stairwell in the back. "The trail from the mall ends here. The diseased magic leads down the stairwell for those who are not observant."

Tracy shuffled a little closer. "It looks way thicker here than at the mall."

I spotted an evacuation map that displayed two floors and stepped closer. "Here's the layout of the basement."

Quin appeared next to me. "You do not have the energy to clear an entire basement."

Tracy moved to my other side. "We're fine. Maybe we don't need to clear the whole thing. We can clear just enough so you can use your vampire thingy to see what's going on."

"By all means, let's use Quin as cannon fodder," He scoffed. "It is never smart to rush into a Bellicose lab."

My eye twitched. "Bellicose lab?"

He turned toward the basement and cocked his head. "Yes. It is not the first one I have found for those who did not listen when I explained it the first time. Eliminating them takes careful planning."

"Right." I paced so I could think. "In order to do that careful planning, we need to know what we're up against. Which means a quick reconnaissance and leave if there's any trouble."

"Perhaps." Quin rubbed the stubble on his chin. "I have a dislike for places I cannot easily escape."

When his eyes met mine, I saw a flicker of fear. "You're afraid."

"I am not afraid," he drawled.

I'd never seen Quin scared before. But then, I'd never seen magic affect him, either. It gave me goosebumps. "Maybe we should leave and come back later."

He let out an exaggerated sigh. "We do not need to run away."

I shook my head. "I understand why you're scared. This stuff has me on edge, too. I never want to see you go berserk again." I pointed to my healed neck. "If you freak out and kill me, I swear I'll attach my spirit to yours and drag you to the depths of hell."

"I did not...go berserk." He dragged the words out. "I simply succumbed to a disease. Your precious lives are safe with me."

Quin always reverted to sarcasm, but he usually did it better. "Fine. You better not get yourself infected and freak out again. If any of that stuff gets on you, I'll flash you out before you kill us all. Deal?"

He looked down his nose at me. "I do not freak out. That is your area of expertise."

The last remark was true even though he didn't know it. I would totally freak out if the place was dark, damp, and small. No way I'd tell him that, though.

Tracy stepped between us. "No one is freaking out. I mean, seriously, we are all professionals here."

I eyed the magic. "Why does this bother you, Quin? Have you seen something like it before?"

"Like this? No. But I have dismantled a few of their labs. They use many terrible magics on live subjects."

"So, this magic might be an experiment?" Tracy asked.

"Perhaps. All their magical practices share similarities. They incorporate the use of demon magic with witch or mage magic. Often both. Its purpose is always to control paranormals."

I rubbed my arms. "Then let's check it out fast and regroup at the hotel. We can figure out how to destroy the lab later."

Tracy and I cleared the magic from the stairwell, and Quin put his ear to the door. After a minute of listening, he stepped back. "Two guards discussed drinking after their shift. They have more than one person locked in the old offices in the hall on the right." He put his hand on the handle and stopped. "You investigate that hall. I will go left. Do not screw this up. Do not draw attention to yourselves. If I say run, do not delay." He breezed through the door.

The basement hallways were void of the magic, so we didn't have to clear it as Tracy and I crept through the door and slipped down the hallway on the right. Voices echoed from somewhere. We stopped in our tracks and shared a look. They were far away in the direction Quin had disappeared. Tracy pointed to the right side and crept toward the first door.

Heart in my throat, I kept my footsteps as light as I slunk down the concrete hallway toward the rooms on the left. What used to be offices had long, skinny windows with a wire mesh over them and a thick coat of grime. The dark gray doors clashed with the yellowish-brown color of the walls. The bright fluorescent lights burned my eyes. I stretched to peer through the first window. Dark, sludgy magic coated the entire room. I turned down my magic sight enough to see through it and stretched my neck to peer inside.

A skinny, naked girl lay in a heap on a stripped mattress on the floor. Blood matted her blonde hair. Purple and blue bruises covered her body. Her face was so battered it was unrecognizable. My throat tightened, and I fought the urge to charge in and save her. After several deep breaths, I crept to the next window.

It held a full-grown man with a shaved head. Tattoos covered his body. He sat in a corner, knees up to his chest and his arms wrapped around them. He'd once been muscular, but his gaunt form made it look like his skin shrunk and those muscles were strings. Swallowing back bile, I moved on. And found the same scenario in the next three cells.

A loud clang came from the adjacent hallway. Quin flew around the corner so fast my brain didn't register that it was him until he stopped in front of me with a hand wrapped around Tracy's arm. "Flash us," he hissed.

I threw my hands onto their shoulders and glanced back, meeting the eyes of an ogre that stumbled around the corner. I flashed to the car. "What the hell happened? You were supposed to be stealthy. Like when you sneak up on me." I released their shoulders. "What type of vampire makes that kind of noise?"

"I do." He opened the passenger door. "Get in."

CHAPTER FIVE

DRAKE

CLOAKED FROM EVERYONE EXCEPT Jenella, or so she said, Drake shifted into his human form. The smaller form didn't take as much energy to cloak, and he'd learned the hard way that preserving energy was the key to survival. Jenella climbed out of a silver human vehicle with a bright smile on her face. The glamour he made for her took away from her striking beauty but allowed her freedom she wouldn't have otherwise had. It felt good to give her what she wanted most. He'd never told her how difficult the undetectable glamour was to maintain. Jenella's enormous power burned through it at a rate he'd never seen. He could renew it from a distance, but he'd never told her that, either. Seeing her every two weeks was the only thing he had to look forward to since his awakening. She was a joy to have around.

"What are you doing here?"

Drake ignored his cousin. Bastien liked to pretend he could sense him and was adequate at guessing his location, but he was never sure.

Jenella and Tracy approached Tarquin. For reasons that puzzled him, they had a fondness for the vampire.

"You need to tell her," Bastien said in the language of their home realm.

A heaviness settled over him. Drake uncloaked himself to Bastien. "I don't have to do anything."

"It's not an order but concern. You're different since you woke up."

"I'm not." Drake watched Jenella disappear into a warehouse. "I spent thousands of years trying to find my place. I am no longer interested. Nor do I wish to impress anyone."

"You are part of our family. You have always had a place."

Bastien was a smart and loyal dragon, but he often missed subtlety. "I fit in with you and Deva. The other dragons still resent me. Everyone else fears me." Except Jenella. One of his favorite memories was when she slapped him. It was a reaction to the situation, but he knew she'd do it again, or worse, if he tried to handle her like that again. "I am neither a dragon nor a First in anything but title. I still wish to find my place but will no longer grovel for it."

"And you want Jen to help you with that?" Bastien's voice held a challenge. He was almost as protective of Jenella as he was of Tracy.

Drake didn't take it as a challenge. His cousin watched her grow up and loved her like a sister. "Perhaps."

Through the bond, Jenella's fear and disgust surged. She didn't realize that she opened the bond when she got scared, allowing her feelings to peek through.

Bastien must have sensed the same from Tracy because he focused on the building with the intensity reserved for when his mate was in trouble. When the feeling subsided, his focus shifted back to Drake. "You need to tell her."

"No."

"It is not healthy to pretend the bond doesn't exist."

"I'm not pretending."

"No, but you haven't told her, either. Jen hates being the last to learn things. She'll transfer that hate to you if you keep it from her much longer." Bastien shook his head. "When did you initialize the bond?"

Drake considered not answering the question, but he knew his cousin wouldn't let it go. "Jenella initiated it shortly after I woke up. Or, rather, that magic she cannot control did." He remembered when the bond formed. They stood in a gym at Castle Mahri while Jenella wrestled with her past. He'd never felt so helpless, yet he understood it was a war she had to fight for herself. His own emotions overwhelmed his efforts to squash his instincts, and he wanted nothing more in that moment than to help her. Emotions he'd intentionally shut down long before his forced sleep resurfaced. The sting of rejection, the sharp stab of betrayal, and the crushing helplessness to change the situation. After the second queen put him to sleep, he lay in his prison, unable to escape, and pondered them until white-hot rage overtook him.

He tried to resume his life after he woke from the trance, but rage always simmered just under the surface. Until that night when Jenella's magic reached out, clamped his center in a vice-grip, and opened other emotions. Ones he didn't realize he still possessed. Ones he craved. Acceptance, certainty, lust, longing, the prospect of finding love. Though he wasn't quite there yet.

All those emotions raced through him as he stood in what once was a dungeon and watched her wrestle with her internal demons. The urge to pull her to him and erase all thoughts of her tragic past was overwhelming. By the time her magic stabbed into his core, he lacked the strength to reject the bond, so he didn't. It was a mistake.

Drake selfishly couldn't bring himself to care. Jenella gave him hope. And hope was the most dangerous emotion. It made him want things he could never have. A healthy bond being one of them.

On top of that, Jenella craved freedom. She didn't want to be tied to anyone or anything. To tell her about the bond would mean more rejection.

He couldn't live through that kind of pain again. If he lost this new hope, it would destroy him.

"You need to tell her."

"No."

"Her ignorance is not healthy for either of you."

The raging inferno of anger inside of him flared, and he stuffed it back down. "I've told you before that the one thing Jenella wants most is freedom. She will see the bond as a shackle. I cannot give her the freedom she desires because of her title. But I can let her be free of a bond she doesn't want. I suggest you butt out of my business before I make you."

"Except you're not giving her freedom," Bastien ignored the warning. "You're out here like me, compelled to protect your mate. It's not only physically impossible for you to stay away, but it is an insult to Jen to keep it from her. Especially since she admitted she knows you're following her. You want to give her what she wants most? Give her the truth. I guarantee you that's as important as freedom after all the lies Mathias has fed her."

Drake's anger drained, replaced by a sense of hopelessness. He spied on Mathias after he changed the castle wards to let himself through undetected. Jenella's brother kept some interesting secrets. Secrets that would devastate her. Like the fact that her mother was still alive. Rage tried to rekindle itself at the thought of the second queen, and he tamped it down. His longing to hunt her was second only to his desire for Jenella herself.

Pain shot through his chest as the bond slammed shut. He understood that if he killed her mother without her knowing, she'd never forgive him. His cousin was right. He needed to talk to her.

Jenella and her friends appeared beside the car and jumped in as they argued. Five paranormals poured out of the building and followed them.

"Perhaps you're right. I will need to think about it." Drake didn't wait for a response. He morphed into his dragon form, cloaked himself, and followed them.

CHAPTER SIX

JEN

ENTERING FERINE DIFFERED FROM any other pocket I'd visited. Instead of driving off a cliff or into a lake, the gate was inside a business called Quick Stop Oil Change. Tracy pulled in as a grizzled ogre directed the human in front of us to the bay on the right.

She pulled the car forward and pushed the button that lowered the window. The ogre stuck his head in the car and paled when he saw Quin lounging in the back seat, his head back, and his eyes closed. "Go to the bay on the far left."

The bay door opened as we approached, and Tracy pulled forward and stopped. When the door behind us closed, the door in front of us opened, and we drove into Ferine. I liked that approach. It kept us from having to put a spell on the gate that erased human memories and gave us better access control.

I went straight to my room and took a shower when we got to the hotel. I knew Quin didn't mean to get us caught. But after seeing the people in that lab, I couldn't help but feel like we should do more. Like *I* should do more. I hoped they'd hang on until we could rescue them. When the hot water pruned my skin, I got out and dressed. I'd never considered that Quin made mistakes like the rest of us because he always presented himself as infallible. Or maybe that was just my perception of him. It never occurred to me that he wasn't perfect like the rest of us.

I still wasn't sure why he became my detective's mentor. Or his reasons for sticking around as I got better at the job. Quin didn't need things like recognition or respect that came with being my ally. He didn't care about his social status, either. I suspected it was because Mat told him to stay close or maybe because I amused him.

The room was growing dark, so I sent some magic toward the lights as I settled onto the bed to read one of my mother's diaries. They flickered twice before they came on. I frowned. It was unusual for lights powered by magic to flicker. I stood on the bed and stretched my arm toward the ceiling to better understand the spell. The lighting spell was normal, but someone had tried to reverse it, causing the weave to be tattered in one area. I repaired it and flopped onto the mattress as Quin and Tracy breezed through the door.

Tracy shoved a takeout box in my hands as Quin set his carton on the small table in the corner. "A medical lab held a wolf shifter around twelve years old. I rendered the torturer useless and freed the girl. They had a vampire chained to the wall whom I also tried to free. The girl knocked down a tray. The guards attempted to follow us, but I took care of the problem."

"I knew one of them saw us but didn't send out my senses after we left." I perched on the edge of the bed and opened the box of food.

"Of course you didn't." He wiped his hands on a napkin. "They planned to cut the shifter open. I could not let that happen." Quin stopped as if to gather his thoughts. "I do not mind torturing vampires who deserve the punishment. The one they had in that room was young and did not deserve it. I failed to free him."

Tracy waved her fork. "We'll have to move fast to save them. How do we do that?"

My chest tightened at the mention of the people locked in those rooms. Tracy was right. "Mat said he's going to send help."

Quin's jaw clenched.

I held up a hand. "When my brother decides he is going to protect me, there's no arguing with him. He agreed to order the enforcers to stay back."

Quin's chair squeaked as he scooted it out. "Oh, yes. We must appease Mat."

"You know as well as I do what that bug-looking magic means. The Coalition leadership needs the information. No need to be condescending."

"I am not condescending."

Tracy giggled and started toward the door. "Speaking of overprotective, I'll be right back. I left my phone in my room and need to check in with Bastien so he doesn't show up here."

The door blew in.

Tracy flew across the room and smashed into the back wall by the window.

Before I could react, Quin latched onto my wrist and swished us across the room to where she landed. My head spun as I tried to process what was happening. Shifters oozing bug magic flowed through the door. I gaped at Tracy, who lay unconscious on the floor.

Quin latched onto my hand. "Flash us!"

Heart pounding and still not thinking straight, I flashed us to the hotel's roof. Quin threw Tracy over his shoulder and became a blur as he leaped onto the roof of the next building. I ran after him, too stunned to flash. Just as I was getting ready to jump, something tripped me. I flew between the buildings and caught the edge of the next one with my fingertips. Coming to my senses, I flashed myself up and ran with a purpose.

"What was that?" Quin yelled over his shoulder.

I didn't have time to answer because the tainted shifters burst out of the door and rushed toward us. Sweat beaded on my forehead as I peeked over the edge. A sea of tainted shifters waited below. I tried to tamp down my panic as I searched for an escape route.

"Flash us down the street." Quin pointed to an intersection about a block away.

"We're going to have to fight," I said, my voice shaky.

He rolled his eyes and flipped his fangs out. "Must everything be an argument? Flash us, Jen."

I flashed to the intersection. Quin latched onto my arm and went fluid. He stopped in an empty parking lot next to a cement storage shed and stashed Tracy inside it. He locked the door and threw a potion at it so fast I barely had time to blink. The next thing I knew, we were on the other side of the parking lot.

I leaned over, put my hands on my knees, took a few large gulps of air, and tried not to lose my dinner. After a few seconds, I stood and squared my shoulders. "What's the plan?"

"To fight."

"Right." I tried to sense Drake and Bastien, but they weren't within my range. "Can you hold them off until I can heal Tracy?" If we had her help, we'd have a better chance of winning. I knew self-defense, but I wasn't a warrior. Tracy and I could combine our magic and at least buy us some time with the explosion it would cause.

A wolf charged into the parking lot from the left.

Quin's sword appeared, and he cut it down with a single swing. "No."

I tuned my inherent magic to Tracy's neutralizing spell and threw it at a group of tainted jaguars sneaking up from behind. Quin shoved a dagger in my hand. "Use this wisely."

I nodded and ran the magic through the blade like Mat did with his katanas.

Quin blurred and dropped a group of shifters in human form.

A lion swiped at me from the right. I sliced its paw with the dagger and hit it in the mouth with magic. It careened into a pole. Pain shot up my leg. I kicked the hyena who'd latched onto it, but it wouldn't let go. As soon as the bug magic entered my leg, I tuned my healing magic to the neutralizing spell and ran it down my leg and into the hyena.

The ruling magic vibrated, eager to put the attackers in their place. Before I could react, it tuned itself to a knockout spell, escaped, blanketed the parking lot, and knocked out the first wave of attackers. The hyena fell to the ground, limp.

Quin's red eyes met mine. One eyebrow lifted.

I didn't have time to explain. A monkey dove over its downed friends and landed on my head. It slapped my face. I spun in circles and tried to smack it off my head with my free hand, shooting magic into it as I did. "Off! Off!"

Something smashed into my side. I stumbled and caught myself before I fell. The ruling magic blasted out in waves. The monkey slid off my head and hit the ground with a *'thud.'* I gutted a goat who tried to headbutt me with shredding magic, then neutralizing magic in quick succession.

That's when I realized that the tainted shifters weren't paying much attention to me other than to keep me occupied. They were after Quin. I stopped fighting, and they melted away.

I raised myself to my tiptoes to peer over the fight and spotted Quin in the center of the crowd. He ducked, flipped, and carved with his sword. His claws sliced and stabbed. His movements were more like a high-speed, choreographed war dance than a fight.

The metallic scent of blood coated the air as he took down a mountain lion. He reversed his sword to slice a bear that reared up behind him. A snake bit him and lost its head to Quin's claws. All in a few seconds. The thick bug magic coating him didn't even slow him down. I'd never seen someone fight with such precision and viciousness, not even Mat. But he was about to be in big trouble as more shifters closed around us.

I flashed closer to him, then ducked and dodged, punched, and stabbed. Claws dug into my side, sending pain shooting through my entire body. Something bit the back of my leg, and my head swam. I blasted and kicked everything within reach as I fought my way to Quin.

There were too many. We couldn't win without drastic measures. I spotted Quin as I punt-kicked a honey badger. It took a piece of my ankle with it. The honey badger bounced off the side of an emu that kicked at me. My whole body throbbed as I fought to get to him. I got within a few feet when a couple of tigers pounced on me. Gunshots cracked from somewhere nearby. One tiger roared as he dropped to the ground in a pool of blood. I held my aching side with one hand and threw neutralizing magic at the second tiger who crouched down and prepared to pounce.

A group of about twenty baboons hopped off a nearby roof and raced toward us. "Holy shit! Quin! We gotta get out of here!" I yelled as my back hit the ground. A lion lunged at my throat. I blasted neutralizing magic into it and hopped to my feet as my heart tried to explode out of my chest. The ruling magic vibrated so hard my teeth rattled.

I knew what that meant. "Quin! Get down!"

Bright white light shot out of me, turning night into day. Shifters sailed in all directions. Some rolled across the parking lot, while others flew straight up and crashed to the ground. The entire pocket of Ferine shook.

I uncurled my aching body and crawled to a sitting position. More than a hundred unconscious shifters littered the area. I wrapped what little magic I had left around myself and staggered to my feet. It felt like a manticore had hit me. I leaned over and braced my hands on my knees until the twinge in my ribs eased.

Quin rolled to his feet with the grace of someone who hadn't just been in a massive battle. "I will never understand why exploding your magic is your first reaction."

"It gets the job done." It sounded better than the truth: I couldn't control it.

"Call those enforcers Mathias has on hold." He headed toward the shed where we left Tracy.

***

We flashed back to the hotel's roof. A figure stepped out of the shadows in the same place where I tripped. Quin set Tracy down and slammed the person onto the roof. A cloud of dust coated the air. He held his claws to their throat.

"Whooo Wheee, what fun!" The grating voice sent shivers down my spine.

Tracy moaned, so I dropped to the ground and ran a small amount of healing magic through her. "What are you doing here, Emine?" I remembered the gunshots. "Wait, was that you shooting?"

My brother's match and the head of the Enforcers didn't struggle against Quin's hold. "You had it under control. I got a few shots off."

Quin let her go. "I take it this is the backup Mathias sent?"

"I guess so."

"Brilliant. I see why you make such stupid decisions."

I ignored his sarcasm and focused on Emine. "Why are you here?"

"Duh. Mat sent me to help." She pointed at Quin. "You should listen to your friend, Jen. It was brilliant."

"My *friend* was being sarcastic. So, you help us by what? Tripping me? Standing way back here and shooting at our attackers?" I heaved a groaning Tracy up, supported her weight, and limped toward the door. "Go home. We have enough problems and don't need another."

She scrambled to catch up with me. "Ah, come on. It's not like you needed my help. Like I said, you were fine. Besides, you would have gotten away if I hadn't tripped you, and we'd lose all this intelligence." She motioned toward the downed shifters. "I couldn't go near that magic, so I went old school."

Emine didn't share Mat's views about my safety. She loved throwing me into dangerous situations to see what would happen. I made a mental note to ask Mat why he sent her. Although, I was pretty sure it was because she was the head of the Enforcers and someone he trusted. Sometimes love can be blind. Aside from her being insane, she had war magic, so it would be a disaster if that magic infected her.

Quin took Tracy from me and supported her with one arm. She was conscious but unable to walk on her own. I rubbed my hands on my shredded pants. A drop of blood trickled down the gash in my arm and splattered on the floor. Something inside me snapped.

I grabbed Emine by the throat and slammed her against the wall by the stairs. "If you ever trip me and then sit back in safety and watch an attack like that again, I will hang you from the gallows of Mahri and let the crows eat your brains. Do I make myself clear?" Her eyes bulged. "Get your enforcers out here to sort this mess out." I released her. "Are we going to Tracy's room? Mine's ruined."

"Yes." Quin's normal sarcastic tone was absent. Pride might have flashed through his eyes. Although it was hard to tell through his resting bored face. A slight eyebrow movement was about as expressive as Quin ever got.

Chapter Seven

DRAKE

Drake launched from his perch on the edge of town. He'd booked an expensive hotel two blocks away from Jenella's but stayed on top of it in his dragon form instead of going to his room. She returned a few hours earlier, but Tarquin stayed active. He escorted the ladies to their hotel, then led the paranormals following them on a chase. Based on what he saw, this was not one of the safe, if not mundane, cases she usually worked. The bond burst open, and Jenella's panic flooded his senses. He launched into the sky and raced to help.

A figure on the roof shot toward a parking lot where several shifters fought Tarquin. The thick, putrid scent of disease coated the air. Drake recognized the smell from the human mall. He spotted Bastien on top of a small cement structure, half cloaked. Tracy was inside, her mind silent. Drake uncloaked himself enough for his cousin to sense him. *Is Tracy okay?*

She's injured, but nothing Jen can't fix. Should we intervene in this fight?

Tarquin fought in a circle of shifters ten-deep. Jenella stood on the edge of the battle, a monkey on her head. Burning anger replaced the sheer panic he had felt from her. She still contained her enormous power, but he felt it claw for release. Behind her, two shifters approached unnoticed. Gunfire thundered over the sounds of the battle, and they fell before they reached Jenella. The shooter on the roof could only be one person. Mathias had sent his mate to help, and she used a gun to avoid the putrid magic. Smart. He probed her mind to confirm his suspicions and turned his attention back to the ongoing battle.

Jenella and her friends must have stumbled upon the Bellicose in that warehouse. And the keepers weren't happy about it. It didn't surprise him, though he wished he'd paid more attention. He could have burned the lab to the ground and stopped this from happening. Jenella had a way of sniffing out trouble. Even so, she could handle herself. She *preferred* to handle things herself. He hesitated. When she dove into the crowd of shifters, he rocketed toward the fight.

"Quin. Get down!" Jenella shouted.

The vampire took three shifters out as he melted to the ground. Power smashed into Drake. He tried to let it flow over him, but it caught hold and vaulted him into the sky. For the first time in a millennium, he lost control of his flight. He struggled to regain it as he tumbled through the air.

He tried to twist but couldn't catch his bearings before his left wing hit the pocket's wards and crumpled. His head smashed into it next. He shrieked as he spiraled toward the ground. Spots danced before his eyes as he tried to extend his wings to slow the fall. His left one wouldn't respond. With no other choice, he retracted them and braced for impact. His leg crunched as he hit the ground and tried to roll. Rocks bounced off his back as he skidded several feet, face first.

Head pounding, he groaned as he rolled to his stomach and examined his injuries. *"Achoo!"* The dirt up his nose and the dust in the air caused him to sneeze.

"You need to tell her before you get yourself killed." Bastien's voice held a hint of amusement.

"I am not worthy of her."

Laughter boomed through Drake's head. *"We are never worthy of fate's gifts."*

The fates never favored him. He'd received very few gifts from the fates throughout his long life. Cruel jokes? Yes. Torment? Absolutely. But fate's gifts were few and far between.

He crawled out of the crater his crash landing created and took several deep breaths to ease the pain. When he had it under control, he shifted into his human form to help him heal. Though shifting didn't heal him completely, it helped speed the process. His knees buckled, and he tumbled to the ground. Bone-crushing pain shot through his body.

Nope. Shifting didn't help.

He needed food and sleep to fully heal, but until then, he'd have to deal with it. He cradled his left hand to his side and waved his right one. The crater became solid ground. He climbed to his feet out of sheer spite and limped toward the area where he sensed Jenella. It took him a while to navigate the unconscious shifters. Jenella's incredible magic had somehow disabled them but left him and Bastien untouched. If he disregarded clashing with the wards. Once again, the dangerous hope made an unwelcome appearance.

He slid into the shadows and watched as Tarquin lifted Tracy without so much as a glance at Bastien, still perched on the structure. Both he and Jenella were injured but otherwise fine.

Drake realized his initial assessment was correct. Jenella always found her way out of trouble. Though, he knew from experience that she would eventually stumble upon something or someone she couldn't escape. Mathias had a point that she needed to better guard herself.

Drake gave her one last, long look and dragged himself toward his hotel.

CHAPTER EIGHT

JEN

Quin's face didn't reflect his pain as he helped Tracy onto one of the two beds in her room. I pulled a chair over and plopped down beside her. I rubbed my eyes to fight the bone-deep exhaustion, then ran as much healing magic as I could muster through Tracy, healing her two broken ribs and a concussion. Black spots danced in my eyes, so I rested my head on the bed and blinked a few times. "Let me see to your injuries, Quin."

Quin stood in the darkest corner of the room with his arms crossed. "No. I will heal in a couple of hours. Perhaps you should focus on healing yourself."

His soft tone registered, but I didn't have the energy to read anything into it. I turned my attention to Emine.

She held her palms out. "I'm good."

I rolled my eyes and dragged myself toward the magichef.

"One does not need healing when they watch others fight for their lives from afar," Quin muttered.

I suppressed a smile as I pushed a button and waited for food to appear. I liked Quin's sarcasm. Especially when he made my point for me. I shoved a plate into Tracy's hands. "We need to clean up the mess they left in my room."

Emine called in enforcers to deal with the mess on the roof and in the parking lot, then checked herself into a room down the hall. Tracy and I swung by mine, and she neutralized the diseased magic as I gathered my things. Quin stayed in an undisclosed location, where he cleaned up while we showered. Older vampires were secretive about where they slept because humans once hunted them, and they never forgot the lessons they learned from it.

The room Tracy rented was much nicer and had more space than mine. It had two beds, a kitchenette, and a dining table big enough for the four of us to sit. As we ate, we taught Emine how to neutralize the magic.

As a Forte mage, her gift was war magic. While mages of Ahl, like me, could absorb as many spells as we could learn and use them in place of our raw power, Forte mages usually got one gift of a particular type. They could have any gift, from growing plants and architecture to technical skills or a million other things. They could tune it to spells like me, but it could only manifest within their forte. Emine's war magic made teaching her the neutralizing spell difficult because she could only manifest her magic as bombs, grenades, bullets, or other weapons. The hotel room wasn't ideal for those. She needed some outdoor practice, so we agreed to meet the following morning before we raided the warehouse. When we were done, I fell into a dreamless sleep as soon as my head hit the pillow.

The rich scent of coffee, combined with the sound 'spshhh plonk, spshhh plonk,' dragged me out of my sleep. I cracked an eye open, then wiggled my toes to make sure they still worked. When they did, I eased myself into a sitting position. I was still a little sore, but most of the pain was gone. Tracy sat at the table with an open backpack, making ping-pong-sized magical spheres and dropping them in.

I checked my energy levels. Two of the three pools were full. The healing magic worked to heal most of my wounds as I slept, so it still needed time to replenish. I turned my attention to Tracy. "I could make a million ball jokes right now."

She chuckled. "I've already thought of most of them. This is so Quin can neutralize that magic. They're like eggs, only they need intention to break open. I made them with a spritz of vampire magic, so they should work for him."

I rolled out of bed, grabbed some clothes, and headed to the bathroom to get ready for the busy day ahead. When I emerged, I ordered coffee and a pastry from the magichef and settled in a chair to watch her work. She made her special blend of witchcraft and alchemy look easy. "You're a magical genius. Isn't that a big use of energy, though?"

"Oh, don't worry about me. I mean, I have plenty of energy. This is nothing." She zipped the backpack and reached for another one. "Will Emine be more help today?" Tracy tried to sound casual, but had a crinkle in her brow.

"Yes. She said we had it under control. And in the end, I guess we did." I shook my head. "I've seen her take on a dragon without blinking an eye, so I don't know what made her hang back. She thinks in terms of war strategy and could give us an advantage if she's willing to help and tones down the crazy."

Tracy moved to the magichef for more coffee. "Yeah. How did those shifters find us?"

"Good question. I didn't scan for people following us when we left the warehouse. It worries me. I hope they assume we're in too bad of shape to do anything."

"It appears I have picked up an unpleasant attachment," Quin announced as he strolled through the door. Emine strutted in behind him.

We spent a couple of hours debating strategies to raid the lab. Quin had experience dismantling Bellicose labs, and Emine had a couple of enforcer squads she wanted to bring in. We needed to teach their mages and witches assigned to the squads the neutralizing spell, but because we had the most power, the four of us would take point.

We planned to flash to the stairwell from a nearby street. Tracy, Emine, and I would clear the magic. Quin would use his incredible speed, cloaking abilities, and Tracy's spheres to disable the guards. The Enforcers would provide support and sort out the aftermath. Emine insisted they destroy the lab so they could come up with procedures for other enforcer squads to follow. I worried about that part because it was in the human world, but she was confident they could hide our activities.

An hour later, we stood in an alley behind the mall, where Quin found the trail that led to the warehouse. He pointed to the remnants of the magic. "It is lighter and less than yesterday."

"It looks like it faded in the sun," I said. The magic was thick in the shaded areas and thin or gone where the sun touched it.

"I mean, that's good news, right?" Tracy asked. "It's still enough for Emine and the Enforcers to practice. I'm worried what this stuff will do to the pockets since our sun is magic rather than real."

"Yeah," I agreed. "We'll have to test it."

Emine absorbed the neutralizing spell. "You won't have to look far. I'm pretty sure this stuff has made its way into the Cauldron." She tapped her chin. "I'll use tear gas. Stand back, chickees."

I took two steps back and watched as she conjured a canister and set it upwind from magic. The canister went off as the wind shifted, and the tear gas drifted toward us. Quin disappeared, but Tracy and I didn't move fast enough, so we choked and cried for a few minutes because Emine didn't bother disabling the gas. Instead, she added the neutralizing spell to the tear gas. She claimed it was more effective since it would neutralize people in two ways.

"You can stick with that," I sputtered. "But not when allies are close."

A mischievous smile lit her face. "Sure thing."

Her response was way too enthusiastic. I narrowed my eyes. "You said this same magic is in Allure?"

"I'm pretty sure. It looks similar, but it's thicker at the Cauldron. I'll show you when we get back. Right now, we're containing it."

The Cauldron, where the Enforcers in Allure were based, got its name because they hired people of all magical types and was considered a melting-pot. Most paranormals lived in neighborhoods or compounds with their own type, even in the city. There were a few exceptions, like our neighborhood, where many types settled, but it was the exception. The Cauldron was the best example of a large force of different paranormals mixing, hence the name. "We'll head back as soon as we close this case and clear the shifter compound."

I watched Tracy work with the magic users on the enforcer squad. When she was confident they could neutralize the magic, she handed the backpacks filled with ping-pong balls to Quin and a vampire on the Enforcer squad.

I flashed us from our staging area down the street into the warehouse. We appeared at the top of the stairs that led to the basement. Tainted shifters in their animal forms jumped at our sudden appearance.

I stumbled back, my eyes wide. Emine shoulder-bumped me, and I snapped out of my shock. An elk regained his senses at the same time and charged us. I blasted it with knockout magic.

Quin threw ping-pong balls so fast I could barely see them as more shifters spilled out from behind the warehouse shelves and the basement door.

"Enforcer squads, engage," Emine's order echoed through our communication spell.

Beside me, Tracy wove a spell and sent it out. It streamed from her hands and drifted through the warehouse, coating anything that moved in neutralizing magic. I stayed by her side and blasted the ones she missed.

Emine deployed a canister of tear gas. It drifted into the air and dissolved without affecting anyone.

"Switch tactics, Emine!" I yelled as I knocked out a group of shifters charging up the stairs.

"Roger."

It was worse than the parking lot. Two more would come through the door for every shifter we took down. I didn't have it in me to explode my magic again. I tuned my inherent magic to a knockout spell and shoved both hands forward. It knocked out enough shifters to block the stairs. A few of them rolled to the bottom. The door slammed, and their unconscious bodies settled against it.

I spun to help Tracy, who stood behind me but hesitated when the big rolling door groaned, and Enforcers flooded in. I let out a relieved breath and changed direction to avoid knocking them out.

Emine flashed past the pile of unconscious shifters to the bottom of the stairs. "Team stupid, move in!" She blasted a tainted giant with a laser beam. "Urgggh!" she growled in frustration as she realized only a small line of bug magic dissipated across his torso.

Quin went fluid and used his superior strength to shove her aside, clear the shifters, and pry the door open. Something stronger than him slammed against it, causing it to buckle. A wolf pounced over Tracy and smashed into me. I tumbled down the stairs and came to a stop against an unconscious tiger. I ran neutralizing magic over both of us. The ruling magic tried to lash out, so I wrapped it tighter as I hopped to my feet, flashed to the door, slapped a hand on Emine, and flashed to the hallway on the other side.

"I could have done it myself," she protested. "Warn a girl next time."

Two giants thundered towards us. Another dropped from the ceiling. "Holy hell," I muttered.

Emine whipped out a flame thrower. "Get down and cover my ass." She didn't wait for me to get clear before she let it rip.

I hit the floor too hard, and my bones rattled. It took me a few seconds to recover, so I shot magic at the legs of anything I could see. Not that she needed my help. Her flame thrower roared to life and shot dissipating magic down the hall, clearing everything in its path. She cackled as she pointed it toward a charging giant.

He crashed to the floor beside me, and I knocked him out. She aimed the flamethrower at the other two.

My ears rang, and the smell of magic and ozone clogged my nose as more shifters barreled around the corner. Emine aimed at the ceiling, and flying shifters fell like rain. I took care of the strays.

When the hall cleared, there wasn't a black ant-looking thing in sight.

"Effective," I said as I swung the door to the stairs open.

A magic sphere hit me in the chest. Hard. I stumbled backward, tripped over an unconscious giant, and landed on my ass.

Tracy rushed over and offered me a hand. "Oh, no. We didn't realize it was you. Are you okay?"

"Fine." I stood and rubbed my bruised butt.

Quin strode past us, a half-empty backpack dangling from his hand. "Follow the plan." He disappeared.

The cleanup took hours. Tracy and I released the prisoners from their cells while Emine cleared the magic in the basement with her handy flame thrower. I used healing magic to neutralize the dark sludge that infected the prisoners as we released them. Some of them were infected with unique magic that I assumed were earlier experiments. We were relieved when my anti-Jaques spell worked on them.

I moved outside to help heal some people that Quin released. They were in much worse shape than the others. Some were oozing the diseased magic to the point where the enforcers wouldn't go near them.

I kneeled near the first one and tuned my healing magic to the neutralizing spell. I ran it through them, then moved onto the next one and the next. When I got to the last person, I caught movement out of the corner of my eye. My head snapped in that direction. "What the hell?"

The first one I healed oozed the putrid magic again. I used regular healing magic to evaluate the problem. And jerked back. I used Emine's trick and kept the healing properties and also tuned my magic to the neutralizing spell and closed my eyes.

Nestled at the base of his skull, right above his spinal cord, was a triangular bug, for lack of a better word. It felt different from the other magic. More concentrated, for lack of a better word. It pumped out the bug magic at an alarming rate. My stomach churned as I injected it with neutralizing magic until it dissipated. I repeated the process on three more of them. Stunned, I went back and studied it.

Why would they implant those replicators when it already grew upon magic contact? I shook my head and went back to work. It wasn't a today question, but something to ponder later.

Most of the prisoners were in terrible shape. Some were on the verge of starving to death, while others were so severely beaten they were unrecognizable. The enforcers called in several healers and a group of crisis mages. As I watched them work, waves of anger and sorrow crashed over me.

Quin took down eight guards, and thirty tainted paranormals attacked us. Three died in the battle. Not all of them were shifters. Giants, mages, witches, and elves were serving as guards, and they weren't tainted by any magic. Which meant they were immune. If the Bellicose had a way to make people immune to the magic, we needed it. Emine took their files before she sent in a team to destroy the place, so I hoped we got some answers.

The worst part was the bodies. We found twenty-one bodies piled in a room. The Bellicose experimented on paranormals until they died, then cast them aside like garbage. No matter how long I lived, I would never get the horrific picture or the putrid stench out of my head.

As promised, the enforcers set up privacy and illusion spells around the warehouse before we invaded to keep humans from getting curious. They were fast and efficient.

I stood to the side with my arms tucked around myself as I watched two enforcers lay the deceased on a tarp that covered the asphalt. Loud beeping echoed off the buildings as two enormous human delivery trucks backed up to them. I blinked back tears as the enforcers loaded them with a care I rarely saw in paranormals. I couldn't imagine the heartbreak and hurt the families would endure when they received their loved one in that shape.

My chest was so tight I wondered if my heart would quit beating. The deaths were so unnecessary. So senseless. I ran a sleeve across my leaky eyes and turned my head, giving myself a break from the horrors.

Quin leaned against the building next to the vampire he'd mentioned the day before. The young vampire wore a white UV protective suit that covered him from head to toe. A darkened, spelled mask covered his face. It took them about a hundred years to tolerate the sun enough to be out during the day. The UV suits made it so they could go outside during daylight hours. Most hated the suits because they restricted their vision and fluid movements. Two things vampires excelled at.

My eyes slid to a group of enforcers who led or carried survivors to the other side of the parking lot and loaded them into vans. Tracy stood with Bastien a few feet away, watching with a grim expression. I was such an emotional mess that I didn't even sense the Dragon Prince arrive.

I turned my attention back to the senseless death. Guilt stabbed through me and mixed with soul-crushing grief as I realized the deaths were my fault. I'd ignored my responsibilities and refused to listen to Mat when he tried to get me to take a more active role as queen. Instead of taking action to protect paranormals, I was out running around finding bridges for trolls to live under and rescuing useless possessions like I didn't have a care in the world. Pretending to be someone I wasn't while my people suffered. Ignoring the disappearance of entire packs of shifters and the senseless deaths of paranormals who had their whole lives ahead of them. The realization made my stomach sour. Another tear trickled down my cheek.

A hand landed on my shoulder. "Are you okay?" Concern laced Drake's voice.

I didn't jump or acknowledge the flutter in my chest. I didn't deserve to be delighted when someone snuck up on me. Not when I allowed people to die like that. Not when I'd killed some of those shifters myself the night before. I used my sleeve to mop up my tears again, squared my shoulders, and turned to him. "Fine."

His green eyes scanned me from head to toe. "You don't look fine."

I shrugged and turned back to the horrific scene.

Drake didn't touch me again. Nor did he ask more questions. He stood beside me close enough to offer support, but not so close I'd fall apart. I appreciated it but said nothing. There were no words. The grief and guilt were too overwhelming. If I tried to talk, I'd fall to pieces, which wouldn't help the situation. It wouldn't bring back the lives cut short.

We stayed like that until the last truck pulled away.

I found Emine on the other side of the parking lot. She raised a box of cereal and shoved a handful in her mouth. "What's up?"

"Are we cleared to leave?"

She wiped her hand on her leather pants. "Yep. I'll stay here and oversee the recovery. Take that baby vampire with you. He's cleared."

"Sure." I took one last, long look at the warehouse and tried not to think about how my selfishness had caused the mess. "Quin said he took down labs before, so I assume they have more. Notify all the enforcer stations to look for signs. Let me know what you learn from the survivors."

"Will do. Where are you going next?"

"To wrap up my case and then home."

She saluted.

"This isn't the right time, but I need to talk to you about some things," Drake said as he followed me to the car.

No one acknowledged Drake as we walked. As a First, people always noticed him. "Are you cloaked?"

"Yes. You, Tracy, and Bastien can see and hear me. I can wait to talk, but it is important."

Bastien launched into the air as Tracy joined Quin beside the car. "Okay. Can it wait until we get back to Allure?"

"It can." Drake turned his head to the sky and took a deep breath. "I have some things to take care of, and then I will find you."

"Sure."

He gave me one last considering look and launched into the sky.

CHAPTER NINE

JEN

QUIN CLAIMED THE FRONT seat of our rental car, so I slid into the back next to the vampire and examined his UV suit. He turned his masked face to me, and his fangs extended.

"My apprentice is not as defenseless as she looks. Should you attack, she will kill you in a gruesome way and blame me. I am not in the mood." Quin didn't even turn around.

The vampire's fangs disappeared. "My apologies."

I inclined my head and stared out the window. At that moment, I craved someone to talk to, someone who understood. I glanced at Tracy. She understood me better than anyone else, but not the responsibilities of ruling. Or the consequences of not ruling in my case. I needed to talk to Deva, the Dragon Queen, or Ara, Quin's match, and the Vampire Queen.

Tracy's tap on the steering wheel pulled me out of my thoughts. She glanced in the mirror to make sure she had my attention. "Once we clear that magic from the shifter compound, are we going to head home?"

"I'm sure you have plenty of energy left for that." Quin's voice was extra dry.

"Yes, we should go home. And I'm good on energy." I tried not to sound as wrecked as I felt. After healing so many people, my energy *was* a little low. But since Emine took care of most of the warehouse, I had enough to clear the shifter compound.

"Same. I mean, we didn't really have to do that much today." Tracy pulled the car into the lot outside the compound and turned it off.

We left the young vampire and Quin in the car as we cleared the magic from the compound. They quarantined the infected and did a great job keeping the magic from spreading. As a result, I only had to heal six people. The magic we'd found during our first visit faded where the sun touched it, which was good news since it was in a pocket that magically copied the actual sun.

When we were done, we headed back to the car. Tracy pulled out onto the main road. "So, where are you going, Quin?"

"I have a lead to follow." He turned his attention to the vampire, his expression growing hard. "How did you end up in that lab, fledgling?"

The vampire shrunk into himself, trying to become as small as possible. I recognized that posture. It was the same posture I used for years when an authority figure addressed me. The posture of an abuse victim trying not to be noticed. My heart ached for the guy.

The vampire cleared his throat. "I'm sorry, Master Tarquin. I made a mistake."

"That is true, but not what I asked."

"I'm worried you won't believe me. No one ever believes me," he whimpered.

Quin's creepy vibe amped up so high that I considered opening the window to get some air. "Explain."

"Master Jedediah turned me. I belonged to his house until about twenty years ago, when I witnessed something I shouldn't have. He hunts me."

A shiver ran down my spine. My first case involved Quin's son, Jedediah. He was awful. I couldn't imagine what it would be like to be hunted by him. It explained the guy's slumped posture.

"What did you see? And do not lie to me." Quin used compulsion.

The young vampire's tension drained. "About twenty years ago, Master Jedediah kept a young girl in a shed at the back of his property. She was...special. Master called her an abomination. A gate guard who witnessed her arrival said she was Master's biological daughter."

"Explain."

"My name is Scott. You can check the records to verify that I was present when that explosion took out his defenses, Master. I'm not lying."

"What explosion?" I was so interested in their conversation that I didn't realize I'd asked out loud. It wasn't really my business.

Scott rubbed his face through the UV suit. "She was only a kid. Couldn't have been more than twelve or thirteen. The girl was desperate for knowledge about her vampire heritage and more powerful than most mages. She was a hybrid or something. I've never seen anyone like her."

Quin's only reaction to the revelation was a subtle head movement. "And you say this hybrid was Jedediah's natural daughter?"

"Yes, Master. After her arrival, I was one of five guards assigned to the back wall. We taught her how to do basic things like going fluid and shadow blending. We made sure she had food and clothing. She got comfortable with me enough to tell me that her mother was a powerful mage. She said she was a natural-born vampire and was unfamiliar with Jedediah until the day her mother left her at the house."

"Natural born." Quin's voice wasn't as smooth.

I fought not to gasp at the realization that the girl would be his natural-born granddaughter if the story was true.

"She grew three inches in the nine months she lived on the property. Turned vampires don't grow."

Quin's silence spoke volumes. I'd never seen him shaken before, and, to be honest, it wasn't very different from when he was bored. After a few seconds, he inclined his head. "A child that age rarely survives the change. I witnessed one vampire turned at birth who survived. He grew into adulthood but was never right in the head. However, changing a mage, even an infant mage, is impossible. That does not explain why you were being held in that lab."

Scott fidgeted in a very un-vampire-like way. "The Master tried to eliminate his supposed daughter and everyone who knew about her. He sent men to kill her. She blew them up, destroyed the cottage, and took out half the back wall. It allowed her to escape without a trace. After that, I witnessed two of my friends die at the hands of Master Jedediah, so I ran. Mistress Vesna took me in for a while, but she is no better than him. I learned she intended to use me as a bargaining chip against him and ran again. I've been running for over five years."

Vesna was Quin and Ara's natural-born daughter and Jedediah's sister. I'd heard they had a strained relationship but never paid much attention to the rumors. Neither caused trouble for the coalition, so it wasn't my business.

The red glow of Quin's eyes peeked through his dark sunglasses. "And you've kept control how?"

"I don't want to be a monster like Jedediah. Donor centers in the pockets are open to everyone and don't request house affiliation. I never stayed in one place long, but Vesna almost caught me twice. A month ago, she caught up with me in Ferine. I fled to the human world and hid in that warehouse district where they captured and imprisoned me. They used me to learn how to alter their spells to affect vampires. At first, I'd become lethargic before my natural immunity eliminated it. So, they altered their disease and administered it again. They mixed mage and demon magic with a human blood disease."

Quin tapped his fingers on his leg. "I will blood bond you to break Jedediah's and Vesna's hold." He waved a hand. "Jen and Tracy are mine. They will protect you during the journey back to Allure. You now belong to the House of Umbra. Tell my love everything. Learning this news will displease the queen, but she will not take it out on you."

"Yes, Master Tarquin." Scott didn't seem enthused about the idea, but I knew Ara took care of her vampires. I'd trust her over Jedediah any day. She was a tough but fair ruler.

Ferine had a rental car return service, so we turned the car over to them and headed to the transport station, the vampire in tow. He'd been quiet since Quin blood-bonded him, and I was grateful. My mind was overwhelmed, and I didn't feel like having a conversation. I needed time to process the events that unfolded and reconsider my path. I took out my phone to make a list of things I needed to do.

As a condition of taking the throne, I was required to work a job for at least two years. If I counted the time I spent studying for the licensing exam, I had four months left. Then, I had to work under Mat for a while before I took over the full duties of the queen. In addition, Mat had to remain regent until I was forty. The Bellicose was growing, and too many people were suffering. If we didn't start taking initiative, the Coalition wouldn't last that long.

I flipped my phone from hand to hand. With my lack of confidence and aversion to being a queen, taking the throne could make things worse. After all, I let Mat push me out at the first sign of conflict. I was so caught up in my first taste of freedom that I didn't pay attention to what was going on like I should have.

I rubbed my chest, trying to ease the ache in my heart for all the people my selfishness killed. I didn't know how to make it right. For a split second, I wondered if maybe Jaques should have killed me when I was a kid. If I'd realized what a selfish ass I'd become, I would have taken matters into my own hands. And wasn't that a sunny little thought? I turned my attention back to my to-do list. I needed to talk to someone before I couldn't stop the intrusive thoughts.

The transport landed, and Elsie, one of Ara's trusted generals, took the young vampire into her custody. She inclined her head to us, then disappeared.

"You okay?" Tracy's voice cut through the silence as we headed toward the main square.

"We should have gone with Elsie. I need to talk to Ara."

Her mouth moved like she had more to say, but she closed it and turned onto my favorite street, leading toward the flashing circle. Not even the scents of freshly baked bread and barbeque could lift me out of my funk. Tracy pushed through a group of dwarves, who blocked the path. "Have you noticed gargoyles hanging around the main square the last few weeks?"

"Yes. I meant to ask Mat about that." We trudged down the street in awkward silence. Frustrated by the tension, I blurted the truth. "I'm having an internal crisis and need some advice from another ruler."

"And you think Ara can help?"

"Yes. No." I shook my head to clear it. Deva, the Dragon Queen, was too close to the situation since she got kidnapped by the Bellicose and held captive for months. She liked me but lacked sound judgment in handling the rebellion. Meaning she wanted to burn them all to a crisp with her dragon fire and eat them for dinner. Because of that, Ara was the right choice. "She might be able to help."

"Sounds good," Tracy said in a clipped tone.

"Why are you mad at me?"

She threw a hand out. "It's not you. I'm pissed about this whole situation. I mean, what was Quin doing in Ferine? My guess is because he knew people were being tortured and killed. He's supposed to find their leaders, but instead, he's wasting time shutting down labs. And where the hell are the Alphas? The people who attacked us are more their responsibility than yours. And, yes, I'm pissed because you could rule more effectively than Mat. But you have it in your head that you need to sit outside looking in.

Kind of like how you treat our friendship. You feel sorry for yourself and whine while he tries to herd you in the direction he wants you to go. It's maddening."

I stopped in my tracks. That was a lot to unpack. I grabbed Tracy's arm and dragged her to a bench in front of a shop to sit down. "You're right about Quin and the Alphas. It's part of what's bothering me. You're also right about me." I shook my head. "When I watched them remove those remains, I realized a few things. Like their blood is on my hands. While I'm out here doing meaningless bullshit and pretending to be someone I'm not, people are dying. And it's on me.

"As far as our friendship goes, I wasn't sure until yesterday that we *had* a friendship. I've been telling myself to keep my distance since the incident where I found out you and Quin made that bet about me. I was open to it until then. After...Let's just say I remind myself regularly that I am your job, not your friend. For that, I'm sorry. But in my defense, I've never had a friend before, so...."

"So you're an idiot. Jen, we *are* friends. We've *always* been friends. Which is why I can tell you to stop second-guessing everything and just be you. Because you are powerful, good, and strong enough to do whatever you need."

I rubbed my eyes. "Thank you."

She nodded. "Get your shit together and decide what *you* want to do. Don't let your brother push you around. Figure out what needs to be done and do it. Geez. Now, I'm going to grab Bastien and go see my dad. He can help us create potions to use against this magic, and it's a good place for me to start. You go talk to Ara and figure out the best path forward without getting in your own way. I'll meet you at the house." She stood and marched toward Dragon Headquarters.

The list of things to do rattled around in my brain as I waited in Ara's human-style kitchen. She loved to cook, and I liked her food. We had lunch about once a month. It built a certain camaraderie that came with being surrounded by people but still alone. I wasn't technically alone, and neither was she. She had Quin, and I had Mat and Tracy. But Ara and I somehow understood each other in ways I couldn't explain.

I typed up my list of things to do while I waited.

1. *Fix magic (how?)*

2. *Figure out what Mat's hiding (ask? Demand?)*

3. *Find Bellicose leaders*

4. *Talk to Drake*

5. *Take the throne*

6. *Fix the hybrid situation*

Ara bustled into the kitchen, opened the door of a big rectangular gadget, and pulled out a pitcher of iced tea. "Hello, Jenella."

I added 'learn more about human behaviors' to my list and slid my phone into a pocket. "Hey, Ara. Sorry to interrupt your day."

"It couldn't have come at a better time." She poured two glasses of tea.

Ara wore her long dark hair swept into a high ponytail. Though she was over six thousand years old, her hairstyle, jeans, T-shirt, and small stature made her look like a teenager. I wouldn't give her a second look if I met her on the street and couldn't read her power level. Unless I saw her shrewd brown eyes. They were unmistakably ancient. I wondered if the young and innocent look was by design. It wouldn't surprise me. "How's the new vampire settling in?"

She took the chair across from me. "He's doing well, considering his history. As with all rescues, it will take time for him to trust us."

I nodded. "I'm glad we found him."

She took a sip of tea and focused on the glass. "I do so love tea. What can I do for you?"

"I need some advice."

Her face lit up. "My favorite. What type of advice?"

I fought not to shiver at her predatory smile. "Ruling. Or lack thereof."

"Is that so?"

I set my glass down. "No. That's not what I meant." I rubbed my face. "What I mean is that I'm failing."

She leaned back in her chair. "Perhaps you should start from the beginning."

I explained about the diseased magic and the tortured paranormals. The bodies. My realization that I was wasting my time. She already knew my magic never merged, but I told her about that, too. And how inadequate I felt. When I finished, I shook so hard I had to keep a death grip on the glass of tea.

Ara did this weird vampire trance thing where she stared at me without blinking. After a few seconds, she reanimated. "I'm unsure which brother damaged you more, Jaques with his cruelty or Mathias with his insistence that you are flawed and weak."

"Mat did the best he could."

"Yet you sit before me an emotional mess, and he has done nothing but fan those flames." I opened my mouth to defend my brother, but she waved me off. "I know you love him, dear. I do, too. However, I find your relationship odd. He orders you around, and you follow the orders while squawking like a duck. Strange, since you are the ruler, and he is not." She tapped her chin. "As far as your concerns about your work requirement, your mother only mandated things that directly benefited her. You need to ask yourself how she would benefit from the rules she put on your ascension. You also need to understand that Mathias serves you, not the other way around."

My eyebrows drew together. "What?"

"Laws, rules, and codes are important to keep the peace and maintain order." She leaned forward. "They are also a handy tool to use when you wish to control someone. Ask yourself why your mother made new laws surrounding your ascension and why Mathias still enforces them. Then decide if they are necessary. If they are, then you are on the right track. If they are not, eliminate them."

"Eliminate them? Can I do that before I fully take the throne?"

Ara's eyes narrowed. "Are you or are you not the coronated queen?"

A ton of bricks landed on my shoulders. She gave me a lot to consider in the short time we talked. I realized that ruling wasn't much different from driving in the human world. Well, it was significantly different. But it's still about rules. I couldn't get it through my head that the rules applied to me when I drove, so I did it my way. Yet I obeyed Mat's instructions to take safe cases and followed my mother's work requirement mandate without ever questioning it. I had my doubts in the beginning, but I didn't make a big deal out of it since it gave me a taste of freedom. So, how was driving any different from the stupid work requirement my mother put on me? How was it different from Mat's insistence that my magic was flawed or that I take safe cases? Unlike the rules of driving, which had consequences, I didn't have to follow any rules surrounding the throne if I didn't want to. I would, but I didn't have to. "Thank you."

"Of course, dear. You can come to me any time. I do like your company."

We sipped our tea in silence as I added 'break the rules' to my list. Then I changed the subject. "Did that vampire tell you about the girl he met at Jedediah's?"

Her face turned to stone. "He did."

"So she really exists?"

"He is not lying. If true, my son has some explaining to do." Her ominous tone made my skin crawl.

"Jedediah never told you about her?"

She shook her head. "I didn't have a third child to inherit ruling magic. Because there were only two of my line, my children decided I'd name one of them as my heir. I didn't tell them the truth because their power struggle kept them out of trouble. Nor did I tell them about my mother's actions surrounding the inheritance of her ruling magic."

My mother changed my ascension, too, so I understood. "What provisions? If you don't mind me asking."

She waved a hand. "If this hybrid exists, it will come out. But if I tell you, you must promise to keep it to yourself for now."

"I promise to keep anything you tell me about the inheritance of the First Lilith's magic to myself until you choose to reveal it."

My head tingled as the magical contract snapped into place.

"Lilith did not appreciate that I became so powerful when I came of age. As a result, we butted heads many times. After Vesna was born, Lilith decided an heir would give me too much power and respect. So she approached a witch, and together, they created a spell. She summoned me to her under the false pretenses of dealing with a band of vampires feasting on the people of Paris. Instead of going on a hunt, she hung me on the wall, gutted me, and took away my ability to have children."

Tears sprung to my eyes. "Why? Why would she do that to her own daughter?"

"You did not know the Firsts, dear. They were not all heroes like the history books portray them. Some, like your grandmother and Jonas, the First Shifter, created paranormals so they could pass on their magic and perhaps rule over them. While others created species that were hard to kill because they liked torture and control. Lilith fell into the latter category. Unlike the rest of us, she could conceive children without a match, so she used three different Firsts for her purposes. I am the product of her and the First who created the gargoyles and Cerberus, among others. Lilith ensured I had none of his traits, though I don't understand how. However, she underestimated how powerful his magic would make me. She resented it."

"That's…"

"Yes." She cut me off. "In those days, there was no such thing as the psychology of childhood trauma. She often hung us up and gutted us as a punishment for the smallest infractions. She said it would make us tough and enable us to survive. It did in all the wrong ways. When I met Tarquin, he was human. I knew he was my match immediately, so I turned him because I did not understand concepts like consent and free will. He was not happy about that." She paused, a small smile ghosting her face as if reminiscing. As soon as it formed, it melted into an iciness so cold that I visibly shivered. "Lilith took him away, staked him in the sun, starved him, injected him with experimental magics, and flayed him daily. It took me several months to find him in the cellar of her home."

It explained why Quin was so terrified at the warehouse basement. I needed to remember that I wasn't the only one with issues. What he experienced was much worse than anything Jaques did to me. "But you found him."

"Yes. He was...changed. He gained abilities and became much more jaded. I often wonder what we would have been if...Well, never mind that. My point is Lilith removed my ability to have an heir. Then, she did a ritual that included slaughtering my sister, her second born, to pass her magic on to my heir instead of me."

"That's awful." I wanted to hug her or puke. Or do something. I couldn't, so I focused on my tea. "So, she ensured you couldn't have an heir and then passed her magic onto them."

"Exactly so. My children wrongly assumed that because I didn't have a third child, one of them would inherit it." She leaned forward. "As you know, that's not possible. Only the third-born or third-made can be an heir. If this hybrid exists and she *is* Jedediah's natural-born daughter, she is the third born of my line. The magic of Lilith got passed to her."

My mouth fell open, and I had to force it to close. "So, the vampire heir is out there running around the world without supervision?"

"Perhaps. Perhaps not. I suspect Jedediah knows where to find her. If she has the power of Lilith, then she does not need a blood bond to control herself, so that is of no concern. But I would very much like to meet her."

I swallowed. I wondered if Ara wanted an heir or if she would eliminate the girl. But vampire matters weren't my business, so I had to be careful. "What will that look like?"

"I am not Lilith." Her sharp tone made me flinch. "I will love her because she is my granddaughter. If she inherited Lilith's power, I intend to support her in becoming the leader Lilith's successor is meant to be." She leaned forward. "Just like how I'm assisting you in becoming the leader you are destined to be."

I swallowed. "I believe you and Deva share that goal."

Ara nodded. "The Dragon Queen and I have been friends for thousands of years. We agree on many things. Including the fact that you will either be our salvation or our demise. We wish it to be the former."

CHAPTER TEN

JEN

A TANGLE OF THOUGHTS ran through my head as I left vampire territory. The hair on my neck stood up as I drew closer to the flashing circle where Tracy and I fought a group of chimeras and where I got kidnapped. We were distracted and didn't notice the illusion spell until it was too late. I stretched out my senses to make sure it was empty. I planned to go home to the little house we rented in the mixed-magic neighborhood to gather my thoughts first. Shaking my head, I eased back and marched toward the palace. It was only a couple of miles. I could think about everything on the way.

I'd only made it a few steps when I sensed Drake. He swooped down and landed in front of me. He morphed into a deer shifter with long, blonde hair before he dropped his cloaking magic. "Hello, Jen."

"What are you doing?"

"I'm looking for you. You promised we would talk." He tilted his head. "Are you scared of that flashing circle?"

"No." The lie hung in the air.

I knew he caught it when a smile spread across his face. "Ahhh. I see. You're practicing avoidance."

"I am absolutely not practicing avoidance." I totally was. Running away when things got difficult was a bad habit. I'd been trying to break it for over a year, but my efforts to break the pattern were fruitless.

Drake shrugged. "I won't tell anyone about your fear."

"Just walking to clear my head."

"Yes. I see that."

I laughed at his dry tone. "What are you doing here again?"

"I told you I need to talk to you, but I see it's not a good time."

"We can talk. Let's start by how you've been following me for over a year, yet you didn't step in to help us during that shifter fight in Ferine." I wasn't mad at Drake for that, but I still wondered what he was up to. I figured my overprotective brother hired him for extra security. Except he wasn't always around. He'd stop in, check on me, and leave.

He rubbed his scrawny left arm. "I attempted to help you during that fight. Your magic hit before I reached you."

My eyes trailed his hand. "I hurt you."

"Yes. I bounced off the ward and could not maintain flight."

The thought that I hurt Drake made me queasy. "I'm sorry. Screwing up and getting people hurt seems to be my special gift." I latched onto that arm and tried to run healing magic through it, but he was fine, so I pulled him into a grove of trees and removed the glamour earrings.

He shifted to his usual huge, rugged self. His green eyes examined me. "Where is that coming from?"

"It's my fault that all those people died. I—"

"Don't take that on, Jenella. It's untrue and unhealthy. You didn't kill those people."

"Bullshit. They died because I refused to rule. I'm out here all 'yay freedom.'" I punched a fist in the air. "And taking useless cases instead of solving the coalition's problems. How is that not my fault?"

He ran a hand through his hair. "If it's your fault, then it's also Tarquin's. It was his duty to find and eliminate their king. He failed. Would you punish him for that?"

"No. Quin is a brilliant detective, but the Bellicose are widespread, and he's only one person. He's also not the Queen of Ahl. I am. It's my responsibility."

"It is also Mathias's responsibility. What has he done aside from hiring Tarquin?"

I couldn't answer that question. I'd avoided spending much time at the palace. "Who knows? It's not like he'd tell me if I asked." I rubbed my face. "My head is spinning with the things I need to think about. It's part of the reason I decided to walk to the palace. I need to figure out what to do."

Drake tilted his head back and stared at the sky. "I suggest you don't go to the palace until you have a clear head. Let me give you a ride home?"

"Why?"

"You need time, and I need to talk to you."

My stomach flipped because I had a pretty good idea of what he wanted to talk about. I had to lock my knees to keep myself from running away. "I can't handle any more truth bombs today."

"You need to understand—"

I jammed my fingers in my ears. "La la la la. I can't hear you."

"Mature." Humor laced his deep voice.

I yanked my fingers from my ears. "Not today. I'm overloaded today. I'll be glad to talk to you after I untangle my thoughts and rest. But you're right that I shouldn't go to the palace without a clear head."

"At least let me give you a ride home."

When his eyes met mine, the desperation and pain that flashed through them made my stomach sink. He expected me to reject him like almost everyone in his life. It made my heart ache for him. "This is really important to you, isn't it?"

"Yes."

"Okay. You can take me home."

I'd forgotten how free it felt to fly on the back of a dragon. Drake shifted, and I flashed onto his back. He didn't wait for me to clutch my favorite spike before he launched into the air. He climbed straight into the sky at a breakneck speed. The wind whipped my face, and my stomach flipped. The ruling magic wrapped around him and held me in place. As soon as it settled, he did a full loop. I screeched and slung my arm around the spike. His laughter boomed through my head. He did a couple of barrel rolls, another loop, and rocketed up, taking us as high as he could. I laughed like a loon as he dove back down, spinning through the air in a playful pattern. He swooped left, slowed almost to a stop, and did it all again. I laughed so hard tears streamed into my hair. He climbed one last time, then shot down and landed in the alley behind the little house where Tracy and I lived.

I flashed to the ground, the grin on my face stretched ear-to ear. "That was fun."

He shifted into his human form and swiped a piece of hair out of my face. "I'm glad you liked it."

My smile melted when I saw the intensity in his eyes. I flung my arms around my stomach. "Thank you, Drake."

He nodded. "I'll come back tomorrow to talk."

I cleared my throat. "You won't let me avoid this conversation, will you?"

"Not a chance." He shifted into his dragon form and was gone.

I put my glamour earrings back in before stepping out of the alley Tracy spelled to hide our influential visitors. Then, I headed to my office to study my mother's diaries. I hadn't read several of her diaries because they were so dull and awful. But I wanted to figure out how she created the pockets and what she wrote after I was born. After finding them, I stacked them on my desk and flipped open the first one. I doubted they'd give me much insight, but at that point, I'd be happy with any clue about why my magic didn't merge. I pulled out the first one and cracked it open.

Tracy didn't come home that night. She texted me to let me know she needed to work with her dad on some potions and planned to stay at Bastien's place. She should have lived with Bastien, her match or mate, for more than a decade. But she refused because of the stigma that still surrounded mixed-magic couples. It bothered him that his mate wouldn't put herself under his protection, and it caused a lot of tension between them. So, I was glad she stayed with him.

Focusing on the diaries, I tried to suppress the smoldering anger that grew as I read my mother's awful thoughts. Thoughts like she only had me to stop people from asking her about an heir. And that once she saw how Mat adored me, she sent him away so we wouldn't get too close. I skipped to the part when I was three and developed healing magic. My mother ranted for ten pages about how unfair her life was because I was so powerful at such a young age. On the last page of the rant, she said it was all because her mother hated her and favored me.

My brain screeched to a halt. I stared at that part for a long time. It was my understanding that my grandmother handed the throne and the ruling magic over to my mother and went to sleep. Every history book I'd ever read reinforced that. But then, my education included a candy-coated version of events. Like how paranormals cherished kids and how my mother was a good person. Lies, all of it. I tapped my chin. "What if my grandmother is still awake? What if she didn't go to sleep but retired instead?" I threw the diary into the safe and flew up the stairs to get ready to go to the castle.

As I stepped out the back door, I tilted my head. "Don't you ever sleep?"

Drake dropped from the roof in human form. "I slept. Where are you headed, and where is your guard?"

"My *friend* is spending much-needed time with your cousin and her family. I'm headed to the castle."

Drake fell into step beside me as I made my way to the flashing circle. "We need to talk."

"We do. I'll swing by, and we can have that conversation later today. I just found something that might help solve a big problem, and I need to talk to my brother."

He raised an eyebrow.

"No. I can't just blurt it out in the back alley, even if it's spelled to hide us. I'll fill you in when I come to see you later."

We stopped outside the neighborhood flashing circle, and Drake shook his head. "It's important. Promise me you won't run away from this. From me."

There was that pain in his eyes again. I put a hand on his arm. "I understand why you assume I'd do that. It's kind of my go-to. But I'm done running. I can't even begin to express how done I am. We can have a conversation when I'm done at the palace. I promise."

Drake inclined his head. "I'll hold you to that."

I landed in the hidden flashing circle near the family entrance at the castle and removed my glamour earrings. It was still early, but the place was already bustling as I stepped through the door and slunk through the back halls toward my brother's office. I hoped he was there. No way I'd go to his apartment, and I didn't want to wait.

Mat wasn't at his desk, but I found him down the hall in a briefing room addressing a bunch of palace guards. His golden eyes focused on me as I entered the room and leaned against the back wall. I'd never attended a palace guard briefing before. One guard saw me, and her eyes widened. I shook my head, and she turned her attention back to the meeting.

Mat finished his briefing, and the guards filed out. Some of them stopped and bowed to me. When the last one left, I focused on my brother. "Hey. Do you have a minute?"

Mat swept me up in a hug. "I wasn't aware that you had returned to Allure."

"I'm sneaky like that. Can we go to your office? This might take a while."

"Of course."

I pounced as soon as he lowered himself into a chair in his office. "I'm considering taking over the duties of queen."

Mat's expression didn't change. "Is it yet another impulsive decision?"

"Are you kidding? Never mind. I see by your eye twitch that you're not. It's been on my mind for..." I tapped my chin. "I dunno. My whole life."

He leaned forward. "That's not what I meant."

"Right. When we took out that demon and so many paranormals died for no reason, I pondered it. At the time, my focus was on my freedom from your bubble, so I ignored it. I wanted freedom so bad that it was all I cared about. As I worked one boring case after another, I considered how I could help people as a queen. I thought about it every time I came here and learned that you hid more things from me, even though you promised you wouldn't. Then, I watched the Enforcers drag bodies out of a warehouse yesterday and realized that the Bellicose is winning.

"Don't get me wrong, I love living on my own and being out from under your control. I'd take the whole three years of freedom if the coalition could survive that long. But I stood among all that senseless death yesterday." I paused. "It was awful, Mat. Most of them suffered a torturous death. They were just kids with their whole lives ahead of them. I couldn't help but understand how selfish pursuing freedom over responsibility made me. My freedom isn't worth their lives. It's a waste for me to pretend to be a detective when I can make a real difference here." Tears filled my eyes, and I blinked them away. "I can't just sit around doing nothing anymore. I'm going to fight the Bellicose, and I'm going to win."

When I finished, my hands shook so hard that I had to clasp them together to hide it. I had a deep-seated fear of being trapped by my throne. Yet there I was, fighting for it. I wondered if I was insane or stupid for not fighting for more freedom instead. With my family history, it was probably the former.

Mat's eyes scanned me for too long. His face gave nothing away. Then he inclined his head. "Very well. Get your magic straightened out, and we'll talk." He stood and strode toward the door.

Working as a detective was supposed to fix two problems. The first was to get me out of Mat's protective bubble so I could learn about the real world and the people I was supposed to rule. I'd done that, sort of. The second problem was my magic. While most people with more than one magic naturally integrated them as they became adults, my three magics refused to mix. It made me less powerful than I needed to be to rule. I didn't care. "Wait. You understand what I'm telling you."

He stopped with his hand on the doorknob. "I understand. The fact remains that you have not served your two years of employment and have not corrected the issues with your magic. I see your concerns, but it will do more harm than good if you take over before you are whole."

I raised an eyebrow. "Whole?"

"Fix your magic, and *then* take the throne."

I wanted to curl into a ball and hide under the desk. I wanted to lash out. Instead, I squared my shoulders and unwrapped my magic. Not fast, nor did I tune it to a specific spell. I slowly and methodically unwrapped it. I saved the ruling magic, my biggest pool, for last. It made the air in the room so thick it was hard to breathe. I rarely let it show. I learned to hide it as a kid when Mat and I were being hunted by assassins because it made me a beacon for anyone to find. So, I learned to hide it. Between that and Mat's intimidating magic that ramped up as mine did, the amount of power filling his office made my hair stand on end.

My brother's expression didn't change, other than a slight tick in his jaw.

I leaned forward. "You don't believe I can fix my magic. You always point out that I'm flawed. Why is that?" I held up a hand when he opened his mouth to speak. "Don't bother lying. It's so you can hold on to power and control. It's a tale as old as time, and it never works out well for the usurper. If you want to waste time fighting to hold the throne while the Bellicose tears the coalition apart, then you will accomplish their goal of destroying us for them. You better ensure your hunger for power is bigger than your love for the coalition and me. Because I am not as broken or stupid as you think. And as much as I love you and don't want it to come to that, I will crush you before I let the Bellicose win."

I flashed to the hallway that led to my office.

Verity, a curvy middle-aged woman with gray streaks in her dark hair, and my assistant sat at a large, ornate desk that forced visitors to go around her. She looked up as I approached, and a smile spread across her face. "Good morning, Je.... uh, Your Grace."

"Hey, Verity." I kept my hands pasted to my sides and offered a shaky smile as I headed through the double doors marked with a crown. Verity followed behind me and shut the door. "Great job hiring the staff. What do they all do?"

She harrumphed. "If you'd pay even an ounce of attention to my reports, you'd learn who they were and what they do." She slammed a packet of papers on my desk. "Seriously."

I loved her fierce attitude. "You're the most competent assistant on the planet. I trust you."

"Well, I have it on good authority that you shouldn't trust anyone completely, so maybe you should read the damn reports."

"Mat strikes again." My voice was a little too rough.

"Just who am I supposed to turn to for advice when you're never here?"

Verity was a mage who could judge and punish people's crimes with a touch. She spent most of her life in the human world, so she didn't understand our value system. I needed an assistant and was lucky enough to snatch her up after some mind-controlled dragons kidnapped us and shattered her world views.

I plopped onto the chair behind my desk. "How's your Juror training going?"

"I hate it. You people are brutal and lack morals. The other day, I watched a witch spell a dryad into driftwood because one of his branches touched her shoulder as she passed. Titus said it was a fair punishment because dryads who touch you claim you, which is taboo without permission. The dryad is in the nursery recovering, and the witch went about her business." She shook her head. "Brutal."

Titus was Verity's match and the crown's, or my main juror. Mat hired him to integrate Verity into paranormal society. When Titus realized they were a match, he talked Verity into moving to Allure and working with me. His position as the Crown Juror allowed him to stay close to help her integrate.

I grinned. "It is fair. Those small punishments keep the two factions from going to war over a minor incident."

She shook her head. "Whatever. Now, let's talk about you. If your brother is forcing you to be here, I'll kick him in the balls."

Did I mention Verity was fierce? "Thanks. Mat had nothing to do with it. If anything, he would prefer I piss off so he can keep the throne." I closed my eyes as soon as the words left my mouth. "Forget I said that."

She lowered herself into a chair in front of my desk. "What's going on between you two this time?"

Mat stormed through the door. "Leave, Verity."

She scrambled out of the room.

I kept my face blank, even though my insides wanted to revolt. "What do you need, Regent?"

My brother's glowing eyes narrowed. "I don't know what's gotten into you, but it needs to stop now."

"Does it?"

He shook his head. "You agreed to work out the issues with your magic and to work for two years. You are not ready to take over as queen."

"See, here's the thing. I wanted freedom from your control, so I was excited to take a job outside the palace. If I had all the information I have now, I would have realized the mistake."

His eyes narrowed. "Following the law is not a mistake."

"A wise person recently told me that although laws keep the peace and help maintain order, they aren't always necessary. When they become unnecessary, we should eliminate them. I am eliminating the ascension law put into place by mother and reverting to grandmother's version."

"You've been talking to Deva." Mat lowered himself into the chair Verity abandoned. "She is great at manipulating situations for her own benefit."

"Aren't we all? And it wasn't Deva."

His eyes flared. "Not me. I'm good at cracking heads to get my way. Subtle manipulation is beyond my abilities."

"Then why are you so opposed to me taking the throne?"

"I'm not opposed to it. In fact, I want to hand it to you. But I want your rule to have a sound foundation, and doubt ascension based on a passing emotion is the best route."

"You just can't help but condescend me, can you?"

"I'm not trying to be condescending anymore than I'm attempting to be power-hungry."

"Yet here we are."

He ran a hand through his hair. "I'm trying to protect you. You'll need your full strength to take the throne."

My eyes narrowed. "What aren't you telling me?"

He shrugged.

"I'll find out."

"I hope so. I'm under contract and will tell you as soon as I can get around it." He stood and headed toward the door. "You do not want to kick that beehive. You also do not want to take the throne until you fix your magic."

"Okay."

Disbelief flashed across his face. "Okay?"

"I'm tired of fighting with you, Mat."

"As am I."

"So, here's the deal. I want to take over as queen, but I'll listen to you about the best way to do that." I held up a hand. "But don't expect me to become you because that will not happen."

"Fair enough."

CHAPTER ELEVEN

DRAKE

Drake waited outside Prince Mathias's office. Speaking to Mathias was the right thing to do, even if it interfered with Jenella's life. It was unfortunate that she no longer trusted her brother. Yet Mathias couldn't care less, and Drake wondered why. He wanted to ensure that she had a place to belong. Something he'd never known.

Mathias rounded the corner and motioned him in. If Drake's presence surprised him, he didn't show it. He wore a neutral expression that only came from years of practice.

When the door shut, Drake turned to Mathias and inclined his head. "I know about your mother."

The young prince lowered himself into a chair. "Do you?"

"I have hunted her and found evidence that she is still alive, though I haven't found her yet."

"If you are here to blackmail me, it will not go well for you."

Drake threw his head back and laughed. "You may be stronger and more vicious than most, but you are not even a blip on the screen to a multidrakelandarnarian. Especially one with ruling magic."

Mathias's eyebrows drew together. "I was unaware you had ruling magic."

"That is by design."

"Is Jenella aware?"

"She knows I am more powerful than her and that I have no desire to rule."

Mathias shrugged. "My mother got to you."

"By bribing a dragon whom I trusted to incapacitate me. The only dragons I now trust are my aunt and cousin. Good luck bribing them."

"Tell Jen about your magic if you want to keep her trust. Otherwise, she will find out and hate you as much as she hates me."

"True. She deserves the truth. So why are you keeping secrets like your mother's existence from her?"

"Because I love her with the same intensity and protectiveness as I would my own child."

"I don't doubt that. But you also refuse to allow her to fly. You keep information from her and undermine her. Those are not actions of love, but control."

Mathias's eyes flashed with anger. "They are the actions of someone who has information that would kill her."

"I disagree. Jenella is much stronger than you think. She can do anything she puts her mind to, including fighting demons, whether imagined or real. I've watched her take down multiple enemies unassisted twice." He rubbed his arm. "Even my aunt respects her power."

"Jen likes you. She would never try to harm you."

"Correct. Because she has a big heart and worries about causing me more pain. I am unsure if she feels the same way about you, though she wants to."

Mathias sighed. "I am aware of my sister's disdain."

"The least you can do is honor her by telling her about your mother."

He tapped his leg. "I cannot."

"Why?"

"That is a long story."

Drake leaned back in his seat and crossed his arms. "I have time."

Mathias's eyes flashed. "Are you sure? It could cause you more problems."

"I wouldn't be here if I weren't."

"Very well. When we ran from Castle Mahri, I got fatally injured fighting through the small army Jaques had amassed. I carried Jen as I fought and took a gunshot to the leg that caused me to bleed out. We were almost free when I realized the problem and started healing myself. But I knew I was too late. I was certain we'd both die because of my stupidity. But that broken, bruised, abused little cherub of a girl used her budding healing magic, not on herself, but on me. Because of her gift, I healed and got us out."

Mathias paused. "We made it to a farm a couple of miles outside Mahri in the human world and took refuge in a hayloft. While my injuries healed, she still bled. I asked her why she saved me and not herself. She said, 'Because you were dying, and I've lived through worse.'

"I'd fought and lost major battles and managed our abusive parents for years. Yet I'd never been so humbled as I was that day. I cleaned the blood off her as best I could, healed her, and replaced her bloody white nightgown with a shirt I stole from a clothesline in a human village. When I told her to get some rest, she put both hands on my cheeks and said, 'You saved my life, dear brother, and we are forever bound' just before she passed out from exhaustion.

"Those words sealed our fate. Back then, I considered myself an honorable man. That day, she taught me what true honor was. I vowed to protect her and have dedicated my life to that vow. I will continue to do so until the day I die. So do not stand on your pedestal and lecture me about honoring Jenella. I honor her every day in every way I can.

"As far as our mother goes, she found me when Jen was still a child. She snuck in here and waited in my office. No one saw or sensed her. I knew the blows Jaques gave her that fateful night wouldn't kill her because she had almost instant healing abilities. For years, I'd sent teams to hunt her. She killed every single one of them."

Drake leaned back in his chair. "You are afraid that if Jen knows she is alive, she'll look for her."

"Yes. Mother is no longer as powerful as she once was but just as lethal. When she visited me, our lovely mother presented a spell showing Jenella sleeping in her bed here at the castle with a knife against her throat. She used my love for my sister to extract a vow that I wouldn't send more hunters after her. She also made me vow I would enforce her unrealistic ascension rules. In exchange, she agreed to leave Jenella alone." Mathias rubbed his face. "I cannot tell anyone, including Jenella, without paying the price."

"I understand your need to protect her. But Jenella has powerful allies that will help her. Allies you helped gather. You both deserve to put that chapter of your lives behind you. Moreso than even I do." Drake rubbed his chin. "You are not stupid, Mathias. This will alienate her."

"It's a sacrifice I'll make to ensure Jen lives a long and happy life." He leaned forward. "The contract stipulated that I couldn't tell anyone awake and aware then. You were not. But you cannot tell Jen any of this."

Drake's eyebrows drew together. "Why not?"

"By having this conversation, the contract now applies to you, too. If I do not follow Mother's ascension rules or tell Jenella she is still alive, magic will extract its price from everyone involved. Before you conclude that doesn't apply to you, you'll have to ask yourself if you want that future for her."

Icy dread settled in Drake's chest as he pondered the situation. "Why? Why would you let her back you into a corner like that?"

"To protect my sister. My mother spent years programming me to do her bidding through cruelty laced with a nugget of praise. So much so that I never considered not following her orders out of fear of the consequences." Mathias rubbed his hands over his face. "I have since realized the error in judgment. If I had it to do all over again, the outcome would be much different."

Drake couldn't breathe. "So now I'm also forced to lie to her."

Mathias shook his head. "I apologize for that. Jen has it in her head that she can take the throne without following the ascension laws and fix everything wrong with the coalition. If she does it without my help, it circumvents the contract, though I'm unsure if she's making the decision out of guilt."

"It's not an impulsive decision," Drake muttered. "But she still doesn't want to be queen."

"Correct. And she expects me to push back on that decision, so I do. Perhaps she can rescue me from the worst choice I ever made."

"She'll hate us both now."

"Perhaps."

Drake stood, still numb from the predicament he'd put himself in. "I don't know who I hate more for this, you or myself." He paused, an idea forming. "Jenella is very perceptive and hates not knowing things. She'll figure out that we're both hiding something from her. If she learns your mother is alive on her own, does it negate the contract?"

"Yes, though the information may destroy her."

Drake inclined his head and left. He had a lot to think about.

CHAPTER TWELVE

JEN

MY PHONE BUZZED WITH a text as I signed off on Verity's new hires.

Emine: Remember that problem at The Cauldron? BM. Need your help.

Me: BM?

Emine: Bug magic, dummy. I need you and Tracy, maybe more. Bring Mat.

I texted Tracy to meet me there and headed toward Mat's office.

I made a ball of magic containing the neutralizing spell as soon as I stepped through the door. "Emine needs our help at The Cauldron. Absorb this. It's the spell that will neutralize the strange magic we found."

It took him less than thirty seconds to absorb it. I texted Drake next. I promised to talk to him later and didn't want to stand him up, and if Emine asked for my help, it meant they were in trouble. Drake was great at helping me get out of trouble. "We're not done talking about the ruling situation."

"Noted."

As we marched out of his office toward the family flashing circle, I couldn't help but think something was off with him, but I didn't comment.

The Cauldron was located downtown in a three-story glass building two blocks from Dragon Headquarters. As we approached the steps, Drake and Bastien descended and changed to their human forms, already dressed in glamoured clothes.

Tracy popped out from behind Bastien. "Hey, Jen. What do we have?" Like me, she wasn't wearing her glamour earrings.

"They have an infestation of that magic. Emine asked for help."

Emine met us in the lobby and waved for us to follow her. As she led us down a hall, people dodged out of our way. Some bowed. One of the first things I needed to do as queen was end the bowing. I hated it.

The Cauldron lobby's glass windows and plush waiting area were deceiving. They made the place seem welcoming and open. As she led us through the labyrinth, the décor became sterile. Thick stone walls, cold steel doors, and a tangled web of wards replaced the glass. The acidic scent of cheap cleaning spells had the two dragons rubbing their noses. Drake sneezed.

We wound around a corner, down another hall, and through what looked like a lounge area. Emine veered left and down another hall, then down four flights of stairs. I doubted I'd find my way out without directions, which I guessed was the point.

She stopped in a square holding area with solid light beige walls coated in monitoring spells. I rubbed my arms against the eerie feeling and raised an eyebrow at Quin, who stood in the corner, his arms crossed over his chest. His brown eyes scanned our group. "Your ability to choose the right people for the job is unique."

"Thanks." I ignored his sarcasm.

Mat leaned against the wall beside me and shot Drake a look I couldn't read before turning his attention to Tracy. "You were the one who found the spell that eliminates this magic, correct?"

"Jen helped. At the mall outside Ferine in the human world. It was where we were first infected."

"Yes. Please tell me the entire story. Leave nothing out. Especially the part where you two let the Queen of Ahl get infected with black magic."

Tracy swallowed.

I rolled my eyes. "Don't blame her. I didn't get infected. Much. Tracy and Quin did."

He leaned forward. "Do you have any idea how many people would like to kill you or, worse, control you? Some may even use black magic to accomplish it."

I threw out my hands. "Hardly anyone knows who I am when I wear my glamour."

"That you are aware of."

"I guard that secret like a dragon guards his treasure." I glanced at Bastien. "No offense. Besides, I plan to take the throne, so it's a non-issue."

"Yet you have solved none of the problems needed to do that," Mat growled.

Bastien watched the exchange with a bland expression. "Perhaps we have gotten off track."

Mat's scary aura expanded, and I laced my hands together to keep them from shaking. He turned his attention back to Tracy. "Please tell us about this magic. How did you figure out how to neutralize it?"

"Well, it took me a while. I mean, my version of Jen's anti-demon magic repelled it, so I knew it had at least some demon magic in it. So, I separated that out and recognized three additional spells woven in. One was an insect repellent witches learn in school. It took me a while to figure out the third element, a disease spell discovered in the fourteenth century. Humans called it the black death, or bubonic plague. Once I got that one, the last piece stumped me for a long time. When Quin went crazy, the answer popped into my head. I mean, I should have recognized the touch of dragon magic right away." She patted Bastien's arm. "I've had a lot of experience with that. I mixed all four elements into a shield for Jen before the magic got me."

"You knew how to counteract dragon magic?" Mat asked.

"Sure. I've been practicing that for years. But it's probably best if we don't tell anyone."

"Correct," Bastien growled.

"Where did they get the dragon magic, Bas?" I asked.

"I don't know, but I'll alert my mother. Perhaps it came from their attempt to take over the dragons last year."

Emine leaned forward. "Which is not why we're here, ya idiots. We have a problem in this dunge — er, jail. I need Tracy and Jen to help me clear the magic. It's about ten thousand square feet, give or take. And about a hundred prisoners."

Tracy shook her head. "No. No way the three of us can do that much at one time."

"How many magic users do you have?" I asked.

"We have a bunch."

"Then why not train them on the dissipating spell and split the area into sections?"

"Right," Tracy agreed. "An area that big would require at least twenty people to keep anyone from burning out. How much time do we have? I mean, mages can dissipate the magic without much trouble. And it should be easy to train some witches to take care of the balls so non-magic users can protect themselves, but those things take time and energy."

Bastien cleared his throat. "That they do. It would have been a disaster if you two weren't in Ferine. Dragon magic is not adaptable to spells in the same way as mage magic is. I tested it against my dragon fire. It repels the magic but doesn't eliminate it."

"I can be of use," Drake said.

I nodded. "We can help train the magic users, but they need to understand their limits so they don't become another casualty. Tracy and I were exhausted when we cleared the mall and we're powerful. If your mages burn out, they'll get infected."

"Sure thing. Let me show you how bad we fucked up." Emine ran a puff of magic over a scanner. The door on the opposite wall opened with a 'click.'

"How did this happen?" Mat asked.

"Hell if I know. I discovered it right before I left to help Jen." Emine tapped her chin. "I bet it's been around Allure for a while."

"If that's true, then we're not just inept, but we're also the most unobservant people who ever existed." I turned to Mat. "Isn't everyone supposed to be looking for stuff like this?"

He inclined his head.

I moved next to Quin, eyed the door, and then spun toward the group. "Right. Yet here we are, in the biggest Enforcer station in the country, and no one noticed stinky, ugly, wiggly magic until it took over? You're right, Quin. We're a bunch of idiots."

"Yes."

Drake's face bloomed into a smile. It wasn't a polite smile or a quirk of his lips. But an amused smile that lit up the room and sent a lightning bolt through me. I'm pretty sure my mouth dropped open because the next thing I knew, Quin poked me in the back. "Keep it professional, shall we?"

"Jen's right. We should've noticed this before it became a problem. I'm going through our ranks to find out why we didn't," Emine said as she swung the door open.

My thoughts screeched to a halt when Emine agreed with me. It was turning out to be a weird day. I let it go and followed her into the guard station.

The room was small, with two occupied cots on one side and two sickly-looking guards against the door. "We need to clear that room and help those guards. This stuff exploded when I threw a pea-sized magic ball at it and infected Quin. I don't want to find out what it would do to a dragon, so you two hang back."

Drake said something to Bastien with his mind magic, then turned his attention to me. "What about you?"

"I can neutralize it, so I'm good. Tracy, Emine, we're up. Mat, watch our backs."

Mat latched onto my arm. "The First is right. Emine and Tracy can handle it. You should stay here with us."

"No." I jerked my arm free. I refused to go back to a half-life inside Mat's little bubble of control. "Emine, you flame throw the place. Tracy, take care of the door guards, and I'll help the guys in the cots."

We crept through the door, and Emine lit up her flame thrower. The guards jumped. Tracy hit them with a spell. I blasted the guys in the cots before they could move. It only took a few seconds to clear the room. I ran my healing magic through the guards. "Bubble wrap my ass."

"I would, but that would be creepy, don't ya think?" Emine said as she dragged a guard away from the door.

"That wasn't meant for you."

"Duh."

Tracy chuckled.

Emine rested an arm on my shoulder. "More of that nasty magic is behind door number two."

I shook her arm off. "Drake, can you disappear those doors so we can see without getting too close?"

He examined the walls and ceilings. "There isn't a lot of room to maneuver here. How fast does this magic spread?"

"It'll send out tendrils that look like black ants marching. It moved slow in Ferine. We should be able to neutralize them if you don't step in front of me and give it a tasty snack." I shivered at the thought.

Bastien put a hand on the door. "I will do it."

Tracy touched his arm. "Wait, hon. Let me just—Emine get on his other side. I'm going to throw a spell as soon as the doors are gone. If any of that stuff comes out here, you get it."

Emine elbowed me out of the way. "Sure thing."

Bastien held up a hand, and the doors disappeared. Tracy threw a neutralizing spell, and Emine shot magic with a smaller version of her flame thrower.

I couldn't even see past the entrance because it was so thick. "Have your people been using magic on it, or did it naturally grow?"

Silence.

"Great." I slapped my hand on the wall to feel the wards. They were designed by a competent witch and fed by several other magical beings to bolster them. I added neutralizing magic to them. "This neutralizing magic might keep it contained until we recruit more magic users. Any ideas?"

Quin leaned against the back wall, his arms crossed. "I suggest we do not drain the three people who can eliminate it."

Tracy chuckled. "You're funny, Quin. Drake, can you tune your magic?"

"Maybe. I need one of you to show me the spell."

Tracy handed him a shield like the ones we used at the mall.

He studied it, asked me to conjure a ball of the magic, then nodded. "I can manage that."

Emine clapped her hands. "Great. Let's do it."

Tracy created several shields and magic balls while Emine gathered magic users.

Mat called some local healers in, and we trained twelve of them, but only seven grasped the spell. They were all mid-to-low level mages. It worried me because of the virus thing I found in Ferine. If they burned out trying to eliminate it, the magic would take them over. As we made our way to the conference room Emine had arranged, horrifying images of infected enforcers and healers running wild in the Cauldron filled my mind.

People dove out of the way and bowed.

I glanced at Mat. "Are people diving out of your way or mine?"

"Both."

"It's kind of creeping me out. How come I never noticed it before?"

"Because you were in a perpetual state of denial and refused to acknowledge your position."

"Huh. Funny, I remembered the bowing, but not the diving out of the way."

He patted me on the head. "Perhaps that is their reaction to me."

"Exactly." No one feared me, and I wanted to keep it that way.

I stopped inside the door and scanned the room. Tracy sat in a chair in the corner, making ping-pong balls. Quin was at the table talking intimately with a tiny, dark-skinned woman with a thick waterfall of hair that fell past her waist. I waved at Ara, who smiled. My skin crawled, and I shook it off. I knew from experience that she meant to be friendly. Emine sat in the center of the table near the wall, her chair leaned back on two legs as she watched Tracy work.

Drake and Bastien sat on opposite sides of the twelve-person table, a 3-D hologram projection of the people we trained going in and out of the basement door playing between them. I didn't see dark magic seeping through the doors as they worked, nor did anyone look infected.

Relief flooded me as I lowered myself into the chair beside Drake. "Hey."

Drake tapped a green dot that hovered in the air, and the scene changed to the inside of the jail. "A quarter of the area is clear."

Mat kissed Emine on the cheek and gently pushed her chair until it landed on all four legs. "How much energy do you have left?"

Emine's expression softened for a second before it snapped back to crazy. Their bond was beyond my understanding, but it was unmistakable. "I'm good. How about you, Jen?"

"Same." I reached across Drake and tapped a hovering yellow dot. The view zoomed in to where a group of mages worked. A couple of healers followed behind. "They're slow but making progress." I punched a blue orb. Another view popped up just as a barrier lifted and moved back. Three witches stepped into the frame, wove a spell, and sent it through a jail cell. "They're making barriers?"

"Emine's brother, Rayar, is down there. He's keeping the magic contained as they work." Bastien's head looked distorted on the other side of the hologram. "At this pace, we won't be able to clear the back three halls until they recover their energy."

Emine's brother had architectural magic and was great at it. The barriers were brilliant. I turned in my chair. "We can clear the rest."

"We?" Mat asked.

"You, Emine, Tracy, and me." I turned my attention back to the monitors. "If the four of us aren't enough to clear the back halls, we can add Quin and Drake and split up into teams of three to clean up the rest of the dungeon."

Mat shook his head. "You need to learn to delegate. More than that, you need to stay away from that magic. I know you don't like it, but we have an entire team down there."

"I agree with Mathias," Drake said. "If it infects you, we are all in deep trouble. You're our last hope of having a strong coalition. You need to consider your safety."

Fates save me from overprotective idiots. I stabbed a finger toward the hologram. "I don't know what's gotten into you, but I don't like it. Quin, Tracy, and I will take the south side while Drake, his new buddy Mat, and Emine take the north. Once we meet in the middle, we'll work together in the larger hall until we reach the other group."

Drake's green eyes flashed with...were those flames? He shook his head, and it faded. "I don't want to hold you back, but I also don't want you hurt or kidnapped again."

It was odd behavior for him. He usually supported me. "Right. Because I'm incapable of taking care of myself."

"No, because you are an adrenaline junkie who rushes into things without thinking."

"Where did you even hear the phrase 'adrenaline junkie'? Look, we have more power in this room than twice the number of people working down there. If we use all our resources, including me, we'll wrap this up in no time."

Several emotions flashed across Drake's face. Emotions I didn't want to see. Hurt, worry, desperation, and fire. "You are terrible at self-preservation. You don't heed warnings and often find yourself in trouble because of it." He drummed his fingers. "Still, you have a point. But please try to take care of yourself for once."

I frowned at the Mat-like statement. "What's going on, Drake? Why the sudden protective streak?"

His jaw clenched. "You realize this is the work of the Bellicose?"

"Yeah. I got that right away."

"Their entire mission is to kill you and take over the coalition."

"Don't forget the human world. They seem to want complete power."

"You think you're funny."

"No. But I'm not stupid, either. I not only discovered their last plot but have done countless hours of research on them. And it's not only me they're after, but everyone in this room. I don't understand why you're suddenly so Mat-like."

Drake's eyes met mine. I almost choked at the raw emotion in them. "Because the world has become much more interesting since you came into it. I don't want to lose that."

I was so confused by his answer that I jumped when Mat said, "I'm going with Jen."

Drake dragged his eyes away from mine. "Are you sure about this, Mathias?"

"Does it matter? This is Jenella we're talking about. If we don't let her go, she'll figure out how to do it without us and probably drag Tracy and Tarquin with her. She considers the word 'no' to be a cage."

"Oh, yes. I'm so easy to drag," Quin mumbled.

I ignored him. Mat was right that I had issues with cages, but I didn't want to help for selfish reasons or because someone told me no. "That's not why. I want to save the coalition. I can't do that from behind a desk."

Drake's eyes met mine, and he gave me a slight nod. For a second, I wondered if he picked up that last thought. The expression was gone so fast I couldn't gauge it. "Very well, I will help."

Emine cracked her neck. "I'll go with Quin and Tracy through the south doors. Mat and Drake can go with Jen through the north, so the rest of us don't have to listen to this nonsense anymore. Bastien can continue to monitor our progress."

Ara linked her arm with Quin's. "And what shall I do? Find a fainting couch in case Jenella gets the vapors?"

Emine grinned. "You can help Bastien coordinate."

Mat flung the door open, and I shot an enormous blast of neutralizing magic through it. The bug magic was so thick that it only cleared a small area. I frowned, increased the inherent power, and hit it again. The ruling magic picked that time to reach out and wrap itself around Drake. My skin tingled when his foreign magic flooded me. It mixed with the neutralizing spell and burst into the basement. My mouth fell open. "Um..." I leaned forward and peered in. "The hall's cleared."

Mat grabbed my arm, shot Drake a death stare, and yanked me through the door. The magic in the hallway was gone, but the cells were writhing with it. Thick tendrils stretched out and wiggled across the floor and ceiling. Mat cleared the first one, dragged the prisoner out to the hall, and returned to clean up the rest. I healed the unconscious prisoner, double-checking for those virus things. I didn't find any.

Drake stood at a cell across from Mat, working some kind of magic I'd never seen before. It wasn't as quick as ours, but it worked. He dragged the second prisoner out, and I healed her. After doing three more that way, I took over dragging people out of the cells. It was quick and efficient, and it wasn't long before we met the other group.

Mat left to heal their prisoners while the rest of us cleared the main hall. I trailed behind Drake as we approached the last cell. Ray's barrier sat beyond it, neutralizing any bug magic that tried to crawl that way. It was a straightforward job and not worth all the arguing. Lost in thought, I didn't realize Drake stopped until I smashed into his back. He reached out to steady me and gestured to the guy in the cell. "This one is different."

I leaned past him and studied the prisoner. I couldn't tell you anything about his appearance other than he was small in stature. Bug magic crawled over every inch of his body, distorting his looks. It jiggled and vibrated as it rotated around him in broad swaths. Then he smiled. The magic slithered out of his mouth, climbed out of his eyes, and dripped out of his nose.

I gagged. "That's gross."

In one smooth motion, the guy jumped to his feet. A thick stream of the stuff separated from him and barreled toward Drake. I dove in front of him. A thousand tiny knives dug into my chest as my back slammed into Drake so hard we collapsed on the floor.

Drake landed in a sitting position, legs spread. I landed between them. Wheezing, I fought through the stabbing pain and tuned my healing magic to the neutralizing spell. The tiny knives digging into me eased, and I sighed in relief.

Hot anger boiled in my stomach, and I threw my hand out toward the guy. The ruling magic kicked in, and a torrent of magic slammed the mage against the wall. It was so thick it made Emine's flame thrower look like a small trickle. I didn't care.

Drake snaked one arm around my waist, and I felt a tug from the center of my chest. Green dragon fire joined my white magic, creating a minty glow. The prisoner's ear-splitting scream echoed throughout the jail and slumped to the floor.

My ears rang. I could hear the others running toward us, but it sounded like they were far away.

"Never do that again." Drake's deep voice vibrated against my ear.

I shivered. "That magic is dangerous. You're one of the last remaining Firsts, and the coalition needs you. You need to consider your safety."

He pulled me closer, his warmth and closeness sending heat through me. His hot breath tickled my ear as he chuckled. He abruptly stood and lifted me with him. "Touché."

I shook out my hands and ignored the sudden chill.

Emine skidded to a stop beside Drake. "What the hell, Jen?"

Quin dropped from the barrier while Tracy and Mat sprinted toward us from the other way. Tracy examined the cell. "Where the heck did this one come from, Emine? I mean, is he the one doing all of this?"

Emine's forehead creased. "I have no idea. But you can bet I'll find out."

Mat kneeled and reached toward the guy. "This one's different. I can feel that magic from here. Are you okay, Jen?"

"Yep. And so is Drake, who was his target."

Tracy's eyes trailed up and down Drake. "Did he infect you?"

"I'm fine." He shot me a look I didn't bother trying to read, then patted the barrier. "We can't take that down until we contain him."

We formed a semicircle around the guy. The bug magic was already bleeding through his clothes.

"As much fun as this is, I'd like to go home, so perhaps you can take action." Ara's voice rang through the communication spell.

Black dancing circles appeared all over the mage's torso. The stuff still gave me the creeps, no matter how many times I saw it. "We'll need to run healing magic through him." I turned my attention to Mat. "Can you tune your healing magic to the neutralizing spell? If you can hold it back, I can look for the virus."

"Virus?"

I explained the triangular pieces of magic we'd found in the prisoners at the lab and how I neutralized it.

Mat's face grew harder as I talked. When I was done, he leaned his head back and pinched the bridge of his nose. "Yes, I can help with that." He dropped his arm. "Consider this your safety lecture."

I fought the smile that tried to form. "Sure."

Mat slapped a hand on the guy, and the spots forming on his skin and clothes disappeared. I moved to the prisoner's other side and searched for viruses. He had five of them implanted in him. The one at the base of his skull was twice the size of the other ones I'd found. Another one of equal size was at the base of his spine, one in each hand and one implanted deep in his brain. Mat's magic probed them as I worked, but he didn't interfere. I pulled the last one out rather than neutralizing it. "Tracy, do you have a way to contain this so you can study it?"

A vial appeared in front of my face, and I guided the virus into it. Tracy wove a sealing spell and held it up. "Got it. I need to take this to my dad."

I let go of the mage and stepped back. "Did you get that, Mat?"

"Yes. That's...interesting."

"It's terrifying. And one of the many reasons we need to become more proactive."

Emine's brother, Ray, walked through his barrier. "Can I take this down now?"

"Has the rest been cleared?" Emine asked.

Ray's face screwed up in disgust as he shifted his attention from the unconscious mage to her. "Yes. We put this wall here to contain that guy. He's different."

"Then yes."

I drifted over to Drake. "Can you read his mind?" Drake's mind magic was more powerful than any dragon I'd ever met. So powerful the ruling magic let him into my head all the time. It wouldn't let anyone other than him and the Dragon Queen, Deva, communicate with me. And Deva got thrown out more times than not. It got flat-out violent when other dragons or mind mages tried. If anyone could read the mage's mind, it was Drake.

He shook his head. "His thoughts are madness. I'll come back and try again later, but I doubt it will do any good."

"Are they single-minded thoughts, like when the dragons were spelled?"

"No. More like he lost the ability to organize them."

"Let's get out of here. We'll discuss the magical properties later," Mat interjected.

As we filed back into the conference room, Ara stood. "So, crisis averted?"

"We've determined that we don't need that fainting couch," I answered.

Mat ignored the exchange and focused on Emine. "Train everyone who can tune their magic on the neutralizing spell. One or two people per enforcer team. Do not tell them it contains elements that work against dragons. The last thing we need is Deva going on a rampage." He tapped his chin. "I'll ensure the healers learn it. This magic is highly contagious, so send out an alert. Jenella is right that we need to inform the coalition leadership about the threat."

I squared my shoulders. "Verity already emailed the leadership, but we might need a council meeting to answer their questions." I paced so I could think. "I bet you anything that mage didn't end up in the Cauldron's jail by accident. They wanted to infect the enforcers."

Mat nodded. "It's a strong possibility."

"And how were they able to do that without us knowing? Why are we always one step behind?" I stopped pacing and faced the table. "Well, aside from the lack of communication. That needs to change first. And don't think for a second that I'm going to sit back and let everyone else fight this without me."

Mat's eyebrows quivered. He really wanted to say something about that. Instead, he turned to address the rest of the group. "Until we understand what we're up against, no one works alone. That includes you, Tarquin."

Tracy shook her head. "Jen, Quin, and I make a great team, so I don't see any reason to change that. But I can't be her guard anymore."

My heart sank. I knew one day Tracy would quit, but I wasn't ready for it just then. "What? Why?"

"Because you don't need a personal guard." Her eyes slid to Mat. "You never did. Besides, I've become your friend, so it doesn't seem right. Also,

I'm going to work with my dad to come up with some potions that will help with this situation and other magics that we found in that lab."

"What about the witches?" I asked. Tracy got harassed by witches all the time when she wasn't with me or wearing glamour. It was one reason I hired her as my guard.

"They're still a problem, but not when I have my glamour earrings to protect me."

"And me," Bastien said.

Tracy didn't roll her eyes, but I could tell she wanted to. "Right. I'm not abandoning you, Jen. I mean, it's time to change things up."

The tension in my shoulders melted. She *needed* to work on her relationship with Bastien and spend more time on her business and her dad. And I loved the idea of having a genuine friend who wasn't obligated to spend time with me. "How about an official advisor position? That way, the witches can't act against you even when you're alone."

She raised an eyebrow. "You want me, a commoner, as an advisor?"

I couldn't help the smile that spread across my face. "Sure. That way, you can still tell me what to do, and I can still ignore you."

"Sounds great. It'll be like old times."

"I will be Jenella's guard," Drake interjected.

Mat's expression hardened. "No."

Butterflies exploded in my stomach at the thought of spending more time with Drake, and I had to tamp them down. "I agree with Mat. I need to be seen as a powerful queen. If I'm guarded by a First, the entire coalition will see me as weak. The more ambitious leaders will claim you're running things."

"Only until they realize you don't listen to me any better than you listened to Bastien and Tracy. Your magic likes me. Did you not realize I used it on that mage in the dungeons?"

I knew I was in denial of our connection, and I wanted it to stay that way. So I gave him a flat look.

He ignored it. "We need to destroy the Bellicose labs before they find a magic we can't combat. You need every resource at your disposal to do that. That includes working with someone on your level." He leaned forward. "Spoiler alert. I am the only one in this pocket who is on your level."

My head whipped to Mat. I saw the resignation on his face, so I looked at Tracy for a lifeline. She looked away. Quin had his head back, eyes closed. Ara and Emine watched the conversation with too much interest. I cleared my throat. "Spoiler alert? Where did you even hear that?" I shook my head. "Aside from the weird human phrase, I get what you're saying. It's a bad idea to start my reign as Queen by giving my power to a First."

Ara leaned forward. "You're not giving up power, dear. You're forming a bond."

"That doesn't make it any better."

"No one is forming a bond with Jenella," Mat growled.

I held up my hand. "Not your call. You've had my back since I accidentally woke you up, and I'm grateful for that. It'll still look bad to start my rule with a First at my side."

Ara's ancient eyes lit with mischief. "Perhaps if you didn't care what others thought, it would not be a problem. He will be good for you. Even Deva likes the idea. She believes the fates have decided on the match."

"I seriously doubt that," Mat grunted.

I rubbed my face. The ruling magic liked Drake. It always had. I needed to figure out how to combine my three magics. Drake *could* help me work on my to-do list. Still, he unnerved me, and I didn't want a bond. I was too young. Too naïve. Not as naïve as I once was, but I still had a long way to go. "I don't know." I glanced at Drake, expecting to see hurt or disappointment, but only found determination in his beautiful eyes. The urge to fall into them made me shift in my seat. They were distracting, and I needed to make a sound decision. "I just don't know."

His lips formed into a small smile. He'd caught that last thought. "My glamor is no longer as effective because ruling magic does not enjoy hiding in the shadows. If you didn't want to be shackled to me, you shouldn't have initiated a bond." He leaned so close his face was only a few inches from mine. "A bonded dragon does not do well without his partner."

"You're not a dragon," I squeaked. It was something he always said because he was different than other dragons.

A smile ghosted across his lips. "A multidrakelandarnarian, then. The point remains that this magic could spell the end of the coalition if left unchecked. Working together, we could find more answers."

My face flushed. I knew the ruling magic had reached out to Drake, but I tried to ignore that it formed a bond. That was on me because I knew better than to ignore my problems. The first time I accessed his magic, I should have researched it. But I was so self-absorbed and high on freedom that I didn't bother. And this was the consequence. "Are dragon bonds forever?"

"Yes."

As I worked on my small cases, he'd always pop up. At first, I thought Mat hired him, but I knew after I accessed his magic that first time that something was different. My instinct to run away from anything I didn't want to deal with kicked in and I'd almost convinced myself that it hadn't happened. But the truth was standing in front of me in all its rugged glory, and I couldn't avoid it anymore, so I decided to use it to my advantage. "I have some conditions."

The bastard grinned. "I would expect nothing less."

"The first one is that you won't hold me back in the field using some bullshit safety excuse. If I'm going to lead the war against the Bellicose, I need to be seen as the most powerful supernatural in the Coalition. Powerful people don't cower behind guards." I motioned to Ara. "Also, I plan to investigate this like a detective, so don't lecture me if I decide to follow a potentially dangerous lead." I pointed to my brother. "That goes for you, too."

"We'll discuss strategy later." Mat turned to Emine. "Train your people, and I'll do the same with the healers and palace guards."

Quin kissed Ara's hand. "We shall take our leave." They disappeared.

"Bas and I will stick together. As your advisor, I suggest you listen to Drake. I mean, you won't, but you should, considering he's old and knows a lot more than you," Tracy said.

CHAPTER THIRTEEN

JEN

THE SUN ALMOST TOUCHED the horizon when I returned to the castle. I'd gone to the house and searched the maginet for incidents that could point to the gross magic. One report from the pocket of Pyron of paranormals getting sick sparked my interest, as did rumors that shifters were going missing on the East Coast. But not enough to justify the numbers that attacked us in Ferine.

The hidden family flashing circle was in the back and had a strict access spell on it that tasted our magic when we landed. I waited for the tug, straightened my rumpled clothes, and shuffled toward the family entrance. As I reached for the handle, it swung open. Helen, the griffin that helped Mat raise me and the matriarch of a large griffin family who adopted us and nested at the castle, stood by the door, a stern expression on her face. "Have you eaten today?"

"Um."

She looped her arm through mine and dragged me to the kitchen table we used daily so we didn't have to sit in the enormous dining room. "We'll have a meal together before you go flittering off again."

I sighed and took a seat. "Sure."

As we ate, I told her stories about my small, mundane cases and the amazing people I'd met. She caught me up on all the castle gossip. The tension that plagued me drained, and I lost track of time as we talked. I missed her fussing over me. Don't get me wrong, I loved being independent, but it was nice to have someone who cared enough to make sure I took a break and ate.

Stomach full, I rounded the corner, heading toward my office, glanced toward the small sitting area reserved for my visitors, and stopped in my tracks.

Drake sat on one end of the sofa, an ankle crossed over a knee, one arm resting on the armrest, the other thrown over the back of the couch as if he didn't have a care in the world. He wore jeans and a green T-shirt that matched his eyes. His hair swooped back in a professional style that contradicted his rugged face. My body heated at the sight. I'd sensed him but was so used to him following me around I ignored it.

My eyes slid to the other end of the sofa, where Deva, the Dragon Queen, sat, shoes kicked off, her legs curled under her as she scrolled through her phone. I hadn't sensed her. And it looked like they'd been there a while. It was an insult to let dignitaries wait when they came to visit unless I was busy, which I wasn't.

"Um. Your G-g-grace."

My attention turned to the urban sprite who sat behind Verity's desk. Her green hair pulled into a professional bun. She blushed, causing her gray skin to have a slight pink undertone. The sprite was a recent addition to the team whose name I couldn't remember.

She grinned and gave me a half-wave. "The Juror, Verity, left for the day. I'm Charlotte. Um. Yeah, so the Dragon Queen and the First Drake are here to see you. Um. Your Grace." Her hand shook as she pointed at them.

Considering my guests could have eaten the tiny sprite as a snack, it was a valid response.

As she stammered, I didn't miss the sparkle of humor in the dragons' eyes. "Thank you, Charlotte. Will you send in some refreshments?"

"Oh, of course. I'll do that." She spread her wings and flew toward the stairs so fast I didn't have time to tell her that George and Helen had a strict no flying or flashing in the castle rule.

"Come on in Deva, Drake."

I led them to the sitting area at the far end of my office beside a large bank of windows overlooking the front lawn. They took a couch on one side of the bank of windows while I perched on the other. "I was going to head your way when I finished up here."

Deva raised an eyebrow. "You are the queen, love. You don't chase after people. You summon them. Or did you assume that big summoning room was just for magic outbursts and horrible jokes?"

The room allowed me to bring in any paranormal from anywhere in the world in the blink of an eye. My mother left it in Deva's care. Her assistant summoned me to see Drake one time while I wore nothing but my pajamas. Then Drake used it to contain my magic when the ruling magic grew on my thirty-fifth birthday. Deva and Drake thought it was hilarious. Me? Not so much. I'd decreed no one use the stupid thing on me again and swore I'd never use it on others unless I didn't have a choice. "Yeah, well. I'm not much on protocol, and I hate that summoning room."

"It's not a matter of what you like. It's a matter of establishing your leadership. You don't want the other leaders to see you as a pushover who will do their bidding."

She had a point, even though it felt like another bar slammed into place around me. I planned to figure out a way to make sure I stayed free while ruling. "Right. So, what brings you here?"

"Why am I seated in a position of power in the upcoming council meeting?"

My eyebrows drew together. I asked Verity to include the dragons more in Coalition affairs, but I didn't track the steps she took to accomplish the task. She was a brilliant assistant, so I let her make those decisions. "Because you're a powerful leader."

"I do not have an official seat on the Council. It's against coalition law to give me one."

I grinned. "I found a passage in one of my grandmother's diaries about how she navigated the coalition signing. She didn't like that the other Firsts ostracized Drake. Or that the treaty left out the dragons. So, she eliminated the provisions that restricted the dragons from the Council and added you as a member of the coalition before signing it. She gave you a council seat about five hundred years later. Her exact words were, 'I have righted a grievous wrong while working in the shadows. Deva and the dragons have much to contribute to these endeavors. It is a shame to exclude them.'" I memorized the passage because I wanted Drake to find his purpose and was looking for something to help. It didn't help Drake much, but I was glad my grandmother recognized how dumb it was to exclude the dragons. "The question is, why did you let them treat you like crap for so long? You have the power to take over the coalition, so don't pretend you don't. You could have done it any time you wanted, especially after my mother's death."

The door burst open, and Charlotte fluttered in with an enormous tray filled with meats, cheeses, fruit, tea, and coffee. She set it down and fluttered out without a word. Deva tapped the arm of her chair. "I considered Lissa a friend."

It was weird to hear my grandmother's first name thrown out so casually. No one ever used her first name in front of me. People usually referred to her as the first queen. "From what I've read, the feeling was mutual."

She inclined her head. "Unlike the other Firsts, who were extremely jealous, she was happy that Drake's family followed him to this realm. She agreed the Firsts should have support when they traveled to new realms. I did not want to upset her plans, so I stayed in the background. That changed when your mother started hunting the Firsts and forcing them to sleep. I pursued her relentlessly when she got her dirty hooks into Drake. When she…Well, I eventually came to an agreement with Mathias to protect you until you could protect yourself. I planned to kill you if you turned out like your mother. I am pleased that you did not."

Mat worked tirelessly to protect me as a kid. His agreement with Deva didn't surprise me. "That's why you sent Bastien to guard me."

She nodded. "Yes. The agreement was that the dragons be close enough to protect you. In exchange, Mat would ensure that you didn't turn into a murderous bitch. I inserted Bastien as insurance."

A couple of years before, the declaration would have shocked me. Then I met Drake. He helped me realize my mother was a selfish, power-hungry tyrant who eliminated her competition without remorse. She cared more about petty revenge and her own image than paranormals. Her diaries reinforced that reality. "I've narrowed down the locations of the resting places of a couple of other Firsts."

"Oh?" Drake's deep voice vibrated through my bones.

I ignored the feeling. "It's a strong possibility that one is in Pyron and one in Mage Mountain. Though she didn't mention which ones were there. She put you in Allure to taunt your aunt and was very proud of it."

"You didn't tell me that."

"Nope. Just like you didn't tell me why you've been following me for the last year. Communication goes both ways."

Deva threw her head back and laughed. "You have come out of your cocoon as the most beautiful butterfly, Jenella. I consider my contract with Mathias complete."

"Okay…"

"However, I still owe you a debt."

"You don't…"

"As an extension to saving my life, you saved the dragons. You found my nephew, brought him back to us, and gave me a prestigious place on the

Council. In our culture, that means I owe you both a life debt and a blood debt. I am here to repay it."

"I didn't..." Deva's magic crashed into my chest and wrapped around me. The ruling magic lashed out, but Drake blocked it using the stupid bond we hadn't talked about. A sense of betrayal stabbed through me as the magical bands tightened. I bent over and clutched my stomach. Tears streamed down my face, and the salty taste of blood filled my mouth. The healing magic raced through me, trying to find the injury and numb the pain. I convulsed, fell to the floor, and lost control of all three magics. They snapped out, searching for a target to destroy, but the two dragons contained them.

It only took a few seconds for the pain to ease, but it seemed like hours. When it subsided, I wheezed as I dragged myself off the floor and sunk into the sofa. I rubbed my stomach and shook my head as I tried to regain my senses. That's when I noticed the yelling.

"You have no right." Mat's gravelly voice pierced my addled senses.

"I have *every* right," Deva answered in a calm, collected voice.

"You cannot force contracts on the Queen."

I held up my shaky hands. "Wait. What?" I coughed and patted my chest. The ruling magic was pissed as I reeled it in. It zapped Drake twice before it allowed me to retract it. "What was that?"

Deva and Mat stood to the side of the square coffee table, nose to nose. They stopped arguing and spun toward me in unison. Mat leaned down and examined my face. "Are you okay, Jen?"

"Yes." I turned my attention to Deva, who casually lowered herself to her seat and began devouring the snacks. "What was that?"

She held up a piece of cheese. "It is like a magical contract, although it goes a little deeper with dragon magic."

"Wait. What?" I'd used the phrase too often since we found the bug magic. In my defense, Deva always unsettled me. I needed to get a handle on that.

"I pledged my allegiance and that of the dragons to you. You are officially a member of our family and the only person I've ever let rule over me. It also means that I accept your offer to become an advisor."

I shook my head. I didn't ask her to become an advisor, though she was on the shortlist. Besides, people had warned me my whole life to stay neutral. I couldn't do that with the dragons hovering. I opened my mouth to say so, but Mat put a hand on my shoulder. "It is a great honor, Jenella. It will help keep you safe."

I growled in frustration. "I don't give a shit about staying safe! They blocked my magic and forced a bond on me without my permission."

Drake flinched. "I didn't block your magic, just softened the blow."

"That doesn't make it better."

Deva's eyes softened. "I am truly sorry, Jenella. I did not realize that you were unaware of the ways of dragons. You saved my life, eliminated that mind-control magic, nursed me back to health, and offered me a place to regain my strength. Then, you bonded with my nephew and gave me a seat of honor in the leadership council. In dragon culture, that means that I must return the kindness. I simply made a magical vow that you are now considered one of us and have my permission to rule the dragons. As a multidrakelandarnarian, the agreement does not include Drake."

My eyebrows drew together. "And if I don't want that...honor?"

She waved a hand. "Our support will provide you with significant advantages."

I decided she wouldn't budge and needed time to process, so I changed the subject. "What was that pain?"

"It was the bond of thousands of dragons. Should you need us, use it, and we will come to your aid."

I looked at Mat for help, but he hadn't taken his eyes off Drake, who didn't take his eyes off me. "What's going on with you two?"

Drake shrugged.

Mat grunted.

Deva clasped her hands. "Welcome to the family, love. Now, Mathias, let's discuss accurate historical facts and the block on Jenella's magic."

She dragged Mat from the room, leaving me alone with Drake.

"So that happened." I stood and made my way to the conference table where I'd thrown my bag.

"I didn't know she was going to do that."

"Yet you helped her."

"Yes."

"Why?" I ignored another stab of betrayal as I lowered myself into a chair and flipped through the 'to do' list on my phone.

"Because you need the support."

"I don't like other people deciding things for me. Even if they think it's for my own good."

Drake pulled out a chair across from me and sat. "I know."

"I shouldn't need to rely on a legion of dragons or a witch of Tracy's caliper to protect me, and I hate that I'm not powerful enough for this job."

"You're powerful enough. But you need all the help you can get, especially in the current political climate. It's only logical to take it when it's offered."

"That's the problem with you ancients. You all have this annoying ability to remove emotion from any situation. Is it because life has beaten you down for so long that you no longer feel? Or is it because you are wise?"

Drake's lips twitched. "It is the latter, of course. And I'm not asking you to remove emotion, only to see the reality of your situation."

"By removing emotion."

"By viewing your situation from a different perspective." He leaned forward. His unique scent of wood smoke and delicious masculine soap washed over me. "When I fly high in the sky, people are insignificant, barely dots on the ground. Buildings and streets are mere scars on the land. I can see the layout of cities, where civilization ends and the wilderness begins. Flying high gives me a bigger picture and helps me navigate. However, if I flew high all the time, I couldn't see that one of those ants on the ground was a powerful ruler who intended to put me to sleep or kill me. I'd never know the wilds were filled with vicious shifters and territorial dryads.

"In contrast, when I fly lower, I can see more definition and read the minds of those I pass. And, when I am on the ground, the buildings tower over my head and obstruct the view. It may be an ambush or a friend waiting around the corner, and I couldn't see which."

"Except you can still sense them and read their minds."

"True. My point is that the different perspectives affect my view of what's around me and my reactions. Right now, your perspective is so close to the situation that you cannot tell a friend from foe or safety from danger. Deva is trying to show you who your friends are."

"And you?"

"I only want to help you fly."

I sat back to distance myself from his delicious scent. "Okay. I'll concede that you're right that I'm too close to the situation. I want to fly. But you need to realize that I am on the verge of being stuck in this safety bubble. Bubbles skew the view."

"People care about you and want to protect you, not confine you."

"It's been my experience that there's no difference between the two. Do you know that when Tracy and I first moved to that little house, I couldn't clean up after myself or use a magichef? I didn't even realize that clothes needed to be cleaned or how to make my bed. Tracy had to teach me all of that."

"I don't see why that's relevant."

"I also thought my mother was a saint who cared about the people of the coalition. It was easy to keep me ignorant and incompetent in the name of safety. I'm not okay with that anymore."

Drake was silent for a few seconds. "Then I'll figure out how to keep you safe without imprisoning you and making you clueless."

I stared at the table, unsure how to process his statement. "I'm not sure you can do that, and neither are you. There are rules and protocols surrounding me that regular paranormals don't have. They restrict me, and if you stick with me, they'll restrict you, too."

He leaned forward. "I am a First, and you are a Queen. We can do what we damn well please."

"Yeah. Except I need to get people to follow me, and I can't do that by going rogue. And you are compelled to stalk me. I don't see how that's doing what we damn well please."

"The bond you avoid forces me to see that you're safe. It does not determine how I do that."

"Right. So, to accomplish that, you flew all over the country, stalking me, instead of shooting me a text asking to have a conversation."

He threw his head back and laughed. "I'm still getting used to how easy it is to communicate with technology. Keeping the bond closed tight triggers my instincts, which is why I checked on you regularly. I had no choice but to stalk you."

"Yet you believe we can do whatever we want."

"Yes. I didn't mean we wouldn't have responsibilities to other people. But you don't have to follow the rules so rigidly. It would be a shame to tame your wild streak."

I knew nothing about dragon instincts. I didn't even understand what opening and closing the bond meant. Well, I knew what it meant but not how to do it. I flipped my phone around so he could see it. "This is my to-do list. If you're going to hang around, then make yourself useful and try to figure out how to accomplish some of this stuff. Also, I need you to tell me things about the Firsts not found in books. It would give us a huge advantage if we can wake the ones my mother put to sleep and get them on our side."

CHAPTER FOURTEEN

JEN

Tracy showed up a while later, and we headed to the flashing circle at the back of the castle as the sun sunk beyond the horizon. With a flash of light, we landed in a much smaller circle at the edge of the mixed-magic neighborhood. I waved at a palace guard neighbor who stood outside his house dripping spells on his lawn. When I found out that Mat stacked the neighborhood with guards, I was livid. But we'd become friendly with some of them, and I learned they were good people. Our raccoon shifter neighbor, Penelope, stood on her front porch, watching over her kids, who squealed as they played in the yard. "Do her kids ever age?"

Tracy chuckled. "Yes. She just keeps having more."

"Really?"

We ducked through the front door, headed straight to the kitchen, and grabbed some food. When we finished eating, Tracy took a sip of water. "So, you and Drake have a bond, huh?"

I shrugged. "I'm pretty sure the stupid ruling magic made that decision for us. He wants to find a purpose and thinks I'm part of that. I have my doubts."

"Of course you do. You don't let anyone get too close to you." She waved her fork in the air. "Dragon bonds don't work like that. If you have a bond, he's not going anywhere, and you need to deal with it."

"I gave him my to-do list and told him to make himself useful."

Her shoulders shook with laughter. "Of course you did. What's up with Deva? I saw her and Mat leave your office, and he looked pissed."

"She put herself and the dragons under my rule and made me part of their family. I'm not sure what that means yet. The magic she used in the contract knocked me for a loop."

Tracy put her dishes in the magiwash and watched it until they put themselves away. "I don't know what her deal is. She's been different since her kidnapping."

I nudged her out of the way. "No one's ever bested her before. That makes powerful people nuts. Deva probably aligned with me to ensure it doesn't happen again."

"Or maybe she likes and respects you."

I sighed. "Maybe." I moved to the living room and plopped down on one end of the sectional. "What am I going to do about Drake?"

"You should let him in. I mean, it's a little too late for second thoughts if you two already have a bond. Besides, he'll be good for you."

"What exactly are the dragon mating rituals? I've looked it up in books and saw that they try to find the one thing their mate wants and give it to him or her. Is that right?"

Tracy blinked. "It's different for every dragon. And it's the one non-material thing that matters most to their mate. Material things are easy for dragons to come by since they all have hordes. They figure out what that one thing is, then prove their loyalty by supporting and protecting it. Most of them do it with flair, so their actions aren't mistaken for anything other than what they are.

"Bastien figured out that I treasured my dad and my potions. He worked as my dad's lab assistant for months. He added dragon magic to my dad's alchemy." She chuckled. "They came up with some crazy stuff. Then, he found the spell that contained our family photos dating back to when my mom was pregnant with me and did a giant magical slide show over the village. After that played, he added his magic to the village wards to prove he could keep my dad safe and sang a song about how he cherished me and my family. It was so corny, yet so sweet, considering Bastien's disposition. If I wasn't already in love with the idiot, I would have fallen then."

I wondered if Drake found the one thing most important to me. Probably not, because there were a bunch of things that were important to me. Mat, the griffins, the people of the coalition, my new friends. Mat was probably the most important person, even though I considered George and Helen family, too.

My stomach fluttered. He tried to give me my freedom when he took me on that fun flight. Because he wanted me to feel free for a few minutes. Or something like that. My shoulders slumped. There was no way Drake, or anyone else, could give me freedom because of my title. The only chance I had was to carve out a small slice of it for myself. "What about the non-dragons? Did you do something similar?"

"No. Dragons understand that non-dragons do things differently, so it wasn't part of the deal. Wait, are you planning on doing something for Drake?"

I gave her my best innocent look. "Not right now, no. Though, if I wanted to, I know his most important thing. I was just curious."

We sat in comfortable silence for a few minutes before she broke it. "My dad said he has a potion to protect people from the bug magic."

My heart skipped a beat. "That was fast. A protective potion or one that dissipates it?"

"Both. He wants me to go to his lab and look at it tomorrow. Do you want to go?"

I shuffled through my schedule in my head. "Sure. He lives on the outskirts of Allure, right?"

She nodded. "Yeah, it's easier to fly to the settlement than flash, so ask Drake to give you a ride. My dad likes you and will be thrilled you're interested in his work."

Tracy's dad was the Vice President of Covens. I didn't realize he was her dad when he rode with us to my coronation. I wished I had taken the time to talk to him more. My focus was solely on my first case and my worry about returning to Mahri. I only cared about my own anxiety at the time, so I didn't appreciate the people who took time out of their lives to wish me well, nor did I bother spending much time with them. I regretted it. Looking past my own feelings to see others was an ongoing struggle. "How can he stand to work with…" I trailed off.

Tracy shook her head. "He ran for the Vice President position right after my mom died to protect me. He drinks a potion that makes him immune to spells when he works with her."

Witches elected the President and Vice President in separate elections. I never paid much attention to them until Tracy came along. Her dad was brave to take on the Vice President position and work so close to the woman who killed his match and tried to kill his daughter. "What time are we going to his villa?"

"First thing in the morning would be best."

I texted Drake to ask if he'd go with me, and we talked for a while longer. Having a friend who didn't expect anything from me was nice. When my eyes drooped, I stumbled up the stairs and crawled into bed.

Clang!

Barely conscious, I jerked my eyes open and scooted to the back of my cage. The smell of filthy people and urine filled my nose as I made myself as small as possible. If the man came back, I couldn't escape. If it was a guard, I didn't want them to see me. I cowered behind the chamber pot.

"Where is she, Jacques?" It sounded like my father's voice. A scuffle and some more shouting, and everything quieted. Heart pounding, I worked up the courage to peek. Father lay on the floor in front of my cage in a pool of blood. The mean man fought with my mother by the entryway.

"Mother, I'm here!"

She turned for just a second as the man brought the axe down on her head.

I startled awake, threw the covers back, and pulled out the bottom of the clean purple t-shirt I wore to bed to remind myself it wasn't a blood-soaked white nightgown. Sweat trickled down my back as I stumbled out of bed and dragged myself to the bathroom to splash water on my face. I used to have nightmares all the time, playing pieces of my traumatic early childhood over and over in my mind. I'd done a lot of work on myself, and, as a result, I rarely had those kinds of nightmares. Not wanting to dwell on it, I headed to the kitchen to grab some water and curled up on the couch to read one of my mother's diaries. Her bragging always put me back to sleep.

CHAPTER FIFTEEN

JEN

THE HOMESTEAD WHERE TRACY'S dad lived sat at the edge of Allure, just past a warehouse district. It was sandwiched between a high desert where the snake shifters lived and a neutral area with several businesses that accommodated people as they moved in and out of the pocket. Thick wards obscured the view of the village, even from the air. Drake agreed to come with me without asking a single question. It seemed off because I was so used to fighting Mat, who made sure that nothing ever came easy for me. I often wondered if he did that on purpose

The passing warehouses looked nothing like the ones we saw in the human world. Most of them had retractable skylights that allowed the occupants to see out and monitor or allow access to flying paranormals. They were much smaller because they didn't store cereal and other goods. Although some paranormals used them for personal storage, others used them for large gatherings, labs, and magic classes. I spotted a small one that had wards like the ones around the castle. Wards that were created by the sorceress Ann Marie. I wondered about it because she lived in the human world. Not that it was any of my business. Ann Marie could own a warehouse if she wanted. Still, something about it bothered me.

My mouth dropped open as Drake followed Bastien through the thick wards of the Alchemist Coven's homestead. What I thought was a homestead was a well-manicured village that spread several blocks. It looked like something out of a human fantasy movie, with its neat little cottages, lush green lawns, and vibrant flowers. Parks dotted the village, and I could picture families gathering, having picnics, or enjoying a warm spring day. Shrubs flanked the main street, each one trimmed into the shape of a paranormal creature. I spotted a kraken, a dragon, and a griffin and grinned. Every house had an herb garden that perfumed the air with a pleasant mix of flowers and spices. As we flew lower, I noticed the flowers color-coordinated with the houses.

Drake and Bastien morphed into their human forms as they landed. I barely had time to flash to the ground. Tracy landed gracefully next to me and led us toward a stone cottage with a steep roof. "Don't be fooled by appearances. I mean, my dad's a clever guy, so he is good at making himself look unassuming." She pushed through the door and motioned us in.

The inside of the cottage was cavernous. The entryway sat at the edge of a spacious family room with a brown leather overstuffed curved sectional and round coffee table. Hallways led from each side, and a gleaming white kitchen sat beyond in an open floor plan.

A tall, muscular man with skin two shades darker than Tracy's strolled out of the hallway on the right. "Ahhh. The best daughter in the world has come to visit." He wrapped Tracy in a hug.

Calvin Cordalia was a big man. At six foot five, he towered over the other witches. He had broad shoulders and well-defined muscles without being bulky. Like his daughter, he was so blindingly beautiful it was hard to look at him for any amount of time. His dark skin and sense of style were flawless. As were his sparkling brown eyes.

Bastien's expression softened. "Hello, Calvin."

"Bastien." He turned his attention to Drake. "And a First. Welcome."

Drake offered a polite smile. "Call me Drake. It's nice to meet you, Sir Cordalia."

"Very well, Drake. Please, call me Calvin." He turned his attention to me. "And the queen herself. I will always be grateful to you for welcoming my daughter into your home and keeping her safe."

"You can call me Jen. And it was a two-way street. Tracy saved me, too."

He nodded. "She talks about your friendship often."

The first time I met Calvin, I didn't realize he was Tracy's dad. I'd banned the President from my transport heading to Mahri, and he filled in. When I later realized how similar they looked, I blurted it out. Tracy laughed at me for two days. In my defense, Tracy's dad rarely left his village unless he needed to. And he never spoke up in council meetings. After that, I educated myself to recognize every council member, anyone they considered part of their inner circle, and their families.

Calvin led us down a staircase to a bright lab. On one side were a bunch of neatly organized and labeled jars full of colorful dried leaves. I bet he had every kind of herb imaginable. The opposite wall held shelves lined with books that ranged from recent to ancient. Two counters ran down the center and contained vials, beakers, scales, and what looked like human cooking devices and pots. I spun in a slow circle, taking it all in. "This is quite the setup."

"This is my life's work. I have a knack for biological potions, so I mainly focused on flora and fauna. Tracy has steered me toward protection potions in recent years, and I find them fascinating."

"I needed his help with a few things. You weren't easy to guard," Tracy added.

I shuffled toward the first counter and leaned down to look at a series of beakers that contained the diseased magic. "How did you contain that?"

Calvin picked one up. "Tracy was kind enough to provide them, along with the initiator spell you gave her. Watch this." He uncorked a bottle of pink liquid and poured it into a container of bug magic. It disintegrated.

"This potion is intended to be safe for paranormal consumption. Once thoroughly tested, it may be more effective than healer magic."

I eyed the now brown liquid. "What are the side effects?"

He cleared his throat. "They should be minimal. I haven't tested it on a live subject, but the ingredients are consumable."

"I see."

He laughed. "With all due respect, you don't. It's a very complicated alchemy."

"Right. So you haven't tested this at all?"

"I added this potion to the wards surrounding the village. It neutralized the magic when Bastien dragged an infected person through it."

I narrowed my eyes at Bastien, but he pointedly ignored me.

"It's effective for both people and wards but needs more testing," Calvin continued.

Tracy sat on a stool, her face screwed up in concentration. "I wonder if we should test it on different wards before we give it to people, though. It's a lot like the neutralizing spell. I can recreate it. But we'd need a bunch of alchemy witches to make it in larger quantities. My dad's right. We need more time."

Time we didn't have. "How much time do you need?"

Calvin tapped his chin. "A couple of months. Maybe more." He held up a hand. "I understand we may not have that much time, but I don't like to deploy my potions until I have thoroughly tested them."

"How can we test them faster?" Drake asked.

"How can we get the witches on board?" I asked at the same time.

Calvin set his beakers down. "I can help with both issues. As the leader of the alchemy witches, I can tell you very few are fans of the President. We have an upcoming election, and I plan to run for the position."

It would solve a lot of problems if he won and figured out how to lure the witches to our side. We could use their cooperation and support. "Can you win?"

He nodded. "I have as good of a chance as the President."

Tracy put a hand on his arm. "It will take you away from your potions. Why would you do that?"

"The witches are in turmoil, sweetheart. If I win, I can reform them into the honorable covens they once were."

"It'll be good for the witches, but what about what's good for you?"

Calvin's eyes focused on me.

I scooted closer to Drake, who leaned against the wall. I didn't like the way Tracy's dad looked at me. Like he saw my inner turmoil and knew how much I didn't want to be the queen. Like he believed I should try harder to lead. I didn't like it because he was right.

He nodded once and turned to Tracy. "I care more about what's good for you, Tracinia. And the hatred toward you needs to stop. The best way to accomplish that is to become their leader."

"Don't do that for me. I mean, I'm doing okay."

He waved a hand. "Your well-being is only one reason."

Tracy clenched and unclenched her fists. "Promise you'll be careful."

"I plan to be very careful. I also plan to give them a kick in the ass." He patted her arm. "Don't worry about me so much."

She sighed. "I can't help but worry."

Bastien's weight shifted from one foot to the other. "I hope you win, Calvin. Let me know if I can be of assistance. Witches taste sour, but I can bite a few to help you make a point."

I rubbed my hands over my face. "What do you need from us to make more of the potion?"

Calvin turned back to his workbench. "Thank you, Bastien. I'll keep that in mind. We need more supplies. If we don't have enough material, there's no point in bringing in more alchemists to mass-produce the potion. After we have them, the production will take a couple of days." He handed me a small vial of pink liquid. "Test this on someone infected with the magic."

I held up the vial. Tiny bubbles surfaced as if it were boiling, though it was cool to the touch. "You're sure it's safe?"

"The ingredients are not harmful." He handed one to Tracy with a paper wrapped around it. "That's for you to use as a template and the list of ingredients. As always, try to improve it."

Tracy unwrapped the paper and read the ingredients. "Okay. I mean, it's not too complicated. Wait. What's gorshma root?"

"Yes." He turned to me. "Gorshma is an ancient root that is nearly extinct. It is difficult to find in this realm. I hoped you would help with that."

I'd never heard of it. "What type of climate does it grow in?"

Calvin shuffled some supplies around. "It grows best in humid climates."

"Can I take a sample?"

He dug in a drawer and handed me a bag with a curly yellow thing that resembled the number six. "That's dried. In bloom, it is much more vibrant."

Drake leaned over my shoulder. "I remember this. It grew in a pocket in the South Pacific at one time. I have not seen it in any other pockets."

"Correct," Calvin said. "That pocket is now heavily populated, and the plant is almost extinct. It might not be possible to find in the quantities we need."

I held up the bag and examined the crinkled thing. "Can the elves grow it?"

"Perhaps. I don't have a working relationship with the swamp elves, so I haven't asked."

"I'll ask them about it and growing the other supplies in large quantities."

Calvin shook his head. "Make sure the sample works first."

How would I do that? "Sure."

CHAPTER SIXTEEN

JEN

I GLANCED AT MY phone after we landed on the roof of Dragon Headquarters. "Thanks for the ride. Did you have time to go over my list?"

Drake ran his hand through his hair, making it stick up. "Yes."

"Any ideas where to start?"

"I appreciate you want to wake the other Firsts, but I suggest you focus on the diseased magic. I have a lead on the Bellicose leadership and need to contact some old allies before we go to Pyron or Mage Mountain."

His assignment to find the Bellicose leadership was news to me. "What kind of lead?"

"The kind I'll tell you about when I learn more." His eyes sparkled with humor. "Don't worry your pretty little head about it."

I elbowed him. "Where do you even find these expressions?"

"They're funny."

Unexpected joy filled me with the teasing. A wide grin spread across my face. "They're human insults." We just didn't insult each other like that in the paranormal world. Saying that to the wrong person would get you maimed or killed.

"Yes. I heard it on human television. I only remembered it because I knew using it would cause that little crinkle in your forehead."

"I don't crinkle. And you need to stop watching human television before those weird insults get you killed. Now, about this lead?"

His humor drained away. "It's something I've been hunting for a while, but I can't tell you about it because I am under a silence contract."

"Fair enough." I sighed. "I need to go see the Sorceress Ann Marie."

I leaned against a spike and gazed over the forest as the wind whipped my braid. Except for a brief kidnapping attempt, I'd never flown over the human world. Butterflies fluttered in my stomach from the excitement of the new experience.

The world is beautiful from up here. I sent toward Drake's mind.

It is a different perspective.

Do you fly over the human world often?

I did right after you woke me. It helped me learn current culture and slang. Then I continued for other reasons.

Smart. I could spend all day, every day, up here.

Drake's carefree laugh bounced through my head, and my heart fluttered.

He wrapped his cloaking magic around us as we approached the gate. The guards in Allure didn't even look up as we flew above them, nor did the humans below. *Drake?*

Yes.

Will Ann Marie even see me?

The wind tickled my face as he swooped low over the trees. The sensation of a warm hug surrounded me. *She will. The hybrids need your help, and you need their support. She knows this.*

It would be great if we could support each other. Ann Marie and her match, the First Jonas, grew frustrated with me for not taking more steps to address the hybrid situation. Another shrugged responsibility as I bounced around, pretending to be a detective for the last year. What I needed to do was get my shit together and take care of my responsibilities like Mat always did. The hybrid alienation being one of them.

I closed my eyes to make a mental list. I needed to talk to Ann Marie, find and wake the other Firsts, and learn the secrets of Mage Mountain. Then there was the bug magic. I didn't like that we came across it in the human world. It could mean someone was trying to expose us, which would be a disaster. I hoped Ann Marie would help Calvin counteract it. In addition, Quin had made little progress in finding the Bellicose leadership. So much so, Mat had Drake working on it with a silence contract. Which meant I needed to touch base with Mat first. Because Quin probably made more progress than I knew. Not that I'd asked. I realized that being a queen wasn't much different from being a detective. It was a bunch of networking, asking questions, and problem-solving. A little weight lifted off my shoulders.

Jonas and Ann Marie First lived on a ranch in the human world. A sprawling two-story white farmhouse sat a couple hundred feet back from a two-lane road. Across a wide graveled area sat a sizable red and white barn, horses meandering in the field behind it. A herd of cows grazed in an adjacent field. The sound of a rooster crowing rang through the air as Drake descended. I found it odd, considering the First Jonas was a shifter. They saw owning animals as enslavement. Apparently, Jonas didn't share that opinion.

Drake landed on a deserted narrow road at the end of the gravel driveway and transformed into his human form. He wore glamoured jeans and a black T-shirt. I glanced down at my gray slacks and white dress shirt. It wasn't exactly a ranch outfit. I reached out and knocked on the wards three times. "So, this is where they live?"

"Yes. It's...odd."

"Yeah."

A young man with a mop of brown hair strolled out the front door and twisted his head in our direction. The ruling magic slapped him back when he tried to burrow into my head. I didn't even feel the tingle I always felt when mages or dragons tried to read my thoughts. The man shook his head at the slap-back. "Mom. You have visitors."

A petite woman with blonde hair stepped onto the porch. Ann Marie was the last sorceress in existence. According to my grandmother's diaries, she created sorcerers and sorceresses as her first magical species. She infused them with a mixture of mage and witch magic. It made them extremely powerful. Too powerful. Most of them couldn't handle the amount of power, and it caused them to go insane. My grandmother couldn't cure them, so she killed them and started over. A necessary culling, she added after explaining her reasons for killing them. Ann Marie was the only one who didn't go crazy, so she was allowed to live. She matched with Jonas the First when she was still a human and somehow stayed sane through the transformation.

Ann Marie strolled down the gravel driveway and stopped at the wards. "Your Grace. Drake. What can I do for you?" Her tone was as icy as her blue eyes.

I fought not to shiver. "I wondered if you had a few minutes to talk."

"About?"

"About hybrids and the Bellicose."

Her eyes slid toward the house. "I'm busy today."

She was hiding something. I sent my senses out, but they couldn't get past her wards. "I'll be brief."

She stepped out of the wards and pointed at a trail. "We have a picnic area just beyond those trees where we can talk. I'm short on time."

Drake scanned the house. "Is Jonas around?"

"Yes."

"May I enter your wards to see him?"

Ann Marie pushed him through the wards. "He's in the garage." She motioned for me to follow her across the road, up a hill, and past a cluster of trees. The picnic area had four faded wooden chairs around a fire pit and a plastic picnic table. Ann Marie settled on one side of the picnic table. "What is this about?"

I lowered myself to the opposite bench. "Right. I'll get straight to the point. Would you be interested in being one of my advisors?" I held up a hand when her eyes narrowed. "Some council members think I'm too young to make sound decisions, so I'm looking for more experienced people to advise me. I want you as an advisor because I want to pull the hybrids into the coalition."

The anger drained from her face, and she drew in a breath. "That'll go over well."

"I don't care. A wise woman recently told me I am the queen, and they are not, so I get to decide. I choose you. I'll offer the same to Jonas, but he's made it clear he's not interested in any position within the coalition."

Her shoulders shook with laughter. "You are not at all like your mother."

"I hope not, considering what I've learned about her. If you accept, how or if you advise me is up to you."

"Clever. I'll consider it. You said you wanted to discuss the Bellicose?"

"Yes. We're trying to track down their leadership." I explained the bug magic, then held out a ball of dissipating magic. She didn't even need to touch it to absorb the spell. "Could you tell me about my mother? Drake wants me to wake all the Firsts she put to sleep, so I'm trying to locate them. He said he was aware but unable to wake up, and it's cruel to leave them in that state. I have an idea where a couple of them are, but wondered if you knew anything about it."

Ann Marie crossed her arms. "I don't. We avoided your mother and her reign of terror. I suspect she bragged about it to someone, though. It wasn't her style to keep her...accomplishments to herself."

"Yeah. Which of the Firsts went to sleep willingly?"

"Six slept willingly and passed on their power. Your grandparents being two of them. Lilith, Herschel, Lena, and Brogan followed. Your mother took care of the other five. Jonas was spared because he'd retired from a leadership role. Well, that and I am much more powerful than your mother ever was, so she couldn't get to him."

I knew Lilith created the vampires, ghouls, and goblins. Ara told me about the screwed-up way she passed on her power. Herchel created most of the flying paranormals, and Lena created the dwarves and brownies, among others. Brogan created the sea creatures. I wondered how my mother found him, considering he never left the human oceans. Her diaries brushed over Gorman, who created the ogres and trolls, and Cynthia, who created kelpies and chimeras. I suspected Celia, who created the centaurs and minotaurs, was near Mahri. And Razazia, who created the elves, was somewhere around Pyron. "My grandfather created all the healing creatures, correct?"

"Yes. Your grandfather's main purpose was to heal. Your mother inherited his magic but rarely used it on anyone but herself and her match. Mathias inherited a small slice of it."

"What are the pros and cons of waking the other Firsts?"

"Too many to list. Razazia will probably leave you alone. She always preferred the company of her elves to outsiders. But the others?" She shrugged. "Your mother's actions caused a lot of animosity toward the crown. You will take the brunt of their anger. I advise making sound decisions, but prepare yourself for the consequences."

"Thank you." I pulled out my phone and made a note. "Did you have time to read my proposal to make the hybrids their own magical species?" Verity and her match, our Crown Juror Titus, drew up a proposal. I approved it and sent it to Jonas and Ann Marie the day before. I didn't tell Mat I'd sent it. It was petty, sure. But if he could play the information blackout game, so could I.

"Yes. The hybrid leadership is resistant. Like I said, there's a lot of animosity. Most of the mixed couples and hybrids hate the Coalition. I commend you for trying, but it won't be easy to get most of them on board."

"I won't stop trying. Call me if you need anything."

Ann Marie tapped the table. "There are a couple of things you can do. I need to introduce you to someone. Also, the Bellicose are amassing in the Treasure Valley. They recently tried to abduct my son for his mental magic."

My eyes grew wide. The man who tried to read my thoughts must have been her son. "What do you mean they're amassing?"

"They're buying entire apartment complexes near hybrid neighborhoods."

I sucked in a breath. "What are those idiots planning?"

"We'll figure it out, but we could use some backup. If the hybrids see you care about them, they'd be more likely to support your proposal." She tapped the table. "I need a safe place for my son to stay for a while."

"He can stay at the palace. He'll be protected, and we'll treat him well. If he's not comfortable with that, the dragons or vampires will take him in. The dragons own a hotel. Staying in it will give him protection, and he can come and go as he pleases. When he leaves, they'll cloak themselves and watch over him without being intrusive."

She stood. "Yes. Deva is sneaky about protecting people when she wants to be. We'll consider it. My son wants to handle the problem himself. My daughter believes she can protect him. They're young but not stupid."

"Sure." I could relate. Mat told me I was young and impulsive all the time. "Send them our way. We'll do our best to protect them."

The knowing smile that spread across her face raised the hair on the back of my neck, and I wondered if I'd just made a mistake. She held out a hand. "I'd like to flash you to the person I want you to meet. I swear you will come to no harm, and I'll send Drake to collect you when he's done gossiping with Jonas."

My head tingled as the contract settled over me.

"Okay." I reached out and took her hand.

We landed in the backyard of a small farmhouse. I sent out my senses. An enormous amount of power emanated from it. Like at Ann Marie's house, I couldn't feel beyond the wards. I made a mental note to tell Tracy about it. She'd love to learn how to make those kinds of wards.

I scanned the area. Most of it was farmland. Hay bales dotted the field in the back while a massive herd of cattle roamed the one to the west. A field of well-manicured rose bushes and other plants that formed a pattern separated the farmhouse from a mansion with an expansive lawn. I tilted my head. "Is that a maze?"

Pride reflected in Ann Marie's eyes. "It is."

I raised an eyebrow, but she didn't elaborate.

I forgot about it as a man radiating enough power to blow up the planet stepped out the farmhouse's back door. Long blonde hair trailed down his huge shoulders and back. He was as big as Drake. The guy's face looked almost angelic. His electric blue eyes lit up when he saw Ann Marie. "Hello, Ann Marie. I am pleased to have visitors."

Ann Marie latched onto my arm and dragged me toward him. "Hello, Cavil. This is the Queen of Ahl. Ahl is the official name of the Coalition of Paranormals. Jenella, this is the God, Cavil. He's new to the realm."

I blinked. "A god?"

Cavil's brilliant smile melted. "Yes. Please, come in and have a cup of tea. I have many questions."

Ann Marie patted my arm. "Cavil wants to make some connections and buy a home in Allure. I'll send Drake to collect you." She disappeared.

I stared at the space she'd occupied for a couple of seconds, then blinked and shuffled through the door. The farmhouse-style kitchen was old. A long rectangular table that had seen better days took up the center. White subway tiles covered the walls. Scarred wooden countertops wrapped around three sides and accented with new silver human appliances. Cracks ran through the blue and white tile floors.

I plopped down in a chair at the end of the table and stared at the funky blue and gray magic enveloping a laptop and phone on the other side.

Cavil put a metal container on a contraption similar to one I'd seen in Ara's kitchen. "It will take a few minutes for the kettle to heat."

"Uh huh." I didn't understand what he said, but didn't want to advertise my ignorance. "So, you're new to the realm?"

He nodded. "Yes. I came here a few days ago. Lily took me in and taught me about stolen human technology infused with magic. I wish to establish myself among the magic users in this realm."

I guessed Lily was someone Ann Marie knew. "If you want to join the coalition, I doubt you'll have a problem. Paranormals respect magical power, and you've got a ton."

His grin stretched from ear to ear. It felt like the sun peeked out of the clouds and blessed me with warmth on a winter day. He leaned forward. "Will you answer a few questions so I can learn more about this realm?"

I didn't feel safe with the guy. He was way too nice. He seemed genuine, but with his power level, it was smart to be wary. I checked the stupid bond. Drake wasn't too far away, but not moving in my direction. He could get to me fast, but not fast enough. My thoughts screeched to a halt. Since when did I need Drake to get me out of trouble? I could get myself out of any situation. All I needed to do was appease this too-nice guy and get out. I squared my shoulders and pasted a congenial smile on my face. "Sure."

He tapped his phone. "What are the current male hair fashions? This device shows me many things, and I cannot determine which one is best."

My shoulders relaxed at the simple question. "Um. That's not really my area of expertise. From what I've seen, paranormals and humans have all kinds of hairstyles."

"I wish to blend in with the masses, both in your mini realms and with humans. Which hairstyle will help me accomplish that?"

Not a chance. The guy was too good-looking and charismatic to blend in, no matter what he did to his hair. I pulled out my phone and searched the human internet for actors. When I found a big blonde one, I flipped the phone around. "That hairstyle would work for you. Several humans and paranormals wear it."

"Very well." Dark blue tendrils of magic shot from his head, and his hair transformed into the exact style as in the picture. "Is that right?"

"Um. Yeah."

A piercing sound screeched through the kitchen. I dove to the floor. The ruling magic vibrated through me, waiting for an attack.

The God threw his head back and laughed. "Our tea is ready, my queen."

I crawled back into the chair and tried to ignore my flushed face. "Sorry about that. I'm not familiar with human kitchens. And you can call me Jenella or Jen."

He poured steaming water into two cups and put a bag in each. "You'll want the bag to sit to get the best flavor. I am also unfamiliar with these noisy devices. Alex taught me how to make tea."

I didn't know who Alex was. Nor did I know how to make tea. I pulled the cup closer to me and peered into it. A bag with a string sat in hot water. I wondered if it was really that easy. "Okay. Thank you."

"Tell me what I need to establish myself in your world. Ann Marie refers to it as 'The Coalition' or 'The Coalition of Ahl.'"

"Yeah. Most people call it The Coalition." I described our real estate market and some fundamental laws. Afterward, I directed him to a website on the maginet where he could study. I doubted I helped him much, but he seemed pleased with what I explained. After a while, I stopped believing his niceness was an act and considered that maybe it was his genuine nature. I still didn't trust it. "So, you're a god?"

He nodded. "I come from the Realm of the Gods. This is not the first realm I have tried, but it is the most pleasing. I wish to establish myself here."

"This might sound ignorant, but what exactly is a god?"

His eyebrows drew together. "You've never met a god?"

"Nope."

"Our power stems from our followers. The more people who follow us, the more powerful we become. You should know this."

I sensed Drake drawing near. "I'll do some reading if I get some spare time."

He shook his head to clear it. "May I ask what type of magical being you are?"

"A Mage of Ahl with ruling magic."

"I see." He took a sip of tea.

Relief flooded me as Drake landed outside the wards. I stood. "Well, here's my ride." I shuffled toward the back door.

The God followed me. He eyed Drake, still in dragon form. "I did not realize you had dragons in this realm."

"Yeah. They came here a long time ago."

"Interesting." He inclined his head at Drake. "It was nice to meet you, Jenella."

"You as well, Cavil." I dashed through the wards and flashed onto Drake's back.

As we flew away, I eyed the maze in the field between the two properties. I wondered if most humans had those. I needed to ask Verity. She knew a lot about human habits.

What was that about? Drake's voice rang through my head.

A god that recently came to this realm. Is that even possible?

It happens from time to time. They never stay long.

This one said he wants to establish himself here. He's learning our ways.

Interesting. Is he a threat?

Not that I saw. But he's too nice, and it makes me nervous.

Keep your guard up. Gods can be as deceptive as demons.

The ruling magic was silent during my brief visit, but I'd still monitor him when he moved to Allure. *Ann Marie left me with him after we finished our talk. She doesn't like me much.*

She has many people to protect.

Yeah. She said the Bellicose are taking over human apartment buildings and are after her son.

Hold on.

He climbed high into the sky, then shot down and plowed through the entrance to Allure and transformed into his human form. He caught me bridal-style and gently sat me on the ground, a big grin on his face.

I rubbed my fluttering stomach and grinned back.

A gate guard cleared his throat. "Um, S-sir First, you can't land in the vehicle path. Um, the dragon landing is that way." He pointed to the left.

Drake strode in the direction the guard pointed. I watched him for a second, then focused on the gate. Five guards stared back at me. "How are you?"

A female mage inclined her head. "We're good, Your Grace."

I shuffled around so I could see Drake as he moved to the center of the dragon landing area and tilted his head back. He was huge, even in his human form. He stood well over six feet tall, with broad shoulders and muscles that bulged through his clothes. I wanted to reach out and trace his scars. Or lick them. I shook my head to bring myself back to reality. "Any trouble with the Bellicose?"

"Not today. I heard about a task force working on the problem," the mage answered.

"Yeah." I tore my eyes away from Drake and focused on her. "Are you interested in joining?"

Her face flushed. "No. But we need reinforcements out here. I heard the Bellicose are gathering in Boise, and there's no other way to enter the pocket."

"Yeah, I heard that, too. I'll send you more help."

She braced her hands behind her back. "Thank you, Your Grace. We'd appreciate that."

Drake strolled back toward the gate, winked at me, and rested a hand on my back. His intense gaze landed on the shifter. "I apologize for breaking your rules. I didn't see the separate entrance for flyers."

The kid turned bright red. "Oh, uh. Sure. Uh, Sir First."

The mage shouldered him out of the way as she stepped forward. "We're on high alert, so using the proper gate is helpful."

"Of course. My apologies." Drake's tone was dismissive as he used the hand on my back to guide me through the gate.

He transformed back into his dragon form, so I flashed onto his back and waved at the guards. *They're scared.*

Yes. Did you enjoy the ride?

My stomach flipped. *It made me feel free.*

I cannot offer you freedom from your responsibilities, but we'll fly any time you wish to feel free.

The smile melted off my face. He was courting me by trying to give me what I wanted most, a dragon tradition. Unsure how to respond, I hugged his spike.

CHAPTER SEVENTEEN

JEN

We landed in the alley behind my house. Tracy stayed behind with Bastien to help her dad, so it was empty when we stepped through the kitchen door.

I glanced back at Drake. "Would you like something to drink?"

"No. I wish to have that conversation now." He lowered himself into a chair. "You won't like it."

"I figured. While we talk, I need to ask you about something else."

"You can talk to me whenever you want should you open the bond." He tapped his temple.

"Right." I didn't plan on opening anything because I didn't want any-one to have access to my thoughts. "We should start with Mage Mountain," I blurted.

"Is that so?"

"Mage Mountain's weird magic has always called to me. I read some bragging in one of my mother's diaries. The mountain used to be in Switzerland. She used it as an anchor to create the pocket and somehow moved it to the American state of Montana. She bragged about the cold climate. A place few wanted to live. Her diaries are filled with bragging about how she put people in their place. It was an attempt to convince herself that she was more powerful than them, I think."

He shrugged. "That sounds like her."

"So we go there first?"

"If you want to. What did she say about the one in Pyron?"

"Not much. She bragged about how innovative she was and how her work would hold out long enough. Long enough for what is anyone's guess."

"There are also reports of diseased magic and missing shifters in Pyron, where there are none in Mage Mountain. Perhaps we should start there."

The magichef spit out two bottles of water, and I lowered myself into a chair. "That's fine with me. What did you need to talk to me about?"

Drake rubbed his chin. His eyes flicked to mine and then lowered. "I want to talk about our bond."

He lied. I didn't know why or what about, but I knew it wasn't what he wanted to talk about. "Do you?"

A slight shake of his head. "Yes." He rubbed his face.

"Are you sure?"

His eyes slid to the door like he wanted to leave. "I want to explain and see what you think about it."

My eyes narrowed. I knew he was lying. He knew I knew he was lying. It wasn't like Drake to act like that, so whatever he originally wanted to talk to me about, he couldn't. Someone put him under a magical contract. And what was up with these powerful men suddenly showing me their fear? I appreciated it, but it was jarring. Especially coming from him. "Okay, go ahead, then."

His lips twitched. "Very well." He leaned forward and met my eyes without hesitation. "You are smart, funny, and everything I hoped for in a mate. I want to give you what freedom I can. If you run from me, I'll understand. I've experienced many rejections throughout my life. They've made me very patient. I will wait until you stop running and decide to talk. But even when you're running, I'll still fight for you. For your freedom. It is not possible to give up on you."

I pointed to my feet. "Still here. I'm not sure what to say about the bond. To be *honest,* I haven't processed it yet. But I'll be glad to explain why it worries me."

"Please do."

"Okay." I'd thought about it a lot since we cleared the magic at the Cauldron. I closed my eyes and sucked in some air to wrangle the chaotic knot of thoughts into something I could explain. "Neither of us has found our place in the world yet. I don't know where you're at on that, but I'm just now learning who I am and who I want to be. How to stay free and rule at the same time. I also need to consider political angles. Mat's right that you being a First complicates things. Then there's the enormous age difference. That's a huge thing to consider in this whole--" I whirled a hand around. "Whatever it is." I met his eyes. "I'm sure I didn't think of everything, and we need to have a lot of conversations besides this one, but that's the gist of it."

"Which is why we're here."

"So you say. Look, I'm not rejecting you or running from you. It's a big thing that needs a lot of work. And there's already too much work to do. I don't have the time, energy, or emotional capacity to add it right now. I'm trying to save the coalition from imploding. Again. On top of that, I need to wake the other Firsts, fix my magic, and do a million other things." I held up a hand when he opened his mouth to say something. "I understand that this conversation is not the one you wanted to have *and* that you're hiding something. You have sharp instincts, and I'm making them worse. I don't have a clue how to handle this in a way that works for both of us, so my default is to worry about myself. I'm working on not being so selfish, but I fail more times than not."

He rubbed his face with both hands. "Holy hell, Jenella. I'm not comfortable keeping secrets from you. But I can't utter a word of what I'm hiding."

I raised an eyebrow. "Oh?"

"Yes. I'd tell you if I could. No matter the consequences."

"So, Mat swore you to silence, huh?"

Drake nodded.

"See, that's something else I need to work on."

"I understand." He stood. "Let me consider what you've said, and we will talk again." He stopped with his hand on the doorknob and lowered his head. "Please remember that the last thing I ever want is to hurt you." He swept out the door.

His words rolled through my head for a long time. He knew something big. Something that would hurt me. Mat knew what it was and swore Drake to secrecy. Probably for a good reason. Because whatever made that honorable dragon lie to me had to be bad. I vowed to figure it out.

When Tracy came in and started making noise the next morning, I crawled out of bed and tried to make myself presentable. Everything running through my head made sleep all but impossible. She sat on a stool at the kitchen island and picked at her food.

"Morning," I grunted.

She watched me for a long minute, then refocused on her plate. "Hey, Jen."

My stomach couldn't handle food, so I ordered a coffee from the magichef and climbed onto the stool beside her. "Drake's hiding something big."

"What makes you say that?"

"He made a big deal about us having a talk and, at the last minute, changed his mind about the subject."

She shoved her plate away. "Why would he do that?"

"He said he's under contract. I'm going to talk to Mat because he swore Drake to silence."

"Do you want me to go with you?"

"No. I need you working on the potion with your dad, and you have your own life to live." My hand shook as I sipped my coffee. "I'm going to try not to start an argument."

She nodded. "I don't believe you."

I breezed past Mat's assistant, shut the door to his office, and leaned against it. "Can I ask you something?"

Mat's face softened. "I'm always here for you to talk to, Jenella. I'm sorry if you ever thought otherwise."

"Drake's hiding something from me. Something big. Do you know anything about that?"

Mat's expression didn't change. "No."

My stomach tied in painful knots at the lie. "So, you're both hiding something."

"That is a big stretch."

"Is it? Because I don't think so." I held up a hand. "What aren't you telling me, Mat?"

"I'm under a magical contract."

"But you told Drake."

"Yes."

"Great." I rubbed my sweaty hands on my pants. "This is me trying to restrain myself from flying into a rage over it." I met his eyes. "So, you tell Drake something that would wreck my world. Something that would devastate me. And the two of you make a contract, so he can't utter a word because you're not confident the loophole you discovered is solid. How am I doing so far?"

Mat blinked. A signal that I'd surprised him. "You will make a great queen. Especially since you've bonded that undeserving dragon."

"Don't insult him. Especially since you're the one who put him in a terrible position. Drake's bond allowed me to use his well of power like a battery when we rescued Deva and took out that demon. And let me tell you, he is much more powerful than he lets on. I'm strong enough to rule with his power boost, even if my magic doesn't combine. The idea of being shackled to someone for eternity is the problem because of my emotional issues. They caused me to block the bond and pretend it didn't exist. It gave me my freedom, but it's killing him. That's not the actions of a stable person. Then, just when I recognize it for what it is, you swoop in with this colossal secret that neither of you can tell me and destroy the trust we've built." I realized I was babbling and snapped my mouth shut.

"That wasn't my intention. I wouldn't have sworn him to silence had he not eavesdropped on a private conversation in the first place." He held up a scarred hand. "I'll try to stay out of it and give you space to work out your bond."

"A conversation with who?"

His lips flattened.

"Quin?"

"Perhaps. But it doesn't matter. If the First hurts you, I will kill him, and he won't see it coming, no matter how powerful he is."

"I'd expect nothing less. Now, about this big secret."

"None of us can discuss it with you without breaking the contract."

I took a calming breath. "I don't like it, but I understand. Will you at least work on a way to tell me?"

"I will try." He shook his head. "When I made the contract, I convinced myself I was doing the right thing."

"Okay. I'm not the same person I was when I came to you with my plan to be a detective. My understanding of choices and motivations is a million miles ahead of where it was back then. I might even understand you better."

His eyes met mine. "I doubt that. You will never understand why I killed anyone who dared come at you. Far more paranormals than you know.

Nor do you understand my motivations for agreeing to this contract. You won't understand it because I ensured you weren't raised like I was. That you cannot be used the same way I allowed myself to be used. You won't ever fully understand my motivations because you never had to pull your baby sister out of a cage or take on a million responsibilities you weren't prepared for. Although I regret I allowed myself to be put in the position to agree to the contract, I'd make it a million times over if it meant I could spare you from becoming me.

"When you decided you wanted to become a detective, I both hated and loved the idea. I loved it because you wouldn't have to take on responsibilities right away, and I hated it because you were unprepared to protect yourself. There are many things I'd have done different while raising you, but making that contract is not one of them."

My eyes stung with unshed tears. "Wow." I cleared my throat. "What I meant was that you've never made a single decision unless it was out of love. I understand you were trying to do the right thing. It chafes, but I get it. Thank you for explaining, though." I closed my eyes and took a deep breath. "You gave me a good life after that whole mess. I need to stop running from things that make me uncomfortable and deal with them. Everyone in my life deserves better from me." I opened my eyes and met his. "Whatever your secret is, I'll figure it out. I won't be able to help myself."

"Of course you will. And, for what it's worth, I'm sorry. I never meant to hurt you."

"I'm sorry, too." My emotions churned like a hurricane, so I changed the subject. "I have an idea to fix my magic."

"Do you?"

"I think...No, I'm almost certain Mage Mountain holds the key. Drake has agreed to go with me."

"I'm going to go with you."

"I don't want an entire legion of guards involved or to make it a big deal. It's too personal, and I doubt I'll find anything on my first try."

Mat rubbed his face with both hands. "Very well. We will discuss it when you're ready to go."

"Okay." I wouldn't give him the chance to go with me. My brother didn't realize how oppressive he was and never would. I just needed an excuse to go without raising suspicions.

Mat stood and pulled me into a hug. "I love you and will do anything within my power to help."

CHAPTER EIGHTEEN

DRAKE

DRAKE PERCHED ON TOP of the castle and watched Jenella as she made her way to the flashing circle near the family entrance. She didn't spare him a look, even though she sensed him. As soon as she disappeared, he launched from the roof and headed toward her house.

The sun sank over the horizon as he landed in the back alley. He flinched at an ear-splitting shriek coming from the raccoon shifter house. The high-pitched noises from the many children never bothered Tracy or Jenella, but it made his sensitive ears ache. He swung his head their way, then focused on Jenella as she lumbered down the alley, deep in thought.

Her head came up, and the mixed emotions in her eyes almost brought him to his knees.

"I'm angry. I'm sad. And I've had enough lies and withholding information for a while." She made her way through the wards and up the steps. "Give me time. Don't call me, I'll call you. I'll catch you on the flip side. You pick the human cliché."

He lowered his head so it was even with hers. *Where do you even get these things?*

She slammed her hands on her hips. "No being funny." Determination replaced the sadness in her eyes and she turned toward the back door. "Fine. Change and come in. If you plan to help me check off the things on my list, then we need to plan."

Drake's heart soared with hope, but he tamped it down. A dangerous and fickle emotion that. He morphed into his human form and glamoured himself in jeans and a green T-shirt. Jenella liked it when he wore shirts that matched his eyes. "Thank you. I cannot tell you how sorry I am. It's not my secret to tell."

Her hand froze on the door handle. "No. Nope. None of that." She flung open the door and stepped inside. "Do you want something to drink?"

"No." He followed her in and closed the door. "I flew over the Treasure Valley last night and saw where the Bellicose has settled their troops."

She motioned him to follow her toward the plush sofa in the front room of her cozy house. It was warm and welcoming and made Drake wonder if it reflected Jenella, Tracy, or both.

She lowered herself into a chair. "How bad is it?"

"Not too bad yet. But it is a problem. Have you talked to Deva about housing Jonas's kids?"

"Not yet, but I will." She tapped on her phone. "I need to commit to taking the throne if we're going to wake the Firsts and take on the Bellicose. Which means giving up my detective gigs." She sighed. "How do I do that and keep my freedom?"

"Yes. Let us discuss this fantastic scheme to wake the Firsts."

"Gah!" Jenella jumped at Tarquin's voice. "Damnit, Quin. Stop sneaking up on me."

"One would expect you to pay attention to what your senses tell you."

Drake leaned back to enjoy the show. Jenella adored that vampire, though he didn't understand why. Tarquin was old and crotchety and not entirely sane. Drake sensed him when he entered the house and wondered why Jenella hadn't. Her senses were much more advanced than his.

She did not disappoint. "It's not about my senses. It's about personal boundaries. This is none of your business."

Tarquin didn't move. "Of course it is."

"Fine. You break into my house, you make yourself useful." She stomped to the kitchen, dug into her bag, and pulled out a book. She flipped it open and handed it to Quin. "Read that and tell me what it means." She swung toward Drake, and he wished she'd remove the glamour so he could see the fire in her golden eyes. "And you." She pointed to the kitchen. "I'm starving. One of your delicious meals sounds great."

A plate of grilled chicken and roasted asparagus formed on the coffee table, along with a glass of wine.

Her face lit up as she picked up the plate. "Thanks." She took a bite of his offering and moaned. "So good."

A satisfied smile spread across his face. He would show up every day and conjure meals just to see that reaction. To hear that moan. He enjoyed taking care of her and wanted to spend the rest of his existence hearing it. Hope soared through him, so he erased those thoughts from his head.

She ran her eyes over his face and chest, then focused on a scar that ran up his arm. Her head jerked back to the plate of food. Drake's heart sang. Perhaps he read the situation wrong. She couldn't help being attracted to him and didn't like it. He could work with that. "If you're free, we can search the pocket of Pyron tomorrow."

She finished her food and set the plate on the coffee table. "Sounds good. But I'll need to let Tracy know where I'm going or she'll have a fit."

"I'll invite her and Bastien as backup. Your presence might anger the other Firsts, like when you woke me. We'll need to proceed with caution if you want them to help fight the Bellicose."

Tarquin set the diary on the coffee table. "I will go with you. The Enforcers have several recent reports of diseased magic from there. It is the more logical focus."

Jenella raised an eyebrow. "Oh?"

He pointed to the book. "This is an idiotic idea. Your dragon is too enamored to oppose you. You lack the emotional capacity to understand that. My presence is required for you to stand a chance."

She picked up the diary and flipped through the pages. "Five Firsts sleep willingly. Jonas and Drake are awake, so there are five more to wake."

"Two opted for permanent death," Drake interjected. "So there's only three left."

"Ann Marie must not have known about those two." She pulled out her phone and tapped on it. "Eight pockets reported outbreaks of what sounds like bug magic."

He picked up the diary and read the page where Anitta bragged about having a party after the last First was out of the way. A plume of smoke streamed from his nose. "Why are you showing me this?"

"My mother bragged about the party because it was when Mat was conceived." She visibly shivered. "Ick. So, according to my theory, she put one in South America and two in North America. She bragged about destroying her enemies. I assume she's referring to the Firsts."

Drake's eyes glowed as he read more of the cursed book. "Where are you going with this, Jenella?"

She leaned forward. "How pissed were you when I woke you?"

"Very."

"And if Bastien and I didn't slap some sense into you?"

Fiery anger flared within him, and he fought not to roar. "I would have gone on a rampage like this world has never seen."

"Exactly." She took the diary from him. "What if a First woke up and remembered the Bellicose? What if that person was so angry summoning demons sounded like a good idea? Or taking over dragons?"

The theory was solid. He'd considered it a few times himself. The first time he fought the Bellicose, they were not much more than a group who rejected the idea of forming the Coalition. The Firsts, including Drake, agreed that having all the magical species under one banner was the best option for their survival. It gave them a sense of community and allowed the Firsts to keep their creations, or in Drake's case, his family, from preying on humans to the point of extinction.

He doubted extinction was a possibility since humans were more numerous and had powerful weapons. At the time, it made sense. Those who liked to prey on humans formed the Bellicose. The Firsts banded together and raised an army that wanted a coalition. Together, they fought many bloody battles against the rebellion and won. He couldn't imagine a First siding with them. Still, Jenella was good at solving problems, so he wanted to hear what she had to say. "You theorize their so-called king is a First?"

"It's a possibility. For someone to claim to be a king capable of taking over and running the coalition, he must be powerful. A First or a ruler. Quin hasn't found him in a year of searching, and he has a worldwide spy network."

She had a point. Vampires historically made the best spies because they hid in the shadows. Between that and their ability to go fluid and move fast, they were almost as undetectable as cloaked dragons. Like dragons, they had superior senses. It made them great spies. If Tarquin and his network hadn't found the self-proclaimed king, no one would.

Perhaps he could find another First. Even though they rejected him, he'd spent many years with them. He knew and understood them. "If he is a First, he is most likely searching for other Firsts. Is that your point?"

"No. Yes." She shook her head, and, once again, Drake wished she'd take off the glamour earrings. "I never considered someone else looked for the other Firsts. Only that their leader is powerful and elusive. Did any of them have a grudge against you, Deva, and the shifter alphas? Possibly Jonas?"

"Perhaps, but I can't imagine one of them working against the organization they spent years fighting."

She tapped the arm of the chair. "I bet Mat has already considered it."

Drake inclined his head. "And concluded it's not worth pursuing."

"What about you, Quin?"

The vampire leaned against the wall with his arms folded and head down. Drake knew he'd listened to the entire conversation, along with their heartbeats and breathing. Tarquin came out of the stupor, which allowed him to put his senses on full alert, and met Jenella's eyes. "I am a detective, not a spy."

She grinned. "Right. But is it a good theory?"

"Perhaps." Tarquin disappeared.

The disappearance didn't faze Jenella. She turned her attention to Drake. "Now, about going to Pyron."

Drake thought about that exchange for a long time afterward. It wasn't anything Tarquin did. But because of Jenella's reaction to him. Dangerous people didn't bother her, nor should they, since she was their queen. His instincts told him he needed to protect her. He resisted them so she didn't develop the wrong idea that he didn't trust her to defend herself. Drake didn't trust Tarquin and never would. That vampire was as deadly as he was sneaky. It didn't sit right that he snaked his way into Jenella's life and gained her trust. She trusted too easily. Yet she didn't. "When do you address the leadership council?"

Jenella rubbed her face. "I enter my captivity in a couple of days."

She was not nearly as naïve as she once was, but she still didn't see her situation clearly. "It's not a cage. Although I understand that responsibility may seem that way to you. Mat has not attempted to impede you since the incident with the dragons, and no one can or will hold you captive." He leaned toward her. "If you don't blow them up first, I will swoop in and eat them."

The look of disbelief on her face spoke volumes.

"I swear it." He smirked when she jumped as the magic contract settled over them.

She shook her head. "You are so screwed."

Drake stood and headed toward the back door before he got himself in more trouble. "One can hope."

CHAPTER NINETEEN

JEN

Sweat rolled down my temple as Drake stretched his wings and glided toward the entrance of Pyron, a pocket northeast of a town the humans named Holbrook. It was in an area they called the Painted Desert. The maginet said it had a hot and dry climate. I had a feeling that it was a subtle way of cautioning anyone who dared to go there that they were entering an oven disguised as a pocket. I ignored the sweat as I leaned over and admired the breathtaking orange landscape with its vibrant plateaus.

Drake flew through the entrance and landed but didn't shift into his human form. I flashed to the ground to get a better look. His gigantic head swooped in front of me, and I pushed his chin, but he didn't budge. "Stop it."

I stepped forward and tilted my head back to see what bothered him. Tracy slid down Bastien's wing and landed beside me in a crouch. Her eyebrows drew together. "What do you suppose happened here?"

I shook my head. "This is bad." I sensed Quin come through the gate and zip around the two dragons.

He stopped beside the broken gates that lay in a twisted metal heap. "It appears the Bellicose has been here."

"Yeah, no shit." I moved to the ledge just inside the gate. In the valley below, the town was a wreck. People ran in every direction, some violent, others slumped over as they shuffled around. Screams echoed throughout the desert. Red, orange, and yellow dragons circled the town but didn't land. A man darted out of a dust cloud, tripped over something, and fell on his face. I tore my eyes away as two more people emerged and attacked him.

Children's toys and other debris littered the streets. Human vehicles sat abandoned, some on their sides or roofs. The houses were smaller than my little house in Allure. Meaning most of the paranormals were working class. They were just trying to live their lives when something or someone came through and destroyed the entire town. A tear slid down my cheek at the sight of the utter destruction and the scent of desperation in the air.

I focused on the black squirming magic that coated almost the entire pocket. It crawled across the ground and swirled around the wards placed by the homeowners. I flinched when one house exploded with a plume of bug magic. "Did that stuff just eat that house?" A man, a woman, and two children ran out the back and into the desert. A yellow dragon swooped in and picked them up, then settled them on a ridge across the way with several others. I pointed. "Quin, can you see if those people are infected?"

"I am thrilled to be your personal telescope." His eyes narrowed. "No."

"No, they're not infected?"

I shivered at his icy glare and turned my attention back to the valley. Tendrils crept toward a group of running people. It got one, and they fell to the sand. My sadness seeped away, replaced by red-hot anger. The ruling magic vibrated, wanting to reach out and end everything in the valley. I wrapped it tighter. "The magic isn't affecting the dragons, right?"

Drake's wing twitched. *No. Only the people they are trying to save.*

"Do these dragons live here?"

Yes. We have colonies in most pockets.

Bastien launched into the air and roared, then swooped toward what looked like a main street running through the town's center. He cocked his head back and blew a stream of dragon fire down the road. The bug magic retreated but didn't dissipate. I rested my hand on Drake's toe and pointed. "The magic doesn't like dragon fire. That's good." I took a step toward the ridge to climb down and help.

Quin's fangs extended. "You cannot fight this alone."

"We're not alone. We have a bunch of dragons."

"Oh, my fates, Jen. Do you see that?" Tracy pointed toward something at the edge of the town.

An object about the size of a house glimmered in the sun. I leaned forward. "We need to check that out."

Bastien landed next to Tracy and morphed into a naked man. "That object is not native to the area."

A dragon shot a stream of orange fire toward it. The thing flickered. The bottom opened, and tainted paranormals spilled out. They headed toward the ridge where the dragons were dropping people.

My heart pounded as the people on the ridge screamed. A red dragon shot a stream of dragon fire into the infected, and they dropped like flies. "Tracy, can you help slow them down?"

"Sure. Bas?"

Bastien morphed into his dragon form, tossed her on his back, and launched into the air. He rocketed toward the people, and Tracy launched a spell at the group on the ground. As soon as it touched them, the bug magic dissolved.

I ran my sleeve over the sweat that trickled down my brow and pointed to a narrow trail leading into the valley. "Drake and I will start neutralizing it from this side. Quin, will you be our over-watch? Call the Cauldron and tell them to send some enforcers and a couple of healers who can neutralize this stuff. If anything goes wrong, try to pull us out." I tapped my chin. "Check with Emine, Deva, and your vampire network. We need to know more about what's happening in the small pockets. We didn't know it was this bad here, so it's safe to say there are others."

His eyes flashed red at my orders. "Anything else, Your Grace?"

"No," I snapped. "Wait. There is one thing. The next time Mat insists you lie to me, don't. I'd rather face the pain of a thousand hard truths than one lie."

Quin's expression didn't change. He didn't even move except for a slight incline of his head.

Drake melted into his human form and latched onto my arm. "Not the time for pettiness."

He was right. I was being an asshole. I blamed the heat and the pressure of the situation because it was too hard back then to admit that I *was* an A-hole.

"Sure." I turned and started down the trail.

Drake, still in his human form, followed me. When we were away from Quin, he rested a hand on my back. "Tarquin made a good point."

"He often does. If anyone can stop this mess, it's us with our combined power. Should we fly?"

"Hiking in is fine. It gives us a better perspective." He stepped off the ridge and reached up to help me down. I didn't need his help but took it.

"You're appeasing me, but it's true. Together, we can probably clear this whole pocket." Butterflies exploded in my stomach when he grinned. "Don't get all cocky, Sir First. I just mean that we're formidable."

"Yes."

I chuckled. "I said don't get all cocky."

"Never."

Heat spread through me, and I fanned myself. "Mat believes the bond is a bad idea."

"Do you?"

"No. If you wanted to rule, I'm sure you could have pulled a Bellicose during my mother's reign and taken over."

"True. Just to be clear, I don't have any desire to rule. I never did. But I'm not above standing behind you and showing my pointy teeth to make a point."

A sloppy smile spread across my face, but I didn't comment. I liked having his support and his pointy teeth behind me.

As we made our way down the ridge, Drake realized I was competent at hiking, so he quit trying to help but kept his eye on me. We moved faster that way. When we got near the bottom, we stopped to gauge the damage. From the ground, it looked like the bug magic cut a large swath through the town and ended at the strange object. Tendrils chased the fleeing residents. I saw it devour two more. "This is bad."

"Yes." He hopped on a boulder the size of a car, making it look effortless. "Our magic might not be enough."

"We can wait for backup. Emine has bombs and flamethrowers."

"She can't use bombs with all the civilians around."

"True. She gets out of hand when she uses explosive weapons." She did it gleefully, too. "I can explode my magic like I did during that uprising near Mage Mountain, but it will wipe out my energy."

"No."

"Right. Probably not a good idea." I put everyone in town to sleep for a couple of days. "You know, the enforcers never figured out what happened, and Emine won't tell them. She said watching them puzzle over it is fantastic entertainment."

"You're not exploding your magic here."

I pondered how the pocket of Ferine shook when I did it a few days before. Pyron was less than half the size of Ferine, so I risked destroying the whole pocket. "I'm not. It's too much and too dangerous. What do you propose we do?"

Drake pointed. "Do you see that outbuilding?"

I leaned into him to see where he pointed. "The tan one or the gray one?"

"The tan one. It's in the center of the village. I'll be our anchor while you link our magic and direct it toward that object. Eliminate as much magic as possible, but be careful not to drain us. The enforcers and Tracy can take care of what we can't get."

"Operation magic up the whazoo. Check. Is our link strong enough to do that?"

He ignored my joke. "If you open the bond and let me in, then yes."

I hopped off a rock. "How do I do that? I'm not good at letting people in, and the ruling magic has a mind of its own."

"The ruling magic won't interfere. It not only created the bond but insisted on it after I rejected it twice. It's not the problem. You are. You need to stop seeing the bond as a shackle and open yourself for this to work."

"Contrary to popular belief, I don't *hate* the bond. I'm just not sure I'm ready for it."

"It exists even if you're not ready for it. I'll give you time to adjust, but I'm becoming obsessed because you won't let me check on you through it. I cannot do anything about that. It's pure dragon instinct. But that's not my point. You've used my magic through it before, so you can do it again."

My stomach flipped at the thought of using his amazing magic, so I focused on the mayhem. I needed to do everything I could to help Pyron, not ogle Drake. "And you think it will be enough to save these people?"

"I think it's our best chance."

"Okay. I'll try it."

He stopped and spun around so we were face-to-face. Hunger flashed through his eyes. "Are you sure you can trust me enough?"

I tried not to fall into those beautiful green eyes as I pondered the question. Did I trust him enough? I liked Drake. He helped me gain my freedom and keep it. He also lied to me for a year.

On top of that, everyone had ulterior motives. I knew Drake had an agenda, but I doubted it had anything to do with me. I wanted to trust him. I wanted to lean into him and open that bond to learn what made him tick. And that terrified me. "Trust and intimacy are difficult, but I'm working on it. I trust you more than most paranormals, so I'm willing to try if it will save this pocket."

His eyes stayed locked on mine for a long minute before he turned and started down the hill. "To be successful, you'll need to do more than try. I understand it's hard for you, especially since your brother locked me into that silence contract. But I promise I won't ever betray you and will do my best to help you in every situation."

The magical contract zinged through me, and I swallowed the sudden lump in my throat and smacked his arm. "That was a little extreme."

"No, it wasn't."

Tendrils of bug magic stretched toward us as we reached the bottom, so we sprinted in a zig-zag pattern toward the building. Or we tried to sprint. Sprinting in the sand wasn't easy and made it painfully slow, especially after we realized bug magic crawled under it. Drake moved faster than me, so I put a little magic into my speed, slapped a hand on his back, and flashed us to the top of the building.

It was solid, with a metal roof and magically enhanced foundation. Drake tilted his head toward the sky. I drifted to the edge to get an idea of how to neutralize the magic buried in the sand. "It's climbing up the wall. We only have about a minute."

When he didn't respond, I glanced back. He stood in the same spot, head thrown back, his eyes glowing. The glow intensified until it bathed the entire roof in an eerie green light. Before I could stop myself, I leaned in and reached for his face.

He grabbed my hand. "Don't touch. I'm getting information."

I stepped back and unwrapped all three of my magics. His eyes lost their glow a few seconds later, and he focused on me. "I'm sorry."

I shook my head. "Don't be. It's amazing that you can ..."

He reached out and pulled me against him. His mouth covered mine. Lightning zinged through me from head to toe, and my whole body tingled. Heat pooled in my core. I laced my fingers through his hair, pulled him closer, and fell into the kiss. It became hot and hungry. All my inhibitions disappeared, and I matched his hunger. He tasted like love and Drake.

A roar rolled across the desert, and Drake pulled back and brushed a curl out of my face. Hunger and triumph reflected in his eyes. "We're linked."

The building exploded.

We landed inside in the center as debris crashed down around us. Splinters scratched my face and ripped through Drake's shirt. His grip on me tightened enough to bruise as he formed scales to protect us.

I wrapped a blanket of dissipating magic around us, threw my hands straight up, and drew on the gigantic pool of magic inside him. His foreign magic flooded me. Every hair on my body stood on end. The ruling magic grabbed it and pulled. Drake pulled us to our feet and turned his face toward the sky. I tuned the magic torrent to the dissipating spell, raised my arms, and let it go.

I didn't know if it was because the bond was open or the adrenaline, but our magic was way more powerful than when we linked before. The ruling magic flowed up and branched out across the town, entered buildings, and burrowed into the sand. My hair whipped around us. A thousand bee stings from the sand beating at us made it hard to concentrate. I slammed my eyes shut and buried my face in Drake's chest. I gave one last push.

When the atmosphere became lighter, I eased back. Something in the wind clanged, and I cracked my eyes open. I coughed as the healing magic tried to expel the sand I'd inhaled and repair the damage to my skin. When the dust cloud cleared, I realized Drake's human-shaped skin still shimmered in the sun from his scales. He didn't have a single scratch on him. I glanced down at myself. Sand coated every inch of me, making me resemble a frizzy-headed, sweaty sand monster. It was good to be a dragon.

The shed was gone, the silence deafening as we stumbled out of the wreckage. I turned in a slow circle and let out an astonished, albeit hoarse, laugh. "We did it."

Drake's lips quirked up as he watched the other dragons doing loops through the sky. "Operation magic up the whazoo accomplished."

I chuckled as I grabbed his arm. "Come on. Let's look at that object."

As we got closer, I realized the object was shaped like a pyramid. The dark magic swirled around it in thick waves. It wasn't crawling on the ground toward us, which I found odd.

"Are we still linked?" I asked.

Drake nodded. "We should be able to clear the outside."

"I'm worried about what's inside."

"As am I."

I moved to the right a few paces, trying to see it from a different angle without getting too close. "Did you see a bunch of tainted paranormals rush out of this thing?"

"Yes. Like it's a people storage."

"Yeah. I wonder if this is how they collect people for their labs."

Drake ran a hand through his hair. "I doubt they've used this method before. Otherwise, someone would have reported it."

I tilted my head toward the sky. "Tracy can figure out the inside. She's got some potions and knows more about how it works than me. Let's clear the outside."

"We're exhausting our energy. And I doubt Tracy has enough potion left to clear the whole pyramid."

"True. We'll have to wait for the enforcers." I started forward, tuned my inherent magic to the dissipating spell, and tested the glob of wiggling bug magic. A tug in my chest told me Drake drew on the ruling magic. We barely made a dent.

"No more," Drake said. "The bond provides us with mind communication and an energy boost, so we don't get as tired, but it's finite. Clearing this on top of what we just accomplished will exhaust us both."

I took a couple of steps back. "We need more witches. I'm going to have to play nice with the President of Covens."

He rubbed his chin. "I suppose. Let me try dragon fire." He strode toward the pyramid.

I trailed behind him and then veered left to get a better look. Smoky glass peeked through in a few small areas and gleamed in the sunlight. It reminded me of a building I once saw in the human city of Las Vegas, only much smaller. The hair on the back of my neck stood up when I realized the glass was clear, not tinted. Bug magic swirled inside, giving it the smoky appearance. I crept forward. Not glass, but something magical. I shuffled around to the other side and tilted my head. "We should probably get–"

Drake's green dragon fire engulfed the pyramid. I backpedaled and covered my ears against the roar. When the fire extinguished, the bug magic was gone, and the glass had gone from smoky to deep black. His fire didn't dissipate it but caused it to retreat. Interesting. I skirted around the object and headed toward Drake.

A gale-force wind kicked up around the pyramid. I flashed toward Drake and bounced off something. The wind increased and tried to draw me toward it. I dropped to my knees in the hot sand to brace myself and tried to flash away. It didn't work.

Drake burst into his dragon form and roared. He dove over the object and extended a talon toward me. Again, I tried to flash to him, but something blocked me. Pain slashed through my side as I bounced off an invisible barrier. The wind increased, and I got swept into the air. I spun around the pyramid so fast my head pounded. My momentum carried me face-first toward a hole near the top.

I realized it was small enough to catch myself on the sides, so I flung my arms and legs out in the starfish gesture. I hit the pyramid beside the hole with a *'crack'* and rolled across it. My butt got sucked into the tiny opening. I latched onto the edge and gave myself a magic boost.

Drake's massive dragon form bounced off some kind of barrier, his roars deafening.

Tracy ran at a full sprint toward me, anguish on her face. She yelled something I couldn't hear over the wind and Drake's roars. She threw a spell, and a bright light zipped toward me, made it through the barrier, and smashed into my face. I tried to flash again but couldn't. One of my hands slipped, so I concentrated on holding on. I gripped the edge of the hole and pulled at my butt. I drew some of Drake's power to give myself an extra boost. My efforts made me slip further in. I clung tighter to the edge and sent pulses of neutralizing magic into the thing.

Something latched onto my wrist. One of my legs slipped and got sucked in.

"Hold on." Quin's dry voice sounded muffled through the clutter of noise. I swung my head toward him and met his glowing red eyes. He was in full vampire form. His toe claws extended through his shoes, and he jammed them into the side of the pyramid right under the hole. His hand claws curled around my wrists.

"Get out of here," I screeched over the howling wind and dragon roars. The wind picked up, and both legs shot out behind me into the hole. Quin strengthened his grip on my wrists.

He used the leverage the claws on his foot gave him and his unbelievable strength and pulled. He was going to rip me in half. His fangs clicked twice. "Flash."

"I can't! The magic around this thing won't let me." The wind howled louder, and I swayed back and forth. *'Crack!'* White hot pain shot up my arms as my wrists broke.

His eyes grew enormous as he quit pulling and switched his grip to my elbows.

A tear escaped and rolled across my temple and into my hair as the wind whistled around us. "Let me go." I didn't see any other way. I just had to figure out how to fix the mess myself. My attention swung back to Drake, still beating against the barrier. "Let me go."

Quin's eyes narrowed in defiance. He withdrew his claws from the building and threw his arms out. Blinding pain shot through my ribs as he smashed into me and used his strength to hold on. "I do not let my people die without a fight," He growled.

We tumbled through the pyramid and landed in a heap against the wall. Blood trickled down my face as I dragged myself to a sitting position and rested my useless hands on my lap. Darkness surrounded us. I couldn't see more than a couple of feet, even with my magic sight. The ruling magic was silent. Pain and exhaustion overtook me, and I leaned my head back. A white glow reflected from somewhere. I tilted my head toward Quin, then focused on my hands, realizing the glow was coming from us. Tracy's spell, I realized when the bug magic crawled the other way. "Why did you do that? You could have gotten out."

Quin leaned his head back and closed his eyes. "Oh, yes. Let's just hand the Bellicose what they want most."

His sarcasm calmed my nerves. "Okay, that was a stupid question."

We were both bloody and bruised, and I fought to keep my eyes open as the healing magic worked its way through my body. I threw some dissipating magic at the side of the pyramid. Daylight peeked through for a few seconds. I could make out several unconscious supers around us before the light faded.

The pyramid shook. I was in too much pain to throw my arms over my head as the top came off. Neutralizing magic flooded in, and a giant green eye peered through it. The roar that followed was so filled with pain and longing that I wanted to curl into a ball and cry. I shook my head to clear it. It wasn't my pain, but Drake's. His pain and longing for me through the bond ached in a way I never realized a person *could* hurt. It was half gut punch and half wake-up call.

Something in the corner beeped, and Quin threw himself over me. I screamed as more pain speared through my entire body. A bright flash and the pyramid shifted. All the trapped paranormals rolled in the same direction. We got hurled to the other side, bounced off a couple of unconscious people, flew straight up, and slammed back on the floor. Everything faded to dark.

CHAPTER TWENTY

JEN

SHARP PAIN RADIATED ACROSS my face. I grabbed the hand and shoved it away. "Stop."

"Oh, good. You're not dead." Quin wiped his hand on his ruined suit.

I groaned as I sat up. My mouth was dry and filled with a nasty, gritty taste. I swallowed several times to clear it. We were on the floor in what I assumed was the pyramid. The sun was still out and light filtered through a hole high above our heads. The stench of body odor made me want to gag. "Where are we?"

"Inside that strange object."

I sighed as I examined our surroundings. A tangled mess of about a hundred unconscious paranormals surrounded us. Remnants of bug magic splattered around them, wiggling and growing. My power was about three-quarters full. "We've only been here a couple of hours. My magic isn't at full strength, but it's close." My head ached, and my wrists still throbbed. At least I wasn't awake when they reset themselves. It was always the worst part.

Quin eased down beside me. "Yes. I am sure magic level is an accurate measure of time."

I dug in my pocket for my phone, but it was gone. We needed to save these people and get out. I didn't bother to tell Quin that I knew how to measure time based on magic because I used it to pass time while locked in a cage as a kid. "It's accurate."

A mage oozing bug magic appeared in the center of the room. Like the one at the Cauldron, it crawled out of his mouth, nose, and ears. A piece dropped to the floor and slithered toward an unconscious man.

I hopped to my feet and charged, sending a blast of neutralizing magic toward him. He didn't see it coming, so he smashed into the wall and slid down, leaving a smear in his wake. Healing magic in neutralizing form shot from me as I tackled him. It was so fast that he didn't have time to react. I searched for those virus things that generated the bug magic. He had five placed in neat intervals along his spine. When he was magic-free, I climbed to my feet. He opened his mouth to say something.

His head rolled across the floor and bounced off a man's leg.

My mouth flopped open, closed and opened again. I raised my eyes to Quin and snapped it closed as his sword disappeared.

"Do not give these traitors the benefit of the doubt. It will not go well." He melted to the center of the room and tilted his head back. "The First and the Dragon Prince are conspiring with Tracy to release us from this hell."

I blinked. Between his extreme violence and his casual statement, my brain got whiplash. "Okay." I stumbled around the unconscious people and put my hand on the wall to feel the spell holding us in.

The pyramid shook. I braced myself to keep from falling. *Drake! Stop moving the pyramid.*

Are you okay, Jenella?

Yes. I'm going to reverse the spell so we can get out of here.

Don't use all your energy.

I ignored the warning and placed my hand on the wall and sent my senses through it. The spell was sticky and more than a little dark. It felt like I'd walked into a thick spiderweb and the spider was poised above me, ready to strike. I jumped when the ruling magic cocooned me in and spread through the spell. The weave was far more advanced than anything I'd ever sensed. It was so tight that I had difficulty distinguishing between the different threads. It wasn't mage or witch magic. Or any type of magic I recognized. I removed my hand, relieved as the sticky feeling retracted. "This magic isn't anything I've ever come across."

"What do you mean?" Quin asked.

"It's not from any of the magical species I've met. And I've met them all. It's far more intricate and advanced than our magic." My theory that a First woke up and was running the bellicose ran through my head. "Maybe Drake or Deva can identify it." I sent the information to Drake through mind-speak.

A few seconds later, he appeared in the center of the room, a mage enforcer at his side. As Drake picked his way toward me, I couldn't tear my eyes away from him. He moved far too gracefully for his size. His ripped T-shirt allowed his solid muscles to peek through. It was all I could do not to throw myself into his arms. Our eyes met, and he stopped in his tracks. Relief, longing, and heat reflected in those gorgeous green eyes.

"Oh, yes. This is the perfect time to ogle the First." Quin's dry voice came from beside me.

It broke the spell, and I tore my eyes away and chuckled. "Hey, Drake."

He made it to me in two strides. His arms came around me and I got pulled into his warm body. His scent washed over me and for a second, I was sure everything was going to be okay.

Drake stepped back and ran his eyes over me, then glanced at Quin. "The enforcers have arrived. We can flash people out, so no need to break the spell."

I pointed to the wall. "Do you recognize that magic?"

He set his hand on it, then shook his head. "No."

My head exploded in pain. I grabbed it and lowered myself to the floor. Quin leaned over. "Problems?"

"My head."

"Great time for a migraine." He paused. "Do you get migraines?"

"No. Never. My head's never hurt like this."

Drake's warm hand landed on my back. "Someone is trying to dig into your head."

Mind magic usually tingled, and then the ruling magic threw it out. Something warm touched my temple. The pain eased, and I straightened. Drake stood in front of me, one hand wrapped around my back, the other on my head, his eyes closed. When they opened, fire burned in them. "Bastien had an urgent message for you." He turned and barked orders at the enforcers popping into the pyramid.

"Shall we leave? Or do you wish to remain here?" Quin failed to keep the concern out of his sarcasm.

I marched after Drake as enforcers flashed in, grabbed people, and flashed out. "You really are an ass sometimes. Why hang around all the time if you think I'm stupid?"

Quin's eyes flickered with something I didn't recognize. "You and Tracy are the first friends I have had in a thousand years. I do not want to lose you."

I considered Tracy a friend, but Quin only tolerated me. He did what he wanted and no one ever called him on his crap. No one dared. I made a mental note to ask him about that one day. Not that he'd answer me. The only one who he ever listened to was Ara, who scared people even worse than him. With his surly attitude and terrifying wife, making friends would be even more challenging for him than it was for me with my title. "I understand."

Drake swung toward us. "The pain in your head was Bastien trying to force his way in. Use my mind magic and toss him out if it happens again."

"Sure." I couldn't help but wonder why the ruling magic didn't react. It liked to get violent with Bastien. Though he wouldn't have used brute force without a good reason. And probably Tracy telling him to. "Where are we?"

"On the outskirts of the town. The pyramid was supposed to go somewhere specific, but I broke the top off and it malfunctioned."

"To a lab, I bet. I'll flash the three of us out." I pointed to the broken top. "Is that Tracy leaning in?"

"Yes. We couldn't get in, so we built a platform."

I flashed us to the top and found myself wrapped in another hug. "Oh my fates, Jen. I thought we lost you again." Tracy's voice was raw, like she'd been yelling.

"I didn't do that on purpose. We were being careful this time."

"Yeah, Drake told me he was only a few feet away when it got you."

"Yep." I pointed at the pyramid. "Do you recognize that magic?"

"I can't even feel it. I mean, I can, but not like you. It makes me want to run away."

"I doubt it's from this realm." I remembered the God Ann Marie took me to meet. "Drake, does this feel like god magic?"

"No. God magic feels...different. Lighter."

I flashed to the ground where Quin stood, staring out at the crowd that had gathered in the center of town. Drake conjured a large canteen of water and handed it to me. I took it and sipped as I eyed the disheveled, beaten-down residents. "They need hope. Will they listen to me?"

Quin came out of his vampire trance and frowned. "You are worried people won't follow their queen?"

I was worried. I didn't have my mother's authoritarian personality or my grandmother's charisma. Establishing myself was important, and I wasn't sure if I could do it. "Yes."

Quin said nothing as he shed his tattered jacket and took a canteen from Drake. His shoes had holes in the toes where his claws had punctured them, and his dress pants and what used to be a white shirt were torn, giving him a more feral look. His hair was still perfect, though.

In contrast, my hair was in such tangles I could feel it pulling. Blood glued my hair to the right side of my head. Nothing I could do about that, so I moved away from the pyramid. Drake and Tracy followed. She handed me a potion. "Drink this. It'll clean you up a little."

I uncapped it and gulped it down. "Thanks."

The enforcers, along with a bunch of other support personnel, worked their way through the people and healed them. They were going to be okay and didn't need a pep-talk from me, so I continued through the town. As we passed through, a few people bowed.

I waved a hand. "That's unnecessary. Please, just take care of yourselves and your families." My eyes strayed toward Quin, who stared into the distance. Drake glued himself to my side but didn't speak. I moved toward a family of Devil Monkeys. Devil monkeys were created and later abandoned by a First who lived in the desert for a short time, though I couldn't remember which one. They resembled a mixture of a camel and a guerilla in their animal form. They weren't much better looking in their human forms with their hunched backs and monkey-like faces. Even the kids. I stopped in front of them. "Are you okay?"

"Yes," the woman said. She pointed to the other side of the town. "Our home is untouched. We're here to help our neighbors."

I nodded. There were no words amid the complete wreckage of the only town in the pocket. An apology seemed shallow and phrases like 'good luck' or 'I wish you well' were lame. "We'll see what we can do to put the town back together and help everyone."

"Thank you, Your Grace." The man started to bow, then straitened. Well, he straightened as much as his hunched back would let him.

I moved on, deciding not to engage with anyone else. The whole situation made me ill.

"They will follow you," Quin muttered from behind me as we moved away. "They see your kindness, your compassion, and your leadership in an unpleasant situation. You do not have to pretend to be someone else or go to great lengths to prove yourself. You simply need to lead."

I blinked. Quin never said that much at one time. Or use informal words. "You're a good man, Quin. At least you are once you get past all the sarcasm and bored expressions."

"I am an ancient vampire who has killed thousands. We will not be having a touching moment or a heart-to-heart. You made me an advisor. I am advising." He walked away.

A feeling of dread washed over me and I fought the tingle that signaled a panic attack. I took some deep breaths and tilted my head toward the sky. About fifty dragons, colored in shades of yellows, reds, and oranges, circled the area. "Those dragons have been flying a long time. Are they going to be okay in this heat?"

Drake's hand settled on my back. "Dragons don't just like the heat. We thrive in it. Heat energizes us."

His touch and his casual explanation grounded me. "Too bad you're not a dragon." It was what he said when he offered me the first ride on his back and I protested.

The warm tone of his chuckle vibrated through me, extinguishing the anxiety. "Fortunately, I share some of their traits." He leaned in, his breath hot on my ear. "It will be okay, Jenella."

Goosebumps coated my skin, even in the wretched, oven-like heat. "Thank you."

As the sun sunk toward the horizon, it cast pink and orange hues across the desert. I'd felt a tingling to the north since we arrived. But as the sun set, the prickle grew stronger. The town was teeming with activity. Architecture mages worked on rebuilding houses, Desert Elves replaced rock gardens and plants. A coven of witches worked on the wards as Tracy added the new potion to prevent the mess from happening again.

Drake worked with the enforcers to come up with a better defense for the smaller pockets. I helped for a while, but realized it wasn't my area of expertise, so left them to it.

When I reached the northern end of town, I kept going for about a half a mile until I ran into a golden ward where the pocket ended. I followed it around to the newly restored gate and crossed my arms. *I know where the First is.*

Don't do anything with all these supernaturals present, Drake replied.

I doubt I can do anything but I need to try. The day I woke him, I'd been repairing a crack in the ward in a remote part of Allure. The wall sucked my magic dry, and he woke up soon after.

A dragon with yellow hair took a couple of swigs of water as he manned the gate. "Can I help you, Your Grace?"

"No." I slipped outside the wards and stood on the edge of a plateau. I turned north and frowned. A hill in the distance rose to a peak and created a black lump, interrupting the perfect horizon. "That hill isn't very far from here, is it?"

"Distance is deceiving in the desert. That hill is miles away."

"Thanks." I meandered back inside the pocket and drifted back toward the square. If the First was there, I needed to do something.

"What are you scheming?"

I didn't jump when Quin appeared, because I'd kept my senses on alert since I woke up inside that pyramid. As a result, I sensed him a full second before he spoke. "Scheming?"

"I did not realize you had a hearing problem."

"I'm not scheming, I'm thinking." I eyed the gate where several enforcers had joined the yellow dragon. No way I'd make it past them all without them noticing. I swung my head toward Quin, an idea forming.

"No."

"You don't even know what I was going to sa–"

"No."

"Fine. I'll do it myself." I strode toward the gate.

Quin appeared in front of me, blocking my way. "Should you ever decide to remove your head from your anus, now would be the time."

I flashed past him. "What you mean is pull my head out of my ass. And I'm not doing anything."

"Irrelevance followed by a lie. Brilliant."

I slammed my hands on my hips. "Fine. I'll get some backup, but I need to check something out." I spun and headed the other direction.

Quin disappeared.

The sand was still warm when I flashed to the base of the hill. I was already coated with a thick blanket of grit, so the sand that plumed into the air as the wind stirred it didn't bother me. I waited for Tracy and Bastien to join me, then moved closer. "The buzzing is coming from here."

"This is not wise," Bastien said, not taking his eyes off the hill.

"Not even a little." I decided Quin was right, that it was stupid for me to go alone, so I fessed up to Tracy and Bastien about my search for the Firsts. They already knew because Drake told them why we went to Pyron before we left Allure. Drake didn't like being sneaky. Unless he was stalking me, then it was perfectly acceptable.

Drake! I pushed the mind-speak through the bond. *I found the resting spot.*

Please don't yell at me. His mind-voice sounded tired.

Right. I didn't need to yell for him to hear me, even when he was far away. *Bastien and Tracy are with me, and I suspect Quin is around. But if I wake this First, I'll need you. Can you fly my way without alerting anyone?*

He was silent for a beat. *I can't tell if you're trying to insult me, or you truly believe I'm incompetent at cloaking.*

Butterflies exploded in my stomach at his teasing tone and I tamped them down. *Well, I sensed you during your stalking phase, so....*

Unusual for my prey. I'm headed your way. Stay safe until I arrive.

You stay safe, too. I flinched at my automatic response. Drake had been around for a long time. His scars marked him as a seasoned warrior. He didn't need to be reminded to stay safe. *And I'm not prey. We'll hunker down here and wait for you.*

He grunted in agreement.

Bastien morphed into his dragon form to scare off predators and perched on a rock. I sat at the base of the rock beside Tracy and watched the sun sink over the horizon, and tried to sense Drake.

The air became significantly cooler, and I pulled my legs up and hugged them. "Are you drained after today?" I asked.

"No. I mean, I'm tired, but not completely drained. What about you?"

"I'm tired, but still have access to Drake's magic, so I should be good."

"So, you can just use his magic whenever you want to now?"

I shrugged. "I don't know how dragon bonds work."

She shook her head. "Sharing magic with a match is a mage thing, not the trait of a dragon bond."

The ruling magic vibrated at a low hum. A signal that something was wrong. Unable to stand the sensation anymore or the worry churning in my gut, I stood and climbed to the top of the pile of rocks beside Bastien's toe. The ruling magic's vibration increased. I scrambled down the rocks and tried to distance myself. The vibration rose to a volume that made my teeth rattle. "Something's happening. You two need to get out of here."

Bastien threw Tracy on his back and hovered in the air above me as the ruling magic exploded. It burrowed into the pile of rocks and unwrapped itself before I registered what happened. A whirlwind of dust and rocks spread out in every direction. Gritty sand coated my mouth, and I realized I'd been thrown to the ground and landed on my face. I choked and spit to clear it as I rolled to my feet. "I woke someone."

Quin appeared beside me. "Perhaps a little caution is prudent when faced with unusual things."

Relief flooded me. He was always excellent support in dangerous situations. "Your sarcastic insults are slipping."

The rock pile shifted. Strands of yellow magic snaked from the cracks.

Quin drew his sword. "Do not explode your magic."

I didn't plan to. I grinned. "It *is* a First."

"Yes."

Has it ever occurred to you to engage your brain before you act? Bastien's voice boomed through my head. The ruling magic didn't reject it, which meant we were in serious trouble.

"Yes." Unfortunately, that pool of power had a mind of its own. Sometimes I could control it. Other times, it did what it wanted. I didn't mind most of the time because it acted in my defense.

The rocks exploded again. Bastien flew higher as stones rained down on us. I threw my arms over my head and squatted. The ground underneath us shook, and I left one hand up and threw the other out to catch my balance.

A skinny woman with tangled red hair rose out of the ground in a plume of dirt. She lurched forward, her translucent wings dragging on the ground. Her pale skin was covered in blisters and sores that oozed a green liquid. Wild blue eyes settled on me and filled with rage so intense I had to focus on her chin.

She charged.

Heart in my throat, I shot raw inherent magic at her on reflex.

Bright-white light flashed as my magic hit her. She rolled across the sand and landed in a heap. I took two steps forward before she bounced up.

Yellow magic lashed out at me.

I ducked and saw a flash as it zipped over my head. The ground behind me cracked open and an oak tree rose from the desert and towered over us.

Quin went fluid and elbowed her in the jaw before she could lower her hands. Her head snapped back. A blazing stream of vines engulfed him but didn't stick. He punched her in the nose. Or I thought he did. His movements were a blur, but her nose wasn't bleeding before her head whipped back.

A boulder lifted off the ground and hurled toward the fight. Quin and the boulder skidded across the sand.

I sprinted toward him, but he didn't need my help, so I skidded to a stop as he picked up the boulder and threw it at the woman.

A series of vines sprung from the ground and caught it.

Tracy threw a spell from Bastien's back. The First threw a gust of wind, and Bastien tumbled through the sky.

I tried to access the ruling magic, but it moved like a pool of sludge, so I tuned my inherent magic to a sleeping spell and tossed it in her direction.

It was a mistake.

Her face turned beet red, her rage burning thick and hungry as she stomped toward me.

Quin blurred again and sliced an arm, then parried and cut her leg. The First's magic didn't bother him, but the rock that smashed into his back did. He sailed forward and crashed into a giant cactus.

I threw both hands in front of me. "We're not here to hurt you." I couldn't help the wobble in my voice.

"That's rich coming from you." Her voice was raspy and dry.

I wasn't sure why both she and Drake mistook me for my mother when they woke. I didn't look much like her, other than I had the same color of hair and eyes. In fact, I looked more like my grandmother, whom the Firsts adored. "I'm not Anitta," I squeaked, ignoring Drake's frantic screams in my head.

Vines and tumbleweeds sprouted out of the ground in front of me. The ruling magic turned them to ash using...was that dragon fire?

The woman's eyes narrowed. "You stole dragon magic?"

I knew from experience that I was no match for a First with my magic split into three pools. So I tried to reason with her. "I'm not Anitta. That was my mother. I'm Jenella."

Rocks came at me from every direction. I flashed away, tripped over a vine when I landed, and rolled across the ground. So much for reasoning. I boosted my speed and charged. The First didn't expect a physical attack, and we both hit the ground. I punched her in the ribs twice, raised up and smashed a palm into her already broken nose.

A rock bounced off my shoulder hard enough to stun me. She hooked her legs around me and reversed our positions and pulled her fist back.

I ran healing magic through her.

She froze with her fist in the air. "What are you doing?"

"Healing you. You're not in very good shape." Blinding pain vibrated through my head when her fist collided with my cheek.

Her weight lifted, and I staggered to my feet. My forehead crinkled as my one good eye glared at her. She backpedaled a couple of steps.

Green and black scales blocked my vision and an earth-shattering roar rattled my bones. My hair stood on end and the urge to run was so strong I had to lock my knees. The First tumbled across the sand and landed on her ass. Drake hovered over me and bared his teeth. A drop of blood coated in bug magic splatted on the ground.

The woman stumbled to her feet. "I always knew you were a traitor."

Jenella is nothing like Anitta! The anger in Drake's voice was unmistakable, and I fought to hide my wince.

Her icy stare bore into me. After several seconds, she dropped her eyes and her shoulders sagged. She released her traps. "Where is Anitta? I have a score to settle."

"She's dead. I'm the incoming Queen of Ahl, Jenella."

"What a shame."

Drake's colossal head swung toward me, and he opened his mouth. *Clean.*

"So, now I'm your toothbrush, huh?" Another drop of blood trickled down a razor sharp tooth and landed in the sand. Bug magic wiggled within it. The magic looked like it was trying to escape. It didn't like dragons. I raised my hand and sent neutralizing magic, then cleansing magic into his mouth. "Got it."

His chuckle echoed through my head.

"Oh, my fates, Jen." Tracy came out of nowhere. "Don't you ever do that again."

"That's excellent advice. Thanks." I turned my attention to Quin. "You okay?"

"Of course." He picked a quill out of his arm and strode toward the new First. "Do not attack the queen again, Razazia. I will disembowel you."

She inclined her head. "My apologies, Master Tarquin. I have been in isolation for too long and lost myself. For years, I saw nothing but darkness and silence. Then I saw who I thought was Anitta." She glanced at Drake, then her eyes settled on me. "I assume you woke me?"

"Yes. Though, I wouldn't have if I knew you'd attack us." I totally knew she'd attack us, but wanted to see her reaction.

Her eyes narrowed. "You have no room to talk, considering what your mother did."

The reaction was exactly what I expected. "I'm not my mother."

Quin shuffled closer to me. "You owe Jenella gratitude for not leaving you to roast in the desert. However, if she knew you…"

Drake huffed in agreement. I set a hand on his massive foot. "Razazia, is it? Do you need a place to stay? If you do, I can help. The pocket of Pyron isn't far, but it's in ruins. We could take you back to Allure with us, though."

She shook her head. "I would not take your help if you were the last paranormal in the realm. I will locate the sand elves."

I nodded. "Some Sand Elves are helping to clean up Pyron. Don't cause any trouble and I won't bother you. Bring yourself into the current times while you recover. If you need help, contact my office. You can call Drake or Quin if that works better for you." She didn't have mind magic like Drake, so I doubted she knew about modern customs like he did when he woke up. "A lot has changed in the world."

She spread her translucent wings and flew away without acknowledging me.

Quin watched her until she faded into the horizon. "That First is going to be a problem."

"I don't care. It was the right thing to do, even if it causes a little trouble." It was one of the few problems within the coalition that I knew how to fix. And much less complicated than bug magic and the anti-hybrid movement.

CHAPTER TWENTY-ONE

JEN

Mat and Emine waited by the gates when we entered Pyron. A shiver ran down my spine as I flashed to the ground. Drake's tail crashed down with a thump, sending a plume of sand into the air between us.

I coughed as I patted his toe. "It's okay." I waited for his tail to lift and focused on my brother. "That magic wrecked this pocket. Did either of you receive reports about it?"

"Good to see you, too." Mat stepped forward and hugged me, his hold so tight that I struggled to breathe.

"Mat, I stink. You don't want to smell like this."

"I don't care how you smell, only that you are alive. Are you all right?"

"Yes, I'm fine." I stepped back and lifted a hand. "Hey Emine."

Her lip curled in disgust. "You're right, you stink. And what the hell happened to your hair?"

I patted my bloody, matted hair. "Lovely, isn't it? And this is after Tracy used a cleaning potion." I motioned toward Pyron. "We found the place wrecked. The whole pocket was in turmoil. They have some kind of device that infects the area and picks up paranormals and transports them. It picked me up, and Drake tore a hole in it. We saw townspeople pour out and attack their neighbors. Some were unconscious inside."

Mat's eye twitched. "I see."

My heart kicked up a beat. I had to admit his self-control in restraining that anger was great. "It's coated with some kind of magic that none of us have ever seen, so tell your people to be careful around it."

"Sure thing." Emine marched toward the Enforcers in the town square.

I turned my attention back to my brother. "Then I woke another First."

"What?" Mat growled. He didn't wait for me to answer. He strutted toward Drake.

Drake morphed into his human form. "Don't."

Mat jabbed his finger into Drake's chest. "You tricked my sister into bonding with you and influenced her to investigate the other Firsts."

"Wait, what? No." I slid between them.

Mat didn't take his blazing eyes off Drake. "He's using you. Yet you continue to feed the bond."

"Says the man who mated an assassin," Drake said.

I could have used that fainting couch just then. I was unaware Emine was an assassin before she matched with Mat. And he was wrong. Drake didn't trick me into anything. "He wasn't around when I woke Razazia." I met Drake's eyes. "You didn't influence me to do that, did you?"

He shook his head. "I'm not so sinister as to do that to you, Jenella. Our connection began in Mahri, and I have never attempted to sway you. I would never soil our bond that way, nor would I become another person who tries to manipulate you." He glared at Mat. "Unlike your brother. And Razazia may be a problem in the future, but she is weak and lacks connections."

I took a sip of water. "She'll be fine. Maybe."

Mat's hard eyes settled on me. "Be careful. You are playing with fire, and I cannot protect you from this."

Everyone turned their attention to me. I threw up my hands. Water sloshed out of my canteen, causing Quin to take a couple of steps away. "You can't be mad about this, Mat. I did everything I could to stay out of trouble and I handled it. I even brought backup."

All eyes turned to him. "Yet here we are. Again."

Heads swung toward me. "Stop it. This isn't a spectator sport. Yes, here we are again. We can't just sit around and wait for their next terrible spell."

"Eliminating their leadership is the key," Bastien interjected. "Or we might not stop the next one."

I nodded. "Exactly. What more can we do besides wake more Firsts and try to get them on our side?"

Mat rubbed his chin. "I don't like being reactive any more than you do. But putting yourself in danger by waking other Firsts isn't the answer. We have people working on finding their leadership, but progress is slow."

"Then we need to speed it up." I closed my gritty eyes. I needed people to rally around the cause. There had to be more I could do. A pang of guilt over the dead and infected caused my eyes to snap open. "I need some sleep and time to figure out how to rally people."

"Very well. We'll discuss this disaster later." Mat's eyes lost their glow. "Emine and I will deal with the fallout here, and I'll call for an emergency council meeting."

I wanted to respond, but bone-deep exhaustion settled over me. I put a hand on Drake's arm. "Sure. Let's get out of here. Will you give Quin a ride?"

"I will." He morphed back into his beautiful dragon form.

Quin eyed Drake's foot. "I do not do well when confined."

"No problem." I flashed us onto Drake's back and slumped against my favorite spike. I was too tired to care that I'd just declared a dragon spike as one of my favorite things. "Drake says he's not a dragon, so I'm sure he doesn't mind a non-bonded passenger." I patted a scale. "You might want to hold on. He's kind of an adrenaline junkie." My eyes drooped, so I gave in and closed them.

Singing in my head woke me as we landed in the concealed alley behind the house Tracy and I shared. Quin was gone, so I thanked Drake and stumbled into the house. A quick meal and a shower later, and I fell into bed and a deep, healing sleep.

CHAPTER TWENTY-TWO

JEN

I WRANGLED MY CURLS into a professional knot at the back of my head and dressed in a crisp white shirt and brown pants. The woman who stared back at me in the mirror was muscular and her eyes burned with power. The innocence from being sheltered had faded, but the wonder of new experiences still made my soul sing. I looked like a strong, competent woman. Too bad it was a lie. I headed to the castle.

Verity followed me into my office and shut the door. "What's going on, Jen? I can't help you if you don't talk."

I told her about the bug magic and our trip to the Cauldron, and that Drake and I were forming a bond. I didn't bother leaving anything out because Verity was a juror who could and would extract the truth from me with a single touch.

When I was done, her mouth hung open. "Well, this place is certainly never boring. I'll give you that."

"I want to talk to the Shifter Alphas before the meeting today. That magic is targeting shifters more than any other group."

"I'll set it up."

"Thanks. You really are the best."

"Yes, I am," she said as she sailed out the door.

The Shifter Alphas arrived an hour later. Gabe strutted in, his overly muscular body flexing as he walked. He always looked like he was ready to pounce on the next person he saw. His sharp amber eyes softened when they landed on me. "Hello, Jenella."

Linda strode in behind him. Her dark brown eyes scanned every corner of the office. "Please tell me you called me here to show off this office. It is gorgeous."

"Thanks, Linda. Hello, Gabe." I stood and motioned to the seating area by the window. After we settled in, I tapped the arm of the couch. "I've been working as a private investigator to learn about the concerns of regular supernaturals."

Linda's face lit up. "You've worked with Travis, then?"

I didn't dare tell Linda that I no longer considered her son a friend. Or that he was a selfish prick. "Travis knew what I was doing and helped with a mentor. I've worked minor cases for people with little power or influence because I wanted to understand what made them tick. Figure out their everyday concerns. I recently took a case involving a missing shifter kid." I filled them in on the case, and the bug magic. When I was done, Gabriel's eyes glowed with anger. Linda looked like she needed to punch something.

The urban sprite fluttered in and set iced tea, coffee, and a platter of meat sandwiches on the table. "Thank you, Charlotte."

She jumped. "Yes. Your Grace."

Linda watched her leave. "You have done a lovely job hiring staff, Jenella."

"I wish I could take the credit, but Verity hired them. She's amazing."

"You're the leader, so you take the credit and the blame for what your people do." She grew serious. "We've received the report about your work from Alpha Roberts. He's grateful for what you and your assistant did for his family."

Gabe filled a plate with meat sandwiches. "We have noticed an uptick in packs not reporting in, but that is cyclical. Occasionally, we need to remind them a power structure exists."

"Most of the tainted shifters came from pockets on the East Coast. I've asked Emine to get you a list since the enforcers took custody of the ones we found."

"So why call us here instead of covering that at the emergency council meeting?" Linda asked.

"Because I didn't want to blindside you." I spent a lot of time with Gabe and Linda as a kid. I didn't want to ruin that relationship with lack of communication. Not only because Mat considered them friends, but because they lead one of the largest magical species in the world. I needed them on my side.

I poured myself a glass of iced tea and waited for them to eat. Shifters had a singular focus when it came to food. They wouldn't talk until their plates were empty.

When Gabe was done, he refocused on me. "We appreciate the heads-up." He paused. "The Bellicose are trying to use this magic to take over the coalition?"

"That's the working theory."

"And what does Mat say?"

"He agrees. They call themselves the Sentinels now, but we're still going to call them Bellicose because older paranormals recognize the name from their previous attempts to take over. Our sources say they rebranded to make themselves seem more noble and modern."

"And what are we discussing at the council meeting?" Linda asked. "If this is a shifter problem, then we should handle it."

I knew they'd make that argument. The individual leaders handled their own problems, and we only stepped in if the factions clashed or if a problem affected multiple groups. "It's not just a shifter problem. It's a Coalition problem. Shifters are the primary target, but several types of paranormals have been infected. If the magic takes over the pockets, it could be disastrous. That's why we're having a council meeting."

Gabe rubbed his face. "I doubt they'll agree on a course of action."

Since there were over a hundred leaders with varying cultures, we never got them to agree unanimously on anything. The last time I attended a meeting, it took over an hour for them to approve an agreement that had already been signed between mages and witches to improve public building wards. "We don't have time for their posturing, so I'm going to step in if they can't agree."

When Gabe and Linda left, I drifted back to my desk. I needed to figure out the best way to handle the situation. Technically, Mat still ruled as my regent. I could override his decisions, but I didn't want to do that for many reasons. What I needed to do was to make a statement big enough they understood I wouldn't play their games without alienating them. I hated politics.

Mat and I stood shoulder to shoulder behind a spelled wall that allowed us to see out, but no one could see in or sense us through it. Verity and her staff settled members of the council into their seats and set up communication spells for those who couldn't attend in person. Mat's assistant, Pablo, set up the oversized desk at the front where Mat and I would sit. Two smaller desks were on the side of it for him and Verity.

The leaders took their seats in the stadium-like rows, shaped in a half circle in front of our desks. Some popped into their seats as holograms. The front rows were reserved for the most influential, while the leaders of the smaller groups sat in the back. A few royal blue plush seats were empty.

I turned my attention to the entrance in the back where Titus, the Crown Juror and Verity's match, stood at the door, reading each person who came through. From the scowls on the faces of the leaders, they didn't like that. My shoulders were relaxed, and I didn't feel even a tinge of anxiety. While I was extremely awkward when dealing with regular paranormals, I was calm and in control in the council chamber among the various leaders. Only Verity and Titus knew about my plan for the meeting. I glanced at Mat, wondering if I should update him, then dismissed it. I didn't want to argue.

Mat leaned forward as the Snow Elf King entered. "Your assistant is perhaps the most organized individual I have ever seen."

"She's amazing, and she doesn't put up with any bullshit."

"Especially yours."

"It's a relief. I have enough people willing to kiss my ass."

"It will be worse when you let your magic show. They'll be drawn like moths to flame. What is Titus doing?"

His job was to determine truth in legal matters at the crown's discretion. Reading the Council wasn't part of that, but he agreed to help with my plan. "He's checking them for involvement with the Bellicose."

"The Council members are under magical contract to work in the best interest of the Coalition."

"Yes. And every voluntary member of the Bellicose is sure they would be great for the Coalition."

"What do you plan to do with this information?" he growled.

My shoulders tensed. So much for my confidence. "Expel and arrest them. Publicly."

"Oh?"

"Yep." I watched Deva saunter in, Drake on one side and Bastien on the other. "Good. I was worried Deva wouldn't attend. At the end of the meeting, I'm going to announce the first members of my advisory committee."

"I don't hate this idea, but you better make sure taking the throne isn't an impulsive decision because I won't be able to hold it for you after this. You also might consider changing your ascension mandate today." He tried to keep the concern out of his voice and failed.

"I already changed it and sent you a copy. It's not an impulsive decision. We have a lot of problems that stem from the death of our parents. I plan to fix them before the Coalition implodes." Titus closed the doors and strolled toward the front to take his seat. I took a deep breath. "We need to work together for once, instead of a bunch of individual groups that coexist. I'm going to act swiftly and decisively to accomplish that." My chest grew tight, and I clenched my hands to keep them from shaking. "I hope."

Mat's eyes glowed with pride, though the worry and doubt radiated from him in waves. "Very well. I'll start the meeting and let you take the lead."

My stomach churned, and I swallowed. Both the meeting and starting my ascension were my idea, but I still hated being queen. Handling the Council in the way I planned meant taking responsibility for the consequences. Another imaginary bar snapped into place around me. "Right."

Mat squeezed my shoulder. "Don't worry. You have a lot of support and I'll help you in any way I can."

"It's not the lack of support that bothers me."

"It's not a cage."

I swallowed. "It is, but at least it's my choice this time." I motioned toward the chamber with its thick marble columns and blue and gold accents. It was a giant, domed auditorium in the back corner of our property outside the castle walls. The Council floor held about three hundred seats. The visitor seats surrounding the entire top floor of the circular room sat empty except for the support staff some members brought.

Mat dropped his hand from my shoulder as Verity burst into the room. "We're ready for you. Let me know when to run the presentation. Titus is off to your left with his list."

I glanced down at the floor where Mat's assistant, Pablo, and Titus stood waiting for us to enter. "Let's do this." I squared my shoulders and marched into the room.

Mat cranked up his intimidating magic as we walked. It helped calm me down enough to unwrap the massive ruling magic that I kept concealed. By the time we took our seats, my power was on full display.

Mat eyed the crowd as they bowed. "We have called you here to discuss a dire problem. I trust you will take this matter seriously. I turn the floor over to the Queen."

Golf claps ensued as I activated the voice projection spell on the table. I clasped my hands to hide the shaking and switched into queen mode. "As you know, we recently discovered that the Bellicose are active. They're currently going by the name Sentinels and use this symbol to show their presence." I waited for Verity to project the symbol I'd found on my first case over the chamber. "Their primary goal is to divide and conquer. We believe they are responsible for creating hatred for hybrids. They also have labs where they're combining demon magic with ours to experiment using vile magic on abducted paranormals. Last year, they tried to take over the dragons and failed."

The ruling magic purred, and I fought not to jump. That was new. "We recently discovered one of their magics and it's unlike anything we've ever seen. It looks like black ants and feels and smells like a disease. No one is immune. Anyone who touches the magic becomes infected and spreads it to others. Once infected, the person becomes lethargic and then violent. That violence is easily pointed at a target. Meaning the Bellicose leadership can herd the violence in any direction they want. Yesterday, they almost destroyed Pyron. If not for the intervention of the dragons and my team, they would have succeeded. Make no mistake, we are all targets." The leaders all started talking at once, and I held up a hand. "Please let me finish."

They ignored me. I pulled out my phone and added notes to my to-do list. It didn't take long for them to quiet, but I kept my eyes on my phone.

Mat cleared his throat. "Your Grace?"

I glanced up. "Oh, am I allowed to speak now? How generous." I set my phone down. "King Olwen of the Snow Elves, in your opinion, what are the top three problems with the Coalition?"

"I'd say lack of cohesion, growing distrust between races, and failure of leadership."

"Thank you. Queen Lidia of the Fairies, in your opinion, what are the top three problems?"

I went around the room with the same question for each leader, saving the leaders of the most powerful races for last. Meaning the shifters, witches, vampires, dragons, and mages. Although the desk designated for the mages was empty. I planned to move Mat to it when he stepped down from his regent position. It would give him something to control other than my life.

The elves would be in the front row if they hadn't split up into separate factions after Razazia went to sleep. Their customs varied so much that they didn't have much cohesion without her. So they compromised and formed independent groups that worked together. They sent representatives from three different factions to the council meetings on a rotating basis. After encouraging them to choose a leader for nearly two years, Mat agreed to the rotation and placed them in the second row with the agreement that should they choose one representative, their status would be restored. I didn't see the problem with them rotating. In my opinion, it was a great compromise until Razazia returned.

I asked the powerful leaders the question last because I wanted to see their reactions to the other answers. As expected, none of them reacted other than the President of Covens, who ruled the witches and hated me because I protected Tracy. She held a sour expression and would occasionally roll her eyes. The Vice President of Covens, Tracy's dad, listened with interest.

"Queen Ara of Umbra, same question." Ara's official title was the Queen of Umbra. Umbra being what vampires were called for centuries until humans renamed them. She kept her original title, though she didn't mind being called the Vampire Queen.

She came out of her weird vampire stupor. "The Bellicose, the hybrid issues that stem from the Bellicose, and unrest also caused by the Bellicose."

Ara knew what I was doing and had my back. I inclined my head to show my gratitude before moving on. "President Claudia of The Witches?"

"You are the problem."

I stared at her for ten heartbeats and then raised an eyebrow.

She folded her arms.

I turned my attention to Tracy's dad. "Vice President Calvin, since your president doesn't know how to count, what are two more problems the witches find with the Coalition?"

Calvin cleared his throat.

The President of Covens shot out of her chair and began a long tirade. I folded my hands under my chin and waited for her to stop. When she started weaving a spell, Calvin put a hand on her shoulder, pushed her into her chair, and said something I couldn't hear. He tugged at the cuffs of his dress shirt. "I agree with the Vampire Queen. The Bellicose and the power vacuum created by the lack of a leader with ruling magic."

"Thank you. Alpha Gabriel of the Shifters, same question."

Gabe and Deva both agreed with Ara, broadcasting to the rest of the leaders that many of our problems stemmed from the Bellicose. "Regent Mathias. As leader of the mages, what are the top three problems?"

"The Bellicose, the lack of a ruler with strong ruling magic, and lack of cohesion are our top problems."

"Thank you. Juror Titus, you have the floor."

Titus stood and pulled out his list. "If I call your name, please step forward." He called out the names of five leaders and fifteen of their support staff. They came forward willingly, then got nervous when palace guards started closing around them. Titus placed a stack of papers in front of me, bowed, and took his seat.

I picked up the first paper and read it, then eyed the first victim. The ruling magic reached out and wrapped around the group, causing some of them to jump. I didn't expect that and hoped it didn't kill them all. "Queen Delaney of the Dwarfs, please step forward."

"Yes, Your Grace."

The ruling magic squeezed her tighter. "The Crown finds you guilty of conspiring against the Coalition by willingly joining the Bellicose, a declared enemy. You have broken the magical contract to work in the best interest of the Coalition, and you are no longer fit to serve on the Council. You will be detained until I decide on a suitable punishment." I leaned forward. "I suggest you consider your actions as you wait." She screamed as the magic from the contract exacted its price for breaking it. The ruling magic released her as a guard slapped spelled handcuffs on her and led her away.

I read the names and expelled them individually. By the tenth person, the Council started getting restless. The ruling magic quieted them when I got annoyed. Beside me, Mat shifted in his seat but said nothing. The only sign that he didn't like how I handled things. When I expelled the last person, I eyed the remaining leaders. "I will not tolerate oath-breakers, schemers, or traitors on my Council. I called this meeting to coordinate a coalition-wide movement to combat the diseased magic and disband the Bellicose. Expelling the traitors among us is the first step."

The floor erupted with chatter. I watched the leaders and noted their reactions. The ruling magic swirled around the chamber, giving me information. Another new ability. But then, I never unraveled it and let it roam, so maybe it wasn't new. I avoided looking at Drake because I could feel his amusement and pride and my stomach was already doing somersaults. I shifted in my seat to calm it.

When the chatter settled down, the President of Covens stood. "This farce does nothing but show your incompetence."

"Sit down, dear," Ara drawled.

"We are here to talk about how to combat the Bellicose," Mat growled. "You will sit down and remain silent unless you have something constructive to say."

She sat down and shut up.

When the rest of the crowd quieted, I explained our neutralizing spell, emphasizing that Tracy created it, and agreed to make the recipe public for anyone to access. When I opened the floor for questions, the Kelpie Queen stood. "What are the non-magic using species supposed to do?"

"Excellent question. If your people cannot use neutralizing magic, rely on people that can. That means that we, as leaders, need to put aside our petty differences and pull together. If we don't, the coalition won't survive." I pointed at the door where the guards dragged the traitors. "They have already infiltrated this Council, caused mistrust, convinced us to discard members of our families, including children, and are torturing hundreds of paranormals. Either we band together, or we fall. Your choice." I sat back and folded my arms.

The vote to band together to eliminate the Bellicose was 121-2 in favor, with the President of Covens and the Kelpie Queen being the only 'nay' votes. I understood. The President of Covens hated me and the Kelpie Queen voted 'no' on everything, even motions she brought to the floor.

They spent the next hour arguing about what to do. I finally had enough and silenced everyone again. "It's no wonder the Bellicose is on the verge of a coup. We can't even come up with a simple communication strategy." I visibly sighed. "I guess that's my fault for trusting you to hold it together until I got my feet under me. Since you can't come up with a viable strategy on your own, the crown will provide you with one. All leaders will investigate their people to identify who works for the Bellicose and educate them on this new magic. Every accused individual will undergo examination by our jurors prior to prosecution." I hoped the Juror examination would stop them from using the mandate to get rid of their rivals, but I wouldn't hold my breath. "If you don't follow these directives, the Regent will step in." Most people were terrified of Mat because of his murder spree as we fled for our lives, so the threat of him showing up was enough for them to get on board. I hoped.

"Now, to move on to other matters. I have chosen some members of my advisory committee. Tracinia Cordalia of the Witches has already agreed to a position. The rest of the chosen people have three days to accept or reject the offer."

As expected, the President of Covens started another rant.

I tapped the desk. "Titus?"

"Yes, Your Grace."

"The President seems to think she has a say in who I pick as advisors. Will you please take her to a meeting room and explain how the advisory committee is chosen?"

His jaw ticked. "Of course, Your Grace."

Two griffins dragged her to a meeting room at the side of the auditorium, Titus trailing behind. When the door shut, I focused on the remaining leaders. "As I was saying, the following people have three days to decide if they want an advisory position. Consort Tarquin of Umbra, Queen Deva of the Dragons, The First Drake, The First Jonas, The Sorceress Ann Marie, Alpha Linda of the Shifters, King Olwen of the Snow Elves, Thaddeus of the Leprechauns, and Regent Mathias of the Mages."

"You've chosen two commoners." The Kelpie Queen's voice dripped with disdain.

"Yes. There will be no repercussions for those who don't want to serve. We will meet at a later date to discuss progress against the Bellicose. If any of you need help to combat the new magic, contact my office."

I gathered my papers and sailed out the door. I kept my head up and my magic exposed as I strode down the trail toward the castle, even though my knees wanted to buckle and my heart wanted to explode out of my chest. Mat followed me, but he didn't comment. I was grateful for that minor miracle.

When I reached my office, I set the papers on the conference table, melted into a chair, and took a few deep breaths. "That was tough."

Mat lowered himself into the chair next to me. "That was bloody brilliant."

I leaned back and closed my eyes. "Yeah? I wanted to make a statement without alienating everyone."

"Yes. You established yourself as a strong but fair leader who cares about the people but is not interested in nonsense."

"I was going for 'don't try to kill me' but that works, too."

"Funny. You understand there's no going back to being a detective after this."

"Yep."

"You're terrified."

"And you're pissed."

"You can't blame me when you show up out of the blue, announce you're taking the throne, and then make rapid-fire decisions without my input."

I cracked an eye open. "Lack of communication has always been our problem. The difference this time is that you're the one left in the dark instead of me."

My brother ran his hand through his golden hair. "I am still Regent. It is not unreasonable for me to expect to be informed."

"Sure. Just like how I am the Queen, so it's not unreasonable for me to expect to be informed. Especially when I've asked repeatedly. Yet here we are, still not communicating."

"The two situations are completely different."

I snorted. "Bullshit. You're just pissed because I yanked control out from under you and your control freak nature can't handle it."

"That may be true, but you still need to inform me of important matters and decisions you make."

"I get where you're coming from. Yet you don't tell me anything unless I pry it out of you."

"So, this is about revenge."

"No. It's about being petty to prove a point. I'm disappointed you didn't pick up on that right away."

It was his turn to snort.

We sat in silence for a few minutes. It was the first time I'd ever rendered my brother speechless. He shook his head as if to clear it. "Then we need to work on our communication."

"Agreed. You go first."

"I'll send you a list of things I've been working on. What was your strategy in choosing those advisors?"

"You want the truth?"

"Yes."

"You won't like it."

"Irrelevant."

"I chose Tracy because I trust her, and Quin won't lie to me unless you're involved. On top of that, he scares the shit out of most people. I chose both the Firsts as a formality. Drake is fine with it because of the bond. Jonas already said no, but his match, Ann Marie, might agree. I chose her because she knows a lot about both the hybrid situation and magic that we don't. I chose Deva because she told me to and Linda because I didn't want to offend her, and we need the shifters to win what might become a war. The Snow Elf King lives in Mage Mountain, and he'll be an excellent source of information. I chose Thaddeus because he is the only leprechaun who lives in Allure full time and can give me an idea about what's going on in Europe. He's also a commoner, and I didn't want Tracy to be the only one."

"Although you made those choices with emotion, they are good ones. We need to talk about your bond with Drake."

"No, we don't."

"You cannot fully bond with a First and hope to establish yourself as a strong ruler."

I snorted again. "Tell that to the ruling magic. Besides, he's a good guy. He tries to help me without holding me back. He makes me laugh. I like and respect him and, like Quin, he scares the shit out of most people. Other than the whole intimacy thing, it's a win for me."

"A bond is forever."

"Yep."

"It will look bad politically."

"Uh huh."

"You don't care."

"Nope. If I'm going to rule, I'm going to do it without losing my freedom. If people don't like it, they can file a complaint with you. You can refer them to Drake. If you both let them live, then I'm sure they'll come around."

Mat snorted again.

CHAPTER TWENTY-THREE

JEN

AN EMPTY HOUSE GREETED me before the sun rose, so I took my time drinking coffee as I flipped through one of my mother's diaries. Unable to concentrate, I set it aside. The coffee tasted bitter as I considered the options to accomplish my goals. If I could interact with the magic at Mage Mountain, I might fix my magic, but it was more than that. I needed to enter a cave. Several people had tried to enter those caves over the years. Some never came out. I didn't believe I'd be one of them, but it could happen.

Then there was the bug magic. Some leaders were resistant to acting against the Bellicose, even though they voted to band together to stop them. That was understandable, considering the division they'd caused. They were going off the basic rule that it was best not to be noticed by predators. I needed them to rally if we were to win, which meant spending more time at the castle.

My phone pinged with a text from Verity, pulling me out of my thoughts. She'd been dealing with the calls and emails from the various leaders that ensued after my little display at the meeting. She said most had questions. Others offered help or criticism. It made me want to tear my hair out, so I sent her a quick answer and slid my phone in my pocket, put my cup in the magiwash, and headed out to get answers of a different kind.

As I landed in the main flashing circle in the downtown square, my eyes settled on the gargoyles who seemed to multiply every time I flashed in. About twenty of them of all different sizes scattered around the square facing the two large flashing circles. Some were tall and lean, others more muscular. A few were only about three feet tall. I'd read those were the vicious ones. Their coloring varied between shades of grays and browns, except one. She had a greenish tint. Their heads had small lumps down the center and two rear-facing horns. One of them unfurled his leathery wings when a kid reached toward him. I approached the green-tinged one that stood guard beside my favorite street. "Are you guys okay? Do you need anything?"

Her enormous head creaked as it swung toward me. "No."

"No, you're not okay, or no, you don't need anything?"

I fought not to step back when she flashed her fangs. I met her sparkling eyes and realized it was a smile. She lowered her head to my level. "We are fine where we stand."

I cleared my throat. "Who do you follow?"

"We go where we're needed as we have for all of time." She squared her shoulders and faced forward, dismissing me.

"Right. Good talk." I kept my eyes trained on her as I headed down my favorite cobblestone street. I dodged a couple of witches who'd stopped in the center to talk and watched a fairy exit the door of a shop carrying a cinnamon roll bigger than him. Gargoyles weren't common in the pockets. They protected humans from demons and usually hung out on rooftops. It bothered me they were showing up in our main square as the Bellicose ramped up their magic attacks. I shook it off as I turned right and headed toward Dragon Headquarters.

Deva's assistant flipped her blue hair behind her shoulder. Intelligent eyes, the exact color of her hair, ran over me and her sharp features pinched into a frown. For some unknown reason, she always wore blue clothes. That day, Karenalla wore royal blue from head-to-toe. She wasn't my biggest fan. She summoned me using my own summoning room after I ignored a request from Drake. Then, I had to march through the building wearing my pajamas, so I put an end to using the summoning room. Since then, she'd treated me with cool indifference. She kept her face neutral as she waved me into Deva's office.

Deva stood by a floor-to-ceiling window, watching over the city. The sunlight shone through and bounced off her long bronze hair. She tilted her head as I entered. "Hello, love."

I lowered myself into one of the plush chairs near her. "Hey, Deva. What's going on with the gargoyles?"

"It's strange they are amassing in the square, but so is their culture."

"I asked one, but she wouldn't give me a straight answer."

"They won't. Gargoyles keep their secrets." She sunk into the chair beside me. "What can I do for you?"

"I need some advice and have a couple of favors to ask you."

Her bronze eyes narrowed. "What favors?"

"Nothing big. I talked to Ann Marie. Her son has mental magic and is being chased by the Bellicose. She requested safe refuge here for her adopted kids. I wondered if they could stay at your hotel."

Deva's face relaxed. "Of course. I adore mental mages. They are so much fun to toy with."

I cleared my throat. "Yeah. This one's good. He almost got into my head. The ruling magic caught him, but I didn't even feel a tingle."

Deva's eyes sparked with interest. "Is that so? Jonas has always been a crafty man. I bet it wasn't an accident that he found such a jewel."

I didn't have anything to say about that, so I changed the subject. "The gate guards at the main entrance requested reinforcements. I'm going to ask Ara for vampire backup, but I wouldn't be upset if a couple of dragons could work shifts, too."

Deva tapped the arm of her chair. "I see. Is there evidence the Bellicose will come through the front gates?"

"I wouldn't put it past them. Ann Marie said they're amassing in the valley, so they're planning something. I have a feeling they're already in Allure somewhere waiting."

"The Council will not be happy with my continued involvement in these matters."

"They'll be less happy when their citizens get slaughtered because we didn't act." I stood and moved to the window. "I'll never understand why the other leaders don't make an alliance with you. It's stupid. Not only because you're so powerful, but because you've ruled for a long time and are wise."

"You flatter me."

"It's the truth. Even my psychotic mother left you alone. I get you didn't take part in politics before, but I need the support. If the Council doesn't like it, they can file a complaint with the crown. I'll be glad to throw it away."

"I stayed out of politics to protect Drake. My dragons were happy to patrol the city without dealing with the rules that come with political alliances. Some are not happy that I pledged our allegiance to you."

"I understand. Your family is your treasure, and they come first. But I could use the help, and Drake won't have to deal with being blamed and ostracized. Not under my rule." I paused because I didn't mean to say that. "I need advice from people who understand what I'm up against. Mat and Helen are great but don't have ruling magic."

Deva's eyebrows drew together. "You are serious about taking the throne."

"I don't have a choice. The coalition is falling apart." I shook my head. "Tracy tells me I put on a persona when I go into what she calls 'queen mode.' Quin said I make stupid choices and should trust that people will follow me. I don't have any idea how to do that because all my training said I had to do things a certain way, so I fall back on it." I turned and met her eyes. "It's difficult to be myself and stick to that training. And I refuse to sit on my throne and order people around. I'm sure as hell not giving up my freedom and existing inside a protective bubble again. How do I get from point A to point B?"

"It's not necessarily a bad thing to have a public persona."

"But?"

"But you don't need one, love. I suspect you think you need to act a certain way based on Mathias's tutelage. He sees things in black and white and rarely bothers with the gray areas. You are nothing but shades of gray. He assumes that fixing your magic will solve all your problems."

"It won't. I'll still be the same traumatized, emotional mess, but with more power." And I'd still lack confidence because, at my core, I didn't want to be queen.

"Correct. There is no magic fix to gaining confidence." She must have picked that thought out of my head. At my raised eyebrow, she continued. "I rule a race that I am mentally connected to, so it is different for me. However, people respect a confident and honest leader more than a leader who pretends to be something she's not. If you solve your confidence problem and learn to be yourself in all situations, you will become a better queen than even your grandmother."

"How?"

"Oh, I'm sure you'll figure it out. You are very crafty."

"Am I?" I'd never thought of myself that way. It gave me a new perspective, just like Drake said I needed.

"Weren't you the one who turned the tactics used by the bellicose against them?"

I had. I'd used their propaganda proposal to erase some of the damage they'd done to the hybrids. "Mat said using propaganda is a slippery-slope and that I should refrain."

"Did he? Interesting considering he convinced you the world is all rainbows and roses."

My lips twitched. "So, how do I get from point A to point B?"

"You need to stop worrying about how you're viewed and do what's needed. You have very good instincts and powerful allies. Use them."

I squared my shoulder. "Alright. I need you to show me how to use that summoning room."

"Why?"

"I want to summon the person behind the Bellicose uprising."

The predatory smile that formed on Deva's face caused me to take a step back. "Do you?"

"No one has been able to find their so-called king. If the summoning room can summon anyone, why not him?"

She tapped her chin. "You must make your intentions very clear when using the room or it will bring anyone who loosely fits the description."

"So I can't just say Bellicose leadership?"

"You can but I wouldn't recommend it."

"What do you recommend?"

The controls to the summoning room were in a solid white, spelled room that only Deva or Drake's magic would open. We stood shoulder-to-shoulder and stared at the three hovering runes that controlled it. She pointed to a peach-colored one with three complicated squiggles and a line across it. "This rune is used to store magic. Never store more than needed for the job as a precaution. It will only accept Dragon or Ahl ruling magic. Your grandmother created these runes and allowed me to infuse my magic in them. It's for you to use should you need it."

"Me, specifically?"

She waved a dismissive hand. "Her descendants."

"Okay. How do I gauge when it's enough?"

"Practice. Not to worry. Drake filled it in my absence and it still holds enough for a summoning. The rune's glow will fade as the magic drains." She pointed to a blue rune with what looked like a primitive drawing of a person. "To summon a person, you put your hand inside this orb and think of nothing but them."

"And the last one?"

"The one with the arrows sends people anywhere in the world. It allows you to send the summoned home."

I took a deep breath. "Once in there, can they break out of the room?"

"Of course not, love. Your grandmother was very thorough in her magics."

"Right." I rubbed my face. "I don't have a name or a description. You said I need to be specific."

"Consider the person behind the Bellicose uprising and you will get the mastermind. If it's their king, then he will appear."

I nodded and shook out my hands. The impulse to run from the room made me lock my knees. I stretched a shaky hand toward the rune.

Deva clutched my wrist. "Relax, love. Intention and concentration are equally important. Do not let doubt or stray thoughts enter your mind, or you may summon the wrong person."

"Right." I closed my eyes and imagined the Bellicose. The division they caused. All the pain and suffering I'd seen, including Deva's and Drake's. Anxiety melted into anger, and I steered it toward determination. I wanted the mastermind behind all the problems. I concentrated on that one person and shoved my hand inside the rune.

I'd expected a grinding noise or tingling. Maybe a flash. None of those things happened. I didn't feel or hear anything.

Until Deva drew in a sharp breath.

I snapped my eyes open and peered through the spelled wall to see what caused her to gasp. "No." I took an involuntary step back.

The woman who stood in the center of the summoning room spun in a slow circle, then tilted her head back and her eyes narrowed. "You have broken your contract, Deva." My mother's cold, hard voice rang through the room, sending a flood of memories careening through my head.

A memory of her standing in her office lecturing me about decorum. The sharp bite of her slap across my face. Bone-chilling fear when those eyes focused on me. An axe swinging toward her head.

"That's. She. No." I stumbled back until I hit the wall on the other side of the room and closed my eyes. It felt like someone took a battering ram to my gut. I bent over and clutched both arms around it. My pain tolerance for physical pain was higher than most. I could take a blow and not even flinch. But the pain of betrayal was an entirely different story. It hurt so bad I wanted to curl into a ball and cry forever. Learning that Mat lied to me about her hurt. But this? This was much, much worse. I dry-heaved.

"Hello, Anitta." Deva's voice carried a coldness I'd never heard as she gently patted me on the back. "What a pleasant surprise."

"Let me out of here now and I won't extract my price."

"Price for what? I broke no contracts." Deva didn't sound surprised to see my mother. At all. Which meant she knew she was still alive.

"You knew." That big secret that Mat and Drake shared popped into my head. "You all knew." I swallowed the pain and straightened myself. The last time I'd seen my mother, she fought with Jaques. Then.... I shook my head and examined her. The gold and red streaks in her hair were duller than I remembered. Her once bright golden eyes faded to more of a caramel color. And her power? She wasn't any more powerful than a mid-level mage. "How?"

Deva turned her bronze eyes toward me, but didn't answer my question. "What do you want to do with this traitor, Jenella?" Her voice rang with glee.

"I...what..." I tightened my arms around my stomach. "Can we hold her? Our restraints won't hold her."

Deva's eyes lit with bronze fire. "If you order me to, I can keep her contained. But you must order it." She raised an eyebrow.

"You're trying to avoid breaking a contract," I muttered.

"Clever girl."

I turned my attention back toward my mother, who stood in the center of the summoning room with her hands on her hips, exuding more confidence than someone in her position should. It sparked a fire inside me I couldn't contain. My magic unraveled.

Her eyes widened, then narrowed. "No. You manipulated that worthless little shit to do your bidding!"

The ruling magic slammed her to her knees. "Contain this traitor so she can't escape. Make sure it's not comfortable."

Deva rubbed her hands together in glee. "Right away, Your Grace."

I stormed out of the room, not bothering to put my glamour earrings back in or wrap my magic. I didn't know which way to go. My emotions swung wildly between anger, shock, betrayal, and...everything. Too many emotions. I wanted to run away more than I'd ever wanted anything in my life.

As I stepped out of the building, I sensed Quin incoming, so I flashed away without using a circle. I needed to get somewhere to release the pressure in my chest from the utter betrayal of everyone I knew. Except Tracy. I doubted she knew. But I'd bet my life that Quin, Ara, Mat, Drake, and even Bastien knew. I rubbed my chest to ease the pain as I marched toward the square to flash...where? I needed to be alone, and the traitors could find me no matter where I ended up. The best I could do was buy myself some time. Changing directions, I headed toward the transport station.

Chapter Twenty-Four

JEN

I STARED OUT THE window of the transport to Mage Mountain and tried to tamp down my anger. I managed to put my glamour earrings in and wrapped my magic around myself. My emotions were so turbulent that it took every drop of energy I had to keep it from unraveling again. The transport was nearly empty. Not many people wanted to travel to a rural pocket that stayed frozen year-round. As a result, the cylinder-shaped transport was much smaller than most, with seats for around a hundred people. The larger public transports were disk-shaped and could seat around three hundred.

The cylinders were newer models with fewer windows than the discs, but they were faster. The cloaking failed a few times during testing, and humans saw them. The pilots had to speed back to the pockets for repairs. The next day, the human internet lit up with stories of UFO sightings. I was told the problem had been fixed, but I hoped I'd witness a malfunction to distract me from my simmering anger. Unfortunately, the ride was uneventful, so I had to close my eyes and concentrate on my breathing. The last thing I wanted was to blow us all up in a fit of rage.

I exited the transport station in Brumal and shivered as I breathed in the crisp, cold air. The magical transports to Mage Mountain only ran every three days, so I could stay in my cabin in Brumal enough time to think. It would give me time before anyone tracked me down. Except for Drake. The stupid bond would probably tell him exactly where I went, and he'd blab to his co-conspirators.

The ruling magic vibrated, so I threw the thought out of my head and made my way toward the cabin.

The pocket of Mage Mountain was deep in the mountains of Montana and had two seasons: light winter and deep winter. Because of the unfavorable climate, it was sparsely populated. Villages were sprinkled throughout the pocket, but most only housed one faction of paranormals. Brumal was the largest and most diverse village, with mages being the majority. Sasquatches roamed around the pocket in family units but stayed near the gate on the other side, near the Rübezahl village, so they could come and go from the human world. There was a coven of witches and a house of vampires in the pocket, but I didn't remember where. The snow elves, including King Olwen, lived near the base of the mountain in the center. When I reached the end of the main road, I flashed to my cabin on the outskirts of town.

When we got sent there against our will, Quin had stolen or bought me winter clothes spelled for warmth. I headed straight to my bedroom in the two-story cabin, dry heaved twice, took a long shower, changed into them, and added a few more layers. Then I headed back downstairs, tuned my inherent magic to a fire spell, and lit the fireplace in the family room. The magichef was fully stocked, so I ordered water and settled into a chair in front of the fire to work through my emotions.

I stared out the window at the morning sun. Or was it afternoon? I wasn't sure. The motivations my mother put in her diaries ran through my head. After reading about them, I understood how calculated and selfish she was. She never did a single thing that didn't benefit her. So why insist I work a job for three years and then spend another two transitioning into my role of queen? If she were still queen, then it wouldn't matter because I'd take on the role as her second until she passed the title to me. Unless she couldn't hold on to the power anymore. She was diminished. She either broke a contract, or someone took the ruling magic away. I closed my eyes and tried to remember when I'd gotten my first power upgrade.

I couldn't. But I remembered she slapped me across the face for it.

I rubbed my sour stomach and tried to work through that. If the ruling magic came to me before she faked her death, then she likely planned that entire scene in the dungeon.

"She planned the whole thing," I said out loud. "But why?"

Was she trying to look like a hero so I'd trust her? Did Mat throw a wrench into her plans when he became a killing machine to protect me?

She didn't have the power to hold the throne, so she what? Rekindled the Bellicose so she could swoop in and save the day after they tore The Coalition apart? If anything, it explained Mat's overprotective nature toward me. He feared her and thought keeping me in a bubble would keep her away. Idiot.

All this time, she was just out there plotting her plots and living her life like the battle in Mahri never happened. Like Mat and I didn't almost die several times. Like he didn't kill all those people to save me. In her world, everything was A-okay and going as planned. Meanwhile, here in the real world, everything was far from fine. I gasped as the dull ache in my chest grew. I curled into a ball and let the tears come.

When I'd cried my last tear, I sat up and tried to look past the sharp pain of betrayal to figure out why everyone knew she was alive but me. To work through it. Deva, Mat, Quin, and Drake all knew. Maybe Bastien, though I doubted it since Deva kept her secrets so well.

She was smart and manipulative. So much so that I wouldn't doubt she gave herself an out when she pledged the dragons to follow me. And she knew exactly what she was doing when we summoned the person behind the Bellicose. I was sure of it. But why? I wanted to think it was a convenient way to skirt around any contracts my mother forced her into. But her reasons probably had multiple layers like everyone else's.

Then there was Mat. He flat-out told me why he'd made the contract, but in my ignorance, I didn't understand the gravity of the situation. He was a lost cause when he believed he was protecting me. I almost couldn't be mad at him because he was being himself. Almost.

And Drake? Deep, dull pain spread through my chest, so I rubbed it as I took a sip of water. I believed he was on my side. Someone I could rely on. More than that, I was convinced the ruling magic created the bond to help me. But what if I was wrong? With the way Deva acted, she could have manipulated the whole thing. She said it herself that dragons were hive minded. What if Drake wasn't bonded to me by choice or fate, but because Deva manipulated the whole thing? The thought that I was stuck with someone who didn't want me hurt worse than the betrayal. And that pissed me off.

I remembered Drake's devastation when he couldn't tell me the secret he held. The pain that came through the bond when that pyramid device snatched me out of his grasp. It was honest. That he kept the bond and the big whopper of a lie to me for a year hurt, and he'd answer for it, but I didn't think he did it for nefarious reasons. At least, I hoped not.

I stood and paced. It felt like I'd been thrown into a game of chess that had been going on for centuries. I couldn't change the game because I was just another piece on the board. Nor could I see past the other pieces to get a clear picture of the players or the score. I couldn't win that game as a pawn, nor could I sit by and wait for the next move. I wasn't built like that. If I wanted to win, I'd need to flip the board and cause the other pieces to scatter and then burn it down.

I whirled around and grabbed my coat from the rack by the door, and shoved my feet into my boots. I needed to find some cross-country skis and get to the mountain. Then find out which cave held the First. If I got lucky, it would fix my magic and I could go back to Allure and kick some asses.

The town of Brumal had a tight-knit community, and the people were wary of outsiders. I didn't blame them. They had to fend off people trying to wield the unique magic of the pocket every few years. The last time I'd visited, I'd accidentally put the entire town to sleep when the ruling magic got out of hand during a chimera fight. By the anxious looks as I passed the locals, they hadn't forgotten. Though I'd spent some time there, they still considered me an outsider. I tried to tamp down my anger and look friendly as I headed toward a shop that carried spelled winter sports gear.

After buying a pair of cross-country skis and the accessories required to use them, I went to a secluded area and tried to remember the instructions. Mat took me cross-country skiing a few times when I was a teenager, but I hadn't been on them in a while. Butterflies danced in my stomach. The skis had a spell on them that would allow me to move super fast. I made sure my winter clothes covered me from head-to-toe, put on a pair of goggles, and picked up the poles.

The first mile was slow. I didn't want to leave the well-groomed trail or activate the spell to move fast until I got the hang of it. Once I did, my confidence grew. A big, sloppy grin lit my face as I left the trail and headed toward the mountain. I giggled when the speed spell activated and hurled me through the trees. I tuned my inherent magic to a wind spell and used it to cover my tracks.

When I hit a small slope, I tried to slow down. The skis jerked to the left. My left leg moved with them, but my right one jerked the other direction. I lost my balance and fell sideways, rolled through the snow and banged my back on a tree. I groaned as I sat up and ran healing magic through myself. When the pain in my knee receded, I stood and tested it, then searched for my skis.

I'd just refastened them when my head exploded in pain. Drake realized I was gone. Burning anger replaced the determination and joy. I bent over and put my hands on my knees and closed my eyes. The bond wasn't hard to find. The source was anchored near my core and wrapped in both dragon and ruling magic. I reached through it, flipped him the magical equivalent of the bird, and stuffed it with healing magic and slammed it shut. The pain eased enough for me to function, so I set off again at a slower pace.

I stopped inside the tree line as I reached the first cave. My stomach sank. A boulder that hadn't been there before blocked the entrance. I shielded my eyes against the colorful magic that swirled around it. Mage mountain held a magic like no other. It shot out at unpredictable intervals in beautiful plumes of all different sizes. The colors were so vivid the mountain looked like a dreamscape. Every color had hundreds, if not thousands, of tones. Some of them weren't even colors that I'd seen anywhere else.

I moved on to the next cave a couple of miles away. Like the first, I stayed back to hide from the search team that I knew Drake would deploy. Just before I got to the second cave, a sense of foreboding washed over me. I shivered and headed toward a crop of trees and bushes that provided cover but still had a partial view. After I removed my skis and switched to my snow boots, I scooted to the edge and peaked out.

My phone vibrated in my pocket and pulled me out of my stupor. I was running out of time. Heart hammering in my chest, I stood and flashed about ten feet in front of the cave.

A flash of light and two katanas blocked my way. "What are you doing, Jenella?" Mat's rough voice asked.

My magic unraveled, and I shoved both hands into his chest. "Fuck you, Mat! You knew. You knew she was alive. Yet you let me think I watched her die. Let me grovel in my grief and pain and never so much as uttered a word. You can go straight to hell."

He ignored my outburst and moved toward the cave. "Please tell me you're not upset that people care about you enough to protect you from pure evil."

I shook my head and elbowed him out of the way. "You think I'm upset that you care?" I leaned in and ran a hand over the rock that blocked the opening. "That's dumb. I'm pissed that you pulled everyone I care about into this mess and let them manipulate me. That you betrayed me. I'm pissed that all this time..." A tear streaked down my face and froze before it dropped. The rock was wedged into the entrance so tight I'd never get in. "Just leave. I'm not playing this game anymore."

Mat's head tilted. "Oh?"

Drake strode through the trees, ran his wary eyes over me, and inclined his head toward Mat.

The sense of betrayal and hurt flooded me at his appearance. I folded my arms and made sure the bond was closed. "And you can fuck right off, too."

Mat ignored me again and poked at the rock. "Mage Mountain draws many people, but no one can wield this magic. What were you hoping to accomplish here?"

I shook my head. "None of your business."

Drake reached for my hand. "Jenella..."

I jerked away from him. "Don't you have someone else your aunt wants you to pretend to care about?"

He flinched. "My aunt has nothing to do with our bond."

I shoved at the rock. "Uh huh. I'm sure your expert manipulator of an aunt never so much as gave you an ounce of encouragement."

"You're being irrational."

I spun around and the ruling magic smashed into him so hard it would have obliterated anyone else. "Do. Not. Tell. Me. How. To. Feel."

Drake released the barrier he'd formed with his own ruling magic. The bastard didn't even have the decency to look bothered by my attack. "That's not my intention. We bonded when my aunt was missing and I hadn't had contact with her in a very long time."

"Against your will."

"There's no such thing as bonding against your will."

I wondered if he was right as I worked to pry the rock out of the cliff. If that was the case, then I chose him instead of the ruling magic. I wasn't sure what I felt about that. I blasted him again.

"What are you doing, Jen?" Mat asked.

"Not that it's any of your business, but this place calls to me." I headed to the bushes where I stored my stuff, grabbed my backpack, and flashed back to the entrance. I left the skis behind. "If I'm right, the First inside this mountain is grandmother. If I can fix my magic, I'll become powerful enough to rule without Drake."

Drake cleared his throat. "So, it's your opinion that this magic is the key to controlling yours?"

"Yes."

"And you came here alone to try."

"Yes."

"And you're making this decision out of anger? Even when I made it clear I wanted to tell you but couldn't?" Hurt laced his voice.

"I'm not arguing with you right now, nor do I want to be reasonable." I beat my fists against the rock, then tuned my inherent magic to a shredding spell. The colorful magic snaked out and dissolved it before it hit. I threw my hands up in frustration. "I just want to go inside the mountain and figure out why it calls to me. After that, I'll give you five minutes to reason with me." I leaned in to find a crack.

Mat folded his arms. "And me?"

"You've already explained. Funny how that doesn't ease the pain and anger." I ran my hand over the rock. "Every time I come to this pocket, the compulsion to go into these caves gets stronger."

Drake's hand landed on my back. "Compulsion?"

I shook his hand off. "Does no one take my anger seriously? And yes. It's a compulsion."

He focused on the cave entrance and shook his head. "And it's urging you to come alone?"

I sighed. "No. That part was all me, since everyone in my life is a traitor."

"I see."

They didn't see. They didn't understand how hard it was to ignore that call the last few months, nor did they see how wrecked I was inside because of their actions. I wasn't emotionally capable of forgiving them just then. That didn't mean I wanted them to get hurt or killed by helping me. As Quin would say, it was a stupid idea. "You two need to leave."

"No," they said in unison.

Drake leaned forward. "You are justified in your anger and can feel it for as long as you need to. But your anger does not negate the fact that we care about you. If you go in there, I'm going with you."

"As am I," Mat said.

The cave groaned, and I forgot whatever argument formed in my head. Two enormous bodies moved in front of me, blocking my vision. I shoved at them. Neither moved. I leaned to the left to see what was going on. Without warning, the colorful magic snapped out and grabbed us, and we got sucked through the entrance. Colors whirled around me as I spun in tight circles.

The cave walls zipped by and alternated between cramped to cavernous. It felt like my brain got replaced with cotton. I got dumped on my feet and stumbled two steps to catch my balance. Mat and Drake crouched a few feet away, fire in their eyes as the colorful strands danced around us. My stomach bubbled, and a laugh escaped me. My body tingled as I turned in a slow circle. The cavern had carved stone with copper, purple, silver, and blue ribbons through it. A polished stone bench sat in the center. The magic shoved me toward the bench. I let out a giggle and danced toward it.

Drake latched onto my arm and tugged me back. "If you ever want to reconsider before you act, now would be the time."

I swung my head toward him, a sloppy grin on my face. "I have an overwhelming compulsion to punch you in the face and sit on that bench. Do I completely trust either compulsion? No. But it sure would make me feel better to release some of this anger and not feel inadequate for once." I laughed again when the magic danced at my words.

"You are not yourself," Mat growled. "And this magic is unnatural."

I didn't comprehend Mat's words. The feeling that I'd reached the moment I'd been waiting for my whole life flooded me. I embraced it and pulled it in until I thought I'd drown. The magic felt clean and made me want to focus on it. The bubbly happiness in my stomach replaced the burning anger, and I clutched it like a lifeline. Something in the back of my head told me it wasn't right, and I shook my head to clear it. "Do you feel giddy with this magic?"

"There is a certain rush to it. There always has been," Drake said.

"Ah. Another secret. Let me guess, you can't tell me about this, either."

He rubbed his eyes. "I've existed for a long time, Jenella. As a result, I know many things you don't. I'm not telling you that you can't embrace it. I only want you to use caution."

His words cleared my head a little, and I leaned toward him. "Oh, yeah?" I pointed to myself. "This is as cautious as I can be. Get used to it or leave. I don't care which."

Mat latched onto my wrist and yanked me away from the bench. I tried to pull away, but he tightened his grip and moved me to his side. "What aren't you revealing about this magic, First?"

Drake's eyes met mine, his hunger and pain so intense I fought the urge to hug him and tell him everything would be okay. Or jump him.

A gurgling sound escaped my throat. Damn it. "I don't know how to react when you look at me like that."

Drake focused on my mouth. "Don't. You need time to process your emotions, and I want to give you what you need."

"Why?" I squeaked.

"Because you are smart and funny and everything I hoped my mate would be."

Mat pulled me closer to his side. "This is not the time."

I closed my eyes and tried to tamp down the excitement and joy shooting through my stomach by remembering the reasons for my anger. My head swam with the high the magic created, so I couldn't quite spark the fire. "I wish I could be this easy and carefree all the time. Self doubt is my default and I'm forever trying to decide how to present myself. On top of that, rage simmers right under the surface and it's a toss-up as to which one is going to win. Maybe the mother induced Bellicose will kill me and put us all out of our misery."

Mat's eyes glowed and his scary magic ramped up. "We need to get her out of here."

The pity and hatred I expected to see in Drake's eyes was absent. Instead, he eyed me like I was a puzzle he wanted to solve. "I agree."

I shook out of Mat's grasp, danced to the bench, and lowered myself onto it. The strands of magic wrapped around me and tickled something deep inside, and I laughed. Without warning, the giddy feeling disappeared, replaced with an overwhelming sense of sadness. "Will I ever gain my confidence and pull myself together?"

Mat's eyes met mine, his face hardening at what he saw. "You're not yourself right now."

Drake lowered himself to the bench beside me. "You will. The first step is to stop saying you're a mess. You're not even the biggest mess in the palace. One only needs to look at your brother and his mate to see that." His lips formed a small smile. "Even your anger issues are benign compared to us."

"Again, not the time," Mat interjected.

"I'm trying to be less self-centered and see things from a different perspective, but every time I make progress, some asshole lies to me or hides the fact that my mother is alive and well and running the Bellicose from me. It makes self help...difficult."

"You're not failing as bad as you assume." Drake rubbed his chin. "And Mathias is right. This cave is clouding your judgment."

Drake was so patient and kind. He always knew just what to say. He deserved better than me. At least after I punched him in the face for lying to me. I opened my mouth to say so.

The colorful magic kicked into a gale-force wind. I latched onto Drake's arm as we jumped to our feet.

The magic gained speed as it swirled tighter around us, herding the three of us into a corner and forming a cocoon. It lifted us off our feet and spun us in circles. I lost my grip as I catapulted into the air. My lungs constricted, and I gasped for air. My stomach tried to revolt but was empty from all the rage puking I'd done earlier. I fought to stay conscious as it slammed into my core and fused with my magic. I screamed at the electric charge that lit up my body. It was worse than even the summoning chamber. A thousand needles with barbs on the ends dug into my skin. I screamed. I thought I'd die.

Without warning, it melted, and I landed on my feet. I bent over and slapped my hands on my knees as I tried to orient myself. I couldn't see anything but swirling colors, so I concentrated on catching my breath. My lungs burned, and every inch of my body ached.

A large wedge of the magic stabbed into my chest.

CHAPTER TWENTY-FIVE

JEN

Icy air burned my lungs. I wheezed as I released the death grip on my chest and stood. The rock that covered the cave sat to my left and once again sealed the entrance. Mat stood a few feet away, his arms folded and his eyes hard.

I bent over and dry heaved, then leaned my forehead against the icy rock.

"Are you okay?" Drake's deep voice came from beside me.

"What the hell just happened?"

He pulled out his phone and held it up. "You found another First. We didn't lose time."

"How is that possible?" I checked my own phone. Sure enough, only five minutes had passed since we entered the cave. "Did I wake someone else?"

"No. And you shouldn't come back here."

"Why?"

Drake tried to take my hand, but I pulled away. He sighed. "Only one First can erase memories and change time. She is not to be trifled with."

I swung back toward the cave, my eyes wide. "I was right."

"Perhaps."

A plume of colorful magic shot out, and I shuffled toward Mat out of habit. The plume swirled around me once, trailed over Mat and punched into Drake's chest. It came out of his back and formed the shape of his dragon before dissipating.

I fought a smile as his eyes narrowed.

Mat ignored the exchange and pointed to a black splotch in the snow a few feet away. "That is the diseased magic, but diminished. The vampires reported finding something similar here this morning."

I leaned down to get a better look. It was bug magic, but it wasn't wiggling. The normally wiggly black ant-like things had faded to gray and were curled into crusty little balls. I'd never seen dead magic that didn't dissipate.

I glanced back toward the cave entrance. "It's dead." I rubbed my chest. "What happened to us?"

Mat shrugged as he scanned the tree line. "We need to move."

"We can't just leave that stuff there." I tuned my inherent magic to the neutralizing spell and...nothing happened. As a matter of fact, I couldn't feel it. I clutched my chest. "I don't have any magic," I croaked.

Mat stopped scanning the forest long enough to turn his hard eyes toward me. "What do you mean, you don't have any magic?"

"I just tried to tune it, and it's gone. I can't feel anything."

Drake's hand settled on my shoulder. "I can feel your magic. It's stronger and tastes different."

My eyes strayed back toward the cave. "Is it fixed?" I held out my hand and tried to conjure a ball. Nothing happened. "If so, why can't I use it?"

"We'll figure it out." Drake handed me my pack. "Do you want a ride? Or are you going to ski?"

My blank stare landed on my pack. If I couldn't use my magic, then we were screwed. For the first time since our mad dash across the world, I felt truly, completely vulnerable.

"You can't wrap your magic around you?" Mat asked.

I shook my head. "I can't feel it."

"I'll ski with Jen." He moved toward the bushes where I'd stashed my skis and returned with them, and another pair that I figured were his.

I stumbled over and put on my skis. "I'm going back to the cabin. You two can return to Allure."

Mat snapped on his skis and scanned the area. "The Rübezahl have information, but they'll only share it with you."

I tried to wrap my magic around myself out of habit and stood on shaky legs. "They always have information and it always wastes my time. Kind of like trying to wrestle the truth out of you."

Drake morphed into what he called his third form. A creature bigger than an elephant with long black fur tipped in green. He lowered his koala bear like head, his long, sharp fangs inches from my face. *I'll go with you. Are you going to be okay?*

"I'm fine." I turned and started down the path back to the cabin, the events of the day spinning through my mind. My head ached as I came to a stop just before we met the well-groomed trail that led back to Brumal. "I can't wrap this magic around myself, and the mages in Brumal are already wary of me." I tapped my chin. "We need to keep my new captive and this magic issue to ourselves."

Lying, even by omission, rarely leads a person down a positive path. If you need an example, I'm right here.

"Stop being so wise and reasonable."

Very well. I'll keep my rational thoughts to myself. Just know that Tracy and Deva will know your magic changed. My aunt will guard that particular prisoner well. Dragons talk. It would be better if you gave yourself time to process and then tell those close to you the truth before they find out on their own. He padded through the trees beside the path without making a sound.

"Can't stop yourself from being reasonable, huh?"

His laughter boomed through my head. *No.*

"I agree with both of you," Mat said. "If word gets out that you can't use your magic, our enemies will seize the opportunity to eliminate you. If they find out mother is alive, it will split the coalition. You should inform your inner circle so they can better protect you."

"Ha. Jokes on you. I didn't summon mother. I summoned the person behind the Bellicose. And if I'm not mistaken, they've already divided the coalition." I activated the spell on my skis to move as fast as they could go and zipped toward the cabin before he could answer. I sensed people inside the cabin as we approached and came to a stop. My heart pounded as I removed my skis and my now useless glamour earrings. "Great. More people." I stormed through the door and bolted to my room.

Tracy followed me and used a spell to dry my hair and braid it after I showered. She wouldn't leave when I tried to pretend nothing was wrong. As I put on some fresh clothes, I told her about my adventure to the cave. She listened without comment. When I was done, I perched on the edge of the bed. "There's one more thing. I had this bright idea that since we couldn't find the Bellicose leadership that I could use the summoning room to catch the person responsible." I closed my eyes. "My mother is still alive and in Deva's custody." The last sentence was a whisper.

She paced back and forth a few times, stopped. Met my eyes and paced again. "Okay. So, you what? See her, flip out, and have an overwhelming urge to run away from the whole thing. You remembered a First was here and came by yourself to check it out as an excuse. Then, Mat and Drake freak out, drag us all here to search for you …" She held up a finger. "Then the three of you got sucked into a cave, maybe got your magic fixed, and came back here. Is that correct?"

"You forgot the part where I can't use my magic or wrap it around myself to hide it, but other than that, yes."

Her eyes narrowed. "Which First were you looking for?"

"I suspected it was my grandmother. This place has always called to me."

"Right. But you still don't know if it's her and something happened to your magic. I mean, that's a lot, Jen." She sat down next to me and slung an arm over my shoulders. "What are you going to do?"

I wiped my clammy hands on my pants. "About my mother? Nothing until I calm down." I swallowed. "I'm going to have to confront her eventually. About Mat and Drake?" I shrugged. "In my dreams, I've relived the trauma of her death a thousand times. I've mourned her, hated her, and blamed myself for what happened that night. And Mat knew she was alive the whole time. Nothing in my entire life has ever hurt like this betrayal."

Emine picked that time to slide through the door. She closed it behind her and lowered herself to my other side, her usual crazy completely absent. "I never met her," she said.

I closed my eyes. "So Mat lied to both of us."

"No, he operated within the perimeter of his contract."

"Right. That doesn't make it hurt less."

"No one is asking you to bury your pain and move on like nothing happened. Not a single person who knew expects your forgiveness, either. But here's the deal. You chose to take your throne early. You chose to use the summoning room without knowing who you'd get. This? This is the consequences of making tough choices. Sometimes you save the Dragon Queen, and other times, your world comes crumbling down around you."

"I mean, I get your point," Tracy said. "But you're not helping."

Emine patted my hand. "Of course I'm helping. Jen hasn't had to face the harsh realities of life since she was a toddler. It's annoying, but true. Now that they've smacked her in the face, she's freaking the hell out. The question is, how are you going to channel that energy? You gonna run? Or are you going to use it to fuel yourself?"

I blew out a breath. "It's impossible to keep Drake at arm's length because he'll just stalk me. I'll work it out with him first. But Mat?" I shook my head.

An elbow smashed into my ribs. "That's not what I meant, dummy. I meant, use it to fuel you in your job. You know, as queen? To lead?

Remember when you went all doll room? Like that. Use all that hurt and anger to fuel yourself until you can process it."

I rubbed my side. "Tracy's right, you're not helping." Still, I got her point. I needed to put on my big girl panties and stop running. As I stood, I glanced at the clothes I'd abandoned in the corner. The thought that after everything I'd learned that day, I'd never be the same person as I was when I put them on that morning popped in my head. "I'm going to go meet with the Rübezahl. Then I'm going to relearn my magic and crush the Bellicose."

Emine stood, the crazy smirk back on her face. "That's my girl."

The Rübezahl were mountain guardians who lived in a tiny village near the bottom of the mountain. Drake, Quin and I had stumbled on it when we got transported to Mage Mountain by the Bellicose. Since Quin, Bastien, Tracy, Mat, and Emine were there, they insisted on going with me to meet with them. I stepped out of the cabin, put my hand on Drake and Tracy's arms and...nothing happened.

My heart skipped a beat. "No." I closed my eyes, concentrated, and tried to flash again. Nothing. Before a full-scale panic attack kicked in, Mat put his hand on my shoulder and flashed us to the outskirts of their village.

No one said a word about my not being able to flash as we hiked through the deep snow toward the town. It was bitterly cold and my face burned, but I couldn't activate my healing magic. The last thing I wanted was to end up in Drake's armpit again, so I pulled my scarf around my face and eyed the village.

Tracy craned her neck. "Wow. This place is really something."

I slowed and walked beside her. "Can you feel the well of magic coming off the mountain?"

"Yeah. Yeah, I can. I mean, it's strange and I couldn't use it. Yours kind of feels like that now."

"Yeah. I'm pretty sure mine's just like it now," I whispered.

Tracy pursed her lips. "It could be worse. I mean, at least it feels clean."

We fell silent as we entered the village and headed down the narrow cobblestone street, common to pockets that didn't allow human vehicles. The snow had been cleared, so walking became much easier. We passed a smattering of businesses but didn't see anyone. I stopped in front of the shop where we got directions during our brief stay in the pocket right after my coronation and dug in my pack for the gift I'd brought. I didn't need to send my senses out because of the magic upgrade. Ten of them crowded into the back room of the shop and a couple of hundred spread throughout the town. I relayed the information.

"I don't like this," Mat said as he scanned the buildings.

"It's fine. They call me in about once a month, so they're familiar with me." I didn't want the others to see how bad the mountain guardians freaked me out. I shoved my pack in his arms and stepped inside, trying to ignore my pounding heart.

The same man I met every time stood behind the counter. I gave him a slight bow. "Guardian. It's good to see you again. I brought you a gift." I set the small wooden figurine of a bear scratching a tree on the counter. It was handmade, and I'd bought it from a struggling artist. Something the Rübezahl would appreciate.

The Guardian studied the figurine. "A very appropriate gift indeed." He set it down. "And completely unnecessary, as we have already established a rapport."

I shrugged. "I liked it, so I bought it for you."

"A gift given without expectations is the purest form of kindness. I shall treasure it always." He hugged the figurine to his chest before setting it on a shelf behind him. The nine other Rübezahl I'd sensed popped through the back door. A woman and eight small children floated over to the figurine. I didn't know how spirits had kids, but they were kind of cute.

The Guardian ignored them and rolled out a map. "The sasquatches found the strange magic here." He pointed to a clearing a few miles away. "You will need snowshoes as your First cannot fly in this pocket." He led me to a display and picked out six pairs. "The mountain does not allow it because flying supernaturals disturb some locals."

A child yanked on my coat. "Your eyes are pretty. Where'd you get them?"

"From my mother." I couldn't keep the bitterness out of my voice.

His mouth dropped open. "How'd you get em out of her head without breaking em?"

The Guardian set the snowshoes on the counter and took the kid's hand. "Mages do not steal body parts, they inherit them. We will study mage physiology later, John." He led the kid back to his match. "My apologies. We are a very isolated society, and it is difficult for the young ones to understand the differences in cultures."

A shiver ran down my spine. "No worries."

He nodded toward the map. "The mage village had a couple of kids get infected with that magic two days ago. The mages shot the one responsible and set him on fire before calling us in. We tracked a second mage to the mountain where he tried to infect the magic. It threw the man off and slammed him on the ground. He then entered the spirit realm. No damage to the mountain's magic was reported."

I wondered if it *was* my grandmother. I hoped so. If it was a different First that messed with me, I was in trouble. "Okay."

"We are concerned that if they keep trying to infect the mountain, they will eventually be successful. The map will guide you, but it's in sasquatch territory. I've arranged a guide to meet you at their border."

I tucked the map in my pocket. "Thank you for calling us in, Guardian. Do we have your permission to cross your territory?"

"Yes. But do not flash. My people are on edge, and there is no telling what will happen should you startle one of them."

I gathered the pile of snowshoes and dragged them and the map to my disgruntled team. I didn't tell the others what happened inside the cave. They noticed my magic was different, though. As far as I knew, Mat and Drake hadn't said a word to anyone about it, either. Except maybe Emine.

We moved through the trees in a loose line. It soon became obvious that Tracy and I sucked at using snowshoes. We clung to each other and wheezed as we trudged behind Drake and Mat. The others hovered around us like we were the weak links.

Tracy wrapped her scarf around her red face to help guard against the biting cold. "These snowshoes are weird."

Emine slapped her on the back. "Pot, kettle, and all that."

Quin took his off and threw them at my feet, then went fluid. He reappeared on an outcropping of rocks and prowled around them. Then leaned over to examine something. He returned as fast as he left and claimed his snowshoes. "There is some unmoving magic."

"Unmoving?" Mat asked.

"Yes. It is not crawling."

I trudged toward it. "We saw this at the base of the mountain. I tried to neutralize it." I clamped my mouth shut to keep from saying I couldn't.

Quin ignored my strange behavior. "It smells off but not diseased."

I leaned over and examined it. Sure enough, a small puddle of unmoving bug magic splattered across the rocks.

Bastien, who'd remained silent the entire way, poked at the magic. "It's dead."

I turned toward the twinkling mountain. A plume of a thousand colors shot into the air and swirled around before dissipating. I cleared my throat. "Mage Mountain magic kills it. Have any of you ever seen dead magic before?"

"How often do you come here without me knowing?" Mat asked.

His question was casual, but rubbed me the wrong way. I had to bite my tongue to keep from saying something snotty. "About once a year. More since we met the Rübezahl."

Tracy nudged Bastien aside and threw a spell at the dead bug magic, erasing it. "Your obsession with this pocket makes more sense now. I've seen dead magic before. It's what happens when a low-level mage or weak witch uses a dissipating spell."

I adjusted my snowshoes. "It's not what we're here to find."

We continued toward the area where we were supposed to meet our guide. A few steps down the trail, a nine-foot-tall creature with long arms stepped into our path. He bent his knees, threw his arms out to the side and opened his mouth, revealing flat, human-like teeth. His roar rattled my bones and had just enough of a high pitch to make my ears ache.

We stopped with more precision than a marching army. None of us screamed and ran like he was expecting.

The sasquatch beat his chest and stomped toward us.

Drake reached out and slammed him into the snow at our feet as if he was light as a feather, rather than a nine foot tall beast.

I shuffled to Drake's side. "Who are you, and why are you trying to scare us?"

The sasquatch's eyes grew large. They darted around the group before landing on me. Recognition flashed through them and he melted into a naked, hairy man. "I'm sorry, Your Grace. The Guardian didn't tell me we'd be guiding the queen and her entourage."

Humans had a lot of names for the various breeds of sasquatch shifters. They called them big foot, skunk ape, yeti, and many others. They were all closely related and usually lived in remote areas as family units. Some lived in the human world but stayed close to a pocket so they could hop inside when the humans got too close. They weren't technically classified as shifters, though. Like griffins, chimeras, and dragons, they could shift but were their own magical species. Most sasquatches stayed in their animal form. They weren't aggressive. The only time one got aggressive was when they were in danger or protecting their family. "You're our guide?"

The sasquatch shivered as he climbed to his feet.

"You don't need to stay human." I motioned toward Drake and Bastien. "These two can use mind-speak."

The look that crossed his face was a strange mixture of awe and anger. It disappeared so fast I thought I might have imagined it. "Strangers have invaded our woods lately." He swallowed, his eyes darting to Mat. "Are you going to kill me?"

I shot Mat a look. "Regent Mathias only kills when necessary. If you don't make it necessary, you're fine."

He scooted away from Drake, who stood beside me with his teeth bared. "The First is not to be trusted, my queen. He is as likely to take over the coalition as to help you."

Drake's eyes flashed with anger. "She's my mate. I would never harm her."

I elbowed him in the stomach. "Why?"

"Because the Firsts are restless and angry. I cannot tell you what to do, but it's best to use extreme caution when dealing with them." He tilted his head toward the sky. "Bwoop. Bwoop. Bwoop." His call echoed off the frozen landscape, and a wall of sasquatches of various sizes stepped out of the trees. "We will guide you to the problem. Follow me." He morphed back into his bigger form and herded us off the trail, away from Mage Mountain.

Tracy latched onto my arm. "Is this okay, Jen? I mean, these things are scary."

"And they stink," Emine said, her voice laced with amusement.

"We're fine. The guardian asked them to guide us, and no one double-crosses the Rübezahl." I sounded more confident than I felt.

"This is colossally stupid. However, it is on par with Jen's usual decision-making skills," Quin said from behind us.

"Just remember who saved your ass twice the other day, Quin." I shot back.

"Which I wouldn't have needed if you did not lead me into another colossally stupid situation."

"Yeah. She's a ball of fun," Emine said.

About a mile in, the sasquatches spread throughout the trees and stopped. "What you are hunting is one-sixth of a league in that direction." He pointed the way we'd been heading. "I dare not take my family any closer."

I didn't know they could speak in their animal form. Neat. I peered through the trees. "Thank you for showing us a shortcut."

"You honor us by visiting today and helping to cure the disease."

His words struck me as odd. I didn't have experience with sasquatches, but I knew they weren't that dedicated to the crown. They appreciated the security we provided, but that's about as far as their loyalty took them. "Sure."

The group gathered around us and took a knee. "We hold you in the highest honor, Your Grace. Good luck with your cleaning." They rose as one and melted into the forest.

I watched them until my senses told me they were far enough away not to hear us. "That was a little much."

"It was the biggest crock of shit I've ever heard," Emine cackled. "We hold you in the highest honor? Hilarious."

"It was hideous," Bastien drawled. "You have never done a single thing to help them or this pocket."

Drake rested his hand on my shoulder before I could respond. "It was a little over the top. Is this place we're heading on the map the guardian gave you, or is the crock of shit going to go to waste?"

A laugh escaped me before I could remember I was mad at him. I held out the map and waited for Mat to take it. "That was pretty cheesy, wasn't it?"

Tracy chuckled. "I wasn't going to say anything, but yeah."

I watched a blur I knew was Quin glide through the tops of the trees, scouting. "It's been my experience that most protocols are a bunch of awkward and cheesy. I get I shouldn't adopt a queen persona, but I have a hard time imagining how that would work."

"You shouldn't. I mean, there's always going to be people who like formalities, but you don't have to let them control you. You're way better with people when you're just Jen, rather than when you put on your professional face and become Queen Jenella."

I wasn't sure how to stop doing that. I added it to the list of things I needed to work on. It was so long that I doubted I'd ever get to everything.

Mat rattled the map. "Let's head out. Try to be quiet as you move."

We trudged through the trees. My senses were in overdrive, so I focused on them. The entire pocket lit up inside my brain, and I clutched my head and tried to turn it down. It didn't work. I concentrated harder until it shut off. I tried to process what I sensed ahead of us.

"Don't try too hard to use your magic until you understand it," Drake said.

"Agreed. You are more likely to harm us than the enemy," Mat growled.

Bastien stood to my left, his black eyes sharp. "What happened to you, Jen?"

"Magic adjustment." I held out my empty hand as if it would explain everything, then yanked it back.

He rubbed his chin. "You can't use it?"

I glanced at Mat in case a safety lecture was coming. "Erm. No. I can't wrap it around me or even feel it. Drake said it's different."

"Adjustment is a good way to describe it," Drake interjected. "I can still access her magic. And she'll figure it out, given enough time."

Bastien's eyes grew hard. "Explain."

The rage I'd stuffed into a box exploded, chasing away the chill from the air. I took a step toward him.

Drake latched onto my shoulder and yanked me back. "This is not the time or place. You have no control over your power and don't want to hurt anyone."

I didn't want to let it go. I wanted to explode. I wanted to go on a rampage and take down everything and anyone who so much as irritated me. The thought made me stop in my tracks. If I went that route, I'd become my mother. The rage drained. Drake was right that I didn't want to hurt the people I cared about, no matter how bad their betrayal stung. "Dang it, Drake. You did it again." I turned my attention back to Bastien. "We can't remember what happened aside from some severe pain on my part. Mat, is your magic any different?"

"No. Have a care, Bastien. Jen is on the verge of losing her temper and she can now kill with a single thought."

Bastien raised an eyebrow. "This is information we should have had before leaving the cabin and wading into danger."

"Yes. A bunch of information isn't shared among this group. Information that has severe consequences when discovered." I waved a hand. "It doesn't matter. Let's find whatever this disturbance is and take care of it."

Drake kissed my temple, sending shivers down my spine. "I'll work on being less reasonable if you work on your anger issues."

"You just can't help yourself, can you? I'm going to start referring to you as Mr. Reasonable."

Bastien threw his head back and laughed. "I never in all my life considered that someone would find that old crotchety dragon reasonable." He shook his head. "What the hell happened to you two?"

I crossed my arms, then dropped them to my sides. "None of your business." Drake cleared his throat, so I let it go. "We need to move. Bellicose are gathering at our borders, and a million other things need attention."

Emine's eyes bounced from Mat to Drake and landed on me. "Gabe and Linda have a couple of packs of shifters heading this way. They've already scouted and found something strange in the clearing we're headed to."

I threw my pack on and headed east without looking back. Drake was right about my magic and that I needed to work on my temper. The ruling magic used to lash out at people for perceived slights, but now I couldn't feel it vibrate with anger. It felt like I'd lost a limb. I'd almost bet my magic merged, and this was how it was always supposed to work, but I was terrified that I'd never learn how to use it. Or that it would kill someone I loved because I had no control. My shoulders slumped. I picked the absolute worst time to come to Mage Mountain and wished I would have listened to everyone who told me to think before acting.

We'd trekked for a long time before I realized I wasn't tired. I always knew that if I got my magic to mix, it would give me an energy boost based on what my mother and grandmother could do, but this seemed different. I didn't have a single sore muscle. Relief flooded me as I realized my healing magic was working without me having to engage it. And it was much more effective.

As we rounded a bend, I sensed a group of about a hundred paranormals. I signaled the others, ducked behind a tree, and lowered myself to the ground. I slithered forward until I could see better.

A demon stood on a stump and addressed a group of paranormals. "When the fake queen gets here, we will eliminate her. Her dragon lover cannot shift, so he will not be a problem. The Bloody Prince, his mage slave, the witch, and the vampire will surrender. Victory will be ours!" He threw his arm in the air.

The crowd didn't cheer. Some stood, some slumped in the snow, while others paced in circles. Bug magic swirled around them, making them look like husks of the people they once were. I noted at least five types of paranormals caught up in the magic. There were a couple of trolls, a few sasquatches, shifters, witches, and mages. I even saw a human-sized fairy, her blue skin bright against the snow.

"We need to call in our backup," Mat said.

"How far out are Gabe and Linda?"

"The shifters will be here soon. Emine has about ten or fifteen enforcers on standby. In addition, we have Ara and Deva en route. Those two alone are equivalent to an army. Can you handle this without your magic?"

I appreciated he didn't order me to stay back, though I knew it was because I was a little volatile. I considered the question. There was no way to reel in my power. If the people in the clearing weren't such zombies, they'd already be able to feel it. "I'm certain I have my full power now. But I need to figure out how to use it."

Triumph and concern reflected in his eyes. "You need to go home."

"No."

"They can feel your power and you can't fight back."

"I can still fight. I'll just have to be smart about it."

Mat's eye twitched. "How?"

I didn't know it was possible to growl and whisper at the same time. "I can ride on Drake's back."

CHAPTER TWENTY-SIX

JEN

AFTER WE RETREATED FROM the clearing, I clamped my hands on my head and tried again to sort through everything I could feel in the pocket. A group of people were moving fast through the forest from the east. Several shifters headed our way in a group from the west. Two of them were more powerful than the rest. One in front and one in the group's rear. It had to be the Shifter Alphas.

The villages were lit with activity, and two powerful people approached from the North. Deva and Ara didn't feel the same as they did before my adjustment. I wondered why for a few seconds before I shook off the thought. It didn't matter.

A black dot in the clearing represented the demon. His infected minions registered as greasy sludge. A few small, tainted dots spread throughout the forest. I counted them.

"What are you doing?"

"Gah!" I was so engrossed I forgot to keep my senses on Quin. "Damn it, Quin. How do you always know when to sneak up on me?"

"It does not take much skill to read an open book."

"I was sensing people. Our backup is about five minutes out. There's a bunch of slightly infected supernaturals watching the clearing."

"I see. Yet you failed to notice what was right in front of your face."

He had a point. "Because I'm surrounded by a group of powerful people who I consider friends and family."

Quin disappeared.

When everyone arrived, we had about thirty people. The infected outnumbered us three to one. I leaned against a tree and watched Gabe, the Alpha Shifter, and Mat discuss strategy. I could feel their nerves and determination. Linda, the other Alpha Shifter, emanated quiet confidence as she formed shifter teams. Deva and Bastien huddled with Tracy and Drake. Excitement, anticipation, and fear emanated from them. Ara and Quin leaned on the tree beside me. A handful of vampires scattered around us. I recognized a few of them from visiting their house. Not a single feeling emanated from any of them. "Goody, a new power," I mumbled.

Ara raised an eyebrow.

I waved her off and stalked toward Mat. "The demon has that clearing locked down and a lot of backup scattered in the forest."

"Gather around," he ordered.

I wrapped my arms around myself to hide my shaking as he directed the teams in different directions. One vampire went with each shifter team. Deva and Ara stuck together, while Quin refused to team up with anyone. When Drake's hand landed on my shoulder, I leaned into his hard body. I was still pissed that he'd kept the fact that my mother was alive from me, but I realized it wasn't his fault. My emotions were all over the place because of it. I soaked up his warmth like a sponge to ease my nerves. Our job was to lead them on a chase around the clearing. That would be easy since my magic was like a beacon.

When everyone was in place, Drake stepped away, and I shivered from the cold. With a bright green flash, a giant creature with long black fur tipped in green emerged. He lowered his koala bear's head. *Can you flash?*

I tried. "Afraid not."

He lifted a front paw, careful not to hit me with his claws. *Climb.*

I climbed onto his paw, and he flung me onto his enormous back. His back was wide, so I couldn't sit like I was riding a horse. I scooted up to his neck. It was still too big, so I shuffled around, laid on my stomach, and dug my hands into his fur. I put my head down and took a giant sniff. His scent calmed my nerves. I blamed the stupid bond. I sat up again and shuffled around until I got comfortable. "Okay. Done."

Drake's chuckle rang through my head.

Emine conjured a scythe and held it up. "This will last an hour."

I had to latch on to Drake's fur and lean way over to reach it. "Thanks."

Magic wrapped around me, holding me in place. When I jumped, it squeezed me tighter. *Your magic usually holds you, so I normally don't bother. I understand if you hate me right now, but I'll do my best to protect you.*

"It's not hate, but betrayal. And no one could reach me way up here." I tried to tune my magic to the dissipating spell, but it didn't work. "I haven't felt this helpless since I was a kid," I whined.

'You're not helpless, just temporarily impaired. See if you can run your magic down the scythe.'

It didn't work. "How come you can use my new magic, but I can't?"

I'll help you with it later. You might want to switch to mind-speak. We are getting close.

I focused my senses on the meadow. *Five tainted people about twenty meters in front of us spread out behind the trees.*

Drake moved through the frozen forest without making a sound. You'd think a creature bigger than an elephant would break branches or the snow would crunch as he walked. But he was so silent that the witch didn't even turn around when Drake reached out with a giant paw and smashed him into a tree.

Green magic shot out both of his sides, and I heard four dull 'thumps.' I glanced around, noting several unconscious or dead paranormals on the ground. *Wow.*

Too easy. These people are not warriors, nor do they have great power. I don't understand why the demons are recruiting the weak.

We initially thought it was because their magic couldn't control more powerful paranormals. With the revelation that my mother is behind them, it makes sense.

How so?

This magic is so strong it infected Quin. If her goal is to divide us or cause an uprising, it's kind of smart to recruit weaker paranormals. If I didn't have magic sight, this would look like a bunch of powerful supernaturals slaughtering the weak during an innocent gathering. It fits everything I've read in her diaries about how she thinks. What do you want to bet there's a spell recording this that she planned to release?

His footsteps slowed as he communicated the information to the others. *Everyone knows what's going on. You made sure of that. Tracy is looking for recording spells. She's already disabled three of them.*

Good. Let's hope she gets them all.

Mat gave a signal, and Emine appeared in the clearing with her flame thrower. She blew an entire line of infected off their feet with the dissipating magic.

Quin raced toward the demon and buzzed around him in a blur. Ara and Deva stood on the other side but didn't engage in the fight. A wave of Deva's mind magic swept across the clearing, and several paranormals fell to the ground, clutching their heads.

Mat followed Emine in and threw his magic into the mix as Tracy wove a spell that blanketed the clearing. She and Bastien sprinted toward the demon and his pet mage, who sat at his feet. Bastien tossed a potion at him. The demon screamed in anguish as the spell smashed into his chest and took hold, freezing him in place.

Shifters and vampires raced in from all sides. The vampires threw spelled ping-pong balls, while the shifters used teeth and claws to knock people out. Good. I didn't want to kill the infected.

Drake plowed through a family of sasquatches, not even trying to be careful. Heart in my throat, I transferred the scythe to my other hand. I ripped off my pack, pulled out vials filled with experiments that Tracy insisted I carry when she wasn't with me, and threw a few into the crowd. One exploded, and the magic ballooned so fast that one of Drake's legs went sideways. I slipped the potions into my pocket and grabbed a patch of fur to steady myself, even though his magic held me in place.

The sasquatches broke out in ear-splitting roars as the magic washed over them. Logs flew toward us. I ducked as one glanced off my shoulder. I didn't even feel the pain. Odd.

Sawdust rained down in thick clouds, and I sneezed. I snapped my head toward Emine. She gave me a thumbs-up before jumping back into the fray.

A horde of mages and sasquatch charged out of the trees. Quin and Emine flanked them and launched a vicious, bloody attack. I turned my head away.

The group veered toward us. They carried clubs and hand-carved spears. The mages blasted bug magic toward some of our shifters. A large gray wolf dove in front of them and tore into the group. When they passed, he lay limp on the ground. A vampire vaulted over him and slashed across the mage's throat with her claws. I lost track of them when Drake spun sideways and swiped, knocking three sasquatches across the clearing. They tumbled like bowling balls, obliterating everyone in their path.

Bastien's black dragon fire came from my right and hit a group of tainted witches. But not before they released a spell that zipped toward a bubble Tracy placed over the demon and his mage. A spear barely missed my foot as an ogre tried to stab Drake. The spear broke on scales that replaced the skin underneath his long fur. I swung the scythe toward the ogre's shoulder. At the last minute, he ducked, and the magical scythe went straight through his neck. "Shit, shit, shit. I didn't mean to do that!"

Drake kicked his rear legs out like a horse, dislodging someone trying to climb up his back. I spun around and got hit by something coming from the other side. A spell hit Drake, disrupting the magic that held me. The creature and I tumbled off his back and landed in the mud near the demon.

The sasquatch let out a squeal of delight as he picked me up and backhanded me across the face. I landed on my shoulder and skidded across the snow. Searing pain shot through my arm as I rolled and came up in a crouch. The fiery anger I'd suppressed exploded through me. I ignored my pain and dug out the vial that Tracy's dad gave me and charged. The sasquatch opened his mouth to roar. I uncorked the bottle, dumped it down his throat, and kind of wish-willed it to work. My wish spiraled out, exploding in the multiple colors common to mage mountain. Every paranormal within twenty feet slumped to the ground. The sasquatch released me, staggered two steps, and fell on his ass. I turned to run, slipped in the sloppy snow, and landed on my back.

Quin's face appeared above me. He held out my scythe as he pulled me to my feet. "Another brilliant plan?" He asked as he swung his sword at a mage.

I didn't bother to answer as I charged back into the battle. I ducked a blow from a sasquatch and slid between the legs of another, punching up into his balls. He hunched over, and I barreled into the side of his knees. He hit the ground and got caught up in a discarded trapping spell.

I craned my neck to find Drake. Mat moved through the crowd of infected, his Katanas glowing blue with magic as he dropped people like they were practice targets. He no longer cared if he killed. Emine sat on the ground at the edge of the clearing, using a laser to cut through legs and cackling. Tracy and Bastien stood on top of a log, protecting the spells she put on the demon. The infected buzzing around them like a cloud of mosquitoes.

Bastien tilted his head, sucked in some air, and blew a torrent of dragon fire at them. Tracy's dark hair had come loose and ruffled in the wind, but she didn't react to the fire.

I spotted Drake across the clearing. He spun in circles and swung his front paws, smashing everything in his path as he tried to reach me. Bug magic skittered away from him as he moved.

I threw my remaining potions at a cluster of tainted shifters, then sprinted toward Drake. Quin came out of nowhere, snatched me up, and hurled me across the clearing. I tumbled through the air and smashed down face-first into familiar fur. I inhaled his scent again, then raised my head. *Hey, you,* I said in his mind as green magic wrapped around me.

Relief and care crashed through the bond. *I'm sorry I couldn't protect you. They were instructed to separate us, and it almost worked.*

My stomach flipped. *We need to end this.*

Two enormous waves of dragon magic hit us. Drake's magic tightened around me as he sidestepped. The remaining paranormals fell to the ground. Deva reached through Tracy's spell, grabbed the demon by the throat, and said something in a language I was unfamiliar with. My mouth fell open when the demon turned to dust. The mage flopped to the ground.

Deva brushed her hands together. "I think we've had enough fun for one day, loves."

I slid off Drake's neck. He transformed into his human form, caught me in his arms, and set me on the filthy ground. My eyes swept the clearing. Bug magic still coated everything, but no one fought. "I guess so."

Alpha Linda limped up, naked and bloody, a big gray wolf in her arms. I could barely sense Gabe's life force. Tears sprang to my eyes. He was almost gone, and it was my fault. I stretched out a shaky hand and touched his bloody head. I wished I hadn't involved the shifters in this mess. Gabe was a good man who stepped up to help us when we needed it most. He offered his pack so I could socialize as a kid and always had our backs. He didn't deserve to die that way. I blinked to hold back the tears, but one escaped and rolled down my cheek. We needed to get a healer for him, or he wouldn't make it. I opened my mouth to yell for Mat, then snapped it shut when silver light flashed from my hand and coated Gabe and Linda in a silver sheen. I yanked it back.

A naked Alpa Gabriel replaced the wolf. Linda dropped him and jumped back. Gabe's eyes fluttered open, and his skin took on a healthy glow. Linda gaped. I turned to ask Drake what had just happened and realized everyone's eyes were glued to me.

I squared my shoulders and pretended I meant to do it. "Anyone who still has energy, take care of the bug magic. Clear our people first. The rest of you move the living to one side and those who didn't make it to the other. Treat them with respect and make sure they're not infected before you touch them. Emine?"

A crazy smile lit her face. "Yep. Enforcers and healers are on their way. Everyone's trained in how to dissipate the bug magic."

"I can help with that," the Snow Elf King said as he picked his way through the crowd.

I knew he was there because I sensed him pop into the field with a few elves halfway through the battle. I wondered if they were on our side until I spotted them clearing magic from the ground. "Thank you, King Olwen. I sensed a few more spots with this magic throughout the pocket. Can your people clear it?" I glanced back toward the mountain. "I'll try to give you an idea of where it is."

He inclined his head, curiosity radiating off him. Probably because my new magic was shining like a beacon. I turned to Quin and Ara. Quin studied his bloody fingernails while Ara watched the cleanup crews with glazed eyes. "Ara, will you and the vampires help?"

She turned her blank gaze toward me. "Of course, dear. We'll help in any way we can."

"Deva?"

Deva raised a dismissive hand. "You already have my vow."

"Gabe and Linda?"

"We will help where we can, but the missing shifters are our priority," Gabe said.

I focused on Ara. "The sorceress, Ann Marie, said the Bellicose are amassing in the Treasure Valley. Send someone to spy on them. Don't engage and steer clear of the hybrids. Figure out how many, where they are, and what they're planning. If you can, find out how many demons they've summoned."

I expected a tinkling laugh from her, but she replied with a small incline of her head. Good enough. I turned my attention to Gabe and Linda. "See if there's a pattern to the missing shifters and send what you find to my office."

Something flashed in Linda's eyes that I couldn't read. They nodded in unison.

"Mat, secure the pockets and hire more gate guards. No one with that magic gets in or out of the pockets. Calvin Cordalia has potions and is willing to deploy his alchemists to protect the wards." I tapped my chin. "What do you want to bet they have bases in Allure?"

"Likely. Along with other pockets," Mat said.

"Find their bases of operation within the pockets and where their support comes from. Have the guards detain anyone who even feels a little off. I'll assign some jurors to gate duty to check people as they enter. Focus on the small pockets first. It's no coincidence that they attacked people in Ferine, Pyron, and Mage Mountain."

"What about you?" Mat's voice was low and dangerous.

"Drake, Tracy, and Quin can help me hit the streets and see what we can find out."

I ignored his scowl as I paced so I could think. A habit our griffin matriarch, Helen, had been trying to break for years. This next part was going to change my life forever. My stomach did a somersault. I took a couple of deep breaths and switched to mind speak. *Drake, what do you think about pigs?*

They're delicious.

I suppressed a nervous laugh. *Have you seen how mean they can be?*

I've heard that, although they are no match for a multidrakelandarnarian.

I rubbed my sweaty hands on my pants. *If I do what I'm about to do and you lie, betray, or withhold vital information from me again, I will suck your brain out of your nose and feed it to the pigs while it's still functioning. And believe me, you don't want your brain anywhere near them. It would be more agonizing than being bonded to me.*

I thought nothing could be more torturous than being bonded to you.

His suggestive tone made my face flush. *I need a promise.*

I swear I will never lie, betray, or withhold vital information from you, Jenella. If you need any information from me, I'll give it to you freely, should you ask. If I'm under a silence contract, I'll tell you. I'll try to be honest with you and request that you do the same. Do not run and hide from me, and I will not hide from you.

It was a little more than I was going for, but it would work. *Agreed.*

The magic contract snapped into place, and I dug into our bond and threw it wide open. Drake rocked back at the force. It felt stronger than before, and I fought not to close it back up. Also, there was no hiding the ruling magic oozing off him. Something he'd spent centuries hiding. The dragons would disown him for it. I closed my eyes. He might have lied to me and stalked me, but he deserved better than that.

I stopped pacing and faced the leaders. "I understand you all have a lot on your plates besides what I've just assigned you. If you can't do what I've asked, now is the time to speak up." No one said a word, and all I got from their feelings was sheer determination mixed with surprise. I squared my shoulders before flipping my thumb toward Drake. "Drake is now in charge of finding and eliminating the Bellicose. This includes coordinating everything I just assigned you and shutting down their labs. You can report your progress to him. We share a bond, so mind your manners."

The feeling of utter shock assaulted me from all directions. I'd just declared Drake my match in public and given him a purpose in the way of the dragons. The wry smile on Deva's face told me she knew my intentions. I ignored her because I still had to work out my feelings about how she manipulated me. There was no way to flip the game board on my own. I needed the people closest to me so I didn't end up dead or chased across the world by assassins. Again. The only people I had were Drake and Tracy. Maybe Mat, though he'd been one of the game players moving me around like a pawn. Either way, if I were going to do things my way, I needed two things. Power and support.

"What are you doing, Jenella?" Mat growled.

"I'm done playing whatever political game this is. I can't win, so I'm flipping the board."

He shook his head. "The game is as old as Ara. You either play it, or you die. There is no flipping the board."

I squared my shoulders and leaned forward so we were eye to eye. "Sometimes, the only way to win a battle is to change your strategy in the field. You taught me that." I waved a hand. "Step one, protect your blind spots. Few people would go against a dragon as strong as Drake, let alone a First." Mat usually only weighed information based on whether I was safe, so I used that. "Step two, break the rules. And step three, win the game."

His face turned to granite. "The Council won't like that. And even if you change the rules, you can't win."

I shrugged. "Exactly. I can't win no matter what I do, so I might as well play by my own rules. Drake will help with that and much more."

"Are you sure about this? It will affect your rule from the start and will make it much more difficult."

"Yes." I talked about the game, but that wasn't why I claimed Drake. Or not the only reason. His unbreakable patience balanced me out in a way nothing else could. He used humor and suggestions, rather than orders, to help me think things through. More than that, he actually gave a shit about me as a person. He made me laugh. Drake deserved to find a purpose and a place to belong. It was what he wanted most. I'd just handed it to him on a golden platter. Sure, it would cause some political problems. And we still needed to work through some major issues. But it felt right. And I needed to feel right after the day I'd had. "I'm not sure if doing things the easy or straightforward way is in the cards for me."

Mat sighed. "This is going to be a nightmare."

"Yes. Funny thing is, I have nightmares all the time, so what's one more?"

His golden eyes examined me as if he were trying to solve a puzzle. "Very well. But I don't like it."

"Noted." I strode back toward the clearing. "We need to return to Allure."

CHAPTER TWENTY-SEVEN

JEN

VERITY TRAILED BEHIND ME as I stormed into my office. "What happened to you?" She reached out and touched my hand, gasped, and dropped it. "Holy hell. Ever consider having a normal day?"

"I have a lot of normal days. Sort of." My shoulders slumped. "I can't run away now. And there's so much I need to deal with." I needed to confront my mother and see if I could push enough buttons so she'd brag about her plans. I lay awake the night before, going over scenarios in my head and trying to deal with my emotions. It didn't help. My stomach was still in knots, and the giant ball of rage made me feel like I'd swallowed a balloon. I stopped by the office before going to Dragon Headquarters to check in. Not because I was procrastinating.

"Right. And your freedom?"

I lowered myself into my chair and rubbed my eyes. "I loved having new experiences and doing what I wanted when I wanted."

"And according to my calculations, you can still have that for two more years."

"Except my magic is a beacon now and I can't hide it. Besides, the coalition might not have two more years."

She leaned against my desk. "And you don't think Mat's been doing the job well?"

"He's a great regent." I couldn't keep the bitterness out of my voice. "But he doesn't have ruling magic."

Her eyebrows drew together. "I've heard you say that before. What is ruling magic, exactly?"

"It's hard to explain. Ruling magic kind of protects and guides. It gives me insight into people, kind of like your magic does, but not as detailed. It makes people *want* to follow me, among other things. I can also suspend other people's magic as a punishment, I think. Though, I don't want to do that. My ruling magic always wanted to beat people down when they disrespected me and offered some protection. When it wanted to."

"You speak in past-tense."

I cleared my throat. "Yeah. I can't exactly use the new stuff. And it kind of did this weird thing to the shifter alpha where it restored him. I need to relearn it."

"Well, that's certainly a problem." Verity moved over to the windows. "You can't be out experiencing life and detecting when everyone can sense you."

"Nope. I can't even return to my house, so here I am." I moved to stand beside her. "It's okay for now. I'll have to figure out a way to have freedom while I rule."

Her calm gray eyes focused on me. "You don't believe you can do that?"

"Not really, no. What about humans? What do their rulers do to keep their identity?"

Verity shook her head. "It's different for them. The media constantly chases them around, so it's hard for them to have a second of privacy."

"Sounds exhausting."

"I'm sure it is. We don't have royalty in the U.S., but I've seen presidents go into office looking young and spry and leave looking old and grizzled.

The only thing I know about monarchs is what I've seen on social media. Most of that's gossip."

"It's probably not a fair comparison, anyway." It didn't really matter. I was born into the position. I had the magic, and I wanted to save the people who were being kidnapped and tortured by the Bellicose. My freedom was insignificant compared to their lives. Besides, we didn't have media that would follow me. Assassins, sure, but not media. I snapped my fingers. "That's it. I'll just go about my business until people stop with the bowing when they see me wondering around. If they don't, maybe Drake will eat them."

She threw her head back and laughed. "You're not going to do that."

I gave her a flat look.

Her laugh cut off. "Are you?"

I chuckled. "The wondering around without an entourage part, yes. It's up to Drake who he does or does not bite." It was one of the things I liked about the bond. I could roam around Allure alone, and he'd show up if I needed help. I wondered for a second if he knew how much freedom that gave me. He knew a lot that I didn't, so it wouldn't surprise me. I turned my thoughts to the Bellicose and their experiments. I couldn't fight that on my own. Mat had used a lot of resources and hadn't even found the leaders. They were bringing demons across, and we hadn't figured out where or how. That had to change. "Let's have a meeting with the magic-wielding leaders. We're going to have to band together if we want to survive."

"That's a little dramatic, but sure."

"Oh, and I declared Drake my Consort. Sort of. I've tasked him with hunting down the Bellicose leadership and put him in charge of gathering information. So, make sure he's involved as much as possible." I tapped my chin. "Do you think Charlotte would transition to his assistant?"

Her eyes narrowed. "Why Charlotte?"

"Because I like her. She's competent, and I like having an urban sprite on the team. Since they can blend into any garden, they see a lot of things no one else does. Drake is patient for a dragon and will help build her confidence, and she'll give him a different perspective. He likes that."

"You are insane if you think that First will let you run his life."

"I'm not interested in running his life. I just want him and Charlotte to feel like they belong. Oh, and give him the office across from mine. He'll just perch on the roof and stalk me if he doesn't have his own place here. Might as well accommodate him."

Verity strode toward the door. "Like I said, insane. I'll set it up."

"And give Quin an advisor's office down the hall. Maybe he'll stop hanging out in here."

Her laughter echoed through the room as she shut the door.

We held the meeting of magic-using rulers in a large conference room on the castle's second floor. I sat at one end of the enormous oval table, with Drake on my right and Quin on my left. Deva sent Bastien to represent the dragons so she could keep an eye on my mother. Tracy got squished between him and Drake. Mat sat at the other end of the oval, Emine on one side, Olwen, the Snow Elf King, on the other. Olwen's long, silvery blue hair gleamed in the light and contrasted against Mat's golden tones. The shifter alphas occupied the chairs beside him, even though they weren't magic users. The centaur queen and a dwarf's Crown Prince sat across from Bastien and Tracy. He'd created a defense system that he incorporated into dwarf properties across the planet, and we needed his expertise.

Several others filled in the gaps, representing twenty-five paranormal races who used magic. Twenty-six if I counted the shifters. I didn't bother asking Mat why they were there because I was afraid of accidentally killing him during an argument. Besides, Quin wasn't a magic user, and I didn't want his presence questioned.

I peeled my eyes away from them when the tension in the room became thick as soup as the President of Covens led her team in. She glared at Tracy as they took the remaining seats.

Bastien growled.

Tracy ignored them and beamed at Calvin. Her dad and the Vice President of Covens smiled back. I was glad he came because he had a calming demeanor that the President of Covens lacked. I hoped he'd help with communication between us and the witches. Still, it had to be hard for him.

I waited for the griffins to finish setting up sandwiches from Thaddeus, my leprechaun friend's deli, and leave before I spoke. "We recently found a demon in Mage Mountain. The Bellicose are targeting smaller pockets for now, but they are amassing in the Treasure Valley. I've called this meeting for two reasons. The first is to develop a strategy to counteract the bug magic and save our people. The second is to inform you that we've captured and are holding one of their leaders. Emine, what have you got?"

She glanced up from a heaping plate of food, then held up her fork. "According to the Enforcers in Mage Mountain, the locals reported Bellicose operatives in the area last week. The locals hunted them down and killed them. Brumal mages take guarding the mountain seriously and have trained to use the neutralizing magic that Tracy created. The Rübezahl notified the queen about an outbreak in a rural area. We went in and took out the demon and brought the rest of the Bellicose to Allure. Very few reports came from Pyron before a recon team stumbled on it. The pocket is still a mess, but we sent resources their way, including architectural mages, healers, and extra protection. We're investigating what happened in Ferine. It doesn't fit with the small pocket theory because it's got a good-size population, and the only target was a shifter compound." She stuffed a big bite of food in her mouth.

"It is too bad your table manners are not as clean as your report," Quin said.

Tracy shook her head. "Geez, Quin, that was rude."

"Yes." Quin turned his focus to me. "I have deployed several vampires to the rustic human city in the valley. They report a large Bellicose presence in areas where hybrids have settled. Their numbers increase daily."

"How many of them voluntarily work for the Bellicose, and how many were abducted?" Olwen, the Elf King, asked. "And what types of paranormals are they?"

"We assume the majority are volunteers, as they do not carry the disease," Quin answered. "There are various types of paranormals, with the majority being shifters."

"We need to communicate better," I said. "And we need a better strategy for finding the traitors among us."

Mat leaned forward. "Agreed. Let's go over the measures we've taken and see where we can expand on them."

I inclined my head.

He motioned toward the alpha shifters. "Linda is working with the PISD to find the missing shifters."

"I've hired several private detectives to find them and gain intelligence about the Bellicose. They are infecting and abducting entire packs. The packs are infecting any low-level magic users they come across. A detective we hired almost got caught in it. We've traced most of them to a few apartment complexes in the human world, but it's unclear if it's another lab or a training ground. We suspect it's the latter."

"I've deployed several magic users to there. They're working with the hybrid leadership, and distributing dissipating spells that non-magic users can activate. It has been an effective defense, but not sustainable," Mat added.

"It's not." Bastien leaned an elbow on the table. "Dragons are patrolling both the pockets and the hybrid communities in the valley. The only activity they report is in a few smaller pockets surrounding Allure. We are monitoring the apartment complexes the Alpha shifter refers to. We believe their next target is the hybrids."

I turned to Drake. "Is Jonas working on that?"

"Yes. Ann Marie is working with the alchemy witches to develop a potion to make them immune. Still, she's unsure if she can protect them all."

Emine raised her hand. "Speaking of witches, the Enforcers have contacted various witch covens to see if they will help to make spells to protect non-magic users. The covens have been resistant. Something about an order from the top."

Heads swung to the President of Covens.

Her lip curled, and her muscles tensed. "You don't have the right to commandeer my people without my permission."

"No, but I do," I said. "I'd rather not because we don't want to undermine you. The written decree the Leadership Council approved allows the teams to access cross-species resources. That means the enforcers can request help from the covens without your approval."

"It's your fault they're in peril. Therefore, *you* can clean up the mess. It's not our problem."

The entire table went still. I kept my face blank and didn't comment because she was just trying to get a rise out of me. After an uncomfortable silence, I raised an eyebrow.

She slammed her fist on the table. "Everyone knows the Bellicose are after the incompetent upstart queen. I do not see why the rest of us must sacrifice for someone so obviously unfit to lead. Look at the ridiculous team she has assembled. Two manipulative dragons, an excommunicated witch, and an insane vampire. We should hand her over to the Bellicose and be done with it." She flung a spell at me.

The spell hit me mid-chest and dug for my heart. I scooted my chair back and jumped to my feet. My new 'fixed' magic eliminated it and pinned her to the wall. It didn't vibrate or warn me like the ruling magic used to. I flung my hands over my ears when a deafening roar came from my right.

Tracy pounded on the side of a now much bigger and harrier Drake to help me. Bastien snaked an arm around her waist and pulled her back. A massive furry clawed hand swiped at the president, leaving gashes across her torso. The wounds closed. She'd taken a strong healing potion before the meeting. That meant she planned the attack.

I put a hand on Drake's fluffy arm and opened my mouth to speak.

She threw another spell.

Drake's magic flooded me, and a green barrier formed and blocked it.

Ice coated her hands, compliments of King Olwen.

Quin became a blur as he lunged.

He didn't make it before two glowing katanas blocked his way. Mat didn't even bother to stand as he conjured them, ran his magic through, and flipped his wrist. The katanas pinned the President's stomach and right shoulder to the wall without wasting a drop of blood. Magic spread through her, paralyzing her and sealing her lips.

The entire room froze. Drake shrunk back to human size and inclined his head at Mat. Quin dropped to the floor in a crouch.

"Tracy, see to Jenella, please." Mat's rough voice was as icy as it was calm. He turned his attention back to the team of witches, his eyes molten gold. "Perhaps you have forgotten who I am. I admit I have become lax since taking on the role of regent, a side effect of being a diplomat." He leaned forward, meeting the eyes of everyone in the room except mine. "Do not underestimate my ability to kill without remorse to protect my sister. You attack her, you will die. I will not hesitate, nor will I bother asking questions. This is your only warning."

Chills ran down my spine at his cold, calm statement. I knew without a doubt that he meant every word. The realization hit that I was one of those people guilty of believing he'd mellowed over the years. Even though I'd witnessed him kill several times when we were on the run. Even though he tried to insist I be more diplomatic. Time and love for my brother had dulled my memory. My anger at him making that deal with my mother drained. I still had issues with it, but I understood it. He made it his life's mission to protect me and he would sacrifice anything, including my trust to accomplish that. I shook myself out of my thoughts and realized the room was so silent I could hear Emine chewing her popcorn. My eyes narrowed. "Are you still eating?"

"Oh, yeah. That was the best show I've seen in a long time. Can we do it again?"

A witch bent over and vomited.

"Let's take a break and reconvene in an hour." I pointed at Calvin. "The President of Covens will be turned over to the Crown Juror for examination and punishment. She is no longer welcome in my leadership council. The witches will need to send a new representative if you want to keep the seat." My voice shook more than I wanted, but I kept my shoulders squared as I skirted around Drake, latched onto Tracy's arm, and marched out of the room.

By the time we got to my office, we had a procession following us. I dragged Tracy in and shut the door in their faces. I waited for the privacy spell to snap into place. "Talk to me."

"He...it...Was that real?"

"Yes."

"But it happened so fast."

"Not really. That was kind of slow for Mat."

Tracy melted into a chair and rubbed her chest. "The witches will not be happy about this. I mean, they worship her. They're never going to believe she started a fight."

"Right." I flung the door open. Verity sat at her desk, eyeing the crowd of people in the waiting area. "Will you send someone to retrieve the observation spell from the conference room, please? Use it to release a statement that the President of Covens attacked me unprovoked and has been removed from her position on the leadership council." I shut the door and turned back to a wide-eyed Tracy. "Problem solved."

She raised her head, her eyes filled with rage and determination. "What will happen to her?"

"It depends on what Titus finds. If she's working for the enemy, she'll be put to death. If she attacked me unprovoked for any other reason, it'll be up to me and Mat to decide her fate."

"I hope she's working for the Bellicose. I'll be glad to kill that monster."

"Will you? Kill her, I mean."

"Yeah. No. Can we just not talk about it right now?"

"Sure. Do you want me to let Bastien in?"

"Yeah."

I opened my office door and a group of people rushed in. Bastien picked Tracy up and swept her out the door before anyone could talk to her. I watched them go, then turned my attention to Drake. "Your new office is across the hall. I've made Charlotte, an urban sprite, your assistant. She's great, but a little skittish."

His lip twitched. "Really. And will I be staying in your apartment?"

I hadn't thought about that. Well, I had, but more as a fantasy than reality. Plus, I had a lot of issues to work through before I could even consider that. "Um..."

His shoulders shook with laughter. "One thing at a time. Let's address the bug magic first, then we'll talk about our cohabitation."

We gathered in a different conference room an hour later. Because Titus was leading the efforts to read people at the courthouse, the President still hung on the wall in the old one. Mat called her continued wall-hanging fair and just, and I didn't bother arguing with him.

Helen forced her way into the new conference room and placed pitchers of iced tea and water on the table, and patted Mat's shoulder. Griffins appreciated decisive violence. Everyone except Quin avoided looking at Mat as they took their seats. Two witches were missing from the original group. Others were pale. Calvin was just as beautiful as always, except for the grim expression on his face.

Gabriel, the Shifter Alpha, eyed Mat. "You are right that we all forgot about your ability to kill without blinking an eye. The shifters will not make that mistake again."

"Smart," I said. "Calvin, update us on your progress with the potions, please." I held up a hand. "I poured your test potion down the throat of a sasquatch yesterday. It worked great."

He nodded. "Very good. We have improved on it. The dragons have provided the needed ingredients and the sorceress Ann Marie shared her knowledge. The elves have agreed to grow the rarer ingredients, so we should have enough to distribute as a vaccine soon."

My eyes slid to Bastien. Deva didn't do things half-assed. It was one of the many reasons I was glad that she agreed to follow me, but couldn't help but wonder what kind of manipulative plan she was cooking up by helping the witches. I dismissed it and refocused on the meeting. "Right. Thank you."

The Dwarf Prince leaned forward. "I have many ideas to increase the overall security of the pockets."

"I'd like to hear them."

"Agreed," Mat said. "Submit them to my office."

A self-satisfied smile crossed his face. "I will do that, Your Majesty."

By the time the meeting broke, I was optimistic that the elves and dwarfs would help, and we already had the vampires and dragons. I still doubted the witches, other than Tracy's dad, were on board. The shifters agreed to work with Mat on strategy, but nothing more. They wanted to find their missing and infected people, they said.

My stomach growled as Tracy and I made our way to the kitchen. I wanted to make sure she was okay and that Helen and George hadn't incited their large family of griffins to start a war with the witches because of the attack on me. You never knew about them. But also because neither one of us ate anything at the meeting.

"What are you thinking and feeling?" I asked as we settled into our chairs.

She let out a breath. "Before I met Bastien, revenge against her was my entire identity. I'd stalk her and knew her every routine. I even made a plan that included sacrificing my life to take her out. Then Bastien swooped

in and gave me something else to live for. I didn't want to lose that."
She rubbed her stomach. "My dad didn't want me to do anything to
her, which I never understood, so he was thrilled that I had something
else to focus on. Dad practically pushed me at Bastien at the first sign
of a bond. I mean, I still want revenge, but..."

"It's not as important as it once was."

"Yeah. I found people to care about and, in the process, sort of lost
the drive."

"But you're still hollow and grieving."

Tracy nodded. "That was...badass, how Mat handled her. Still, I'm
worried about the fallout."

"Me, too. I went into that meeting wanting to build bridges with the
witches, not alienate them."

Tracy seemed confused and disappointed, but not upset. I wondered
if she'd ever see her vengeance. I changed the subject to give her a break.
"So, are you going to work with your dad over the next few days?"

"Yeah. I'm worried about this magic. It's popping up everywhere."

"That's how they designed it, I think. They want to take over the
coalition, so they designed a spell that does the legwork for them."

"Lazy." Tracy stood. "I mean, how are they so sure it won't take over
their people and turn them into zombies, too?"

"Great question. They must have a way to protect themselves." I
tapped my chin. "I'm going to have to confront my mother. Then, I
want to go to the human world and look around."

"Will she talk to you? I mean, it would be helpful, but I picked you
up off that bathroom floor at the thought of going to Mahri. And this
is so much bigger." She leaned forward. "Do you want me to go with
you?"

I shook my head. "No. I need to do it alone. And you need to help your
dad." I rubbed my chest as another stab of betrayal shot through it. Tracy
was right that it was going to be tough. But if I could convince my not-dead
mother to brag like she did in her diaries, then I might learn some vital

information to take down the Bellicose. "If I can't do it, we're screwed. She's the only good lead we've had."

CHAPTER TWENTY-EIGHT

JEN

I SAT AT MY desk, looking over the report Drake sent me about what the various leaders were working on. The Bellicose were actively recruiting in the smaller pockets, so some leaders were consolidating their people into the larger ones. Some had put in requests to expand their territories in those pockets to accommodate the influx. It made sense, but I never learned how to do the magic to expand their territories or the pockets. Not that I could, since my magic was still not working.

On top of that, the number of people the Council sent to us to check for Bellicose involvement overwhelmed the Jurors. I suspected the leaders would use rooting out traitors to settle scores. What I hadn't considered was that the score they had to settle was against me. I rubbed my aching head. I'd only been queen for a few days and already wanted to pull my hair out.

Quin sat at the end of the conference table in his weird vampire trance. Or maybe he was sleeping. It was hard to tell with him.

I yawned and stretched my arms over my head. He didn't come out of his stupor, so I opened the envelope that was delivered the day before from the First, Jonas. As I read through the proposal, a different kind of pain shot through my head. I rubbed it and threw the bond wide open. Blocking the bond had become such a habit that I did it without thinking. Since I made our bond public, Drake started this game where he would wait a few minutes before poking at it. I'd respond by opening it, shouting at him and slamming it shut again for a few seconds. Mature, I know. But I hated the sudden headaches and that he was attempting to train me. And I was still more than a little pissed that he knew about my mother and never said a word. He found the game amusing, so I played it both out of spite and to make him smile.

I left it open this time and continued reading through the proposal. "Hey Quin, have you found more out about that hybrid vampire?"

"We are giving Jedediah a chance to track her down and present her to us before pursuing it ourselves." His lack of sarcasm made me focus on him. He slid into the chair across from me. "Do you have a problem with that?"

"It's not really my business. I was just curious." I handed him the proposal.

He read it at record speed. "Interesting."

"As my advisor, what do you recommend?" I wanted to approve it right away, but knew there would be massive push back from the other leaders. If Quin liked it, I'd run it by Mat. A reasonable, cool-headed stance for me. In the past, I would have whined and threw a fit. But that seemed dumb now because it never accomplished what I wanted it to and did nothing to cool my anger or solve problems.

"You are serious about this advisor business."

"Yes. You even have your own office down the hall."

"Hmm. One would think you would recognize your decision-making flaws, yet you never do." He shoved the papers in front of me. "I suggest you follow your intuition."

I grinned. "My intuition says to sign it right away. I've realized that I'm nothing more than a pawn who got thrown into an established game I can't win. I plan to flip the board." Quin wasn't there when I told Mat, and I thought he might help. "This is a good start. Aside from that, it's a great idea to make the hybrids their own supernatural type and give them a seat on the Council. The magic of the decree might even make it hard for people to treat mixed couples so poorly. If I weren't trying to be less impulsive, I would have already signed it."

"Mixed couples like you and your dragon."

I shook my head. "No, the whole hybrid discrimination thing doesn't apply to me. Coalition law describes me as of all races." The coalition's official name was The Coalition of Ahl. Ahl was the name the Firsts came up with when they started creating magical races. As the queen of the coalition, my grandmother infused her magic into every being they created, so I encompassed all races. If I could relearn my magic, I'd be connected to everyone. The distinction made it impossible for me to bond outside my magical race. "My grandmother's diaries said something about her magic being the stabilizing factor. I should be able to absorb and use the magic from every faction. I'm more concerned about people like Jonas and Ann Marie, or Tracy and Bastien. Or your potential granddaughter. It'll give them a place in the paranormal world."

"Granddaughter." Quin sounded like he was testing the word.

I didn't have time to ask more because he disappeared. A second later, Razazia the First burst through the door. Charlotte's gray head poked out from her. "Um...Your Grace, the First Razazia, is here to see you. Um. She didn't—"

"It's fine, Charlotte. Thanks."

She gave me a wary look as she scurried out the door.

Drake's anger burned through the bond as he moved toward me faster than I knew he could fly.

I turned my attention to Razazia. "What can I do for you, Lady First?"

"You have commandeered some of my people. Why?" She used the ancient language of Mahri.

Drake landed behind the castle as I puzzled through her words. My skills using the ancient language had come a long way since I started reading diaries, but I was far from fluent when people spoke it. "I didn't commandeer the elves. They volunteered."

"So you say."

"Look. If you're going to make it in the modern world, you need to learn some current languages. I suggest Spanish and English, since they are popular with both humans and paranormals."

"Are there no manners in this modern era?" she said with a refined English accent.

"Manners change with time. Your perception of what is rude differs from mine because I was born a few thousand years later than you. But I would expect that people would value the truth in any era."

Her eyes narrowed. "You should take care of how you speak to me. You are vulnerable in this office with no dragons as backup."

Drake strolled through the door, and I smirked. "You were saying?"

Razazia watched him with an expression I couldn't read. "I see."

"You don't. Otherwise, you would have noticed the vampire in the corner." He leaned against my desk, looking far more relaxed than the emotions the bond showed me. "What do you want, Razazia?"

Her head swung around the office and settled on a corner. It wasn't the corner Quin was in, but she had superb acting skills. "Why were my elves drafted to serve the upstart queen, Drake?"

"Because she asked them to help, and they agreed. Unlike her mother, Jenella does not force people to do her bidding. The Snow Elf King was her first volunteer."

I leaned back in my chair. "If you want to help, you can. If not, then I'd appreciate you not interfering with the elves who choose to fight for the coalition."

Her eyes ran over me, then focused on Drake. "I am contractually obligated to help, as are all the Firsts. I don't have a choice."

"Sure you do." I pretended I didn't notice that she wasn't talking to me. "That contract was severed years ago. You can ask Jonas about it." My mother severed the contracts the Firsts made with the coalition as soon as she put Drake to sleep. It was her way of making sure Jonas stayed out of her business.

Razazia turned her glare to me. Her magic swelled as she floated toward the door. Her translucent wings shimmered in the light. "I shall consider your offer. My elves may help you should they choose. Do not control them or you will regret it."

I stared after her, not sure what to think about the visit. On one hand, it would be great to have her help. On the other, she would be a pain in the ass the entire time. "What just happened there?"

Drake shrugged. "If I had to guess, I'd say that between the shock of the modern world and losing control over the elves, she's feeling insecure."

I pointed toward the door. "That didn't look insecure."

He grinned. "You would know better than me."

"Funny. Is she going to be a problem?"

"I doubt it. She seemed placated by your explanation." He rubbed his face. "Do you have a couple of hours to go somewhere with me?"

Quin drifted out of the room, probably to follow the First. "Where?"

"I'm going to do a fly-over of the Treasure Valley to better map out where the Bellicose are staying."

"I'd like that." We headed out the door. Charlotte sat at her desk in front of Drake's new office. "Where did Verity go?"

She wrung her hands. "Oh. Um. She is training with the Juror Titus at the courthouse, Your...um."

"No problem. Will you inform Prince Mathias I'll be out for a while with Drake, please?"

"Yes...umm. Am I being reassigned to the First?"

Charlotte did good work but was awkward around me. It was painful to watch. "You don't have to worry about protocol with me. I'm not a fan, so you're good. And yes, I'm promoting you to the Consort's Chief Aid. You do good work and that's the main thing I care about, so don't worry about all that other stuff."

She hid her shaky hands under the desk, and her eyes slid to Drake. "I'll call Prince Mathias."

"Thank you."

We headed through the family entrance, and Drake threw me on his back since I still couldn't flash. I needed to set aside time to practice my magic. I needed to do a lot of things. Like stop procrastinating and go confront my mother.

He launched into the air and took off so fast my eyes watered. We didn't slow as he burst through the gates and into the human world. I leaned over and lost myself in the mountain scenery. Trees dotted the forest floor, along with gouges where humans built roads to harvest them. In one area, all the trees were gone. A large piece of equipment loaded logs on the back of a longer vehicle. "What is that?"

Drake wrapped his magic tighter. *Humans use the wood for many things. I read somewhere that they also thin the forests as a fire management technique.*

Since they didn't have magic, I supposed they had to use different ways to contain the summer wildfires that plagued the area. *I don't like it.*

You could always go to their government and complain. Amusement fluttered through the bond.

I tapped my favorite spike. There wasn't anything I could do to save the trees. And what humans did wasn't my business. Besides, I already had too many problems of my own.

We started just north of where Jonas and Ann Marie lived and flew in a zig-zag pattern toward the city. I saw at least three other dragons sweeping the area. A white one joined us and had a mind conversation with Drake before flying in the other direction. When we got to West Boise, my senses lit up with paranormals. The hybrids, I realized. Their magic was like bright stars in a dark night and were somewhat clustered together. My stomach soured as I sensed the dark voids surrounding them. I patted Drake on the shoulder and pointed. My cheeks heated when I realized he couldn't see me. *There's a large amount of bug magic to the northwest.*

Drake banked in that direction and descended, then hovered above an apartment complex coated with the stuff. I sensed several paranormals inside. All weak in power. I couldn't tell if they were tainted because the bug magic that coated the apartment complex screwed with my senses. *Is that a hybrid subdivision over there?*

Yes.

Are there more of these apartments?

Two complexes besides this one. The vampires found an office building where they meet. I sensed a demon there last night.

I wonder if Ann Marie knows how many there are.

Yes. Jonas said he planned to send his kids to us next week.

I rubbed my eyes. *We need to do something about this.*

And what do you propose we do? It's impossible to eliminate them here without humans noticing.

True. But they're one step ahead of us, and if they mess with the humans, we're screwed. I need to confront my mother.

Drake was silent for so long, I didn't think he'd answer. *I will go with you.*

We banked north and descended on a warehouse at the edge of the city. His feet barely touched down before he shifted into his human form. He put his hand on the door and a set of keys dropped from the top. He caught them and grinned. "Mathias keeps a stash of human vehicles here. I borrowed one so we can drive back."

My eyebrows drew together. "Why?"

"To give you a different perspective."

I glanced around at the surrounding buildings. The scent of chemicals and something I couldn't quite place assaulted my nose. "Why?"

He threw his head back and laughed. "Come on. It'll be fun to drive back to Allure. The stench will fade as we enter the mountains. Besides, we need to talk about your mother."

The fluttering in my chest died a sudden death at the mention of my mother. I trudged toward the door. "If you say so. Can I drive?"

"No. I have it on good authority that you are a terrible driver."

Tracy, no doubt.

As promised, the air cleared as Drake navigated the two-lane highway into the mountains. I considered rolling down my window to let the fresh scent in the car, but Drake's scent settled my nerves in a way the fresh air couldn't. "Why are they taking over apartments in the human world?"

"It's a mystery. The only logical conclusion is they're after the hybrids."

I had the sudden urge to chase every single one of them down. My eyes narrowed. "Why do I want to hunt?"

Drake's face lit up. "You're picking up on my feelings on the matter."

Great. One more thing to deal with. I watched the river on the other side of the road and thought about the bug magic. "After we distribute the potion and clear the bug magic, then what? The Bellicose will just whip out another nasty spell and we'll chase our tails again." I tapped the armrest between us. "And if they take over the hybrid community, we're screwed. How can we do better?"

"Awareness. You've done your best to warn everyone. Jonas and Ann Marie won't let the hybrids fall to the Bellicose."

"Sure." I took out my phone and eyed my list of things to do. The magnitude of what I'd learned the last few days made it seem silly. I closed my eyes to think, and an idea started to form. "Is there anyone you've heard of who can help me with my magic?"

"I can somewhat guide you, but I doubt anyone else can help. It's complex and unique and, like the magic in Mage Mountain, no one else can wield it."

I'd spent my entire adult life hoping to fix it, but in the many scenarios I'd ever imagined, being useless and unable to wield it wasn't one of them. "I need to at least figure out how to flash."

Drake turned onto a lumpy dirt road with a sheer cliff on my side. "We'll work on it when we return to Allure."

I gripped a handle beside the door, then released it when his amusement seeped through the bond. "I don't want to give up my freedom," I blurted.

"Then we'll work on that, too."

As we crept up the mountain, the road became almost impassable. The cliff disappeared, replaced by foliage so overgrown I doubted we'd be able to pass. The road just before it had been washed out by the spring thaw to the point it didn't even look like a road. Drake stopped the vehicle and waited. My skin prickled as a spell tested me for magic. The road ahead fixed itself and the foliage parted. Drake drove on.

I twisted in my seat and watched it close behind us. A goofy smile swept across my face. "That's handy." I settled back in my seat just as Drake sped up and drove off a cliff.

My white knuckles gripped the handle beside the latch that opened the door, and I tried not to squeal. I wanted to, but I knew how gates worked. If we didn't have magic, we'd end up back down the mountain near civilization with no memory of where we'd been. Since we had magic, we landed on a paved road between the pocket entrance and the gates to the city. Drake took a left and headed toward a gigantic storage spell.

I eyed the outside wards as we walked toward the gates. "I so want to learn how to make those."

Drake took my hand and touched it to his lips. "Give it time. You can't accomplish everything at once."

"So reasonable," I said to hear his laugh.

He didn't disappoint.

Several more guards lined the gates than the last time we went through, including vampires and dragons. It didn't surprise me. Mat was a master at security. A shifter manning the gate bowed and waved a hand. The gates made a hole just big enough for us to fit through and closed behind us.

Drake inclined his head to a purple dragon, then morphed into his own dragon form and flung me on his back. *You can be a queen and still be free. Ara and Deva do it. You simply need to let go of your fear and fly.*

He launched into the air.

When we got back to the castle, we headed straight to my office. Quin was absent, so I moved toward the seating area. "You should check out your new office and get to know Charlotte. I think you two will make a great team."

"I like her, though she needs to stop acting like prey before she encounters paranormals who cannot control their hunting instinct."

"That's why I paired her with you. She needs to build confidence, and I think you can help."

"I can. And I appreciate your attempt to give me a place to belong."

"But?"

"I plan to kick hornets' nests and see what tries to sting me. I don't want to bring that to your doorstep."

Movement caught my eye, and I leaned forward to peer out the window. The griffins amassed by the front gates. More gate guards than usual lined the walkway. On the other side, several people stood to one side, carrying signs. "Am I being protested?"

"The witches are not happy about the treatment of their president."

"Nope. But a protest? Isn't that a human thing?"

"Yes. It's an effective way to draw attention to a cause."

"What do they want?"

"They want her reinstated and an apology."

I shook my head. "What were you saying about hornets and my doorstep?" I ignored his laughter as I headed to the door and poked my head out.

Verity stood by her desk, locking it up. "Hey, Jen. I'm getting ready to call it a day. Do you need something?"

"Did you release the footage of the incident with the witch president?"

Her face turned to stone. "What do you take me for, incompetent? Of course I did."

"Great. Can you project it on a loop out front before you go? The witches don't understand the gravity of the offense."

She shook her head. "You are a frigid woman sometimes."

I grinned. "They're protesting like humans and want me to apologize to them. I'm just showing them the truth."

She shook her head. "I'm on it. Anything else?"

"Nope. Have a great evening." I shut the door and headed back toward the window and folded my arms. The spell activated above the witches, complete with sound. The protesters froze. Some dropped their signs and left after seeing the truth. Others doubled down.

Drake placed an arm around my shoulders, sending tingles through my body. "Don't worry about them. They are not the majority."

"I wasn't going to. There are too many other problems that come with this stupid job."

"Yet here you are, not running away from them." Drake dropped his arm, leaving me cold. "I have a couple of leads on the Bellicose leaders. It's one of those hornet's nests."

"Okay. Keep me updated. I'm going to work up the courage to visit my mother. If I can convince her to brag about how she took over the Bellicose, it'll give us a direction."

He shook his head. "Deva has tried to extract information from her. She's not talking and her mind is sealed. There is no need for you to put yourself through that."

My eyes narrowed. "The same Deva that manipulated me to summon her? The one who knew she was alive and didn't bother to tell me? That Deva?"

His hand ran through his hair, making it stick up. "We were all under contract. Some of it still stands. I understand your resentment and anger, but we were all doing what we thought best."

"Uh huh. Best for the Coalition? For me? Because from where I'm standing, the only one who your silence benefitted was her." My anger simmered so hot I fought to control it.

Drake's eyes lit with fire when it filtered through the bond. "It kept you alive."

"And stupid."

"No one who ever had a single conversation with you thinks you're stupid."

"Coulda fooled me."

"You don't understand it, and your anger is justified. But everyone who knew thought they were doing the right thing. Including me."

"And that's the problem. Everyone thinks they know what's best for me instead of letting me make up my own mind. It makes me weak. And my anger, justified or not, has been simmering for years and it takes every ounce of self control I possess to keep it from exploding." I waved my hands around. "Betrayals like that feed it. It's why I can't play your aunt's or Mat's game. Eventually, my self-control won't be enough and I'm going to kill everyone."

He reached out to touch me, then dropped his hand. "I feel it. And I cannot tell you how sorry I am. I've bungled our entire relationship. I don't want to be another person who you need to guard yourself against, nor do I want to lie to you. By not telling you about your mother before I spoke with Mathias, I backed myself into a corner. I regret it and will not make that mistake again. I swear it. One day, I hope you can forgive me."

As the magical contract settled into place, I closed my eyes. "My head understands that no one meant to hurt me, but the betrayal still stings. I can't help it. And I already forgive you because out of everyone, you at least clued me in that something big was being kept from me. But I can't help feeling betrayed because you're..." I trailed off.

"The most reasonable and handsome dragon you've ever seen?" His smile didn't reach his eyes.

I sighed. "The reasonableness isn't necessarily a good trait. I was going to say sincere."

"So you say." He pulled me to him. "I'm so sorry, Jenella. I will do anything to make it up to you."

For a few seconds, I stayed there and soaked up his warmth. Then I leaned back and locked eyes with him. "Anything?"

"I may regret saying that later, but yes."

I stepped away and rubbed my hands together. "Great. About my magic...."

CHAPTER TWENTY-NINE

JEN

THE SPARRING AREA TOOK up about half of the basement of the castle. I stood in the center and tried to figure out how I'd healed Gabriel. Shifters healed fast, but not as fast as vampires, or those of us with healing magic. He was in awful shape when Linda brought him to me. I wished for him to heal and silver magic shot out of my hand. I opened my eyes and tried to pull from my wells to conjure a ball of magic. It didn't work. "It's like I can't draw from my wells of magic," I said to no one in particular.

"What do you mean?" Mat asked from the bleachers on the left side of the room.

I turned my attention to the small crowd that had gathered. Mat sat on one end, his feet on the floor, his elbows resting on his knees. Quin stood in the corner behind him at the very top. Tracy perched in the center, Bastien by her side. Drake leaned against the wall beside the entrance to the gym. I shook my head. "I always imagined I had three pools of magic inside of me. It was as easy as drawing from the pool, kind of like sucking water through a straw. I can't do that now."

"That's not how I envision mine. Try bringing it from your center and letting it run down your arm," Mat said.

Nothing happened. "Nope."

"I use my mind as the source of my magic. Mathias uses his core. Neither of those will work for you." Drake moved toward me and held out a hand, and I automatically took it. "You said that you envisioned your magic as pools."

"Yes. I could feel them." I tapped my chest.

"Perhaps you need to channel your inner woman and become emotional."

I frowned. "You need to stay off the human internet. Women are no more emotional than men. Especially paranormal women."

His lips twitched. "I'm not implying that you're too emotional. But you do have all those emotions we discussed earlier hidden just under the surface. You can use them to fuel you until you find a better way." He shook his head. "Use the bond to feel what I do and try to mimic it using your emotions."

I sucked in some air and closed my eyes and focused on the bond. His foreign magic flooded me. A tickling sensation spread over me. A ringing in my ears followed. The same vibration the ruling magic used to make rattled my bones, only deeper. Like a growl. When the sensations drifted away, I opened my eyes. He held a plate of cookies in his hand. I caught a whiff of vanilla and chocolate and my mouth watered. "Wow."

He dropped my hand and set the cookies on the bench beside Mat. "Did that help?"

"No, not really. But those cookies smell amazing." And gave me indigestion. I rubbed the bubble in my chest. "I recognized the vibration in your magic. Going on the theory that I need to use my emotions, which I doubt is the case, I'll try."

I didn't think tapping into my anger was a good idea with the people I cared about in the room, so I dug up every ounce of determination I had and focused on a spot on the other end. When a tickle started in my chest,

I shoved the determination into it. Pain burst through my face and I threw my hands up. "What the...."

"Jen. Oh my fates, are you okay?"

I shook my head and tried to focus on Tracy's voice. "Yeah." I pulled my bloody hands away. "What did I do?"

A laugh escaped her. "Bounced off the wall, I think."

I was on the floor on my ass, my face throbbing. A hand I recognized as Drake's lowered in front of me, and I used it to pull myself to my feet. "Did I flash?"

"You did," Drake answered. "Perhaps we should practice this outside."

"Hold that thought." I stumbled toward the bathroom and washed the blood off my face and hands. My nose had already stopped bleeding and the bruises around my eyes faded by the time I finished. When I returned to the sparring room, I rested my hands on my hips. "I used way too much determination. I think I only need a spritz of emotion."

"A spritz?" Amusement laced Drake's voice.

"Yeah. I used an injection. It was too much."

By the time I finished practicing, the energy boost from my new healing abilities had long since worn off. I rubbed my eyes as I stumbled toward the door. "At least I can flash now."

"Do you think you can use that method to do other things?" Mat asked.

"Maybe. Rest first."

I was exhausted when I made it to my apartment and hopped in the shower. I spelled my hair into a braid and fell into a dreamless sleep.

Drake's voice in my head woke me up the next morning. He said something about going to kick that hornet's nest. I told him to shut up and let me sleep. I may have shouted. Instead of leaving me alone, he told me he found one of their leaders and planned to use him to find their headquarters in both the Treasure Valley and in Allure. He'd already touched bases with a few council members who wanted to help. I couldn't tell if he was happy with the purpose, but he was good at it. After that little gem, I rolled out of bed and got ready for the day.

My brother sat at the table in the breakfast nook sipping coffee when I slid into a chair next to him. "Hey, Mat."

"Morning."

Helen, the griffin matriarch who ran the household, appeared with breakfast. "It's so good to have you back in the nest, Jenella."

The scent of bacon, eggs, and pancakes drifted from the plates, and my stomach grumbled. "It's good to be home." The words slipped out before my brain engaged. I took a few seconds to think about that. It *did* feel good to be home, but I couldn't figure out why. "Thank you for all you do, Helen."

She patted me on the shoulder and went back to the kitchen.

I turned my attention back to Mat. "I'm still mad at you about keeping things from me, but it's not all-consuming. You can thank Drake and his reasonable disposition for that."

A small smile formed on his hard face. "Is that so?"

I took a bite of bacon, in no hurry to have the conversation. "Yep. What other bombs are waiting to drop on me?"

"None that I can think of."

I raised an eyebrow.

"Perhaps you should know that Quin and Ara raised me. Not that it matters much."

My eyes blinked several times. "Oh?"

"Mother gave me to Ara to raise on my twelfth birthday, hoping to turn me into an assassin who killed without remorse. As you can see, she was successful, though not in the way she hoped. Ara and Quin were competent guardians. They didn't approve of Mother's methods, so they raised me to have morals." He tapped the table. "Also, Deva was attempting to find Mother when she got kidnapped last year. Quin took over the task for a while but decided you needed him more. We were unaware Drake knew she was alive."

I closed my eyes and counted to ten as the pain of betrayal ripped through me. "Really."

"I deserve your anger."

"Yes, you do," I said through gritted teeth. I rubbed my aching chest. "You're lucky the ruling magic isn't working. Here's the deal, Mat. The witches refuse to help and are staging a human protest. The hybrids hate us because we let people treat them like crap for so long. And the Bellicose are closing in and are way more creative than us. I can't solve these problems alone. That you have my biggest allies lying to me makes me so angry I want to scream." I leaned forward. "There are a lot of reasons I never wanted this stupid title. The lack of freedom, the massive responsibility, the inability to trust anyone, the loneliness. But we need to solve these problems, so I'm willing to face all of that. I need to trust you to have my back."

Sadness filled his eyes. "I always have. I only lied to protect you. Mother put me under a magical contract to keep things from you. It would have killed us both if I broke it. When Drake confronted me, I feared that the contract would transfer to him, so I swore him to silence to protect you. It's always been about you, so your fears are unfounded. I will always be on your side. I won't try to box you in or insist on extra protection now that you have your First. You should still use more caution."

I sighed. "There's a lot to work through."

"Yes." Mat's eyes filled with so many emotions that I couldn't stand it.

I picked up a piece of bacon and took a bite. Then closed my eyes to savor the salty goodness. There was nothing that compared to Helen's cooking. "I think Drake was hunting mother out of vengeance, rather than for me. He also kept the information about the bond from me that entire time because he's a big chicken-dragon. Your motives were to keep me safe. Though I still haven't worked out why you didn't bother telling me that Quin and Ara raised you."

"Because Mother put me under a magical contract, I couldn't tell anyone. You eliminated it."

I stopped with a piece of bacon halfway to my mouth. "It all comes back to her, doesn't it?"

"It always *has* been all about her. She didn't want to be seen as incompetent, so she forced contracts on everyone."

"She really is awful."

"Yes. I'm sorry and I hope you can forgive me some day."

"Forgiveness seems to be the theme of the week for me." I pushed my plate away, no longer hungry. "You're forgiven. We need to stand together if we want to live." I tapped the table. "Drake thinks he found one of the Bellicose leaders. He said he's kicking hornets' nests today. The witches are protesting us and I haven't heard if they plan to replace their president. Gargoyles are amassing in the square and won't tell me why. Here's the question. Who benefits most from all this chaos, betrayal, and mistrust?"

Mat sat back. "The same person who always benefitted from terrible schemes. Mother has an uncanny ability to make everything work for her."

"Exactly. Which is why I can't stay mad at you, Deva, or Drake. She wants to divide us."

"Agreed. Don't worry about the gargoyles. They're drama hounds. If they suspect the Bellicose is targeting Allure, they'll want to watch."

"They're supposed to be guardians that ward off evil spirits."

"Gargoyles *can* ward off evil spirits. It doesn't mean they will."

"I planned to wake more Firsts and ask them to help, but that didn't work so well with Razazia, so I think I might hold off on waking the others. She came to see me and has agreed to let the elves continue to help with our efforts. She needs time to adjust to the world, so I can't count on her." I took a sip of coffee. "The hybrid leadership signed the agreement. They're officially their own magical race within the coalition. The dragons and vampires are watching apartment complexes in the Treasure Valley. Ann Marie was right that they're amassing there. Also, I'm going to learn how to create new pockets when I have a second to catch my breath."

Mat's intimidating magic ramped up. "You've been busy."

I rubbed the dull ache in my chest. "Yeah. But it's the tip of the ice burg where the coalition's problems are concerned. I'm going to see if I can convince Anitta to brag about her involvement with the Bellicose. You've been doing this for a lot longer than me, so what do you think is the best approach?"

"There is no good approach. Mother is a master manipulator. If you give her the slightest tell, she'll catch on to your scheme and spin it in her favor."

"She has nothing on Deva," I mumbled.

"True. But Deva has a heart where mother doesn't."

"I dunno. I think if I can prick her ego enough, she won't be able to help herself."

"It's worth a try, but take someone with you and guard your emotions. Even diminished, she's dangerous, especially when cornered."

That statement taught me something important about my brother. Our mother terrified him in the same way Jaques's memory scared me. The haunted look in his eyes was like looking at myself in the mirror after waking up from one of my nightmares. Heaviness settled in my chest. I'd always thought of Mat as invincible. To me, he was the rock that just sucked it up and took care of business. But in that moment, I could see that he did those things to hide his fear. And if I had to bet, I'd say his overprotective nature and ability to kill stemmed from it.

I reached out and rested my hand on his because I couldn't bring myself to voice the revelation. When he pulled back, I did what I did best and changed the subject. "Have you looked out front? There's more witches today."

The whiplash change of subject wiped the haunted look from his face. "Yes. They've been peaceful so far."

"Sure. They'll be peaceful until they're not. You should have killed the President. She's going to be another problem."

Mat rubbed his chin. "I was under the impression you wanted to build bridges with the witches, not alienate them." He shrugged one shoulder.

"Don't worry about them. George has his best griffins on it. They won't make a move without us knowing."

I slumped in my seat. "I *do* want to build bridges. But I don't think that's going to happen. Tracy's worried that her dad will be a target because he's trying to force an election to replace her."

"He'd make a much better ally. Speaking of allies, I've been working with Gabe, Linda, and a few other leaders on a strategy to recover our people from the labs."

"Good. And?"

He shook his head. "Gabe said he can't be sure how many the Bellicose have because there are too many shifters to track. He assured me it's his top priority."

"You think he's lying to you."

"Yes. But damned if I can figure out what he's lying about. Did Titus read him?"

"He did. They're not working with the Bellicose, if that's what you're thinking."

"I'm not."

"Do you have people on them?"

Mat raised an eyebrow.

I snorted. "Of course you do."

His face grew serious. "If you go see mother today, take someone with you. And be very careful what you say to her."

"I'll see if Deva or Bastien will stay close. And I don't plan to say much."

"For the record, I'm glad you're no longer running away and hiding from the hard stuff. I hoped this day would come."

Every once in a while, revelations like to reach up and smack me in the face. That morning, as the sun filtered through the windows, the slaps kept coming until my face was numb. On top of learning about his fear of our mother, Mat's declaration about running caused something inside me to click into place. I realized I ran away from things because I'd been living in the past. My trauma caused me to run from threats. To hide. And I no longer had a single reason to keep running.

A million pounds lifted off my shoulders and I could finally breathe. I didn't need to run and hide anymore. I could simply be. Well, except for the threat of the Bellicose looming over us. I cleared my throat. "Have you contacted our allies and see if they'll mobilize if we're attacked?"

"Not exactly, no. It would be best to alert the council, but they'd insist on a meeting."

We both winced.

"We have the vampires, dragons, and shifters. Maybe some elves. Who else can we recruit?"

"We also have many mages, the Enforcers, the Castle Guard, and the Gate Patrol. I'll contact the trolls and ogres, but they make up a fraction of the people we'll need based on reports."

"I'll text Ann Marie and see if there's any movement in the human world. Maybe the PISD and see if we can bring in some detectives." It meant contacting my former best friend, which I wasn't thrilled about. "What if we put the city on high alert?"

"I did that when you ordered me to add more gate guards. You need to work on your magic. We're going to need it."

Mat was right, I thought, as I made my way to my office. My magic was key to both defeating the Bellicose and giving me back my freedom. But so were our allies. The weight that had been lifted settled back on my shoulders, though it felt different. I couldn't imagine the sheer volume of responsibilities I'd have after Mat stepped down. He handled so many details.

Verity wasn't at her desk when I reached my office. Charlotte's shoulders slumped when I approached her. "Where's Verity?"

"Um. Training, I think. The Juror Titus trains her for an hour per day and she hates it." Her face flushed. "Um. I don't think I was supposed to tell you that."

I waved a hand. "It's fine. Verity's free to do what she wants, as are you. Have you heard from Drake?"

Her forehead crinkled. "The First talked in my head a few minutes ago, I think. He said something about researching a human address."

I nodded. "He does that to me, too. It's annoying until you get used to it."

"Yeah. Um, can he read my thoughts?"

"He can, but he won't. He's very polite and wouldn't do anything to break your trust."

Her eyes narrowed. "He better not."

I liked the fire I saw there and hoped we could build her confidence and bring more of it out. Inside my office, Quin sat at the conference table with a pile of papers in front of him. "Hey, Quin."

His eyes flipped to me briefly before returning to whatever he was reading. "Jen."

"Didn't I give you your own office?"

"Yes. However, someone must compromise their privacy to keep you breathing."

"And you've appointed yourself."

"A noble sacrifice for the greater good."

I pulled out my phone and called my former best friend. Travis answered on the first ring. "Hey, Jen."

"Hi, Travis, how are you?"

"Getting along. I heard you are no longer interested in being a detective."

"Not true. I'm just too busy." No way I'd tell him the entire story because he'd use it for personal gain.

"Interesting. What can I help you with?"

So, we were going to skip the small talk. "Are there any detectives interested in searching Allure and the surrounding area for Bellicose?"

He sighed. "Many of them are already looking for missing shifters, but you can post the job. That is, if you're asking as the queen."

He was fishing. "It's an official request. When will it be posted?"

"In a couple of hours."

My shoulders relaxed. "Thank you. I appreciate it."

He was silent for a few seconds. "I'm glad you're finally taking your rightful place."

"Yeah, I figured you would be," I mumbled.

"Look, Jen. I gave you space to find yourself. I still consider you my oldest and dearest friend, and I hope you'll remember that when the flood of false friends begins."

Travis was a social ladder climber and used me to gain prestige. I'd distanced myself after realizing it. I needed his cooperation, though. "We'll see. Thank you again for posting the job."

"Take care, Jen." The line went dead.

A guilty pang rattled through me. "Hey, Quin? Do you think I'm doing enough?"

"Enough what?"

"To fight the Bellicose. Because I don't think I am."

"You are only one person."

Although a simple answer, it was the truth. "I need to convince the leadership council to work together."

Quin remained silent, so I moved to the window to think. Except it didn't help because of the witches protesting out front. I leaned forward for a better look. Yep. More of them were out there. And more palace guards perched on the wall. It wasn't what I'd envisioned when I took over the throne. Though, it didn't feel like a cage, either.

Sharp pain sliced through my chest. I doubled over and squealed. My tailbone throbbed, and my left arm screamed. Thoughts that weren't mine flooded my head, along with the scent of blood and sulfur.

Quin appeared at my side. "Jen?"

I sensed Drake coming my way fast. "It's not my pain." I sprinted toward the door. It seemed to take a year to get down the stairs. He was toward the front, so I turned that way and breezed past a few visitors and out the front door.

CHAPTER THIRTY

JEN

A CROWD GATHERED ON the front lawn, their heads tilted toward the sky. My eyes burned from the thick smoke mixed with the pungent scent of sulfur. I came to a stop at the bottom of the front steps.

At the side of the castle, Drake flew in a tight circle as he slashed at a demon nearly as big as him. I ducked around the corner of the castle. The demon was unlike anything I'd ever seen. It stretched its tan wings and made lazy circles, revealing a humanoid body with thickly roped muscles. Dark brown splotches of different sizes covered its body. Six-inch claws tipped both its hands and feet. Its horned, triangular-shaped head stretched, and some kind of acid shot from its mouth. I grunted as a white-hot burning pain shot down my side, mirroring a gash the acid made on Drake.

Several griffins swarmed around the fight but didn't engage.

I tried to tune my magic to the anti-demon spell.

Nothing happened.

The demon spread its leathery wings and used the barbs on the tips to stab down on Drake's back. Drake jerked back, and the demon's wing got stuck on a spike. They spiraled toward the ground, shot into the sky, and descended again. I covered my ears when Drake let out a thundering roar and slammed his barbed tail down. The demon jerked back but wasn't fast enough. My eyes slammed shut as the barbs spiked its head.

A tug in my chest made my eyes open. Green haze surrounded the fight. The demon rocketed toward the ground, caught himself at the last second, and landed in a crouch.

His putrid head turned my way. He grinned.

My heart kicked into overdrive.

A painful roar echoed off the building, but I didn't dare take my eyes off the Demon. Drake's teeth sunk into the demon's torso. A white dragon came out of nowhere and smashed the demon's head on the ground three times. Drake shifted into his human form and chanted something, and the demon melted to dust.

Drake collapsed to his knees. I sprinted toward him and skidded to a stop when all the blood registered. He had a gash down his side that oozed. His left arm hung in an odd direction and his feet looked like they'd been through a blender. He leaned over and braced himself on the ground with one arm. I hissed at the open gashes that ran down his back from a series of wounds. He opened his mouth like he wanted to say something and passed out.

Heart in my throat, I dropped to my knees beside him. I needed my healing magic. I closed my eyes and tried to concentrate. My brain wouldn't work. I scrambled to his other side and tried to stop the bleeding. The echo of his pain zinged through me, and I wheezed. I reached out and touched his face. "Hang on, Drake." A tear escaped, then more.

Emotions flooded me when he didn't respond. So many that I couldn't sort them out. How could anyone, even a demon, hurt this patient, wonderful man? I brushed his cheek as my shock and sadness melted, replaced with the burning anger I kept in a tight ball.

He was mine, and I wouldn't put up with anyone hurting him. Something inside me broke. Silver magic coated me. It poured through the bond from my hands, wrapped around his core, and then fanned out. It wasn't like when my magic exploded before. The silvery haze hovered in a tight circle around us, sinking into our chests. I watched as his wounds knitted themselves together.

Drake's beautiful green eyes fluttered open.

"Hey, you." I tried to offer a smile.

He blinked and dragged himself to his knees, his eyes scanning my face. An arm snaked around me and crushed me to his naked chest. The stench of sulfur and blood assaulted my nose. I threw my arms around his neck and squeezed. "Are you okay?"

Instead of answering, he released me and leaned back enough to see my face. His soft lips met mine. The kiss was gentle, yet desperate. Gratitude flowed through the bond, and I dug my hands into his hair and pulled him closer, deepening the kiss. Emotions like I'd never known flooded me. Warmth, acceptance, a sense of belonging. Heat and lightning shot through my body and a hunger like I'd never known overtook me. I deepened the kiss.

Drake pulled back and ran a thumb down my cheek. "You are amazing."

I blinked as I tried to control myself. "That was all you, bud."

A throat cleared behind me. Right. I'd forgotten that we had an audience. I pulled back and stood. Paranormals of all types surrounded us, including Mat and several leaders. George and Helen flanked Mat, Helen with a hand on her chest and a goofy smile on her face, George with wide eyes. Mat's face was blank, his arms crossed over his chest.

A phoenix hovered in the air above us, grinning at the white dragon. Two mages linked arms with sloppy smiles on their faces, while a group of dwarves huddled together near the gates, their mouths hanging open. "Great." I turned back to Drake to check his wounds. It was a waste of time, because he'd already magically cleaned up the blood and wore clean clothes. I looked down at myself. My jeans and blouse were clean. "That's handy."

Amusement danced in his eyes, and his hand landed on my back. He leaned down and put his lips to my ear. "Hornet's nest kicked."

I ignored the shiver of pleasure. "And you almost died."

"You wouldn't let that happen." His voice rang with such faith my knees almost buckled.

People from the edges of the crowd drifted away. "Right. People."

Drake tilted his head toward the white dragon. "Thanks for the assist, Glac."

The white dragon huffed and flew toward Dragon Headquarters.

"Glac. I've heard that name before."

"He runs the hotel."

I remembered Tracy talking to a white dragon after a fiasco I had at the Bank of Mahri. "And a friend of Tracy's."

"Perhaps. Many dragons favor Tracy."

The crowd broke up as we headed back toward the double doors at the main entrance to the castle. Mat, Helen, and George fell in behind us. Instead of going back to my office, I guided Drake toward the dining room beside the family entrance. Quin reappeared as we gathered around the table. Helen got up to get refreshments, but Drake stopped her and conjured tea and cookies.

"Well, that's handy," she said, as she lowered herself into a chair.

Mat's eyes cut into me. "What was that?"

"Don't look at me. I was in my office. That was all Drake."

"I found two buildings where I suspected the leadership spent time." He tapped his head.

"So you just flew around reading minds until you found something?" I asked.

"Yes. Then I perched on them and listened for a while. I found two demons. One in the human world and one here in Allure. There are others in the human world, but not as strong. I passed that information off to

Jonas. Jenella's magic upgrade affected me, and I cannot completely cloak myself like I did before. The demon sensed it and attacked."

I sucked in a breath. "No."

He took my hand and touched it to his lips. "I'm not worried about it."

"Where?" Mat's question sounded more like a demand.

Drake's eyes sparked with something I couldn't read. "I will forward the locations to you. My new assistant is working on it now."

Helen leaned forward. "You brought trouble to the nest."

"I did." Drake dropped my hand. "I apologize. I feared I wouldn't win against that demon. My instincts guided me toward my mate."

Her eyes narrowed. "Then you will defend us against the evil you brought to our door."

"I will."

I held up a hand. "It was always going to land on our doorstep."

"Agreed," Mat said.

I lowered my hand. "Did you just agree with me?"

His lips twitched. "I did. And I agree with your First's aggressive approach. Many leaders were at the council building and witnessed that display. You said you wanted them to rally around you against the Bellicose. Use the First's power display to do that."

I focused on Quin, who was unusually attentive. "Quin?"

"Do not screw it up."

"Right." I turned to Drake. "I need to go to Dragon Headquarters and confront...the prisoner there. Will you be okay?"

Amusement danced in his eyes because, of course, he'd be okay. He was okay for thousands of years before me and my bullshit took over his life. "I will go with you."

"Sure." I stood and squeezed Helen's shoulder as I padded out the back door toward the hidden family flashing circle. The fresh air calmed me and made it easier to think. "I'm going to try to flash."

Tingles ran through my body when Drake took my hand. My healing him did something to the bond. It became more sensitive. Or raw. "You can flash us both."

I stopped inside the circle. "You'll regret that decision when I overshoot the square, ram us into a building, and you're all bloody and broken again."

"No, I won't. But I will start calling you crash or some other corny nickname."

I slammed my eyes closed and injected determination while I concentrated on the main flashing circle. Drake's tug on my hand was the only sign anything happened.

We stood in the center of the arrivals circle inside the main square downtown. I dropped his hand. "Well, that was easy."

"Yes." He eyed the gargoyles. There were more of them now. They lined the entire square and stood three deep. Paranormals dashed in and out of the gaps they'd left at the intersections, careful not to touch them. A couple of adolescent ogres poked at one beside a tailor's shop. "This is becoming a problem. Do you want me to take care of it?"

"No." People dove out of our way as I marched toward the gargoyle the ogres were messing with. "Hey, you two. Leave the gargoyles alone."

They froze and shuffled a couple of steps away. One managed a clumsy bow. "Yes, Your Grace. Sorry, Your Grace."

I waved a dismissive hand. "Don't worry about it. I don't blame you for your curiosity. Just don't poke at them. If one takes offense, you'd be in trouble."

They gave me more apologies and scurried off. I turned my attention to the gargoyle they'd been harassing. "Why are you amassing in the square?"

His head creaked as it turned toward me. "Our King has ordered it, Your Grace."

"Why?"

"We did not ask why."

I tapped my chin. "What are your orders?"

"To wait here for him."

I glanced at Drake, who shrugged. "Stay out of the way so people can come and go. And don't kill any kids that mess with you."

"Of course, Your Grace."

"I'm going to have to call the Gargoyle King and find out what's going on." A swarm of pixies streamed out of a shop and sailed around the corner in front of us. Everyone else either gaped or dove out of the way. "I plan to wonder around the city until people ignore me."

Drake chuckled. "Both are good ideas. I doubt the gargoyles will side with the Bellicose. They observe more than take part in skirmishes, but it's worth investigating. You're right that people will ignore you when they realize you don't require reverence. I wouldn't go alone just yet, though."

"Right. Safety first," I said as we climbed the stairs.

Learn your magic first. I have an idea of how I can help you with that. Drake switched to mind-speak.

"Okay."

Deva stood outside her office, her arms crossed across her chest. "Hello, loves." Her smile didn't reach her eyes.

Her assistant, Karenalla, sat at her desk and sent me a death stare. "What did you need, Your Grace?"

I shifted my attention from Deva to her. "Why do you hate me, Karenalla?"

"I'm unaware of what you mean."

Deva's chuckle sent shivers down my spine. She waved us toward her office. "Come in, Jenella, Drake. We have much to discuss." As soon as Drake shut the door, she slumped into a chair. "I can't get her to give me a single morsel of information. Her mind is locked down tight, and she is confident she will prevail."

I shuffled over and took the chair opposite. "Let me try. I have some ideas."

Her eyes narrowed. "I don't wish to sound negative, but how can you speak *to* her when you cannot bring yourself to speak *of* her?"

I swallowed. "I think my presence will throw her off. If I can manipulate her into bragging, then she might give us something."

"I can help with your emotions," Drake said.

I frowned. "Like send me reassurance through the bond? Because I don't think even that is going to calm my sour stomach."

"Perhaps not. But I will flood you with enough reassurance and a sense of calm to disguise your nerves."

"I like it," Deva drawled. "Drake and I will go with you. I discovered it doesn't take much effort to cloak myself from her these days."

My shoulders slumped. I'd thought through the emotions about confronting my mother, but not nearly enough. I ran my hands over my face. "We'll try it." The bubble in my chest grew, and I rubbed it as I thought. "I can't show any emotion."

"Correct. Anitta is very manipulative and will pick up on the slightest tell." Deva tapped her chin. "Keep your face blank, your emotions in check, and do not fidget."

"Tell her nothing," Drake added. "She will try to push your buttons. Don't engage. I'll keep you calm, and we'll pull you out should you need it."

They didn't believe I could control my emotions or keep a cool head. They were probably right. I closed my eyes and stuffed my anger, resentment, and every other emotion I felt into a box. It was easier when I concentrated on what I'd read in her diaries. She liked besting people and making them feel inferior. Once she got the upper hand, she bragged about the accomplishment. The question was, how did I make her think she had the upper hand without giving her any information? When my eyes opened, Deva's bronze eyes focused on me with an intensity I'd never seen from her. I cleared my throat. "I have an idea, but I'm not sure it will work."

"We'll pull you out if we need to," Drake said, his voice soft yet firm.

CHAPTER THIRTY-ONE

JEN

DEVA KEPT MY MOTHER in a storage closet next to her private quarters on the top floor. The door was gone, and a bronze glow covered it, with bands of green and black laced through. The closet had a cot, toilet, sink, and table that hovered in the center of the room. My mother sat on the cot and stared at the wall. Her sharp eyes turned to me as I lowered myself into the chair. "Ah. There you are, you foolish child."

Confidence and calm flooded me from the bond. Drake and Deva leaned against the opposite wall, cloaked so well I struggled to sense them.

I ran my eyes over my mother. My memory of her was of a strong woman who glowed with power and carried herself with confidence. In my head, she was tall, beautiful, and powerful. This woman was two inches shorter than me, had average looks, and was as weak in power as I pretended to be as a detective. Her hair had faded from glowing gold with red highlights to a dirty blonde with rust. Her eyes were such a dull gold that they looked light brown. It was her, but she wasn't anything like my memory portrayed.

I inclined my head. "Anitta."

Like me, she didn't have a visible reaction. She slid off the cot and glided to the door. "It's as cowardly as it is stupid to rely on the Dragon Queen to hold your prisoners."

I raised an eyebrow.

She waved a hand. "But then, you always were a coward." She tapped on the magic that coated the room. "Tell me, how is your murderous brother? I hear he's killing allies now."

I ignored the fiery rage bubble inside me and said nothing. It took all the inner strength I had not to lash out at her. If I still had the ruling magic, I doubted I'd be able to control it. Drake sent a flood of calm through the bond, which helped me keep my shoulders relaxed and my face blank.

"I see." My mother said.

"You don't," I said in a calm, sure voice.

Her eyes bore into me. "Oh, I do. Your brother has done nothing but lie to you and manipulate you your whole life. You don't trust him and don't even have the will to defend him. He's made you question your every decision and sapped your confidence. It's made you weak."

Use that. Deva's voice rang through my head.

I let my expression slip, and my eyes flash. It wasn't difficult because she was pretty much spot on. Or she would have been had I not had that talk with Mat at breakfast. I schooled my expression just as fast as I let it slip.

She threw her head back and laughed. "Did he tell you he stole my throne and plans to keep it?"

"No, but it doesn't surprise me." My voice didn't betray the urge to reach out and strangle her. Mat had flaws, but I couldn't stand it when others criticized him. I only put up with it from Deva and Ara because I'd asked their advice. My mother didn't even raise Mat and knew nothing about him. "What I don't understand is why you let him steal your throne."

Anger flashed in her eyes. "Is that what he told you? That I let him?"

I shrugged a shoulder. "Were you not the most powerful person in Ahl? It seems silly that a firstborn, without ruling magic, could just swoop in and take the throne."

Careful, Drake said in my head. *Don't sound too bitter and say nothing more.*

Her eyes flashed with rage. "He used *you.* That's how."

I gave her a sharp look, then pretended to catch myself and returned to my blank expression.

She took the bait. "That's right. He put out a death notice and, before I could react, stole your magic and the throne with it. Or are you too stupid to realize why your magic is fractured?"

I almost gasped at that statement. She knew my magic didn't mix and that I struggled with it. Which meant she had someone on the inside. I wondered if she really believed that Mat broke my magic. I also wondered why she couldn't tell it wasn't fractured anymore. Not that it mattered. It wasn't why I was there. "So Mathias, who doesn't have ruling magic, stole your heir and throne and told everyone you were dead, and you...did nothing? All you had to do was show up, put out a statement that Mathias was mistaken, and resume your responsibilities. Instead, you resurrect the Bellicose, start ripping the coalition apart, summon some demons, and use vile magics to experiment on the very people you swore to protect."

"You ignorant, foolish child. You know nothing about choices and consequences or about ruling. You don't even see what is going on right under your nose."

Drake and Deva started chattering in my head at the same time. I ignored them as I tamped down the hurt and anger that came with her statement and thought about what to do next. If I didn't make the right move, she wouldn't start bragging, and we wouldn't get any information. I let my shoulders slump a tad and shook my head. "And you understand nothing about me, the coalition, or what it means to do the right thing."

Her face turned red. "The right thing? The coalition is failing without me. You aren't powerful enough to hold it. My return is the only way to save it. Yet you are too stupid to see what's happening right before your eyes."

"And you are imprisoned," I said without thinking.

Relief washed over me when it worked. She threw her head back and laughed. The tone was classically sinister. "Neither you nor that sad excuse for a dragon can hold me." She leaned forward. "You think you can do everything yourself, and she thinks she is invincible. I always knew you were worthless, but it's such a wonderful surprise that you're also stupid."

Calm and confidence flooded the bond so fast that I almost dropped my mask. Drake misread the situation, which was rare for him. He thought her words would cause me to react. The only reaction I had was a flutter of anticipation. She was getting ready to strike. I had to make her think she won. I shook my head and let my shoulders slump. Then, I straightened and resumed my blank mask.

A sinister smile spread across her face. "You think you're safe in your little castle surrounded by your filthy griffins. You think you'll be able to manipulate that worthless First into providing you enough power to rule. Yet your world is crumbling around you and you can't do anything to stop it." She leaned forward. "Do you want to know why?"

"No."

Her triumphant laugh echoed through the hall. "Because I am the rightful ruler." Her hand clenched and unclenched. "And because power is all about the people you choose to serve under you. Paranormals want to be told what to do. They crave direction and orders. They want nothing more than to be ruled by a firm hand so they know where to fall in line. Your grandmother never understood that. Nor do you. But I do. I learn what people want, and I give it to them. And they do my bidding because they understand I know what's best even though magic has exacted a price from me for someone else's incompetence. And they will do anything for me. Including getting close to you to ensure you remain encumbered. I created a king and gathered an army that followed my every command while you chased pixie dust. You cannot win this war, and the upcoming battle will prove it." Her mouth slammed shut as if she realized she had given too much away.

I let a slow smile spread across my face. "Thank you, Anitta. You've been very helpful."

She ranted as I stood, slid the chair back against the wall, and left without so much as a glance in her direction.

Drake's hand landed on my back when we got to the elevator. "Are you okay?"

I sighed. "I'm fine. Is it weird that it hurt worse to learn she's still alive than it did to confront her?"

"No. When my mother died and the ruling magic came to me, I became frustrated, but I didn't mourn her."

I frowned. "Your mother's ruling magic passed to you even though you're not in her realm?"

"Yes. About a thousand years ago. I questioned my sanity for a while before I figured it out. It is difficult to mourn the person who sent your life careening in a direction that caused so much pain. Even more so when you never knew them. She dropped me inside Deva's territory and never returned right after I was born. And then volunteered me to come here."

I hugged him. "I'm sorry."

He released me when the elevator opened on the ground floor. "Don't be. It was a long time ago and I've worked through it. My point is, you never really knew Anitta, and she caused you and Mathias a lot of pain, so your lack of feeling toward her is valid."

I thought about his words as we made our way out the door and down the front stairs. People moved out of our way as we turned the corner on my favorite street. I tried to offer pleasant smiles and nods, but most of them avoided eye contact or were too busy bowing. "It doesn't matter. I got some good information from her. I need to see if the leaders are still at the council building. Mat thinks I should capitalize on your demon fight this morning. Do you want to go with me?"

"Not unless you need me to stand behind you and show my pointy teeth."

I grinned. "You joke, but your pointy teeth are terrifying. And difficult to clean."

He put an arm around me as we reached the circle and put his lips to my ear. "They have many other uses that I can't wait to explore."

My face flushed when my whole body lit up. "Um."

His deep laugh sent tingles through me. "I need to return to my new duties. Call me if you need anything." He kissed my temple and stepped back.

Once inside the flashing circle, I met his eyes. The heat and longing in them made my knees buckle. I made a show of fanning myself, activated my new power, infused determination, and was gone.

I had a few options when it came to communicating with the other leaders. The traditional method of calling a meeting, sending out a bulletin email with the viewing spell from outside the castle attached, or let the rumor mill work for a couple of days before addressing it. That was never a good idea because the information got distorted.

I wanted something less formal and more personal. I needed to understand the leaders every bit as much as I needed to understand their people.

I stepped inside the door to the council building and stopped. The main chamber was straight ahead and silent. Two hallways branched off from the entrance. The right one led to the area where me and my advisors were supposed to meet before council meetings, and the left led to the council offices. They snaked all the way around the circular building and met on the other side at another entrance to the main chamber. I turned left and drifted down the hallway.

Voices drifted from an open door. I stuck my head in. A small group of leaders sat around a breakroom table. Drinks and discarded dishes littered the room. A magichef and magiwash lined the wall on the left. The back wall had several tall, skinny windows overlooking the castle guard training grounds. The centaur king stood when he spotted me. "Your Grace. What can we do for you?"

I pasted on a pleasant smile. "Sorry to interrupt. I was just out for a walk and heard voices." Chairs scraped on the floor as the others prepared to stand. I waved a hand. "No need to stand. I'm not big on formal protocols." Some eyes widened. Other faces screwed up in disgust. "Except for formal occasions, of course." It was a lie, but I could compromise if I had to.

The centaur king cleared his throat. "Would you like to join us?"

A sudden urge to run out the door made me lock my knees. "I don't want to intrude. I just heard voices and thought I'd stop and say hello."

He pulled out a chair. "You're not intruding. Please. Come and join us. Would you like a drink?"

I shuffled toward the magichef. "I'll get it. Thanks."

Drink in hand, I moved to the chair and attempted to look pleasant while my heart tried to escape my chest. I'd interacted with these leaders before, but I'd never sat in a room and had a conversation with them. I slipped on my detective persona. "Thank you. It's kind of you to invite me."

"I suppose it is," the sprite queen mumbled. She had gray coloring like Charlotte and wore a sour expression.

"Do you know Charlotte?" I blurted. When her lips pursed, I continued. "She started working in my office recently and is wonderful."

Her eyes lit with pride. "Charlotte is my one hundred and thirty-fifth niece. I'm pleased that she has become useful."

"She's invaluable. I've recently promoted her."

"Good. She deserves much better than the fates have given her."

An awkward silence followed. I was just about to bolt when the fairy queen fluttered her bright yellow wings. "Your Grace, may I ask you a question?"

"Sure. And call me Jen or Jenella, please."

She cocked a bright yellow eyebrow, her yellow eyes sparkled against her blue skin. "I see. We saw Drake the First fight with that creature and...the aftermath. Are you matched to him?"

My face flushed. "Yes. But we haven't made an official announcement yet."

"Why not?"

"For a lot of reasons. Our bond is new and not quite settled. There's also the perception that he's running things, which I can assure you is not the case. But the main reason is we're focused on the growing attacks by the Bellicose."

The phoenix king's red eyes met mine. "No one who's sensed your magic will believe he is running things, Your...Jenella." He leaned forward. "Tell us about that creature he fought."

"It was a demon." I went over the Bellicose plot to summon demons, the bug magic, the labs, and the potions Calvin and Tracy were working on. "We haven't seen one that powerful before. I'm worried there are more, especially since the gargoyles are amassing in the square."

The Minotaur King snorted, shooting a long line of smoke out of his nose. "This is why we meet. We are small communities with less influence and magic than your dragons and vampires. We are attempting to work out an agreement to band together to protect each other."

They were trying to do exactly what I wanted for the coalition. I had the sudden urge to dance the jig. I buried the excitement and kept my face neutral. If I wanted them on my side, I'd have to play it smart because some of them had been leaders for a long time, even if their groups were small. "I apologize for that. I'm new to this job and never meant to overlook you and your people. It's smart to band together, and I'd like to hear more."

I spent two hours listening to their ideas. They'd spent two years moving their communities closer to each other and worked toward unity. They told me about their struggles and triumphs. By the time they were done, I was in awe of their leadership, willingness to compromise, and to sacrifice for their people. "I want that for the coalition," I said.

"You can achieve it, but it will take time and work." The Centaur King said from beside me. "We can provide you with ideas and insight if you wish."

The leaders of the bigger groups would be difficult to convince. They still hated Deva and the dragons for something she did thousands of years ago. An idea formed. "I'd like that. Would two of you be willing to become advisors?"

Eyes widened, and the air became tangy and sour with fear.

"I don't think that's wise, Your Grace," the Minotaur King said.

"Why?"

"As we explained, we are small groups with little influence. To promote us would put a target on our people."

"Who would target you?"

"Any group that feels their power and influence slipping away."

"I see." I wanted to pace. The coalition *needed* to adopt their ideas. I was sure of that. "The last thing I want is to bring more danger to any of our people. But I *do* want your council." I leaned forward. "How do we accomplish that?"

"Friendship," the Pixie Queen blurted from the small box she sat on in the center of the table.

"Preposterous." The Manticore King wagged his scorpion-like tail. "The Queen of Ahl doesn't need more friends. Much less us."

I almost laughed. I had exactly one and a half friends. And I only trusted one of them.

The pixie queen fluttered her translucent wings. "She's friends with the shunned witch, so why not us?"

I held up a hand. "Actually, I've been disguised as a detective for the last year or so and worked for many of your people, so it's not such a far-fetched idea."

"Friendship." The Centaur King sounded like he was testing the word. "I like it."

We agreed to have lunch the following day, where the public could see us together, and I headed back to the castle, my head spinning. I wasn't sure I'd make actual friends out of them, but I hoped so. I liked their ideas, so at least I'd gain some allies. Then there was the information I got from my mother...er Anitta. I needed to stop thinking of her as my mother because Helen was a million times more of a mom than her. I needed time to think and maybe work through the conversation with Mat. He'd have more insight than me since he knew her.

CHAPTER THIRTY-TWO

DRAKE

DRAKE RETRACTED HIS WINGS as he dove toward the empty field, then stretched them out at the last minute to slow himself. He melted into his human form, clothed himself, and released his cloaking. He hoped he was doing the right thing, but one could never be too careful when going to talk to a god. Especially ones that turned up just before a war kicked off. He eyed the mansion across the field of shrubbery formed into a maze. It was odd for humans to have something like that in the western world.

The door to the farmhouse in the human world swung open, and the god stepped out, his face hard. "What do you want, dragon?"

The man was taller than Drake, with blonde hair and bright blue eyes. His power level was substantial, but not as strong as the other gods he'd met. Political posturing and flowery greetings were beyond him after everything he'd learned the last few days, so he got straight to the point. "I'd like to have a conversation. Maybe ask a favor."

His eyes drifted toward the home next door before returning to Drake. "Come in."

The farmhouse kitchen was rustic, with wooden countertops and tile floors. The pungent scent of lemon and bleach clouded the air. Drake fought not to sneeze as the god waved a hand to a small but sturdy table. "Please, have a seat."

"I apologize for barging in. I understand you met my mate, Jenella."

"You're mated to the queen, then?"

"Yes, though it's a new bond."

The god nodded. "She is very kind."

"She is. I'm here to ask for your help on her behalf.

A small smile formed on the god's face. "Oh?"

He reconsidered for a moment. Until his instincts screamed at him to help her. "Jenella's family is fractured. As a result, her magic got blocked. After a recent encounter, we think it's fixed, but she struggles to relearn it. Her grandmother was from your realm, so she has similar magic to yours. I wondered if you could assess the problem and perhaps guide her through relearning it."

"Why is she not asking me this?"

"She doesn't like people to know her weaknesses. I agreed to find someone to help because if you refuse me, no one will hold it against her. If you refuse her, then many paranormals will expect her to act." Drake doubted his own words because Jenella didn't operate like that. She'd never punish someone for refusing an order, though protocol said she should.

"I see." The god moved toward the icebox that humans stored their food in and extracted a drink. "And you want me to pretend you didn't interfere?"

"No. She knows I planned to ask someone for help."

"I can help." The god retook his seat. "For a price."

The tension drained from Drake's shoulders as the negotiations began. He only hoped it didn't backfire on him. "What kind of price?" A growl laced his voice.

"I wish to establish myself in this realm. Since you are important to the Queen, I want you to help me with that." When the god smiled, he swore the room brightened.

Drake squinted against the light. He'd expected a favor, or perhaps gold, but not that. "Establish yourself in what manner?"

"I want to buy a house in the affluent part of Allure and get introduced to the powerful people who live there."

"Why?"

"Because many gods cannot maintain power levels without people believing in us." He leaned forward. "I've found something that interests me here and plan on becoming powerful enough to stay in this realm permanently."

"I will eat you as a snack should you try to harm Jenella to take over her throne."

The god nodded. "An expected response from a multidrake-landarnarian." He waved a hand. "I have no desire to take over. I only want to fit in amongst the other powerful paranormals in this realm."

Drake didn't take his eyes off the man as he thought it over. Power was addictive, and if this man could increase his power level by belief, then he could become a problem. One that might put the coalition in jeopardy and harm Jenella. "I will need a detailed magical contract swearing you will train Jenella and never harm her or attempt to take over the coalition. That you will not rule a single group in this realm."

"Agreed. On the condition that you find suitable homes for me to consider and introduce me to some powerful people."

"I am not the foremost expert on how the powerful gather, but I will help find you potential homes."

"That will work. And call me Cavil."

"You can call me Drake."

They spent thirty minutes on their back and forth before they agreed on the terms. The agreement was ironclad, but still worried him because he didn't want to put his mate in a dangerous situation. He hoped he made the right choice and that Jenella wouldn't hate him for it.

After he left the god's strange home, he swept the city for information. The known Bellicose offices were empty, so he moved toward one of the apartment complexes. Many Bellicose were still there, but not as many as in previous days. The battle would take place soon. Drake banked left and headed downtown. There were many thoughts related to the Bellicose, none of them kind. The lack of the enemy didn't surprise him. The two locations he'd found within Allure were usually empty during daylight hours. Except for that day.

Before the demon picked up his presence and attacked, he'd learned they planned battles on two fronts. The first from within Allure, the other on the hybrid community in the human world. The attack only caught him off guard because he operated under the assumption that demons couldn't function during the day. It was a mistake he wouldn't make again.

The sun kissed the horizon by the time he made it to the human city. Having a purpose felt good, though he wouldn't count on its permanence until the bond was sealed. Jenella didn't understand dragon mating dances. She thought that by giving him what he wanted most in a dramatic way that she was signaling her acceptance of the bond.

To dragons, such a dramatic act meant love. He could not imagine a world in which Jenella let down her guard enough to love him. As a result, her misunderstanding put him in a precarious position. If he didn't return the gesture, she'd think less of him. Or maybe not. She wasn't interested in the nuances of gestures as much as she was at the thought behind them.

The downtown area bustled with humans and hybrids alike, many drinking in bars and soaking up the last warm days before heading into fall. Too many thoughts cluttered the area, so he flew in a spiral, picked up snippets, and steered clear of the other dragons who patrolled. Many hybrids were wary of the new 'pure bloods' flooding the city.

Drake headed toward an apartment complex in the west area of the city and perched on the roof of a building nearby. He thought about Anitta's revelations. Although he knew she had insiders, he chose not to invade the minds of Jenella's inner circle out of respect. He needed to change that. He wanted no part of that burning rage that pulsed inside of her, though. His chest puffed out with the pride he felt for his mate. She handled a tough situation like a champ and went back to work. More than that, she knew exactly how to push Anitta's buttons to get her to talk. The conversation couldn't have gone better.

He still had the urge to kill Anitta.

Vampires darted in and out of buildings surrounding the apartments. It pulled him out of his morbid thoughts. He tilted his head and examined the white dragon, who soared high above. The scent of diseased magic and vehicle exhaust clouded the air and made his nose burn. The other dragons seemed unbothered. But then, the exhaust fumes weren't nearly as bad as the days when human cities smelled of feces and filthy bodies. Aside from bringing Jenella into the world, creating the pockets with their clean air was one thing Anitta did right, even though her motivations were selfish.

Movement caught his eye from the apartment complex, and two mid-level mages and two witches exited and got into a human vehicle. None of them had what Jenella called bug magic on them. He followed them as they navigated the main roads and turned off into a hybrid neighborhood. Their thoughts revealed they were looking for a powerful mental mage. Jonas's son, no doubt. They'd never find the boy because Jonas's protective streak wouldn't allow it. No one, not even Anitta, challenged him and Ann Marie and won.

After a few turns, they pulled into the parking lot of a neighborhood bar. Drake found an adjacent house and changed into his human form.

If they were targeting hybrids for their mind magic, it made sense that Ann Marie wanted her kids out of the area. Her son was a strong mental mage shifter hybrid with more power than most. He scanned the thoughts of patrons in the bar. The bartender thought of inventory and profit margins, while most patrons pondered their problems. He focused on the Bellicose as a few vampires melted from the shadows. After confirming his suspicions, he launched into the air. The vampires could handle them.

The unmistakable sulfur stench of demons assaulted his nose as he reached the outskirts of the city. He counted three demons hidden within an office building. Two mid-powered and one more powerful than the one he fought earlier. Their minds didn't work like humans or paranormals. Their thought patterns were even more chaotic than the mage they'd encountered at the Cauldron. He was debating his strategy when Glacintial's white form appeared above him again. *Do you feel the demons, Glac?*

The dragon circled twice and landed on the roof. A distant cousin and one of the original dragons that accompanied his aunt through the portal, he was one of the few who could be trusted. He'd served as his aunt's general for many years and now ran the hotel across from Dragon Headquarters.

Glac changed into his human form, his long white hair ruffled in the wind. "Drake."

"What do you know about those demons?"

"Nothing. I am charged with protecting Jonas the First's kids. They are as vicious as him and do not need my help, but it is still my duty."

Drake grinned. "You feel it is a waste of your talents?"

"Queen Deva promised your mate that she would take them in. I am here to ensure that she keeps the promise. It's as boring as it is important."

The smile melted off his face. "Jonas and Ann Marie are right to be wary of the number of Bellicose in the area. You are a good choice for the job."

"Yes. I've counted over five thousand in the area. They have a certain taint to them that the hybrids do not."

"Jenella calls it bug magic."

Glac's white teeth gleamed in the moonlight as he attempted to smile. "I suspect there is more than that in Allure. I have sensed this magic in several neighborhoods."

"As have I. I only wish we knew their plans."

"They are planning an invasion."

"Thanks. I may have never figured that much out had you not told me." Drake's voice held an unusual dryness.

Glac chuckled. "You have spent too much time with that vampire."

Movement outside the office building caught their attention, and the conversation dropped. Drake leaned forward and watched two witches exit, followed by a demon who radiated so much power that his stomach turned. Unlike the others he'd encountered, this one's human form was perfect. He stood about six feet tall, his dark hair streaked with auburn, and his movements natural. The demon stopped two steps outside the door, tilted his head toward the sky and said something to a witch, who scurried back inside the building. The demon crossed his arms and waited.

Go, Glac. Tell the queen about this should I not make it back.

Glac melted into his dragon form and flew south.

The front doors swung open, and three demons like the one he'd fought earlier flew out of the door and darted right at him.

Drake burst into his dragon form and bolted toward Allure.

The demons were fast, but he was faster. He led them on a convoluted chase over the mountains. One caught his tail. Drake dove, barrel rolled, and wagged it. The demon smashed against trees and the ground three times, the barbs on his tail dug into it. He shook his tail as he gained altitude and watched the demon fall until the forest below swallowed it.

As the gate came into view, he didn't think he'd make it. A demon came out of nowhere and slashed at his wing. Drake tried to remember what Jenella's anti-demon magic felt like. He got it mostly right and sent it directly into his attacker as he dove toward the gate. He dodged right when he caught movement out of the corner of his eye. And smashed into another one. It spiraled through the gate.

The other two demons attacked.

He didn't think he could win against the two of them, but he wasn't going down without a fight. Drake blew fire at one and bit the other. As soon as his teeth hit it, it turned to dust. That wasn't right. With no time to ponder the situation, he swung toward the last one and raked it with his claws. It dodged, so he smashed it with his tail. Dust rained down around him.

Drake flew through the gate after the last one. Several guards surrounded a pile of dust. He shifted into his human form and glamoured himself in a white dress shirt and slacks as he strode toward them.

He recognized a vampire as one of Ara's generals and approached her. "Elsie. What happened?"

"It came through the gate and disintegrated when a guard shot it with that anti-demon magic that Jen, I mean the Queen, created."

Those demons didn't react the same as the other demons he'd fought. Drake wasn't sure what that meant for the coalition, but he didn't like it. "I fought two others who acted similar. It is as if they're only half manifested. I think they are bringing them through too fast."

Her eyebrows drew together. "Why are you telling me this?"

"Are you not one of Ara's most trusted generals?"

"I am."

"Good. I trust you to report this back to her."

"Thank you, I guess."

The vampire hadn't heard about his new status as Jenella's Consort. He hoped to see her reaction when she figured it out. In the meantime, he needed to do some research on demons and rally some old friends.

CHAPTER THIRTY-THREE

JEN

LUNCH WITH THE LEADERS was at noon, and I was running late. I'd been practicing my magic, but couldn't find the right emotions to do anything useful. Using emotions worked for healing and flashing, but not on anything else. Which meant I needed to reconsider the strategy. On top of my struggles to find the right emotions, I had to deal with the bubble in my chest. The pain became excruciating every time I tried to conjure something.

Verity insisted she accompany me to my lunch. I wasn't sure what she'd do if they attacked us, but agreed because Tracy was busy in the lab and Verity was good company.

I poked at the bond, but it was closed tight. It bothered me not knowing if Drake was okay. He slammed it shut the night before and I hadn't heard a peep since. I understood how he felt when I kept it closed and he couldn't feel me. I reminded myself for the hundredth time that the guy could take care of himself. Still, I'd become attached and didn't want anything to happen to him.

We flashed to the main square and stepped out of the landing circle. The gargoyles lined the entire square and the tops of the buildings. I needed to call their king and find out why they were there. People stopped and stared as we trudged down the street. A few bowed.

I sighed. "How do I make people stop doing that?"

Verity tucked her hair behind her ear. "You could just tell them."

"All of them? That would take hours."

She shook her head. "The other leaders don't have to deal with the bowing, right?"

"No. It's something my mother came up with to feed her ego. I hate it."

"So end it."

She was right. I'd have to be much more decisive and less...scared. I wasn't sure how to do that, but I added it to my list of things to work on.

Thaddeus's deli was a few blocks from Dragon Headquarters, just past the ogre shops. I opened the door and inhaled the yummy goodness of pickles and freshly baked bread. The deli was decorated in shades of green, complemented by pops of yellow, creating a happy atmosphere. Tables lined the walls on each side of the counter. Paranormals of all different types sat at them, conversing in several languages.

"I adore Thaddeus," Verity said as we made our way to the front.

The leprechaun behind the counter looked up as we approached, and his face lit up. "Verity! Jen! It's good to see you both."

"Hi, Thaddeus." I leaned forward and whispered, "how do you know who I am?"

Thaddeus waved his hand dismissively. "Luck of a leprechaun. I saw you put your glamour on outside the castle one day when I catered an event. Don't worry, your secret is safe with me. What can I offer you today?"

He was a former client who hired me as I worked on my first case. I recovered his life savings. Since then, we'd hired him to cater a few events at the castle. He was a good guy. "Have you thought about my offer to become an advisor?"

He nodded. "I appreciate it, but I'm going to pass. I just want to run me deli."

"I understand. Besides, I don't want you to become so busy that your food suffers."

His grin reached from ear to ear.

We both ordered the special and headed toward the table where four of the leaders I'd met the day before sat. The Minotaur King, the Centaur King, the Fairy Queen, and the Pixie Queen.

"Good afternoon," I said as I took a seat.

"Jenella, Verity, it's good to see you," the Minotaur King said. "I thought you brought your witch to most gatherings."

"She's not my witch. Tracy's a friend and advisor and is busy trying to save the coalition."

"My apologies. I didn't mean to offend."

I waved a dismissive hand. I probably should have been more diplomatic. But Tracy got enough shade from the witches, and I was sick of people marginalizing her. "So, how's your day going?"

The lunch went well. We didn't talk about business, but I learned a lot about what made them tick. The Minotaur King had a herd of a couple hundred. When the Bellicose started ramping up their anti-hybrid campaign, he moved them and the mixed couples he protected, including his daughter, to a rural area of Allure.

The pixies were small but many and only cared about their pixie dust business. Paranormals used their dust for healing, poisons, mood stabilizers, and even aphrodisiacs. The Queen worried her business would be affected if the Bellicose took over. The Fairy Queen was concerned about exposure because her people couldn't disguise themselves among humans with their brightly colored skin and hair.

To the Centaur King, the Bellicose taking over was wrong and therefore unacceptable. He liked being part of the Coalition because it let him rule his people the way he wanted.

As we finished our lunches, Drake popped back into my senses, heading my way from Dragon Headquarters. I turned my chair and focused on the door as he breezed through it. Relief washed across his face when he spotted me.

I grinned.

The grin melted off my face when the Firsts Razazia and Jonas followed him through the door.

"Oh my," the Pixie Queen muttered.

I stood. "What happened?"

Drake strode toward me and kissed my forehead. "Hello, Jenella. We need to talk to you."

I eyed Jonas. I hadn't seen the First Shifter since my coronation. He still looked like an unremarkable middle-aged guy with brown hair and eyes. "Oh?"

Razazia stepped around Drake and examined my wide-eyed lunch companions. "May we join you?"

Five sets of eyes turned to me.

"Of course." I stood to scoot a nearby table over, but Drake elbowed me out of the way and moved it.

Razazia slid into the chair next to Verity, who eyed her suspiciously. "Don't touch her."

Verity didn't roll her eyes, but it was implied in her sharp look.

Jonas sat at the end of the table, leaving the chair next to me for Drake.

"What's this about?" I asked.

Razazia's smile didn't reach her eyes. "A lunch among friends." She leaned forward. "Are we not friends, Jenella?"

"No. I rarely become friends with people after I kick their ass." I didn't mean to say that, but it eased the tension at the table as the others erupted in laughter.

She laughed along with them. "Drake is right about her."

Jonas rubbed his chin, not taking his eyes off me. "Perhaps."

Verity introduced the rest of the table to the Firsts, pulling their attention away from me. I loved that woman.

Drake returned, set a tray in front of Jonas, then took his seat.

The Fairy Queen's wings buzzed with nerves. "Why, exactly, did you decide to befriend us when you have the Firsts?"

I had no idea what Drake was doing. I could have used mind-speak to ask, but I wanted to see how this played out. "Because I find the way you banded together admirable and, more than that, I like you. I've enjoyed this lunch."

The Minitour King rested an elbow on the table. "Are you dismissing us?"

"No." I elbowed Drake.

A mischievous smile lit his face. "I apologize for barging in on your lunch. This was the only time the other Firsts were available."

"And?" I asked.

Jonas leaned forward. "And we wish to talk about the Bellicose before they destroy everything we've built."

The hair on the back of my neck stood up. Where Drake was powerful yet playful, Jonas was rigid and intense. I glanced at Razazia. A predatory glint lit her eyes.

"Right." I leaned toward Jonas. "And you think now is the right time for that?"

He shrugged and took a bite of his sandwich.

An awkward silence settled over the table. The other leaders made excuses and high-tailed it out of the restaurant.

I rubbed my eyes. "Thanks, Drake. Now they'll never want to have lunch with me again."

"Sure they will. They're just in awe of our exceptional display of power."

"It's not the time for jokes. They've banded together with several other leaders to protect their people. It's what I want for the coalition. I wanted to learn how they did it and maybe gain them as allies. You just blew my chances."

Razazia shook her head and nudged Verity's arm. "Is she always this uptight?"

Verity's eyes glazed over briefly before she scooted her chair away. She'd picked something up from the First. "I'm a Juror. Don't touch me."

"What do you want?" I asked in a tight tone.

Drake sighed. "I found an office building in the human world where I believe they're summoning demons."

My heart skipped a beat. "Where?"

"One of my…spies stole information from the building last night. She discovered some of their master plans," Jonas said.

I glanced around the Deli, but it was empty. "Let's take this conversation elsewhere."

As we headed toward the main square, people dove out of our way. Some bolted in the other direction. Others stared wide-eyed. Verity was practicing her flashing skills and agreed to flash Razazia, while I flashed Drake and Jonas. After we landed, we headed to my office. Verity followed us in and shut the door.

As soon as the privacy spell clicked into place, I moved toward the seating area at the end of the office by the windows. "What did you find?"

"I've been watching an office building for several days. Last night, a demon more powerful than the others emerged. He sensed me and sent three of those flying demons after me," Drake explained. "They weren't fully formed."

"What do you mean, not fully formed?"

"They disintegrated as soon as I injured them."

"They abandoned that building shortly after and left a plethora of information behind," Jonas said. "One of my people broke in and stole it. We're still sifting through most of it." He drummed his fingers on his knee. "They plan to attack Allure within the next two weeks. After they take over the coalition, they will attack the hybrid communities and enslave them. I believe their end-goal is to subjugate humans."

My hands shook, and I had to pause so I could convince myself not to run out of the room. It tracked with what Anitta said about an attack coming soon. I suddenly wanted my brother. Mat was so much better at that stuff than me. He just took care of business without the fear that plagued me. Or maybe he didn't show the fear.

Drake put his hand over mine. "I'm sorry, but there's more."

I closed my eyes. "Tell me."

"The powerful demon looked exactly like Jaques."

My eyes flew open. "No."

Razazia shifted in her seat. "No?"

"No. It's not Jaques. Mat sliced him into pieces and burned his body." My head whipped to Drake. "Demons are deceptive. They also play on fears. It's not Jaques." I stood and started pacing. "She knew my greatest fear and planned to use it against me. We can use that to our advantage." I pulled out my phone and texted Mat. "The question is, how?"

Mat burst through the door and strutted across the room. His eyes scanned the Firsts. "What is this about?"

I explained.

His eyes glowed by the time I was done. "You are correct. It's not Jaques. A clever plan had you not blown it up."

"Right? Anitta created my greatest fear and planned to use it against me." I took my seat. "Whoever she has on the inside didn't tell her I woke Razazia."

Mat's face grew hard. "We'll find the traitor and make them pay. Let's focus on the upcoming battle." He turned his focus to the Firsts. "Are you standing with us?"

Jonas stood. "I need to sit this one out. The hybrids are my priority, and I need to protect them."

"Thanks for the info, Jonas," I said. "And thank your spy, too."

He inclined his head as he slipped out the door.

"Razazia?" Mat asked.

She didn't answer right away. After a few seconds, she stood. "I hesitate because my elves are scattered, and I don't yet trust you."

I nodded. "That's understandable. I wouldn't trust me either, considering who spawned us. Will you think about it? The Snow Elf King agreed to help, and I'm hoping to engage the local elves. It would be great to have your support."

"I will." She inclined her head and left the room.

Mat slid into her empty chair. "It's not Jaques."

"It's not. But kudos to Anitta for masterminding that little mind fuck."

Mat cleared his throat at my cussing. "She's good at those. I want to hear what you learned from her."

My stomach soured. I wasn't sure if it was from fear or rage. "What she said, or what I interpreted from what she said?"

"Both."

"She called me stupid and worthless, talked about my lack of power, insinuated that I'm using Drake's power to rule, and that you and I had a false sense of security here."

Mat's eyebrows drew together. "Don't take that personally. It's the same thing she's told me my entire life."

"Those insults were just her warm up. Once she thought she had me where she wanted me, she said power doesn't matter, but the people who serve you do. She thinks the only way to rule is with what she called 'a firm hand' and she is the only one who gets it. Anitta figures out what people want and gives it to them."

Drake shook his head. "Not true. She promises them things to bring them under her influence but never delivers."

I pointed at him. "Exactly. But it works for her. She's grown the Bellicose, even though she openly admitted that magic exacted a price from her for breaking her oath to the coalition. Though, she claimed it was someone else's fault."

Mat rubbed his chin. "That's nothing we didn't know."

I held up a finger in the 'wait' gesture. "That's not the best part. She thinks everyone will fall in line because she's just that great of a leader. And she has an army who plans to attack us soon."

"We already knew that, too."

I sighed. "True."

"But you got more out of it than that."

"Yep. She's delusional and thinks she is the best thing to happen to the world. It's a weak point and we can exploit it. There are traitors among us who expect a payoff for feeding her information. She knew about my magic issues, that you're obsessed with security, and that I'm worried about the coalition falling apart. That means whoever is working for her is someone close to us." I tapped my chin. "She also thinks she'll win, so there must be more than one. She's a brilliant manipulator, so it wouldn't surprise me if she planted several people in key positions. But she can't hold them because she's so diminished she didn't feel my power or the two dragons hovering behind me listening in."

"We were cloaked well," Drake said.

"I still sensed you. If she wasn't diminished, she'd sense you, too. Her power level is that of a mid-level mage of Ahl."

Mat ran a hand through his hair. "Where are you going with this, Jen?"

"I thought the reason they targeted low to mid powered paranormals last year was to divide us. At the time, I hadn't read Anitta's diaries. I didn't even know she was still alive." I held up a hand when Mat opened his mouth to say something. "Her diaries gave me insight into how she thinks. Everything, and I mean everything, is about her, for her, or a manipulative revenge ploy over some perceived slight. The Bellicose recruits weaker paranormals because she's diminished and wants to feel powerful. I asked her why she didn't show up and take the throne instead of reviving the Bellicose. It pissed her off. The ruling magic transferred to me the night we ran, and I got a massive power boost last year. My theory is the first transfer happened when she urged Jaques to be awful to please her. And last year was the first time she summoned demons."

Drake put a hand over mine. "You think she masterminded your whole life?"

"No. Just the years of abuse. I think it eats at her that Mat kept me sheltered and she couldn't reach me to steal the ruling magic back. Not that she could." My stomach soured at how close she'd come to getting me the day I rescued Deva. Had that gone a different way, we'd have lost the war before it began. Mat knew she was out there and likely to target me, which explains why he was so adamant that I take an office job and stay close. The ball of rage inside me burned, so I threw those thoughts out of my head. "Once magic exacts a price for a broken contract, there's no going back."

Mat's eyes glowed with rage. "It doesn't matter. We have her imprisoned and Deva will crack open her mind and gain her secrets. In the meantime, you need to work on your magic. I'll gather our allies." He focused on Drake. "Does Jonas have enough support in the human city?"

"Yes. There are vampires and dragons all over. I've requested the new god help Jenella relearn her magic."

"The one that's way too nice? How can he help?" I pulled out my phone and texted Quin.

"He comes from the same realm as your grandmother."

I froze. "Our grandmother was a god?"

"Essentially, yes. However, only this realm calls them gods."

Mat leaned forward. "And what is this god doing here?"

Drake shook his head. "I got the impression he wants to establish himself and stay here to protect an interest."

I nodded. "He told me that, too."

Mat raised an eyebrow. "What kind of interest?"

"A person, I think," Drake answered.

"Great. Bring him in, but don't tell anyone." I was too desperate to turn down the help. "We can't trust anyone, even our allies."

"I'll set up a war council," Mat said.

I tapped my chin. "I'll contact the dwarves and elves. They run the Conservators and know how the pockets are made. I'll use that as an excuse."

CHAPTER THIRTY-FOUR

JEN

I LANDED IN THE flashing circle of the main square and turned left. People still bowed when they saw me. The bowing was becoming my nemesis. I vowed to take a walk every day until they got used to me wondering through.

Gargoyles dotted every building in the square and lined walkways. There were even more than earlier. As one, their heads swiveled toward me. I tried not to shiver as I scurried down a side street and around the corner. Their king hadn't returned my calls, so I still didn't have any information. My best guess was that demons were being summoned inside Allure. I glanced back toward Dragon Headquarters. We still hadn't found their king. I needed to go back to the summoning room and see if I could bring him in. I picked up my pace. The faster I got the first task done, the more time I'd have to take care of other things.

The Pocket Preservation Conservators, or Conservators, were on the outskirts of downtown Allure next to the combined dwarf and elf district. Their land began in the foothills and extended to the pristine mountains.

Although not as big as shifter territory on the other side of Allure, the land was vast. Dwarves lived under the mountains mining magical minerals that were a side effect of the pocket's creation. The minerals they mined fueled a lot of the magitech and other things we used in our daily lives. Because they were busy making a fortune off them, they didn't have the resources to tend the land above. To solve the problem, they offered the surface to the forest elves who had petitioned for their own land after Razazia disappeared and the elves fractured. The agreement included a tight alliance that turned into a friendship. It was another alliance I wanted to study to see how the different groups worked together. I wondered if I could do that as I learned how to create pockets that included foothills and mountains.

Dismissing the thought, I tilted my head to examine the soft pink Victorian-style mansion with wrap-around porches and white trim. The odd color didn't match the gold and black sign with the name of the organization. I grinned and kept my pace even. I'd never been to the building and butterflies danced in my stomach as my excitement to learn more about the pockets and meet the dwarves and elves stirred.

Beyond the wrap-around porch, large windows flanked the double doors, also white. A slate-colored spell shimmered across the front of the converted house. The smell of eucalyptus and minerals enveloped me as I stepped through the doors.

A grim-faced dwarf perched on a barstool behind a podium glanced up. Her face paled. "Hello, Your Grace. What can we do for you?"

I pasted on a professional smile. "I wondered if I could talk to some of the magic users that maintain the pockets."

Her eyes darted to a tablet in front of her. "They don't work here."

I knew that. Most of the people who went out and recharged our wards were prominent and powerful. I took a step closer. "How about someone who knows about the magical properties of the wards?"

Her forehead creased as she tapped on her tablet. "Prince Leebol will be right with you."

I nodded and moved to the small waiting area and thought about the bond. Drake headed my way, though he was far away and coming from the general direction of Jonas's house. I still didn't like that he could track me down and read my inner thoughts, but checking on him gave me a warm sense of comfort.

Footsteps pounded down the stairs, and I craned my neck to see one of the twelve dwarf princes. He was tall for his species at around five feet. Thick, dark hair covered his head and face. A tiny baseball cap balanced precariously on top of it. He bowed. "Your Grace. I am Prince Leebol of the dwarfs. You had some questions for me?"

I cleared my throat and tried to coax my brain to shift gears. "Yes."

He led me up a winding staircase into an office and closed the door. "What can I help you with?"

"I'd like an overview of how my mother contributed to making the pockets."

The dwarf raised an eyebrow. "You don't already know?"

"No. My mother didn't share that information with me and I can't find documentation. I'd like to learn about the magic used and the differences between pockets so I can improve them and create new ones."

"For the hybrids." He ran a hand through his thick beard. "And perhaps the sasquatches. They don't much care for Mage Mountain, from what I hear."

I thought the sasquatches liked Mage Mountain, since there was a large population there. "Something like that."

He nodded, then went deep into magical theory. I knew magical theory, but not to the levels he explained. It was boring and technical. Most of it was based on experience and educated guesses. Magic was unpredictable and did what it wanted.

Just when I thought my head would explode, he paused. "I wasn't there when the teams created the pocket realms. However, I believe they combined their magic with the Queen's. She absorbed their magic, mimicked it, and weaved a spell. Then, the others added their individual touches to create the environment. Switching out the types of elves and elementals provided the different climates. I've heard she summoned climate mages and mimicked their magic to tweak them. It was quite a feat."

My brain stuck on mimicking magic. It wasn't the same as absorbing, but it was close. I wondered if I could do that. Probably, I decided. "I think I understand. So, creating a pocket that contains a hot and dry climate, like Pyron, I'd need to bring in magical beings who prefer the desert, along with mages with skills like fire protection and air filtration. Maybe some tech and architectural mages. Then mimic their magic, weave it into a shell that contains the atmosphere and allow the others to expand it. In a jungle environment, I'd need to bring in paranormals native to that climate and do the same. Is that correct?"

"Somewhat, yes. I believe you can simply absorb their magic and take it with you so they don't need to be present when creating a smaller pocket. Although many elves and dwarfs claim to have played an integral part in their creation. Some of them help maintain the pockets to this day."

My heart thudded in my chest at the thought that I could mimic. I remembered the ruling magic taking away power from the President of Covens when she disrespected me outside my transport on the way to my coronation. That didn't seem right. He said mimic, not steal. I'd need to think about it more later. "Can I be a part of the next recharge?"

"Of course. We'd be glad to have you." He tapped on a tablet. "I'll send you the schedule."

When I saw them recharge the wards, I'd understand better. "Have the dwarfs heard about the upcoming battle?"

His eyes lifted from the tablet. "Of course."

The front door swung open and Razazia marched in, the Forest Elf Queen behind her. Leebol swung toward them. "Madame First. What can we do for you today?"

She waved a hand. "I'm here to see *Jenella*."

I ignored the extra emphasis on my name. "Hey Razazia. What's up?"

Her eyes narrowed. "What are you doing here?"

Something in her tone set off my anger, and I had to take a breath before I answered. "I'm the Queen. The Conservatory falls under my rule. What are *you* doing here?"

Her translucent wings fluttered with irritation. "This is elf land and I am their First. But that is not what I meant." She sighed. "You haven't heard the news."

My eyebrows drew together. "What news?"

"The apartments in the nearby human town have emptied."

Ah. That explained why Drake was rushing toward me. I pulled out my phone. There were several missed texts from Verity, Mat, and Tracy telling me just that and trying to find out if I was okay. One text from Mat informed me that our allies were gathering in the field between the palace and the council building to prepare for battle. "Thanks, Razazia." I texted everyone back.

An explosion rocked the pocket.

I raced out the door. Thick smoke rose into the air from the direction of downtown. A wave of Deva's mind magic swept over the city, and swarms of dragons exploded into the sky. Many already circled the downtown area.

My heart pounded as I glanced back at Prince Leebol. "Move your people to safety and lock down your mountains."

He frowned. "We're under attack and you want us to hide? What kind of cowards do you take us for?"

"Right. Then prepare for battle and meet us in the field next to the palace. And be careful. The Bellicose have infiltrated our ranks."

He ran back through the door.

My phone buzzed. Mat, telling me to go back to the palace for my safety.

I shoved it in my pocket and realized Razazia and the Forest Elf Queen still stood beside me. "We could use your help, but don't feel obligated. If you don't want to fight, protect your people."

I didn't wait for her to reply before I flashed to the roof of the hotel across from what used to be Dragon Headquarters. And gasped. The entire top few floors of the twenty-story building were gone. Jagged edges of dragon glass and rock stuck out in a curved pattern that resembled a shark shifter emerging with its mouth open. Dragons swarmed the area. There were so many, I couldn't even see the sky. Below, several paranormals lay dead or injured on the ground.

Deva's mind magic was laced with anger as she directed dragons.

The bubble in my chest pulsed, and I rubbed it. *Deva!* I called using mind-speak.

The sea of dragons parted, and a bronze dragon darted through them. Deva landed on the other side of the hotel roof. *She's gone.*

My stomach churned. "How the hell did that happen?"

I have a traitor.

"You said you were hive-minded and your dragons couldn't betray you!"

Unfortunately, I don't always monitor those I trust most. I will not make that mistake again.

My knees almost buckled. Deva didn't trust many people enough not to monitor them. Drake and Bastien would never betray her. "Who?"

Karenalla blew up the magic surrounding her while trying to eliminate it. They escaped together in the chaos.

Can you find her?

I already found and eliminated Karenalla. Anitta escaped.

I clutched my stomach. "No."

I'm sorry, love. I failed you, myself, and my dragons.

Her statement rang true. But I didn't believe it. Deva didn't make mistakes like that. Or I'd never heard of her making them. She didn't involve herself in politics until I came along and Mat dragged her in to protect me. "Are you still on our side, Deva?"

Smoke billowed from her nose. "You question my loyalty?"

Drake descended through the dragons and landed on the roof. I flashed to his back. "I'm questioning everyone's loyalty right now. Especially the dragon who let that slimy, manipulative bitch slip through her fingertips."

You may be family, but I will still eat you should you continue to question my loyalty. I have made a vow to you and intend to keep it. Her statement was in the form of a roar inside my head.

Smoke boiled out of Drake's nose and floated away, but he didn't speak.

I held Deva's closest eye for a few seconds. Not because I was confident, but because I needed time to cool the simmering rage that fought to explode. "Then rally the dragons and meet us at the palace. Herd any demons or Bellicose you come across there on the way."

Drake launched into the air. *The Bellicose apartments are not empty but contain fewer paranormals than before.*

"Great. Let's head to the gates and then sweep the city."

Nothing was going on in Allure. We spotted a couple of fights, but there was no sign of Anitta or the Bellicose. The entire time, I pondered how she manipulated Karenalla into working with her without Deva knowing. She said she didn't monitor her as much. We all knew how Anitta operated. And Deva had witnessed it first-hand when Anitta put Drake to sleep. Yet she didn't monitor the dragon charged with caring for the prisoner. Or the spell.

Is Deva okay? I asked.

She's angry and embarrassed about her mistake. I believe her when she says she won't make it again.

He was a loyal dragon.

We descended on the lawn of the palace where our allies were already gathering. Drake didn't bother to shift to make himself smaller, so some had to scramble out of his way. I flashed to the ground between his feet. There weren't many paranormals there yet, just a smattering of mages, older vampires, shifters, palace guards, and griffins. I didn't see any dragons or witches. I hoped more would show up.

Mat picked his way toward me and inclined his head. "You talked the dwarves and elves into helping."

"Not really. They volunteered when Dragon Headquarters exploded."

I rested a hand on Drake's foot. "How many will help?"

"Unknown. I doubt this battle will be conventional. Gabe thinks they'll attack his shifter compounds first and release them on the city, so they only offered a few to help us."

"Did Calvin give him potions to protect them?"

"He distributed them to the individual alphas yesterday."

That was something, at least. "What is your strategy? If they attack people on the streets, we'll be spread thin." I waved my hand toward the clusters of paranormals.

Mat's eyebrows drew together. "I am aware. We have enough powerful allies to win, even if they try urban warfare."

"I don't trust any of them right now," I mumbled.

"Nor do I."

"Where's Emine?" I didn't trust her to have our backs, either, after she left Quin and me to battle a horde of tainted shifters alone.

"She's gathering enforcers and will be here soon."

Drake melted into his human form and shook his head. "Our enemy is coming in from all directions. Deva eliminated a group entering the ogre district. They were also spotted near witch territory."

I thought about the smaller species I tried to befriend. They'd be vulnerable and unprepared. I pulled out my phone and texted the Fairy Queen and the Manticore King. "The witches can hold them off. I take it Deva offered to protect the ogres?"

"Yes." Drake rested his hand on my shoulder. "She's angry, and it's stirred up the others. Dragons are more powerful when they're angry. It would only take two or three to provide them protection."

He had absolute faith in his aunt. I didn't blame him after all she did for him, but I didn't share the sentiment. Not after she manipulated me into summoning the mother I thought was dead and then letting her escape. "Sure. I'm going to go change clothes and touch bases with Verity."

CHAPTER THIRTY-FIVE

JEN

Relief flooded me when I returned, and more paranormals sprinkled the field. We still needed more to win, but it was a good start.

I didn't object when four palace guards fell in around me and helped me make my way to a newly built hill where Mat and Drake stood with several other leaders. My brother was brilliant at taking care of business, and I realized I could learn a lot from him if I ever got out of my own way.

When I reached the top of the hill, I inclined my head at the Pixie Queen, who perched on a nearby branch. I didn't see Quin and Ara in the group and wondered where they were. Quin was always around, so his absence was odd. Tracy and Bastien were at the alchemy compound preparing potions for everyone. On top of that, Drake was also gone. I pang of longing ran through my chest. At least I sensed his presence downtown, so I knew he was okay.

I stopped at the top of the hill, and Mat rested a hand on my shoulder. "A few groups are still en route."

"How are we going to do this?"

"We'll wait until everyone gets here, give a motivational speech, and set up city-wide patrols. When the Bellicose begin their attack, we'll converge."

"That's it?"

He dropped his hand. "We haven't been attacked and if people don't feel like they're contributing, they'll lose faith and become complacent."

"Right." I didn't like it because I had the urge to kill everyone who ever thought of siding with the Bellicose. Especially Anitta. I wanted to bite her in half and...I shook my head. Those weren't my feelings, but Drake's, though my feelings toward her weren't much different if I disregarded the urge to bite her. I turned my attention back to the field.

The wind whistled through the trees behind us as mages filed in from the council building and came to a stop in front of the hill. Griffins descended from every direction and landed among them. Not all of them ours. Vampires melted from the shadows, led by Quin and Ara. Glitter dropped from the sky as a swarm of pixies joined their queen. The Fairy Queen winked at me as she and the leaders of their co-op led their small groups in. Manticores and centaurs trotted away and blended in with the mages. Hundreds of elves and dwarves arrived together and split to take up our left and right flanks. Several other paranormals of all different types intermingled amongst them.

Helen and George, in griffin form, perched on each side of the hill and faced the crowd. Emine marched through the gates, leading disciplined rows of uniformed enforcers to the front. All of them in their human forms.

Silence settled over the field as Drake, Deva, and several dragons descended and landed behind us. Drake shifted and moved to my side. I reached for his hand. He lifted it to his lips but didn't comment.

"As soon as she makes her speech, leave," Mat warned.

Drake stayed silent. He knew I wouldn't leave while other people fought.

Mat activated an amplifier spell. "Thank you for helping defend Allure and the Coalition. As many of you know, a group calling themselves the

Sentinels has gathered in the nearby human town. They call themselves that as a recruiting effort. Make no mistake, they are still the same Bellicose that has fought to destroy the coalition since its inception."

A sparkle from the corner of my eye and the pixie queen perched on my shoulder. "You can't trust them, Queen Jenella."

I kept my face neutral. "Who?"

"Any of them. We spent the day spying on the different factions around the city. Not all of them are as loyal as they pretend to be."

My eyes trailed over the field. I already knew we had traitors, but I appreciated that the pixies took the time to help. "Thanks. And be careful when you spy."

She belly laughed. "No one sees us as a threat enough to bother hiding things."

"They will now that they've seen you on Jenella's shoulder," Drake said.

She fluttered in front of his face on the way back to her branch. "They'll also see that she protects us."

Amusement came through the bond. *You have made some interesting friends.*

She's not really a friend yet, but I'll take all the support I can get.

I missed most of Mat's speech during the exchange, but cheered with the crowd when he was done. Several groups left to patrol not long after. I expected those not on patrol to leave, and some did, but many camped out in the field. The dwarves burrowed into the side of the hill leading to our running trails, and the elves set up shelters for everyone by growing wide-leave plants to use as tents. I sat in the grass on the hill and watched them as the sun sunk and the shadows grew long. Mat and Emine went back to the castle a couple of hours earlier, but Drake stayed by my side.

Silence fell over the field as the darkness descended. I leaned against him and tried to stop my eyes from drooping. "What if they don't attack?"

He wrapped his arm around me and pulled me closer. "They will. Where are the shifters?"

I yawned. "Mat said they're locking down their territory since they've been the targets of the bug magic."

"Let's go back to your apartment and rest," he whispered against the shell of my year.

Goosebumps broke out over my skin. "Okay," I said before my brain engaged.

We tiptoed around the makeshift leaf tents as we made our way back toward the castle.

Just outside the outer wall, my skin started crawling. I sent my senses out. Hundreds of Bellicose surrounded us. "Um."

Drake sniffed the air. "They're here."

I jerked out my phone and texted Mat before I flashed us back to the hill.

The Bellicose melted out of the shadows in a trickle. They came from all directions and met a ward that hid us from their sight and blocked them. As they felt for weaknesses, they got funneled toward an entrance to the left-front of the field.

Mat and Emine appeared next to us as the demon pretending to be Jaques stepped through an opening. Five tainted mages swarmed around him. The ward shook, and sparks shot into the air. I closed my eyes to salvage my night vision. When I opened them, the ward was gone, and several untainted witches stood within the Bellicose ranks. The ball of rage inside me burned hotter.

The vines hiding our allies disappeared, and hundreds of dwarfs charged out of their make-shift caves. Those who left earlier converged behind the Bellicose.

At least a hundred dragons, led by Bastien and Tracy, raced from downtown carrying the alchemy coven and circled the area. Potions rained down on our enemy as vampires melted out of the shadows. Our allies might have disbanded, but they didn't go far.

I didn't have time for a little 'yay' moment, though, because the former President of Covens stepped up beside the demon and smirked. Every encounter I'd had with her floated through my mind. The scene outside the transport before my coronation where I'd almost taken her magic away. How she accused me of being weak at the council meeting. That she tried to kill me. Then the protesters who were hanging around out front, probably gathering information. "Tell Tracy it's time for her revenge."

Drake squeezed my hand once.

I took that as agreement and focused on the demon.

"Take the lead, Jen," Mat growled.

If the demon was surprised to meet such a large force, he didn't show it. He stopped and tilted his head to where we stood on the hill. "Hello, Jenella." He used projection to make his voice heard.

The voice was off. Jaques's voice always held an arrogant, controlled tone with a slight English accent. The demon's accent sounded as American as mine.

I still broke out in a sweat and shook. Drake sent calm and confidence through the bond, and I grabbed onto it like a lifeline. His warmth grounded me enough to speak. "You are a poor imitation of my dead brother, demon." My voice echoed over the field.

The same sinister smile I remembered from my tormentor spread across his face. "Oh, I doubt that. Tell me, are there any cages in this castle?"

I ignored the jab as I counted the flying demons overhead. There were ten of them.

"You are not Jaques. You have one minute to disband and leave this realm before we banish you and slaughter your people, including your pet witch." Mat's voice was firm and commanding.

The demon threw his head back and laughed. "The Bloody Prince has spoken. I'm shaking in my boots." He blasted bug magic at the ward that surrounded the castle walls. It spread over the surface, oozing and crawling. People with more sensitive noses gagged at the stench. With a flash of orange, it dissipated.

The demon turned and barked orders as the witches released a combined spell. It floated towards the wards. They shook but held.

"Tracy."

Bastien lifted off the ground. Tracy stood on his back and swirled her hands in a circle. A spell crashed down on a good portion of the witches. They screamed.

The demon roared.

I reactivated my projection spell. "Engage," I said in a calm, commanding voice.

Bastien swooped over the crowd as Tracy threw a neutralizing spell at the tainted mages.

Hundreds of flying paranormals lifted off the ground. Dragons, griffins, pixies, fairies, and many others filled the sky. The bellicose troops surged forward.

The demon's form flickered, revealing a horned gray creature with a triangular face and wings. It was only a split second, but it was enough. Mat and I shared a look. He conjured his katanas, their blue magic bright against the darkness. "Stay safe, Jen." He dove into the fray.

Emine brought out her flame thrower. "Enforcers are on the way, chickee. Kick some ass." She followed Mat into the crowd.

Drake shifted to his big, fluffy form, and I flashed to his neck.

Dragons swooped down and blew fire, and griffins slashed with their claws and bit with their teeth. Vampire blurs raced through, leaving bodies in their wake. Mages blasted magic. Pixie dust rained from the sky, neutralizing bug magic and rendering people unconscious. Dwarves swung their battle axes, and elven magic created a haze over the field. Thick vines wrapped around the enemy and held them until mages could move in.

The roar of voices was deafening. The scent of blood tinged the air. I lost track of Mat, but Emine was easy to spot as she switched back and forth between her flame thrower and a machine gun. She chased down witches, cackling as she sprayed them with her flame thrower or bullets. She seemed to switch between the two, depending on who she encountered. One coven tried to weave a spell. Emine's bullets cut into them and half of them fell to the ground in a spray of blood.

The President of Covens stood in the center of the group, weaving another spell. Bastien swooped toward her, and Tracy launched herself off his back. She started throwing punches before they hit the ground and got swallowed by the crowd.

Bastien blew black fire toward the remaining witches. Some ran away, others got caught up in it and melted to ash.

The overpowering odor of burning flesh dwarfed the putrid smells of battle. I tore my eyes away from the gore and tried to breathe through my mouth.

An explosion rocked the ground, and part of the wall leading to the palace crumbled. I hunkered down on Drake's neck as he stormed through the crowd, smashing bellicose with his front paws heading straight for the fake Jaques.

A group of untainted shifters of all types stormed through the wall and raced in our direction. Good. The shifters showed up.

It took my brain a few seconds to register their lack of engagement with the Bellicose. They didn't even slow down as they charged past the enemy and toward us. I caught a glimpse of a huge gray wolf seconds before a rhinoceros shifter slammed into Drake's side, pulling my attention away.

He roared and stomped him into the ground, chomped a tiger in half, and used his size to smash anyone who got close while sending out waves of mental magic. It was enough to cause many of the shifters to hesitate or pick easier targets.

"The castle is breached."

"*Gah!*" I slid halfway off Drake's shoulders before his magic caught me and tossed me back on. Quin crouched on his back behind me, his eyes red and his four fangs out. "Damnit Quin. Shouldn't you be fighting?"

"Then you would not know the castle has been breached."

"Drake?"

Deva has deployed people to take care of it.

I relayed the information to Quin.

"Very well. Try not to die in a stupid way." He dove onto the back of a charging elephant and shoved his claws into its neck.

I dragged my attention away from him when shouting came from the castle, and fire shot into the air, heating the entire area. A yellow dragon plummeted from the sky, and one of the flying demons descended on him. Two centaurs rammed the demon at full-speed as a griffin swooped in and bit him. A nearby mage chanted and hurled magic at the demon. It disintegrated into ash.

I rubbed the growing bubble in my chest. I fought the urge to jump in and help.

The fake Jaques demon appeared in front of us and morphed into his true form. His arms and legs thickened, and his wings expanded until he was around the same size as Drake. "Hand over the fake queen, First, and we will allow you to live."

Why do the bad guys always think that line will work? I spoke in Drake's head.

Perhaps they watch too many human movies, too. Drake morphed into his dragon form and struck at a dizzying speed. His teeth sunk into the demon's center, and chanting rang through my head. The demon disappeared. *I missed him.*

I clutched my favorite spike. *He can flash?*

He used a teleportation device.

A blur ran through the gaggle of shifters still trying to attack us, even though they were puny compared to Drake's dragon form. Their heads left their bodies.

Ara appeared from the blur, pausing long enough to let Tracy and Bastien fly by, potions and spells dripping from them, sprinkling the crowd. She turned her red eyes toward me, and her lips formed a feral smile. A drop of blood fell from her fangs. I shivered.

A different roar came from the front of the house, and smoke and dust filled the air as the front of the palace collapsed. There were holes in the walls along the side and scorch marks. Smoke rose from the roof. People streamed out of the family entrance.

My hands clenched and unclenched in frustration. So much senseless death and violence. My heart ached for every single paranormal caught up in the mess. I wished I knew how to stop it. I was utterly useless without access to my magic.

"Retrieve the fake queen," a guttural voice came from the ground. The fake Jaques demon, I realized. He was tall and gangly yet muscular in his true form. His twisted teeth were at least three inches long. The black horns on his head dripped with an oily substance, and his greasy wings were tattered. One hung at an odd angle. He threw a putrid brownish-gray magic at us.

Razazia swung in on a vine, landed in front of Drake, and launched yellow elven magic toward it. It swirled around the demon and formed thick green ropes.

The demon flexed and wiggled as he tried to free himself.

Drake sent a stream of colorful ruling magic toward him. Mine, I realized, though I didn't even feel a tug.

Bastien swooped in as Tracy slung a potion at the demon. A torrent of fire streamed out of his mouth.

The three magics combined just before it hit.

"Boom!"

Drake snatched Razazia off the ground and escaped into the air. I leaned over and peered at the crater as he descended and released Razazia. She dove back into the battle.

The demon still stood, though he had several gashes that oozed a deep brown liquid.

I gagged. "Gross."

The demon took two steps toward us.

Anitta stepped out from behind him and smirked. "I've been wanting to do this for a long time. Consider yourself dethroned." A torrent of bug magic exploded from her so fast I didn't have time to duck out of the way.

Everyone had tried to help me figure out my magic, and I'd made some progress, but I still couldn't do much more than conjure raw, colorful magic and flash. I'd even gone back and skimmed my grandmother's diaries to figure it out. As the bug magic came toward me, all those failed attempts flashed through my mind.

I slammed my eyes shut as it hit us. It blew my hair back. My face and arms tickled as it wiggled around me and tried to latch on. I kept my eyes closed and braced myself to fight the lethargy that overtook people when they were first infected.

The tickling came to an abrupt stop. I cracked an eye open. Dead bug magic surrounded me, sitting limp and useless on Drake's back. Not a single spec of it on my clothes or in my hair. Whatever the magic of Mage Mountain did to kill it, I had done. I hid my confusion. "I'm waiting to be dethroned, weak mage."

Drake let out a deafening roar and descended on the demon. Bright green magic, rather than fire, streamed from his mouth, dissolving the demon's defenses and the bug magic that covered his minions. His neck stretched, and his sharp white teeth clamped down on the demon. He chanted as he tore it apart. Dust floated into the swimming pool. He raised his head and trumpeted.

I released my favorite spike and dove off his back toward my mother. My momentum was enough to smash her into the ground. I wrapped one hand around her throat and punched her with the other.

She screamed and latched on to my boobs as she tried to push me away. Green magic surrounded us and tried to suck me back toward Drake. I wrapped my arms around Anitta and let it take me.

As soon as my feet touched his back, I slammed her body onto a spike.

Her shrill scream pierced the air. I lifted her up and slammed her down again. She squirmed, and the spike went through an ear and out the other side. Mat appeared beside me. A glowing blue katana sliced through her neck. I flashed to the ground, leaned over, and vomited.

The Shifter Alphas darted out of the hole in the wall and sliced through two fairies who tried to stop them. They gathered their horde of untainted shifters and charged a group of vampires.

Bloody and broken people littered the battlefield. Shifters howled, people screamed, and magic flew. The stench of burning flesh, bug magic, and blood coated the air. I pulled my shirt over my nose so I didn't vomit again.

Two demons descended on Drake, causing Mat to slip. He flashed away before he hit the ground. Covered in blood and radiating with rage, his eyes met mine. He inclined his head like killing our own mother was no big deal and raced after the Alphas.

No way I was getting back on Drake's back with the bloody mess of what used to be my mother up there, so I flashed to the top of a section of the wall.

I thought I'd been in battle before. I was wrong. The fight with the demon in Hospa seemed so insignificant compared to this one. It was like comparing a speck of dust to a planet. There was so much death. So much destruction. My heart ached at the sight of what should be allies attacking each other. I wished it would end. I wished *I* could end it.

A flash of bright light and the too nice god appeared beside me, a white haze surrounding him. I backpedaled, almost lost my balance, and flashed back to the center of the wall.

His smile was too bright for a battle as he bowed. "I'm here to help you with your magic."

"Not a good time," I said as I dug through my pack for Tracy's potions.

"I disagree. It's the perfect time." He motioned toward the field. "Or do you not want to end this?"

I wanted to more than anything. I tilted my head toward Drake as he lodged his tail in a demon and slammed it against a tree. Deva swooped by and yanked it out of the tree, and flew off. The Shifter Alphas tore into a manticore that got separated from his herd. "Now would be a good time to tell me what to do."

Cavil shuffled closer as if on a Sunday stroll. "You are trying to pull your power from your core. It's unnecessary. You don't have magic, you *are* magic."

A spell hit him, reversed, and covered the witch who threw it. The guy screamed as he melted to the ground. "Um. I don't know what that means."

"The magic is a part of you in its raw form. Stop trying to force it and just tell it what to do. It will comply. Don't be afraid to get creative." He winked.

A demon scaled the wall and swiped at me, his claws catching my hip and leg and leaving deep gashes. The fiery rage I'd suppressed since I'd learned about the lies and deceit surrounding me reared its ugly head.

I demanded my magic eliminate every speck of bug magic in the pocket and end the fight. That it send the damn demons back to hell. The boiling anger injected itself into the bubble in my chest and it burst.

The entire pocket rocked as silver magic shot from me in all directions, following my orders. It flung me off the wall and lifted me into the air. It turned me as bright as a star as it cascaded over the battlefield and beyond in watery waves. The Bellicose dropped like rocks. The demons melted to dust.

It cut off. I plummeted.

A griffin swooped in a second before Drake got to me and I landed face-first on its furry back. I stayed that way as we landed and waited for my heart to exit my throat. "Thanks, Helen," I said as I slid off her back and caught myself on my weak limbs. I swung my head toward the wall to thank Cavil. He was gone.

Helen huffed at the human version of Drake and launched into the air.

Mat stood frozen a few feet away, his eyes wide, his katanas forgotten.

Emine threw her hand up in the air and hooted.

My knees shook, and I latched onto Drake to steady myself.

All the fighters from our side stood wide-eyed.

I cleared my throat. "So that just happened."

Drake stepped back and examined me from head to toe. "Are you okay?"

"Yeah." I rubbed my chest and noted that the bubble that had been plaguing me was gone. "I feel better, actually."

Mat strode toward us. "What did you just do?"

"I don't have power. I *am* power," I muttered.

"Why must you always explode your magic?"

I didn't jump at Quin's appearance, though I didn't sense him, either. I didn't have the energy to care.

Mat tore his eyes away from me to address Gilbert, a manticore and the leader of the castle guard. "Bring the healers in. And assign people to set up tents for them. Do a battlefield assessment and report back."

"Yes, Your Majesty." His eyes stayed locked on me as he marched away.

We waded through the battlefield and the debris that used to be the castle, helping the injured and taking care of the dead. Tears slid down my cheeks as I helped move and cover people who didn't make it. I didn't apologize for the tears, or offer explanations when eyebrows raised. The deaths were pointless. Those people deserved better from me and everyone else tasked with keeping them safe.

I found Verity and Titus broken and bloody outside of what used to be the family entrance. Mat healed them as best he could, then sent them to the healer's tents near the woods in the back of the castle. I wished five people back to health before I ran out of energy, so I did what I could. Drake stayed with me the whole time, offering his muscles to move chunks of building and sending support through the bond. He occasionally offered a handkerchief or conjured a bottle of water. Anyone who dared to judge me got a multidrakelandarnarian growl in their face. I appreciated that because I was in no mood to deal with the backlash from the mess.

I sensed Quin standing guard on what was left of the roof with several other vampires, but he didn't bother making another appearance.

Tracy administered healing potions. At some point, her dad and his coven showed up with carts full of them and the potions that cleared the bug magic. When Tracy ran out of hers, she found me and dragged me to a food tent Thaddeus and other restaurant owners set up, and she and Bastien force-fed me a sandwich.

When we finished the forced meal, she put a privacy spell around the four of us, leaned back and folded her arms. "Tell me what's going through your head, Jen."

"I'm fine. Just...Are you okay? I lost track of you when Bastien started burning witches."

Tracy managed a small smile. "As okay as I can be, I guess. I finally killed her." Her voice was a little too ragged.

"Tracy—"

She shook her head. "I don't want to talk about it until I've processed the whole thing. What about you? You finally got the person behind the Bellicose leadership."

My stomach soured at the thought of my mother. I barely lived through watching her fake her death. This time? I was numb. "Mat killed Anitta. I just spiked her."

The table fell into silence.

Drake rubbed both hands over his face. "I've never considered my back as a weapon."

His attempt at humor fell flat.

I squeezed his arm. "I think the reason Quin couldn't find their so-called king is because no one expected the Shifter Alphas to be traitors."

"Correct," Bastien said. "There are probably more demons and plenty of Bellicose left to summon them. We still need to find the Alphas, the sympathizers, and their so-called king."

Hot anger flashed through me at his words. "So much senseless death, and for what? Why would Gabe and Linda do all of this?"

"They're not running the Bellicose, even though they are part of the leadership."

"Then who is? Jonas?"

"No." He held up his phone. "Jonas is engaged in his own battle against the Bellicose. We think your theory that it's another First has merit."

I remembered they wanted to bond me, as Detective Hendrix, to their declared king. Since Gabe already had a match, it made sense someone else was running the show. Someone powerful, based on that magic I felt in the pyramid in Pyron. "I summoned the person behind the Bellicose and my mother appeared. Maybe I can summon their king, too."

Bastien shook his head. "We can't hold anyone right now. Both Dragon Headquarters and the palace were destroyed. And the Cauldron might not hold someone that powerful."

Tracy's eyes hardened. "I mean, with Anitta and the former coven president gone, they have to be weakened, right?"

Drake took my hand. "Those are good questions. Ones we'll have to answer later."

I turned my attention back to the castle. The entire front was gone, part of the family wing collapsed. The back had a giant hole in it, the floors hanging on by a thread. Stone scattered across the landscape. Blood soaked the ground. "If a First woke up and decided the coalition needed better leadership, then we're going to have to be creative." I shook my head. "That theory makes more sense, but still doesn't feel right."

Bastien leaned forward. "Your mother didn't reveal who helped her?"

"No. But none of this makes sense. Demons feed off chaos and like to prey on humans, not paranormals. And my mother was as selfish as she was ruthless, so she'd set herself up as the most powerful person in the room. She wouldn't want a First thinking he was going to rule." I shook my head. "I will never understand the Bellicose. Their entire agenda makes no sense if you think about it. We all have a specific amount of power and it's rare to gain more. It's unreasonable to think that you can gain enough to control the entire supernatural population unless it's transferred to you or you're born into it."

Bastien raised an eyebrow. "Oh?"

"What I mean is they want to use spells to control everyone and skip the faction leadership. It's not sustainable in the long run."

Drake nodded. "It's a tale as old as time. They want to separate us, so they prey on minor grievances and inflate them to where people think the prescribed issue is their biggest problem. Then they use mind-magic to give the anger a nudge and do everything they can to fan the flames. The paranormals helping them are most likely under the impression they will gain status or even power. Most won't care if they can target their anger. Using demons is new, though. Demons don't care about long-term control. They only care about causing enough chaos to feed."

"All great points. It's still dumb."

Bastien grunted. "We need to look for people who try to be more powerful than they are."

Like my former friend and son of the traitorous alphas. "Maybe."

Drake rubbed my back. "We'll figure it out. It is my new purpose, after all."

I took a sip of water. "Are you okay with that? The purpose?"

"Yes. Are you going back to your house?"

"Yes."

He leaned in so his lips were close to my ear. "I need a place to stay."

CHAPTER THIRTY-SIX

JEN

THE DRAGONS WHO LIVED in the tower all moved across the street to their hotel. Except Deva. She perched on the ruins of the building and refused offers to stay at my house or in the untouched guest wing of the castle, where Mat and Emine planned to stay. Most of the griffins stayed with them to guard it and help rebuild.

I wiped my sweaty hands on my filthy pants as Drake descended to the spelled alley behind our little house. Butterflies erupted in my stomach at the thought of Drake staying with me.

Neither of us spoke as we made our way to my bedroom. Drake looked around and moved toward the window to peer out. "Your view is odd."

A nervous smile spread across my face. One window looked out the front, where two faced the side of our neighbor's house. "I never open those blinds. I bet the view from the top of Dragon Headquarters is amazing."

"The sunrises are breathtaking. I can't wait to share one with you."

It sounded great. And terrifying, I thought as his arms came around me. Heat soaked into me and I melted against him. "I doubt I'll ever be normal." I turned, buried my head in his chest, and inhaled his scent.

He lifted my chin with one finger until I met his eyes. "Normal is boring and overrated. I'm not sure it even exists, considering how many times it's changed throughout the years. You are who I want."

"Even though I'm screwed up and weird?"

Soft lips brushed across my temple. "I'll eat anyone who calls you weird."

"Ha ha."

"Stop telling yourself you're screwed up. You're no more screwed up than everyone else." He stepped back. "I understand not wanting to nurture the bond until you've established your place in this world. I can wait a little longer if that's what you want."

My heart ached at his words. I wanted *him* to find his place. Mine was established the day I was born. "I'm sorry I did this to you."

"You didn't do anything. The fates decide who we bond with. My point is, I'll give you all the time you need to work through it. I hope you one day realize what an amazing person you are and accept the bond for the gift it is instead of viewing it as a shackle."

"I don't see it as a shackle." More like a bomb waiting to explode, but I doubted saying that would help the situation.

He played with one of my curls. "I've done an abysmal job courting you. I decided many years ago that my mate would never appear. When you did, I thought the fates played a cruel joke giving me my enemy's daughter. As I got to know you, that changed."

"Damn fates."

His lips twitched. "When the Firsts and the dragons rejected me, I thought it was because I was not worthy and needed to earn my place. I spent years trying to become worthy with no success. Because of those experiences, your apprehension about the bond made me hesitant to pursue it. By the time I realized I bungled our courtship, you'd already figured it out and thought I lied to you. I'm usually smarter than that, I promise."

"You are." I ran a hand over the scar on his arm. "You're also as scared of it as I am, you big chicken dragon."

He didn't laugh like I hoped. Instead, he waited until I met his eyes before he continued. "The bond compels me to nurture it. I should have told you and started courting you the minute it formed, even though I knew you were such a scaredy queen that you'd run."

I opened my mouth to say something, but he put a finger on my lips. "There's no need to say anything. As far as the age difference is concerned, you made a good point. Our world views and life experiences are very different. You think your childhood trauma is the worst thing that could happen. And believe me, if I could, I'd go back in time and kill every person who knew what Jaques was doing to you. But I must admit I've seen worse."

My stomach soured at the thought. "I don't want to know."

"No, you don't." He dropped his hand. "The age difference doesn't bother me. Dragons often mate with people much younger or older than them. As a result, we instinctively adapt. It's impossible for us to do anything other than accept our mate for who they are. You can ask Tracy about that if you don't believe me."

"Tracy is angry at Bas most of the time, so I'm not sure that's a good example."

"True. But it works for them. The bond allows us to understand what our mate feels and helps us adapt to them. It goes both ways. When we disagree, it will help us communicate and understand each other." He leaned in so his lips touched my ear. "That, along with the make-up sex, will be glorious."

I choked out a laugh. "What about regular sex? Will it be glorious?"

His lips met mine. Gentle at first. As if he were testing. I snaked an arm around his neck and pulled him closer and sunk into it. Heat transferred back and forth through the bond and my knees almost gave out. His hands lowered to my hip. He tasted like fire, hope, and redemption. I dug my hands into his hair and pressed myself against him as hunger replaced my anxiety.

He broke the kiss and pulled back.

I shivered as I ran a hand over his muscular chest and rested my forehead on it. "Shower."

He chuckled. "We don't have to do anything tonight, or any night, until you're comfortable. I just want to be with you."

I met his eyes. The hunger in them reflected mine. I locked my knees. "It's not that I don't want...I do, it's just I–" I sucked in some air. "I'm messing this up."

He shook his head and slid his hand down my arm. "Impossible."

I headed toward the bathroom. "I got dibs on the shower."

"Dibs?"

"Yeah. Dibs."

"Do these dibs apply to always, or can I join you sometime?"

A tremor ran through me at the suggestive tone. I shook a finger at him. "Nuh uh." I shut the bathroom door.

I grinned as I scrubbed the grime off. My stomach flipped with anticipation. Was I really doing this? The thought made my body ache and my heart flutter, so I concentrated on the task.

After I dried, I pulled out a spell to tame my hair so it wouldn't be a frizzy mess, slipped into my fluffy robe, and padded back into the bedroom.

He sat on the bed, clean and wearing only a pair of boxer briefs, his hair slicked back. I eyed his rugged, muscular body. White scars ran down his sides, a triangular one on his chest. Those butterflies that had been fluttering in my stomach as I showered exploded. I dragged my gaze to his face. His eyes smoldered as I tiptoed toward him on shaky legs.

I slipped between his knees and pulled him close. I ran my hands down his sides before moving them to his shoulders. He reached out and twisted a finger in one of my curls. "You are beautiful, Jenella."

I leaned in and touched my lips to his. I went for tentative, but the heat and anticipation rushing through me took over. Hunger overwhelmed me, and I needed all of him. The kiss deepened. He wrapped his arms around me and pulled me to the bed, his body covering mine. I ran my hands down his muscular back and watched goosebumps roll over his skin. His eyes glowed as his soft lips trailed my body. Heat and desperation roared through me, and my mind went blank as hunger consumed me.

My pillow was too hard and my face sweaty. I cracked an eye open. Sunlight streamed through the blinds and I tried to sit up. A steel band constricted and locked me in place. "Ow."

"Sorry." Drake's sleepy voice rumbled in my ear as the steel band released.

I raised my head and did a drool check. Relieved that his chest was drool-free, I turned my attention to him. A wicked smile worked its way onto my face as memories of our first night together flooded into my head. Energy surged through me. I could have hopped out of bed and ran a marathon. "Morning."

"Hmmmpf." A small stream of smoke trailed out of his nose.

"Not a morning person, huh?"

"No. I should be, since I *can* wake up now." One green eye cracked open. "You look like the cat that ate the canary."

"I am feeling rather energized."

He pulled me closer and kissed my forehead.

The wards pinged.

"Ugh." I pulled back. "Mat's here."

Drake grumbled and gently set me aside as he climbed out of bed. I sat up and admired his impressive ass. He glamoured some sweats. "Stop having those thoughts, Jenella, before you embarrass me in front of your brother."

My face flushed. I felt like a teenager caught doing something wrong. I threw the covers back and stumbled to the bathroom. "Talking to Mat first thing this morning was not what I had in mind."

His soft chuckle echoed through the room.

I cleaned up and tied the mess of hair back into a ponytail and threw on some leggings and a T-shirt. Emine and Mat sat at the kitchen table while Drake conjured breakfast. Emine's eyes scanned my outfit. A big, crazy grin formed on her face and she shot me a thumbs-up.

My cheeks heated.

Drake glared at her as he handed me a cup of coffee.

"I hoped you would wait a while before you solidified the bond. This is going to cause a lot of problems." My brother turned his hard face to Drake. "You better treat my sister like the queen she is, First."

Drake took a sip of coffee. "No."

I slid into a chair next to Emine. "Drake's not really a morning person."

He turned his rugged face toward me. "I will treat Jenella as a mate and a best friend. I will dedicate the rest of my life to making sure she is happy, safe, and never feels alone or as if no one cares. But I will not treat her like a queen. She hates being treated like a queen."

My heart skipped a beat. If I hadn't already bonded with that dragon, I would have then.

Emine held up a piece of bacon. "Googly eyes. Great. Just what I needed for breakfast."

"Why are you guys here so early?" I asked as I helped myself to some fruit.

"Rayar and his architecture team are already working on the castle. It'll take them a few days, so if you want any changes, now is the time to speak up. Also, the witches are back. They agreed to speak to us to settle their grievances. On top of that, the gargoyles have moved from the square to the castle walls. They won't tell me why." Mat eyed my clothes. "I suggest you find something more appropriate to wear before then."

I pushed my half-eaten meal away, my little domestic love bubble bursting. "That sounds like fun."

Guilt flashed through Mat's eyes. "I don't mean to ruin your happiness. I only wanted to inform you of our progress, as we agreed."

The weight of the world settled on my shoulders as I slid off the chair. "I'll see if Verity will work from here."

Drake refused to leave. Instead, he made himself a make-shift area in the corner of my home office. He attacked his new purpose with a singular focus. Several more leaders agreed to help root out the Bellicose. He didn't just talk to people. He gathered information with his congenial and patient nature. As a result, he got more details in four hours than I could gather in a year. Drake's new assistant, Charlotte, came with Verity and helped him sift through it all. They got along well, and her nerves melted away as they worked.

Verity and Titus crammed themselves into my corner with me. Verity eyed my clothes. "Mat's right. Sweats and a T-shirt are not appropriate for a business meeting. At least consider a shower and fixing your hair. Maybe put on some shoes and a bra, for heaven's sake."

"They're leggings." I didn't want to change clothes. They were comfortable, and the thought of washing off Drake's scent made me ill. It made me feel like maybe everything would be okay. The bond was messing with my head, but I didn't care. I rubbed the new bubble in my chest.

She tapped her notepad. "You are a little shit, Jen. I honestly don't know why we all put up with you."

"I ask myself that all the time. How's your Juror training going?"

"I hate it. Your value system makes no sense, and Titus won't let me punish anyone. I don't see why I can't just use my human values. They're more logical."

"They make little sense to me," Titus said. He was a by-the-book Juror who knew every law within the various groups that made up the coalition. While Verity spent her entire life in the human world and adopted their values.

She shook her head. "I don't think I'll ever adjust. But I don't really need them as long as I'm Jen's assistant." She leaned forward. "Clothes?"

"I'll change in a while. How are you guys doing since the attack?"

"I'm pissed. I cannot believe they took out the castle wards." She pointed at me. "You need to clean that shit up."

Verity was fierce, but I'd never heard her swear like that. "The wards around the property are still intact because we disengaged them before the battle. But yeah, they shouldn't have been able to ruin the castle. I'm pretty sure Anitta did that, and she's gone, so it won't happen again."

"Entry access needs to change, too. Maybe a spell to screen people before they enter the building." She made a note. "I'll talk to George and Helen about that. What other changes do you want to make?"

"I want my office to stay the same, but my apartment needs to be expanded to make room for Drake. The ceilings need to be raised and a balcony or something added that he can launch from. Also, reach out the First Razazia and offer her an advisor position."

"I already did. She declined."

"What about the Ancient Ann Marie?"

"The Ancient Ann Marie accepted on the condition that you don't expect much from her."

"I don't. So we have Tracy, Quin, Mat, Deva, Drake, and Ann Marie. Any word from the others?"

"The Alpha is out since she's a traitor and all. King Olwen of the Snow Elves agreed."

"My grandmother had eleven advisors, and my mother had twelve." I thought about Quin's advice to rule the way I wanted to. And Ara's advice to break the rules. I started to see what they meant. Living up to expectations and following protocols was draining. "I can't be what the people want me to be. I can only be myself."

"Right." Verity didn't miss a beat. "There's no specific number of advisors required. The ones you have are enough for now, and you can always add more later. Especially since the ones you chose are all so opinionated."

"I agree. Titus, I want you to be my aide. You can keep your job as legal counsel if you want, but you've been around for a long time and have a lot of knowledge about the human world and the other pockets. I could use your perspective."

Titus sat back and crossed his arms. "I'll think about it."

That was all I could ask. I took a deep breath and stood. "Thanks. I need a change of clothes."

I shouldn't have bothered. A group of witches, including Tracy's dad, waited for us in one of the undamaged sitting rooms on the visitor's side of the castle. Mat ordered them to hold an election to choose another leader by the end of the week. I put them on probation and changed their place on the Council to the second row, giving the elves the option to sit in front. They agreed to clean house and present a leader at the next meeting.

"What do we do next?" I asked after they left.

Mat shook his head. "What do you want to do?"

"I hope Calvin wins and gets his people under control, but that's about all I *can* do unless they're all aligned with the enemy. I don't think they are."

"Calvin's not. I suspect you scared the rest of them with your magic display yesterday." Mat tapped the table. "There has been no further demon activity in Allure, and the witches are spreading the potion throughout the pockets to make amends. We should have defenses in place in every pocket within the next two weeks."

I closed my eyes. "Why do I feel like we're not doing enough?"

"Because we haven't found the leaders."

"You don't think Anitta ran things?"

"No. I think she manipulated someone powerful to do her bidding. Her death probably empowered that person because there's no one left to pull his strings."

"What about Gabe and Linda?"

"That one stings. How did she get to them? Or were they planted as spies from the beginning? I've contacted Jonas. He's spread thin with the hybrid situation. They haven't been attacked yet, but he expects it will come soon. He'll help as much as he can. It'll take time to untie all those knots."

"Time we might not have. What more can I do?"

"You're doing everything you can, Jen. You have earned the respect of many leaders and gave their people hope. We'll figure it out, and we'll win."

"I hope so," I mumbled, suddenly exhausted.

"If it helps, I haven't thought I was doing enough since I became regent. It's exhausting, and there is always one more problem to fix. Once the Bellicose is gone, there will be someone else causing trouble. The best you can do is try to prevent them and work through the ones that you can't."

That wasn't exactly the encouragement I wanted, but at least it was honest. I left the meeting with a new perspective of my throne and my brother. The throne was like one big private detective gig where I had to solve multiple cases at once and make sure my clients, the people, were happy. I could do that. I wanted to do the job for the first time in my life.

And Mat? All the grief I gave him seemed stupid now. I'd often said he was amazing, but I'd always treated his guidance like a burden. I decided from that moment on, I'd listen to him more and try to understand why he made the decisions he made. Did I fully trust him to be truthful? No. But it was a start.

I chuckled at that thought. I doubted my new resolve would last.

CHAPTER THIRTY-SEVEN

JEN

I stood between Mat and Drake as we watched the leadership council assemble and rubbed the bubble in my chest. "Did the witches elect Calvin?"

"The witches are still acting like humans and protesting us, so I'm unsure if they elected anyone," Mat answered.

A short time later, we took our seats, with Drake on my left and Mat and Emine on my right. Jonas sat in the Shifter Alpha's seat. His predatory eyes bore into me. I wondered what that was about.

"I call this meeting to order." Mat's voice echoed through the chamber.

The doors to the left opened, and a gaggle of witches entered. A tall, muscular man strode in behind them, his dark skin contrasting against his white shirt. He wore the crest of the president of covens on his chest. I fought the grin that wanted to explode onto my face as Tracy's dad bowed to us.

Mat inclined his head. "Welcome, Calvin Cordalia. Are you the new representative for the witches?"

"Yes, Your Majesty. The witches have held an election."

I hoped that meant the witches would work with us in the future, but I kept my face neutral. "Welcome to the Leadership Council, Mr. President."

The Kelpie Queen stood. "You have no right to pretend to welcome him, considering you threw out his predecessor. I propose we charge the crown with meddling in the affairs of a sovereign ruler."

Verity threw a memory spell at the wall without me prompting her. Like me, she was done with their foolishness. The projection showed the previous president making several treasonous remarks inside the castle. It ended with her trying to murder me.

I met the Kelpie Queen's eyes. "Motion denied."

The Wyvern King stood. "Your Grace, may I inquire why the First Drake sits in a seat of honor?"

"The First Drake is my match and, therefore, my consort."

The King waved a hand. "You are a mage, not a dragon. This pairing is an abomination."

"State the Coalition law your claim is based on."

"My dear girl. Not everything has to be a law. Mixed couples are simply immoral," He huffed.

"And we all know where you got those wrong-minded ideas." I signaled Verity, who played another spell, showing the Bellicose campaign to divide us. When it concluded, Titus stood and read the matching law. "So, you can see, dear boy, I have every right to match with whomever I wish, as does every coalition citizen."

Everyone began talking at once.

I glanced at Jonas the First. His eyes sparked with interest. Until then, he didn't believe I cared about the hybrids.

Beside him, Bastien's posture stiffened. His face gave nothing away as he watched the scene play out.

I waited a few seconds before I called for silence. "As it has been for thousands of years, magic and fate decide matches, not the Council. Regent."

Mat glared at the Wyvern King. "The First Jonas has uncovered some vital information about the Bellicose."

I listened as Jonas presented several documents his spy stole. The ones that outlined their plan to attack both us and the hybrids. One document was a royal decree from the one they called the king that gave his generals the authority to lodge a full-scale attack on Allure and enslave the hybrids.

"The Queen has charged me and the First Drake with the duty of assisting the First, Jonas, in eliminating what remains of their forces in the valley," Mat said when he was done. "The Shifter Alphas turned traitor and sacrificed many of their people. We will hunt them down and kill them, along with anyone who serves the enemy. If you wish to join us, you will have a seat at the table, but we will enforce strict contracts going forward."

"The dragons vote to support the queen's defense of the hybrids," Deva's steely voice rang out.

"As do the vampires," Ara said.

"Of course you do," The Kelpie Queen growled.

I ignored her and searched the crowd for allies. I had several, but I needed more. It's one reason I tried to befriend the group of smaller leaders. They remained silent and wouldn't meet my gaze.

"The elves support the queen." Razazia's voice came from the corner of the last row. She strode down the aisle and stood next to the Snow Elf King.

Relief flooded me as the place erupted in shouts and chatter.

Drake leaned over and put his lips to my ear. "Is this where I stand behind you and show my teeth?"

Goosebumps coated my skin. "That sounds like fun."

Drake's growl was somehow suggestive. I didn't know a growl *could* be suggestive.

"Silence." He roared.

Mat didn't even flinch. "Thank you for your support, Madame First."

The discussion was exhausting. My head ached, even though I'd hardly said a word. Mat and I hated council meetings for that very reason.

Drake threw an arm around my shoulders as the discussion tapered off. *This is a shit show,* he said in my head, though his stoic expression never changed.

It's exhausting but necessary. I hope we get enough support to eliminate the Bellicose.

You already have enough support to win with the combined forces of the Vampires, Dragons, and Elves. Jonas is confident you can win the hybrids to your side with enough effort.

I hope you're right.

It'll work out.

"Interesting." Tracy watched the team of magic users recharge the wards that kept the pocket intact and functioning.

"Yeah," I agreed. The team was made up of elves, dwarves, witches, and several forte mages. Their fortes included tech, weather, environment, and architecture. Four elementals who represented earth, fire, air, and water also took part.

The witches worked together to weave a spell in the shape of a large basket, and the others added magic to it. As a group, they cast it out without touching the ward. The recharge hit near where I'd fixed the crack when a mind-controlled dragon rammed it. They repeated the process several times.

"I bet they funneled their magic through my mother to create the pockets, and she played the role of the basket. Or does that seem too easy?"

"I believe she stole their magic when she created Mahri. The castle there is the anchor." Quin said from Tracy's other side. "She bungled the first attempt and developed this method. She then ordered others to fix her mistakes."

"So, does every pocket need an anchor?" Tracy asked.

"I am not the foremost expert on the pockets."

I shook my head. "It makes sense. It gives the magic focus and is easier to build around and expand as more becomes available. I wonder how she solidified and cloaked them."

Tracy leaned forward as the witches released another basket. "I could solidify it with a spell, and I bet a dragon could add cloaking magic. I mean, it would take a few paranormals working together for a whole pocket, but it can be done."

"Yeah." I'd have to talk to the dwarf that ran the operation and make sure I understood it, but it seemed doable if I could learn to absorb the various magics.

I thanked the group for letting us watch, and we headed downtown. Quin fell in beside us as we left the flashing circle at the main square. The gargoyles were still perched on the palace walls and turned to stone when anyone confronted them.

We turned left and headed down the cobblestone street, where two witches went from shop to shop, adding a drop of Calvin's anti-demon potion to individual wards. I'd been walking around downtown for a few days, hoping people would stop diving out of my way and bowing. It didn't help. I needed to work on a different strategy.

"My dad is efficient," Tracy said.

"He is. Mat told me people are lining up for the potion. How's your dad doing in his new role?"

"It's been rough. A few covens still won't follow him."

"If those covens are loyal to the Bellicose, they need to be stopped. If he discovers their involvement, I'll step in."

"Sure. How is Drake doing on finding their leadership?"

"He's fantastic at it. So far, he's recovered several paranormals from labs and is working with Jonas to break up their bases in the human world." He also discovered that those who supported the Bellicose movement preferred to display their symbol discreetly on their businesses and homes. The Enforcers rooted out several of them before they caught on.

"Mathias tasked me with finding the former Shifter Alphas," Quin said. "I am following some promising leads."

I nodded. "Do me a favor and take backup with you. I have a bad feeling about them."

Quin didn't respond, but then, I didn't expect him to. His phone buzzed, and he pulled it out of his perfectly tailored suit. His eyes grew wide as he read the message. He slapped a hand on our shoulders and went fluid.

"What the hell?" I yelled as I got dumped beside the main flashing circle, my head still spinning.

"Take me home."

"I'm not your personal taxi," I said as I put a steadying hand on Tracy's shoulder and headed toward the center of the circle.

"There is a disturbance at my home. It may be an attack."

My heart skipped a beat. We had a long way to go to break up the Bellicose, but they had to be insane to attack a vampire house. I slapped a hand on his arm. We landed in the vampire palace's flashing circle.

Bodies littered the ground. There had to be about twenty between us and the gates. I leaned down next to one and checked for a pulse.

"They are vampires. They will be fine."

I stood and focused on the trail of bodies that led to an ongoing scuffle up ahead. I didn't sense any bug magic, but there were two hybrids.

A guard flew over the heads of the others and landed on the sidewalk with a *thud*. Some in the cluster clutched their heads while others groaned. Tracy and I followed Quin through the fight. My ears rang from the shouting when we emerged in the center.

"Alright, alright. I give. Holy hell. Can't a girl go for a walk with her brother in these asshole pockets? Alex, are you okay?" came a woman's voice, followed by a male groan.

Quin parted the vampires as he moved toward the fight. We stayed on his tail, and I peered around him when he came to a sudden stop.

I gasped.

The woman on the ground held her arm while restrained by four of Ara's elites. Power rolled off her in waves. She didn't look as worried as she should have in that situation. Her intelligent whisky-colored eyes scanned Quin and then landed on me. They sharpened as she decided I was the biggest threat. Not whisky-colored, I realized, but brown with gold flecks. The blood in her dark brown hair did nothing to hide a single red streak on one side and a golden streak on the other. I tore my eyes away from her and focused on the man being held down by three vampires. The same man who tried to read my mind when Drake and I visited Ann Marie and Jonas.

I raced to his side.

The woman went crazy. "Don't you touch him. We didn't do anything."

"Relax before you make the situation worse. That guy needs a healer." I wished the guy back to health and kept my eyes on him as his wounds sealed. I stepped back and assessed the woman. She was already healing. "Do you need my help?"

She shook her head. "Who the hell are you, and why are these vampires attacking us?"

"She's a rogue who claimed to be from a dormant house, Your Grace." A vampire changed positions to better secure the woman.

I crouched down in front of her. "She's not feral. She's got a lot of power, though. You can let her go if she promises not to attack." I raised my eyebrow at the hybrid.

"I'll do whatever. Just let my brother go. He has nothing to do with this."

The brother stood to the side, his arms crossed over his chest and his face red with anger.

I turned my attention back to the woman. "It's not my call. You're in vampire territory, so it's up to Ara, though I doubt she'd harm Jonas's kids." I motioned to the tiny woman gliding through the crowd. I leaned closer. "A word of advice. Watch your language around her. She's not fond of swearing."

The hybrid's face hardened in defiance at the sight of Ara. "No problem."

Ara placed one hand on her heart, her other on Quin's arm, and gasped.

I shook off the chills that ran down my spine. I'd never seen the two of those two show that much emotion. "Hey, Ara. I think we found your granddaughter."

The End (for now).

Please take a moment to leave a review on Amazon.

ONE MORE THING.

Whew. What a wild ride. Thanks for hanging in there.

It's not the end, though. Book 3 takes the fight to the human world, deals with the fallout from the mother-spiking scene, and is full of a bunch of mystery and mayhem. In addition, a novella featuring the vampire-mage hybrid Lily is coming soon. She is a fun character, and I can't wait to introduce her. I hope to release them by the end of the year.

Sign up for my newsletter at to stay updated on upcoming releases.

Thank you to everyone who helped me with this book. The editors, proofreaders, beta readers, and ARC readers were all wonderful to work with and continue to make me a better writer, one criticism at a time. The cover designers at getcovers.com did a great job bringing the world to the front with little information. I'd also like to thank my family. Without them, I wouldn't have quite the imagination or a love for the strange.

A special shoutout to my feline assistants, Callie and Gracie, and my canine assistant, Zorro, for keeping it real.

Finally, thank you, the brave reader who, once again, took a chance on a new author and battled your way to the end of the book.

Cheers.

ML Conklin

www.ingramcontent.com/pod-product-compliance
Lightning Source LLC
Chambersburg PA
CBHW060514160726
47991CB00001B/34